THE EMILIE ADVENTURES

EMILIE AND THE HOLLOW WORLD
&
EMILIE AND THE SKY WORLD

ALSO BY MARTHA WELLS

THE EMILIE ADVENTURES

MARTHA WELLS

TOR PUBLISHING GROUP
NEW YORK

THE EMILIE ADVENTURES

Emilie and the Hollow World copyright © 2013 by Martha Wells
Emilie and the Sky World copyright © 2014 by Martha Wells

A Tordotcom Book
Published by Tom Doherty Associates / Tor Publishing Group
120 Broadway
New York, NY 10271

www.torpublishinggroup.com

Tor® is a registered trademark of Macmillan Publishing Group, LLC.

The Library of Congress Cataloging-in-Publication Data is available upon request.

ISBN 978-1-250-87314-9 (paperback)
ISBN 978-1-250-39605-1 (ebook)

Our books may be purchased in bulk for promotional, educational, or business use. Please contact your local bookseller or the Macmillan Corporate and Premium Sales Department at 1-800-221-7945, extension 5442, or by email at MacmillanSpecialMarkets@macmillan.com.

First Edition: 2025

Printed in the United States of America

0   9   8   7   6   5   4   3   2   1

BOOK I

Emilie and the Hollow World

———∽∞∾———

CHAPTER ONE

Creeping along the docks in the dark, looking for the steamship *Merry Bell,* Emilie was starting to wonder if it might be better to just walk to Silk Harbor. So far, her great escape from Uncle Yeric's tyranny hadn't been great, or much of an escape. *It's going to be embarrassing if I don't get further than this,* she thought, exasperated at herself.

Emilie reminded herself failure wasn't an option. She scrambled behind a row of barrels, her boots squishing in foul-smelling muck, and squinted to get a look at the slip numbers next to the pier entrances. It was a cloudy night, the half-moon mostly concealed, and this end of the docks had only a few widely spaced gas lamps. At the other end there had been tap houses and inns, and more people to blend in with, sailors or dockworkers heading for home and passengers waiting for the ships with a late boarding. This boardwalk was empty except for the occasional armed watchman, and if Emilie was stopped, she couldn't very well say indignantly, "I'm not a thief, I'm a stowaway, thank you very much!"

And she had to leave the city tonight; Uncle Yeric was a penny-pincher, but he might very well hire a hedgewitch to track Emilie with magic. Uncle Yeric and Aunt Helena would never lower themselves to hire a hedgewitch under normal circumstances, but considering what they thought Emilie was running off to do, they might make an exception.

Emilie had passed the gaslit graving docks and the warehouses, looming dark and quiet. The hydraulic tower and the smaller pump house, its chimneys still billowing smoke against the night sky, made a good landmark; at least she knew she was in the right place. The *Merry Bell* and the other short-range steamers should be down here somewhere.

If Emilie hadn't spent money on food, she would have had enough to get to Silk Harbor by buying passage on the Coastal Ferry, which had departed late this afternoon. That had been her original plan.

She had formed the plan very carefully, stealing the newspapers out of the scrap paper bin to study the steamship lists and to learn where the passenger ferries berthed and the best route through the city of Meneport to reach the harbor. But none of the newspapers, or the storybooks that featured romantic heroines thrown out by their evil stepmothers (or stepfathers, or stepuncles) to make their own way in the world, had mentioned how painful starvation actually was, how once past the stage of acute pain, it made your thoughts slow and your body weak. It had taken Emilie two days to walk to the city, and by the end she had been footsore, exhausted, and so blind with hunger that she had stopped and bought a pork pie at the first shop she saw. It had fortified her for the walk across the city to the port, where she had succumbed again and bought a sausage roll and tea. Then she had found the booking office for the steamship lines and discovered that she was half the passage price short. If Emilie had had any inclination to see herself as a romantic heroine, this experience would have cured her of it.

I'm not a heroine, she thought, blending in with the shadows as she ran lightly to the next stack of cargo. *I just want to live where I choose, like any reasonable person.* She spotted a posted brass plate with the number 8 on it. *Finally!*

The *Merry Bell* was a passenger steamer that made the short trip up the coast to Silk Harbor every other day, and it was due to leave at dawn. From what she had heard in the shipping office, it would carry a number of passengers, few of whom would bother with staterooms, since the ship would be docking before nightfall. Everyone would be sitting in the lounges or wandering the decks, and it would be easy for Emilie to slip in among them once the steamer was underway. That was the plan, anyway. She only hoped the state of her clothes, a somewhat-the-worse-for-wear shirtwaist, jacket, and bloomers, with stockings and walking boots, didn't call attention to her, especially if she had to swim in them. She didn't have any luggage, either. Before she had left she had made up a small bundle of her belongings and posted it to her cousin Karthea on the overland mail, so no one would see her leaving the house with a bag.

Emilie stepped out from behind the crates and took a careful look up and down the dock. A light mist had come in, clinging to the infrequent gas lamps, and the only movement she could see was far down the boardwalk. Her heart pounding, she darted across the wide expanse to the pier's entrance.

The walkway was roped off, but that must be the bulky stern of the *Merry Bell* tied up at the end. In the dark all she could see was the shape of a long steamer with two stacks and a paddle wheel, with a closed promenade along the second deck. A few lights shone from cabin windows, though there was no movement out on the decks. Only the crew should be aboard now, and most of them sleeping. *Hopefully.*

Now Emilie had to figure out how to get onto the thing. She expected that trying to sneak up the gangplank would be impractical. She was going to have to swim, but first she wanted to see if there was a ladder or net she could use to climb up the hull. She ducked under the ropes blocking the pier and started cautiously down toward the ship.

There was something lumpy between the end of the gangplank and a stack of crates, barely visible in the dark. She thought it was a tarp thrown over a piling. When she was barely five steps away, it stood up.

Emilie flinched back with a smothered curse. The looming figure became a bearded watchman in a battered gray coat. In a voice rough with suspicion, he said, "Hey you, what are you after here?"

Emilie backed away. She should have had a story. "Um, I just wanted to look at the ship. I'm not a thief." She realized a heartbeat later that it was the wrong thing to say. He hadn't accused her of being a thief, just implied that she was a trespasser. Now that she had blurted out the word "thief" like a guilty . . . thief, he was going to think she was one.

"Having a look at the ship in the dark?" He came forward, still looming, and even more suspicious. "Wouldn't be waiting for the mail, now, would you?"

"I'm not expecting any mail," Emilie said, trying to sound innocent. Maybe if he thought she was daft, he would let her go.

It did give him pause. She couldn't read his expression in the dark, but he said, in a different tone, "Are you with old Migiltawny's crew?"

Emilie considered the odds. The only choice was between yes or no, and one or the other had to be right. She took a chance. "Yes," she said brightly.

"Migiltawny the dock pirate!" the man roared. "So you're his look-out!"

"What? No!" *Oh, hell,* Emilie thought. "I didn't know that. I mean, I'm not here for that. I'm not a pirate, either!"

"Oh, you aren't! Let's have a look at you." He flipped the slide on a dark lantern, and in the light he looked bigger and more threatening than before. Emilie started back and he grabbed for her arm.

She wrenched away, heard her jacket rip as she twisted out of his grasping hand, and bolted back up the pier. He didn't chase her and for a moment she thought he would let her go. He had to see she was a young girl, though it would be hard to tell how young in the dark, and she thought herself an unlikely prospect for a mail thief or a dock pirate. But as she reached the pier entrance a piercing whistle split the air, and she heard pounding footsteps. Two more watchmen ran toward her from down the dock.

Emilie stumbled to a halt, looked wildly around, and took the only route left: three quick steps to the edge of the pier and a dive into the dark water.

The cold was a shock; Emilie gasped and swallowed foul salty water. She choked, coughed it up, and started to swim away from the pier.

Behind her the men shouted and light shone on the water as they brought lanterns out. Emilie took a deep breath and went under. She swam as hard as she could and wished she could afford to get rid of her boots. If she ever got the opportunity to try to pass herself off as a legitimate passenger, she couldn't do it barefoot.

She surfaced when her air ran out, close to the pilings of the next pier. She clung to one and looked back at the *Merry Bell,* and was star-tled to see its decks lit by a dozen or more lamps, with crew members running back and forth to gather near the gangplank. She groaned to herself. Running away and then jumping dramatically off the pier probably hadn't helped convince them she wasn't a mail-thief-pirate-robber, but she couldn't tell them the truth, either. She had no idea what they did to stowaways. *It probably isn't as bad as what they do to pirates,* she thought.

This plan was turning into a disaster, and it was her own fault. The *Merry Bell,* as disturbed as a trodden-on anthill, was out. She would have to look for another day steamer, or wait until the Coastal Ferry returned late tomorrow and try to sneak aboard it. In the meantime, she needed a place to hide until they grew tired of looking for her, and convinced themselves there was no gang of robbers ready to descend on them.

She should be better at this. Her mother had been a runaway too, and Emilie had never been allowed to forget it. Obviously it didn't run in the blood. *Uncle Yeric would be so surprised.* She paddled to the end of the pier, trying not to splash too much, and looked for another ship.

There was one two piers over, the decks lit by several lamps. Her teeth already chattering, she paddled toward it for a better look.

It was large, made of flashy bright coppery metal, but shaped like a round top-heavy tub. Its hull was bulbous, and widened out to support platforms along the main deck. There were four decks, and it had three smokestacks, but they were set side by side across the width of the ship. There were no windows on the upper decks and few doors, though there was an open promenade. Some of the windows were lit, and she saw two men walking along the third deck, just turning in to an open hatch. There was no gangplank down, and as she drew closer she saw the ship wasn't tied up to the pier, it was standing at anchor a short distance from it. The name on the bow was SOVEREIGN.

Emilie threw a look back at the dock. More men were gathering with lamps, agitated shadows searching the crates and barrel stacks, darting into every corner. Swearing to herself, Emilie swam toward the other ship.

She had to swim out and around the bow, to get to the side facing away from the lighted pier. *I can't do this much longer.* If there was no way to climb up to the deck, she was going to have to find a piling to cling to. The cold water sapped her strength, and she didn't think she could swim anywhere else after this, not without a rest.

But for once, the first time in three days, luck was with her.

The ship had a cradle for a launch or lifeboat that had been lowered down the side, and sat just above the water. The boat was gone; someone must have taken it to go to shore. The cradle had a small platform with a ladder leading up the side to an open gate in the railing.

Emilie didn't know how exhausted she was until she tried to climb up onto the platform. Her soaked clothes weighed twice as much as she did, at least, and her arms ached with the strain by the time she dragged herself onto the narrow metal shelf. She lay there for a while, breathing hard and dripping, rivulets of water running away across the platform. But it was warmer out of the water than it was in.

After a time her breathing returned to normal, and the metal platform began to feel cold and very uncomfortable. She sat up and started to wring out her clothes as best she could. Listening hard, she could still hear muted commotion from the docks, but she had a refuge for the moment, and that was all that mattered. She could stay here until the men on the dock stopped looking for her, then swim back to shore.

She heard the putt-putt-putt of a small-boat motor. "Oh, no," Emilie muttered weakly. *Out of the kettle, into the coals.* What were the chances that it was this ship's launch, returning? After the events of the past night, she thought the chances were rather good.

She had had time to rest and to let several pounds of water drain out of her clothes, so tackling the ladder wasn't as difficult as it would have been earlier. The motor boat was drawing closer somewhere out in the dark, and that spurred her on.

She dragged herself up onto the polished wooden planks of the deck, and staggered upright. She started toward the nearest hatch, a heavy door with a thick crystal porthole. It stood open a little, and she cautiously peeked inside. It led into a wide interior corridor running parallel to the deck, lined with fine dark wood, the floor covered with a thick patterned carpet. An electric ceramic sconce about midway down provided wan light, enough to show her the richness of the brass fixtures and fittings. *This must be someone's private steam yacht,* she thought, startled. Not a good place to be caught if she didn't want to be mistaken for a thief again.

Emilie heard the boat motor sputter and turned. The launch was entering the slip, the light on its bow giving her enough of a glimpse of the occupants to see that there were several figures in dark clothing aboard. *This isn't the best place to hide but it's the only one I've got.* She wiggled through the doorway without moving the hatch and started down the corridor.

She was still dripping, but fortunately the dark pattern of the carpet didn't show it. Anxious and feeling exactly like the unwelcome, uninvited intruder she was, she took the first turn to a cross passage.

The lights were brighter here, which made her feel horribly exposed. She hurried past cabin doors, but they were all closed, and she was afraid to walk in on someone sleeping, or worse, awake. She passed a narrow stairwell, hesitated, then decided to stay on this deck.

Then the passage opened out into a lounge. It had deep upholstered couches built back against the walls, and glass-fronted bookcases, and a white porcelain heating stove. There was a partially open door at the back. She hurried over to peek inside, and saw it was a steward's cubby, with a gas ring, a tap, and storage cabinets. As a hiding place, it was a good possibility. Surely it was too late at night for someone to want to sit in the lounge and call for a steward—

Footsteps sounded from somewhere nearby, and Emilie whipped into the cubby and pushed the door nearly to, leaving a slim gap. She crouched down on the tile floor, wrapped her arms around her knees, and tried to make her breathing silent.

Two sets of footsteps drew near, and she heard a man's voice say, "Lord Engal, I wish you wouldn't do this." It was a light voice, with a cultured city accent.

"You mean proceed with the expedition, or trust Kenar's word, Barshion?" another man, presumably Lord Engal, answered. His voice was deeper, with the same accent, and Emilie immediately pictured a much larger man. He sounded amused and dismissive. Emilie thought of Uncle Yeric, not in a complimentary way.

"Perhaps both." Barshion's tone was serious. "You know what I think of Kenar. We can't be certain what his motives are. There's too much at stake—"

"Dr. Marlende's life is at stake, and the lives of his crew! This expedition must leave as scheduled. We've already delayed too long." The amusement had gone from Engal's voice, making him sound far more commanding. *Expedition?* Emilie wondered. *Lives at stake?* Fascinated, she edged forward and angled her head to see out the gap.

A man paced into view, slender, with sleek blond hair and the pale skin of Northern Menaen ancestry. He was dressed in a very correct tweed walking suit with a carefully starched neckcloth. He said, "Marlende was . . . is my friend as well." From his voice this was Barshion. "I want to go to his assistance as badly as you do, but if we have the wrong information, we're risking Marlende's life and the lives of his surviving crew, as well as our own."

"I understand your concerns, but we can't wait any longer. Even if

Kenar is overstating the urgency, the entire party must be in real danger." Emilie heard a rustle, the click of what might be a pocket watch, then Engal stepped into view. He was big, burly enough to work on the docks, gray-haired, gray-bearded. Like Emilie, and most of the people she had seen in Meneport, his looks were more Southern Menaen, with warm brown skin and dark eyes. "Hickran should be back soon. What's keeping the man?"

"Ricks said he saw the launch returning a moment ago. It should be coming alongside now—"

Sharp cracks sounded from somewhere nearby, and Emilie flinched and knocked her elbow painfully against the cabinet. Startled, Engal said, "What the—"

"Gunshots," Barshion gasped. "The launch—"

The two men bolted away down the corridor, and Emilie pushed to her feet. *Gunshots?* she thought, astounded. Maybe the guard of the *Merry Bell* and the other watchmen had been so touchy and suspicious for a good reason. *Maybe there really are dock pirates.* She felt a little like she had stepped into a play.

A door banged open somewhere, men shouted, muffled by distance. Emilie bit her lip. She couldn't stay here. The watchmen would be called, the city constabulary too, probably, and if they searched the ship . . . Her disastrous plan was getting more disastrous by the moment. Emilie eased to her feet, peeked to make certain the lounge was empty.

She stepped out of the cubby, heard shouts and running footsteps but couldn't tell the direction. She had to see where the robbers were before she knew which way to flee.

She ducked out of the lounge and headed back to the stairway she had passed on the way in. She hurried up to the next deck, finding a foyer with four closed cabin doors and an entrance to another cross corridor. She ran back toward the starboard side, passed two open doors that led to a darkened dining area, then found a hatch out onto the unlit glassed-in promenade. She went to the railing, looking down through the windows streaked with damp and saltwater spray. *It's robbers all right,* she thought grimly.

There was a fight on the deck below, near the gate in the railing, above the ladder to the launch platform. Five or six men in blue coats common to sailors and several others in dark-colored uniforms. She had no idea which were crewmen and which were the robbers.

A gunshot went off and glass shattered at the far end of the promenade. Emilie jerked back with a muffled yelp. Her throat went dry from fear. If she had stepped into a play, she wished she could step back out of it. She scrambled back through the hatch and down the corridor.

It didn't go straight through to the port side, but turned into a confusing maze of service cabins and smaller lounges. Emilie had forgotten how absurdly wide this strange ship was, and blundered into a smoking room and a small pantry before finally tripping over the rim of a hatchway out into a larger corridor.

Before she ran ten steps down it, three men in black livery shot out of an intersecting passage and slammed past her, heading starboard. She gasped and flattened herself against the wall. One threw her a confused glance but they clearly didn't have time to stop and question stray girls, whether there were supposed to be any aboard the ship or not. In the light of the crystal sconces, she clearly looked a lot less like a scout for robbers than she had to the watchman on the dark pier. *Those must be crewmen*, she thought. *The bluecoats are the robbers.* That was handy to know.

Figuring she had truly used up every bit of her small store of luck by now, Emilie ran faster.

As she reached a passage parallel to the outer port side, the deck shuddered beneath her and she heard the muffled grumble of the engines. *They're casting off?* she wondered, heading for the nearest hatch. A quick look through the small porthole told her that the deck just in front of the hatch was empty, and that this side of the ship was facing the pier. The hatch was closed and locked and she had to wrench the bolts back before she could yank the heavy door open.

Emilie stepped out into a cool breeze, and heard fighting and shouting from the other side of the ship. The vessel wasn't moving yet, but the throb of the engines was growing louder. There were a few deck lamps lit, but there was no one out here to see her.

The ship was anchored some distance from the pier; Emilie would have to swim for it again. She went to the railing and realized she couldn't jump from here: the deck below was wider than this one. Also, she was much higher up now. She hurried along to an outside stairway, tucked into a sheltered nook in the side. She made her steps quiet, but she was only halfway down when someone stepped out of a hatch on the lower deck.

Emilie froze. It was a man in a greatcoat that was far too heavy for the cool night. He stepped to the railing, stretched to look down, then turned away from Emilie and started away down the deck. She just had time to take a breath in relief when a bluecoat slammed out of the hatch just behind him and swung a cudgel.

"Look out!" Emilie shouted in reflex. The man whipped around and ducked, lightning quick, and the cudgel missed completely. Before the bluecoat could recover, the man seized the cudgel, wrenched it away with a quick twist, and delivered two stunning blows to the bluecoat's chest and head.

Another bluecoat stepped out of the hatch, and Emilie surged forward. She had no idea what she was going to do, just that she had to do something. Then she tripped over a water bucket abandoned at the bottom of the stairs, seized it, and flung it at the bluecoat.

The bluecoat cursed and ducked, giving the man time to whirl around and hit him with the cudgel too. As the bluecoat collapsed, the man caught sight of Emilie, and froze for an instant, staring at her. He was standing under a lamp, and the light fell on his face. Emilie yelled in pure shocked reflex.

He wasn't human. The matte black fur, the glitter of reptilian scales were only an impression, but she clearly saw the gold split-pupil eyes and the pointed teeth.

Another hatch opened farther down the deck and half a dozen bluecoats spilled out, brawling with just as many black-liveried sailors. They spread across the deck, shouting and fighting.

Emilie turned to run, but the deck heaved suddenly, rolled under her feet, and knocked her flat. Emilie struggled to her knees, trying to stand. It had to be the engines, an explosion in the boilers. The deck shook again and kept shaking, as if something huge had grabbed the ship's hull from below. The dock lights started to recede, as the ship moved out of the slip and into the harbor. Gunshots sounded nearby, and Emilie looked up to see that two sailors with rifles stood on the deck above, aiming down at the bluecoats.

The strange man—creature—man shouted at her, "Stay down!"

That sounded like very good advice, despite the source. Emilie scrambled under the stairs and huddled back against the wall.

The deck shuddered continuously, the water churning below. She heard splashes, saw two bluecoats tumble over the rail. They were losing the fight, or fleeing the potential explosion, or both. The gunshots stopped and the ship's horn blew frantically. *You have to get off this ship before it gets any farther from shore,* Emilie told herself, her heart pounding in her ears.

She crawled forward and peered around the stairway. Several sailors and bluecoats still struggled at the far end of the deck. She saw the strange not-human man toss another bluecoat overboard, then a door crashed open somewhere on the deck above. She looked up to see that Lord Engal stood at the rail above her. He shouted, "Get off, jump, you bastards, if you don't want to go with us!" He fired a pistol into the air, emphasizing the order.

That seemed to convince the few remaining bluecoats that retreat was a good idea. Three went over the rail. Two others paused to drag a fallen comrade upright and toss him over, then they jumped after him.

The roar of the engines reached a deafening pitch, and Emilie had to follow them, before the ship broke apart. She pushed to her feet, staggered as the deck rolled violently, then flung herself at the rail.

"No!" someone shouted, and grabbed the back of her jacket, jerking her to a halt. "Too late!"

Barely three steps in front of her a glimmering gold wall sprang up along the rail and arched to form a dome over the ship. "What's that?" Emilie demanded. She looked up, realized it was the not-human man who had grabbed her. She tried to pull away, and he let her go.

He looked toward Lord Engal, who was still on the deck above them, and seemed to be studying the gold barrier with an air of great satisfaction. The man said, "The way home."

"Whose home?" Emilie tried to ask, but the roar of the engines blotted out the words. The deck shook and water rushed up all around them, the brown churning water of the harbor, kept out by the gold wall. No, the water wasn't rushing up, the ship was sinking, sinking fast, as if something dragged it below the surface.

As Emilie stared upward in baffled horror, the water covered the dome of light overhead as the ship sank faster and faster, and the brownish water gave way to deep blue.

CHAPTER TWO

"I don't understand," Emilie said, too shocked to do anything but stare upward. She thought it was a remarkable understatement considering the circumstances.

The ship was enclosed in a bubble of gold light, traveling underwater. The view was murky, the only illumination coming from the lamps along the deck. But she saw shapes fleeing the ship's lights, a small school of multicolored umbrella fish, their jelly-like bodies and drifting tentacles remarkably graceful. Feeling a cold shiver in her midsection, she realized she couldn't see the surface. The air smelled salty and tinged with seaweed.

Emilie had seen magic before. Mr. Herinbogel, her friend Porcia's father, was a retired sorcerer and sometimes helped the local physician with healing spells. And there had been the occasional traveling conjurer shows at the local fairs. But those had all been very small magics, not like this. This was like something out of a grand gothic novel.

Beside her, the man said, "It's called an aether current. It's carrying us under your sea, to a crack that leads through the bottom of the world." He looked down at her and added, somewhat unnecessarily, "It's magic."

"My sea," Emilie repeated, seizing on that detail. "It's not my sea."

"It's not mine, either." He cocked his head at her. "I'm Kenar."

The Kenar whose word Barshion didn't trust. Kenar who was something-not-human. "I'm Emilie." It seemed beyond rude to say *what are you?* even though it was one of the questions she badly wanted to ask. As if they were meeting in her uncle's parlor, she said instead, "Where are you from?"

He seemed to hear the original question anyway. He said, "I'm Cirathi, from the coast of Oragal."

"I haven't heard of that place. But . . ." The water was growing even darker. Bubbles streamed by and she realized they were still moving forward, rapidly, away from the harbor. Emilie saw the silvery flicker of a large tail fleeing their lights. The fish was swimming up . . . No, it was the ship that was still sinking, falling down through the water. "This is all very odd, so maybe that isn't a surprise."

A ship's officer turned to look down the deck, spotted Kenar, and shouted, "You, back to quarters!"

Kenar's hands knotted on the rail, and he ignored the command. Emilie stepped behind him, using his bulk to block her from view, hoping the officer would be too distracted to notice her. It was a little late at this point to be thrown off the boat. She hoped.

The officer strode down the deck and stopped a pace away. He said, "You heard me. Go inside."

Kenar's head tilted to regard him, and with a frustrated edge in his voice, he said, "You could use force, Belden."

The officer's expression tightened, but he didn't give way. He said, "We have to make certain none of the pirates stayed aboard. That will be easier without passengers on the decks and in the corridors."

Kenar was still for a long moment, then stepped away from the railing. This left Emilie in full view of the officer, who stared at her oddly, startled, then motioned for her to follow Kenar.

Emilie had no idea why the man wasn't raising the alarm that a stowaway was aboard this strange ship, but decided to stay with Kenar, if possible. He seemed disposed to be kind to her; human or not, he might be her only ally in this strange situation.

Two sailors conducted them through the hatch and forward down a passage, where another sailor stood guard at a door. He opened it and they were ushered into a large lounge cabin, paneled with thin strips of fine dark wood. The door was closed firmly behind them.

The lounge was as luxurious as the rest of the ship, with upholstered couches built into the walls, lamps with milky ceramic sconces. Then Emilie saw the large crystal port looking out onto the deck.

She stepped toward it, caught again by the impossible wall of water just beyond the deck rail. It was very dark now, but the ship's lights reflected off a school of small copper-colored fish, vanishing into shadow as the ship sped past. Emilie had never been afraid of water, but she was beginning to fear it now. If it rushed in on the ship, how long would it take for her and the others to swim to the surface? It had to be far longer than she could hold her breath.

Knowing if she kept thinking about it the sense of pressure would just get worse, she deliberately turned away and looked around the cabin. Dr. Barshion sat on a couch against the far wall, and from his expression he was almost as sour about being confined here as Kenar. And there was a woman standing beside a drinks cabinet, wearing a tweed jacket and a divided skirt. She was Northern Menaen like Barshion, tall and slender, with her blond hair confined in a bun. She turned to Kenar angrily and demanded, "How did those men get on board?"

He folded his arms, but didn't seem to think her fury was directed at him. "They were on the launch. Hickran and his men must have been attacked while they were picking up the last supplies."

The light here allowed Emilie to see his face better. His straight nose and high cheekbones belonged to a handsome man, though they were coated with tiny black scales instead of skin. His brows were feathery fur, and his hair was dark and plush, almost a mane, that didn't quite conceal the extra folds of reptilian skin at the back of his neck. The greatcoat, the dark brown shirt, trousers, and boots he was wearing concealed most of the rest of him, but his hands had scaly skin too, with mats of dark fur across the backs. That combined with the gold eyes and the pointed teeth should have made the whole effect horrific. Maybe the shock of the pirate attack and the steamship plunging underwater in a protective bubble of spells had softened the impact, but . . . *He doesn't look monstrous,* Emilie thought. *He looks like this is how he's supposed to look.* And there was something about his voice that was reassuring.

Barshion frowned at Kenar and asked, "How did you get out of your cabin?"

Kenar lifted one shoulder in a shrug. He said, "Someone left the door unlocked."

"He fought the pirates and threw some of them off the boat," Emilie said. She wasn't certain why she was defending him, except that apparently someone had to.

Possibly it was ill-considered. The others turned to stare at her in blank surprise. The woman said, "Who are you?"

"I'm Emilie." Emilie had no intention of giving her last name, even if she was on a magic underwater steamship. After everything else, she didn't want news of her exploits getting back to her family, not until she was safe in Silk Harbor. She prompted politely, "And you are . . . ?"

The woman blinked, compelled by courtesy to reply, "Oh, sorry. I'm Vale Marlende."

Marlende. She must be related to the Dr. Marlende that Lord Engal had spoken of rescuing. "I'm very pleased to make your acquaintance, Miss Marlende." Emilie took a deep breath and plunged in, feeling it was better to admit the worst and get it over with. Not that it had ever worked out that way at home. "I'm here because I'm a stowaway. But I didn't mean to stow away on this ship. I was aiming for the *Merry Bell.* I'm going to Silk Harbor to live with my cousin at her school for girls and I didn't have the money for the passage ticket."

"A stowaway?" Barshion said, astonished. He regarded Kenar with suspicion. "What was she doing with you?"

Kenar was looking at Emilie, his scaled brow quirked in surprise. "I found her on deck. I thought she was one of Engal's daughters."

Barshion said, "Even Engal wouldn't be mad enough to bring his daughters on this voyage."

Ha, Emilie thought. Lord Engal was Southern Menaen too; she thought the resemblance ended there, but no one would have been looking closely at her during a pirate attack. It explained the crew's reaction to her, surprised but not alarmed. It was too bad she hadn't known that while there had still been a chance to get off this ship.

"You swam over from the dock, I suppose, which explains why your clothes are wet." Miss Marlende frowned at her. "Couldn't your cousin have wired you funds for your trip?"

Emilie set her jaw, sensing an implication that she had somehow failed to think of this sensible alternative. It stung more, since the implication was correct. But she hadn't known she didn't have enough money until she got to the ticket office, and it would have been too late by then to wire and get a reply. And if she had waited a day, Uncle Yeric would have had time to track her down.

She had no intention of explaining that. Before she could think of a reply, Barshion cleared his throat. "We can discuss that later, Miss Marlende." He looked at Emilie, stern and skeptical. "You really expect us to believe that your arrival, at the same time as the ship is attacked, was a coincidence?"

"It was a coincidence for me," Emilie told him, exasperated. Again, she was being accused of things she hadn't done and being questioned like a criminal. *Maybe it's me.* Maybe her face and manner were guilty and suspicious, and she had never noticed before. Whatever it was, she was sick of it. She planted her hands on her hips. "I'm a sixteen-year-old schoolgirl. Do I really look like someone who would be scouting for pirates or dock robbers or whoever those men were?" Surely a pirate's accomplice would be taller, and have dueling scars, or something.

"She has a point," Miss Marlende said to Barshion.

Emilie seized the opportunity to change the subject. She asked Kenar, "Are we really going down through a crack in the bottom of the world under the sea? Is that where you're from?"

Kenar nodded to Miss Marlende. "You explain it better."

Miss Marlende turned to her. "He's from the world inside ours, the inner world. My father, Dr. Marlende, is a philosophical sorcerer, an expert in aetheric currents." She eyed Emilie a little uncertainly. "Your family doesn't take any of the journals of the Philosophical Society do they?"

Miss Marlende didn't seem to think she was capable of understanding the explanation. Emilie would be more angry about that, if she weren't so afraid that it was true. She had done a great deal of reading, but not of any scholarly journals. But there was one thing that she did understand. "I've read about aether navigators, and how they work," she said. There were aetheric currents in the water and the air. They were what sorcerers used to make magic, and were invisible and intangible to ordinary people. Though there were always rumors that they could make people or animals ill, or that if a house was built in or near one it would suffer hauntings. But philosophical sorcerers had invented a way for oceangoing ships to navigate by known aetheric currents, as an alternative to compasses and celestial navigation. The novel *Lord Rohiro of the Far Seas* had explained it in great detail, in between sea battles and pirates and wooing foreign princesses and sea lords.

Miss Marlende seemed relieved. "Oh, then this won't seem quite so odd. Well, not entirely, anyway." She continued, "My father had been fascinated with the theories that there was another world inside the earth, that the center of the earth was hollow and that it was a nexus of aetheric currents. He began experimenting with aetheric currents in the sea, and below it, as a possible way to contact that world. It all

turned out to be far more complicated than the original theory implied, but eventually my father developed an engine that could travel
within the aetheric currents, powered by them, and he built a ship to
test it on."

Caught up, Emilie said in a rush, "And he took the ship on an expedition to the hollow world, and something happened and he and the
crew were trapped, and Kenar came to tell you where he was and get
help." Miss Marlende blinked in surprise, Barshion frowned, and Kenar lifted a brow. Emilie winced at herself. She had to remember, she
couldn't trust these people, and they really had no reason to trust her.
Pretend you're at home, and you have to watch every word you say, she
told herself. But at the moment, there was nothing she could do but
explain, "When I was hiding on board, I overheard Dr. Barshion and
Lord Engal talking about that part. But the rest was new."

"When did you overhear this?" Barshion asked, still watching her
skeptically.

"When you were in that lounge with the porcelain stove. I was in
the steward's cubby," Emilie said, glad she was able to prove it. She was
a runaway, not a liar.

"Oh, yes." Barshion sat back with a sigh. "We did discuss it there.
And only someone who was hiding in the steward's cupboard would
know that."

Mollified, Emilie felt the tension in her shoulders relax. At least
Barshion was willing to admit that she was telling the truth. And she
really didn't want to talk about herself anymore. She looked at Kenar,
reminded of all the questions she wanted to ask him. "Are all the people
down in the hollow world like you?"

"No," Kenar said, absently, looking past Emilie and Miss Marlende,
at the port. "The Cirathi are explorers, traders. We travel far, and see
many different places and kinds of people. We learn languages with
great speed, compared to others; I learned Menaen from Dr. Marlende
and Jerom and the rest of their crew, before coming here." His voice
turning wry, he added, "Lord Engal finds that suspicious."

Miss Marlende said wearily, "Sometimes I think he finds everything suspicious."

She was looking out the port too, and Emilie turned and saw that
the water beyond the rail was now dark as pitch, impenetrable by the
ship's lights. There was nothing out there to betray that they were

traveling through water, not even bubbles. A shudder crept up Emilie's spine. They must be very deep underwater, already, and some distance out to sea. *And we're going even deeper.*

Dr. Barshion stood, moving to the port. With a trace of concern in his voice, he said, "The bubble seems to be holding."

"Seems?" Miss Marlende lifted her brows. "If it wasn't, I think we'd know by now."

Emilie realized the faint sensation of falling, and of forward motion, had ceased. "It doesn't feel like we're going down," she said. But it was growing colder in the cabin, and moisture trickled down the inside of the port.

"The bubble—the spell protecting the ship and allowing us to breathe—compensates, so we don't feel the weight of the water above us," Barshion told her.

"Or we'd be crushed like an egg," Miss Marlende explained.

Emilie nodded. She hadn't thought about the weight of water before, except when she was trying to carry it in a bucket, but now it seemed obvious that all that water above them must be very heavy. Heavy enough to bend or break metal and glass. "How will we get to the hollow world, again?"

"There are fissures in the seafloor," Miss Marlende said, her face thoughtful. "Deep ones, that lead all the way through, connecting the outer layer of the world with the inner. Passing through them would be impossible, of course, except within the aether currents."

"Most of this, of course," Dr. Barshion said dryly, "is theoretical."

Kenar snorted quietly. Apparently it wasn't theoretical for him.

"But Dr. Marlende did it, didn't he?" Emilie said.

"My father took a different route," Miss Marlende told her. "He used an airship, and went down through the extinct cauldron of Mount Tovera, on the island of Aerinterre. Kenar took the same route up. The trip has never been made by sea, before."

That wasn't encouraging. Emilie was still having trouble believing she was here. It had all happened so fast. She asked Kenar, "But why did you come here? I mean, I know it was to get help for Dr. Marlende, but why . . . It must be a long way."

Kenar said, "I owed him a favor." He turned away from the port and said, "So why does a young schoolgirl flee her home?"

Emilie thought, *Uh-oh*. The others hadn't bothered to ask, so she had been hoping to avoid the subject entirely. "I wasn't fleeing," she said, to buy time. It was a complete lie, she had been fleeing, so she was a liar after all, but the last thing she wanted to do was explain why.

She was saved from further questioning by Dr. Barshion, who said in frustration, "There must be some word by now . . ."

He went to the door and opened it, and began to interrogate the guard about where everyone was and what was happening. Miss Marlende moved closer to listen, then turned away, muttering to herself in a disgruntled fashion. She said, "It sounds as if we'll be here for a while. They think there might still be some intruders on the ship." She walked back to the drinks cabinet, frowning at it. "I'm desperate for tea."

"The steward's cubby should have a tap and a gas ring," Emilie said, glad to show that she was a little useful. She didn't know much about aetheric magic, but she could do tea. "We can make some, if there's any here."

"Good idea." Miss Marlende went to ransack the cabinets in the cubby, while Dr. Barshion argued with the guard, Kenar watched the dark water, and Emilie found some mugs and tried to get over the strangeness of doing something so normal in the oddest place in the world.

*　*　*

Emilie made tea, which everyone drank but Kenar, and waited. Miss Marlende and Dr. Barshion talked about aetheric currents in technical detail, with Kenar joining in occasionally. Emilie tried to listen, because some of it was interesting, but it had been a long hard day, and the couch was soft and comfortable. After a time, she drifted off to sleep.

She woke abruptly when the deck shuddered, a vibration that traveled up through the couch and rattled her bones. She sat up, startled wide awake. "What was that?" The wall clock said she had been asleep almost three hours.

The others were sitting bolt upright, frozen, listening hard. Staring out the port at the bubble, Dr. Barshion said, "I don't know. It's not a terribly good sign."

Head cocked to listen, Kenar said, "We hit something?"

"I don't think so." Frowning anxiously, Miss Marlende added, "Perhaps it's just an aberration in the flow—"

The deck shuddered again, more violently, and Emilie's heart dropped to her stomach. She swallowed hard, very aware again of the water pressing in on their fragile bubble. Dr. Barshion strode to the door and pulled it open. The sailor-guard was braced against the wall, looking uneasy. Dr. Barshion said, "I must be allowed to go to the engine rooms. If there is some sort of interruption to the aether current—"

The sailor was saved from the decision to disobey his orders by a thunderous shout from the other end of the corridor. "Barshion!" It was Lord Engal's voice. "Where the hell are you?"

"Here!" Dr. Barshion stepped out.

"Come along, we've got a problem!"

Barshion hurried away, Miss Marlende and Kenar right behind him. Emilie followed, having no intention of being left behind.

Lord Engal led them down the first stairwell, saying, "Abendle doesn't believe the problem is in the protective spells, but in the motile itself."

Barshion said, "By 'problem' he means . . . ?"

Taking the stairs two at a time, Engal glanced up at him, his face grim. "He thinks it's not getting enough power from the conventional engines."

"What's the motile?" Emilie said, keeping her voice low. Her knowledge of the interior workings of steamers ended at Lord Rohiro's fictional pirate ships.

With an impatient glance at her, Miss Marlende replied, "The motile is the engine that my father invented. It lets us travel in the aether by taking in the aetheric stream and expelling it, for locomotive power. The aether helps protect the ship from the pressures and forces outside the current, as we travel through the fissure."

The sound of clanging, banging, and the chug of the engines grew louder until they reached a lower deck with a stained metal floor, low ceilings, and warm damp air. Lord Engal turned down a corridor and led them past several hatches. Passing one, Emilie got a glimpse of a room filled with mist and smelling thickly of wet earth and green plants. She stopped, startled, peering inside. All she could see were clusters of white things like balloons, or like stuffed sheep's bladders. An older crewman in a disheveled uniform was poking one with a dubious expression. The others were leaving her behind and she hurried after them, asking Kenar, "What's that room for?"

"It's part of the spell that cleans the air inside the bubble," he said over his shoulder. "I don't know how it works, either."

The air grew warmer and from the clanging and chugging that seemed to be coming from the deck below them, Emilie thought they must be just above the boiler room. Then they came to an open hatch. Dr. Barshion and Miss Marlende followed Lord Engal inside, but Emilie stopped on the threshold with Kenar.

The cabin was filled with big pipes and tubing, all connected to a round plinth in the center with a large copper dome atop it. Dials and knobs surrounded the base of the plinth, and two crewmen stood there. Tools were scattered on the floor around them, and they were pointing to the dials, arguing. They stopped as Engal stepped inside. "Any luck, Abendle?" Engal asked.

"No, my lord." The man who answered was Southern Mcnaen also, with grizzled dark hair and deep lines in his face. Both crewmen looked sweaty and exhausted, as if they had been battling something down here for the past hour. "The adjustments didn't help. I don't know—"

His voice tense, Dr. Barshion said, "Open the cover, please."

As the younger crewman lifted the copper dome, misty steam filled the room, though Emilie couldn't tell the source. Under the dome was a glass ball, and floating inside it was a bubble of silvery white light. Emilie leaned forward, squinting to see. It wasn't a light, it was a liquid. She could tell from the way it moved. It had an opalescent quality to it, as if it was a liquid drop of pearl. Blue light crackled under the glass, like a miniature lightning strike, and Emilie flinched.

So did everyone else. Miss Marlende said grimly, "That shouldn't be happening."

"What is it?" Emilie whispered to Kenar.

"It's quickaether," he told her softly. "It powers the motile, and the other spells the ship needs to travel the aether currents."

The crackling light inside the glass flickered suddenly. The deck shuddered in response and the ship around them groaned. Emilie swallowed in a suddenly dry throat. *That can't be good.* The ship sounded strained nearly past bearing.

Barshion checked all the dials, spoke quietly to the older crewman Abendle, and turned some of the knobs. Then he stepped back from the plinth. His expression wasn't encouraging.

Watching him worriedly, Lord Engal said, "You look blank. I'd like to believe that's a clever ploy to frighten me right before you tell me that of course you know how to fix it."

Barshion shook his head, baffled. "I don't understand what's wrong—all the spell's parameters are correct, but the engine is still failing."

Miss Marlende took a sharp breath. "Then we've got to surface. How close to the boundary are we?"

Engal said, "We've just passed it. We entered the fissure just off the coast and the current's carried us through, just as we theorized."

Kenar didn't seem surprised, but Dr. Barshion and Miss Marlende stared at Engal. "You didn't inform us," Barshion said, startled and angry. "If you—"

"I was rather busy; we had three dock raiders in the forward hold who decided to fight to the death." Engal lifted his brows. "We may be past the boundary, but we're still some distance from your father's last known position. I estimate several more hours of travel, at least. If we leave the current now—"

"But we can surface, that's the important point," Miss Marlende said urgently.

Barshion waved an impatient hand. "I don't think we have a choice. It's either surface intact now, or surface later as a smashed mass of metal."

Engal nodded sharply. "Then we'll surface now."

Emilie and Kenar stepped hastily out of the way as Lord Engal plunged out of the cabin and back down the corridor. Dr. Barshion stayed behind, but Miss Marlende dashed after Lord Engal, her boot heels tapping on the metal floor. Kenar followed her and Emilie hurried after him. *Boundary, fissure, surface,* she thought. It couldn't mean what it sounded like. Except that it couldn't mean anything else. She asked, "We're not going back up, back to the harbor, are we? We're already there, in the center of the world? That's what the black water meant?"

"Yes." He sounded more relieved than worried, and she remembered they were going toward his home.

"But so fast . . ." She had thought it would take days.

"The aether currents move through water and air at a pace faster than anything could travel without magic." He threw a quick glance down at her. "But we're here sooner than I expected. It must have something to do with the sea."

She meant to ask him if it had been a long journey for him, flying up through the volcano, but Engal was already pounding back up the stairs and Emilie had no breath to talk.

They hurried after him, forward down a passage, passing a couple of short corridors lined with cabin doors. Everything was as rich as the lounge areas, fine wood, polished brass. They went up a set of stairs to the bridge, to a passage that opened directly into a chart room. There was a big table in the center and large cabinets for maps against the walls.

Four crewmen were there, all in the black livery. The oldest man looked up, frowning. It was the officer who had ordered Kenar off the deck and sent him to be confined in the lounge. He said, "Lord Engal, are we—"

"We're going to surface, Captain Belden, prepare the crew," Engal said, moving past the crewmen into the wheelhouse.

The wheelhouse had a curved outer wall, with large ports all along it, now looking out on the black water. There was also a brass-bound wheel, a speaking tube, and an engine telegraph, for transmitting the captain's commands to the men in the engine rooms. In the center was a waist-high cabinet of polished wood, the top formed out of a heavy glass hexagon. Beneath the glass, something was glowing with a faint silver light. Engal stepped to it and carefully lifted off the top. Emilie edged closer, and saw that there were metal plates inside, rings and wheels, something like an astrolabe. He made a minute adjustment, and Emilie felt a sudden push upward, as if the deck was moving up under her feet. She stumbled, vertigo making her head swim.

Kenar and Miss Marlende went to the railing at the front of the wheelhouse. In the chart room the captain was frantically giving orders to secure the hatches, batten down this and that.

The water grew lighter, and Emilie made out a rocky shape, like a cliff face, a short distance off their bow. She gasped, suddenly realizing just how fast they were moving. Faster than the fastest train, as fast as falling down a cliff, only in reverse. It was the most exhilarating sensation, like how she had imagined flying.

Then the rock fell away and the light turned blue-green, coloring everything inside the wheelhouse. The ship moved up through something that looked like an underwater forest, tall stalks of frilly seaweed bending away from their bow and the bubble of magic protecting it. Emilie walked along the port, fascinated, watching the quicksilver flashes as fish raced away from the intrusion.

She could tell the ship was slowing down; bubbles rushed up past the ports as they left the seaweed forest behind. Emilie felt the deck push at her feet again, as if the ship had been lifted on a wave. Her heart pounding, she stepped forward to grab the rail.

A bell rang somewhere in the depths of the ship and Captain Belden took the speaking tube, saying, "All hands, brace for surfacing."

And then the ship rolled over onto its side. Some people staggered but no one fell. Emilie held on to the rail, gritting her teeth against the urge to scream. Water rushed past outside, the whole ship bobbed upright like a wooden toy in a pond, and Emilie wished she hadn't eaten that sausage roll back at the tap house. But then the motion gentled, and they floated on fairly low waves. Emilie stared out the port, but couldn't see anything past the golden bubble.

"We did it," Miss Marlende said, awe in her voice.

Kenar let out his breath in a hiss, then leaned on the railing. His shoulders slumped in relief.

Miss Marlende turned to Lord Engal. Sounding a little breathless, she asked, "Should we lower the spell bubble?"

Lord Engal looked down at the device inside the plinth. "From what Barshion said, I don't think we'll have to. It was about to shatter at any—"

Past the port, the golden light of the bubble dissolved, and they were looking out over a sea.

There is a sky was the first thing Emilie thought. It was crystal blue, bright and pure, streaked with the white of clouds. And the water under the ship was clear as glass. She could see a school of blue and yellow fish, flickering some distance below the surface.

"What is this place?" someone whispered in astonishment.

Emilie turned to look out the other side of the port, and drew in a breath of pure wonder. They were floating past a flooded city.

She moved to the railing, staring in amazement. It was spread out all across the starboard side, made of gray-white mottled stone like marble. The tops of square pylons, columned walkways, and towers with odd spiral curves gleamed above the expanse of clear water. Tall feathery trees stood in the sea, waves lapping against their trunks, their soft emerald-green foliage vivid against the sky.

Emilie looked up at Lord Engal, standing next to her, and said, "It's beautiful."

He glanced down at her, smiling, then took a second startled look. His brows drawing together, he said, "Who the hell are you?"

CHAPTER THREE

The next several minutes were problematic, at least for Emilie. She had thought Lord Engal looked like a shouter, and he proved her right, railing on about spies and stowaways and wasn't anybody guarding the ship as Miss Marlende repeated Emilie's story. To her credit, Miss Marlende continued doggedly, despite the noise and interruptions. At the end, Lord Engal turned to Emilie and demanded loudly, "Why shouldn't I throw you overboard?"

Emilie folded her arms, skeptical. After all the shouting and turmoil at home, being threatened with a dire fate wasn't as shocking as it ought to have been. She said, coolly, "I suppose you should throw me overboard, if you don't mind being a murderer. I prefer being shot to being drowned, if I'm given a choice."

Silence fell as Lord Engal was rendered momentarily speechless. Leaning casually against the rail, Kenar said, "You're not killing a child." There was a cold edge to his voice.

"Of course I'm not killing a child!" Lord Engal thundered. "We're not savages," he added, glaring at Kenar.

"I'm glad to hear it," Kenar said, his tone making it clear that as far as he was concerned, the matter was still up for debate. Emilie could have objected that she wasn't a child, but decided against it. Despite Lord Engal's bluster, she thought Kenar was by far the more dangerous individual. It was just lucky that he seemed to have high moral standards.

Lord Engal pressed his lips together, then transferred the glare to Emilie. "You're very confident, if you are what you say you are."

"What else would I be?" Emilie asked. She was discovering how much she had learned about verbal sparring from arguing with Uncle Yeric and her older brother. And Lord Engal had more important things to deal with than Emilie: outside the ports, the flooded city drifted by, small waves from their passage lapping at the white towers and graceful arches. Captain Belden was standing by the wheel and had cleared his throat three times; obviously decisions were called for.

Miss Marlende said impatiently, "Do you really think she's working with Lord Ivers' men? That seems unreasonable to me, and I've been dealing with his machinations much longer than you have."

"Who's Lord Ivers?" Emilie asked.

Everyone ignored the question. Lord Engal said, grimly, "So you'll agree to take responsibility for her, then?"

"Yes," Miss Marlende said. Then she looked a little appalled at what she had just agreed to. Emilie was a little appalled, also. She didn't think Miss Marlende thought much of her except that she was a nosy foolish stowaway. That that assessment was probably accurate just made it worse.

"Then take her below," Lord Engal snapped.

Miss Marlende set her jaw, unmovable. "I will, once I find out where we are and how far we have to go to find my father's airship."

"Ah." Lord Engal rubbed his chin, deflating as he apparently recalled that there were more important concerns at the moment. "Yes, we'd better ascertain that."

Captain Belden looked relieved. He signaled for another officer to take the wheel and stepped into the chart room. "Here, my lord. I've got the readings from the aether navigator."

Lord Engal strode after him. "Come along, Kenar, we need your map."

With one brow lifted in ironic comment, Kenar pushed away from the rail and followed.

Miss Marlende took a deep breath, still flushed from the argument. She looked down at Emilie and said, "His bark is worse than his bite, you understand."

Emilie nodded politely, if noncommittally. The expression was appropriate for dogs, who were without personal malice and whose job was, after all, to bark; she didn't think it applied to people.

As they stepped into the chart room after the others, Kenar took a folded packet out of his inside coat pocket and spread it on the table, flattening the creases with the blunt dark claws on the tips of his fingers. It was a map drawn in dark ink on thin cloth instead of paper, stained by dirt and grease. There were shapes sketched in, the outline of a coast with a large collection of islands, with notations made in a language with blocky letters that Emilie couldn't read.

"Now where's—Ah, here we are." Engal took the chart the officer held and put it down next to Kenar's map. Emilie had never been fond of geography, but she recognized Menae's coastline, with Meneport next to the mouth of the Seren River, and Silk Harbor some distance below it, and the other coastal cities scattered here and there. "They're not supposed to match up, are they?" Emilie asked Miss Marlende, keeping her voice low to avoid attracting undue attention. Since Miss Marlende was now in charge of her, maybe she would answer questions.

"No." Miss Marlende shook her head, absently tucking back a frizzy curl of blond hair. "According to the maps Kenar has brought us and his own observations, there's no correlation between landmasses."

Emilie nodded toward the port, looking out over the serene sea. Sunlight was glinting off the white facing of a fluted column, the top chipped and worn by weather. "That's not the sun, is it? It's a sun, but not our sun."

"Kenar calls it 'the warm heart of the earth.' There are other solid bodies in orbit around it that cause periods of darkness. One is called the Dark Wanderer, and the people who live here use it to determine directions. West is darkward, the direction the Dark Wanderer comes from, and east is antidarkward, the direction the Dark Wanderer takes when it leaves the sun." Miss Marlende stared out the port, caught for a moment by the view over the crystal water. "I can't believe we really made it here," she murmured.

Emilie couldn't, either. She supposed it would sink in over time.

Captain Belden was using a triangular plotting instrument to mark a position on the chart, and Kenar had his own system, using the widths of his fingers to measure and a stub of pencil to mark the points.

Lord Engal's brow furrowed as he studied the results. He said, "We left the fissure nearly ten hours early, at this point." He tapped the spot on the chart that Captain Belden had plotted, some distance off the Menaen coast. "We know Marlende's party is here, in the vicinity of the Aerinterre mountain fissure." He tapped another point on the chart, the outline of a large island. Then he looked at the other map, where Kenar had marked the same points. "Hmm."

Emilie craned her neck to see. On the hollow world map, the space between those points was blank. Kenar drummed his claws on the table and admitted, "Our ship was still charting this area. It was new territory for us."

Captain Belden said slowly, "If our figures are correct, it should be the same approximate distance between the coast of Menae and the island of Aerinterre. That would be about two days' sail, if conditions are good." He gave Kenar a hard stare. "If there's nothing in the way."

"I don't know," Kenar said pointedly. "If I knew, I would have put it on the map."

Lord Engal let out a gusty breath, still frowning. "We've no choice. We can't return to the upper world until the motile is repaired, and if we can't go back, we must go forward. We'll try to reach Marlende's position."

"We might not be able to go back," Captain Belden said, "but we don't have to go forward. We could hold this position and make the repair."

Miss Marlende stepped forward and slammed a hand down on the table. Emilie jumped, startled. Everyone else stared at Miss Marlende. Teeth gritted, she said to Lord Engal, "The whole purpose of this, the whole reason we contacted you, gave you access to my father's work, was to help him and his crew. If you leave now, when he's within reach, so you can claim the discovery, I will—"

"I have no intention of leaving here without your father and his men," Lord Engal cut her off. "That may not be my sole reason for pursuing this experiment, but it certainly is the most important." He took a deep breath, and added more calmly, "Miss Marlende, you've repeatedly demanded that I trust you and Kenar. I would appreciate it if you would extend a little trust to me in return."

Miss Marlende met his gaze for a long moment, then said, grimly, "Fair enough."

With a pointed glance around, Engal continued, "As I said, we'll sail toward Marlende's position while Barshion and the engineers try to make the necessary adjustments to the aetheric engine. We'll also try to raise the airship on our wireless, though from Dr. Marlende's notes we know that the aether in the air here may interfere with radio waves. If we encounter obstacles, we'll deal with them as necessary. If we can't deal with them, I'll reconsider our course."

Captain Belden didn't look happy, but he didn't object, either. Emilie, as annoyed as she was with Lord Engal, had to admit that this was as

fair as possible, and probably what she would have done in his position. Miss Marlende seemed to agree. She said, with a trace of stiffness,
"Thank you, Lord Engal. I can't ask for more than that."

Then Lord Engal ruined it by saying, "I should think not."

* * *

There was a lot of bustle at that point, everyone putting their heads
together over the maps, and Emilie found herself shuffled out of the
wheelhouse and into the corridor. Once there, she wasn't sure where
to go. Everyone seemed to have temporarily forgotten that Miss Marlende was supposed to be in charge of her, and she didn't want to remind them. And she didn't want to draw too much attention and get
herself locked up in a cabin for the duration.

But her stomach was growling, and she felt sure she wasn't the only
one; somebody would be feeding the crew breakfast.

She went down the nearest stairs to the main deck, and once there
followed the smell of fried bread and sausages down another stairwell
to the crew quarters. The corridor opened into a crew lounge fitted up
as a galley, with long tables and benches, where an older woman and
a boy about Emilie's age were working at a small stove and counter,
dispensing food. Several crewmen, some with bandages, black eyes,
torn uniforms, and other signs of the fighting, were sitting down to eat
or waiting for seconds. Emilie picked up a tin plate and a cup from a
clean stack and joined the line.

She noticed most of the crew were Southern Menaen, like Lord Engal,
or looked as if they had a mix of both Southern and Northern heritage.
They could have all been hired from Meneport, but they seemed comfortable with each other, as if they had been together as a crew for a
long time. They had fought off the attack on the ship in a very capable
fashion; it made her wonder if Lord Engal did this sort of thing a lot.

From the talk she overheard, everyone was unsettled by the fight,
tired, and deeply uneasy about their current whereabouts. Emilie
thought it was a rational reaction to the whirlwind events of the past
few hours.

When it was her turn, the boy who took her cup to fill it at the tea
urn just stared at her, but the woman who was dishing out the food
blinked in surprise and said, "Now who are you?"

"I'm Emilie." She held out her plate hopefully. "I'm with Miss Marlende." Maybe that would come in handy after all.

"Oh, well then, you should really be eating up in the passenger
lounge," the woman told her, but continued scooping sausage slices,
fried bread, and potatoes onto her plate. "Verian, the ship's steward, is
going to be serving up there."

"But this looks so good," Emilie said, and for once it was the complete truth. The sausage was plump, the bread soaked with butter and
sugar, the potatoes nicely browned.

Her sincerity must have been evident, because the woman smiled,
ladled more onto the plate, and said, "If you need anything, I'm Mrs.
Verian."

Emilie thanked her, took her mug of tea, and retreated. She went
back up the stairs to the passenger decks, since she was less likely to
be noticed there. Recalling there were tables and chairs on the glass-
enclosed promenade, she headed for it.

The hatch was already open. Emilie peeked out cautiously, and saw
Miss Marlende seated at a table. Kenar was nearby, perched on a supply
locker built against the wall. They were looking out at the view, which
was so arresting Emilie had to stop and stare a moment.

The ship moved slowly, the low throb of the engines the only sound
as they sailed along the edge of the flooded city. The clear water sparkled in the sunlight, and their wake lapped at the white towers, the
wide pitched roof of a submerged building, a line of artistically twisted
columns that marched away to nowhere. Emilie supposed there was
no time to stop and explore, not before they had rescued Dr. Marlende.
But maybe we'll have to come back this way, and have time to stop then,
she thought.

Her stomach grumbled again, and she stepped out onto the promenade. She meant to say something polite, but then saw the distant
shape in the sky. "What's that?" she demanded, interrupting their conversation.

She couldn't tell how far away it was. It hung in the sky, like a solid
band of heavy gray cloud, except something seemed to be stretching
up from it, a translucent column that vanished high in the air. Miss
Marlende followed her gaze. "Oh, that. It's the other outlet for the Aerinterre aether current, the one that's connected to Mount Tovera in the

surface world." She sounded much calmer than she had in the wheel-house. Perhaps Lord Engal's assertion that he still meant to find her father had reassured her somewhat. "There's so much free aether in the air here that we can actually see it with the naked eye, if the weather conditions are right."

"Oh." Emilie blinked, recalling herself. She stepped toward the table. "I hope I'm not interrupting."

"No, we were wondering where you went—Where did you get that?" Miss Marlende said, as Emilie set her plate down and took a seat.

"The crew galley," Emilie said, and started to eat.

"It's better than what they had in the passenger lounge." Miss Marlende sat back with a sigh. Kenar made a disparaging noise, and she said, "Oh yes, oyster cocktail and salad are fine for you." She explained to Emilie, "He doesn't eat meat, he thinks our vegetables are odd and our fruit tasteless."

Chewing sausage and potatoes, Emilie glanced at Kenar. He had shed the greatcoat and changed clothes. Over the trousers and worn leather boots, he wore a sleeveless red shirt studded with gold disks around the hem, and gold chains woven through his mane. It accented his alien appearance, making it easier to see the dark scales on his arms, and where they gave way to short dark fur that spread across his shoulders. He looked much more comfortable and much more at ease. She swallowed and said, "But you have pointed teeth."

He took an apple out of a pocket and said, "You have flat teeth, and look what you're eating."

"True." Emilie polished off a piece of bread, and decided to try to get a few more answers. She asked, "Who is Lord Ivers, and why is everyone worried about him?"

Miss Marlende's brow furrowed, but she explained, "He's a very wealthy man, like Lord Engal, and he studies aetheric currents, like Lord Engal. We believe it's Lord Ivers who was responsible for the dock raiders who attacked us last night. It wasn't just a coincidence; there were a few earlier attempts."

"He wants the credit for the discovery?" Emilie guessed. She didn't know much about the prominent sorcerers and philosophers of Menae, preferring the more dramatic imaginary versions in popular novels. But in her aunt's society news journal, she had seen mentions of awards and royal honors for philosophical achievement, inventions, discovering places and things, all of which seemed fairly minor compared to this. She thought finding a way to visit the hollow world must be the biggest philosophical achievement of the age. "He's going to steal your father's glory?"

"Well, to put it bluntly, yes." Looking out at the serene sea, Miss Marlende grimaced. "Lord Engal and Lord Ivers and my father were all working—separately, you understand—on mapping the aetheric currents that could be traveled in, the spells needed to protect a vehicle, and perfecting an aetheric engine. My father had an advantage. He's a sorcerer himself, unlike Lord Engal and Lord Ivers, who have to hire sorcerers who are experts in aetheric studies to work with. My father finished his engine first, and rushed to place it on an airship. He took a small crew, and entered the current inside the cauldron of Mount Tovera on Aerinterre. I camped on the island with the ground crew, and waited. He was gone for six weeks. Then Kenar arrived, to tell us the engine had failed and he needed help."

"How did Kenar get back through the current by himself?" From what Emilie had observed, this was impossible, and she couldn't imagine climbing up through a volcano, even a dead one.

"There were several hot-air balloons stored aboard the airship for emergencies, and my father fitted one out with the protective spell, so they were able to travel the current in it. Another man came with Kenar, my father's apprentice, Jerom Lindel." Miss Marlende added bleakly, "He died on the trip."

From behind them, Kenar said, "The journey was . . . rougher than we expected. Jerom said the spell was meant to protect a large vehicle. It didn't work the way he thought it would, and there was nothing he could do to fix it."

"I'm sorry," Emilie said to both of them, meaning it. The man must have been a friend of Miss Marlende's. Kenar sounded as if the trip had affected him severely, and she didn't think he was someone easily overwhelmed.

Miss Marlende sighed. "Originally, the plan was for Jerom to get the materials needed to repair the airship's aetheric engine, and then he would set the spell on the balloon and he and Kenar would return through the volcano's current. But with Jerom dead, there was no one who could manage the spell."

"I hope it doesn't hurt you to speak of him," Kenar said, watching Miss Marlende.

Emilie said, "Did you have an understanding with him? I mean . . ." *Shut up, Emilie,* she thought, realizing belatedly she hadn't been acquainted with Miss Marlende nearly long enough to ask that question.

But Miss Marlende just shook her head, her expression regretful. "He was a good friend, but I wouldn't have married him. I don't intend to marry at all. I'm not sure I ever quite convinced him that I was serious about that." She continued, "But his death also left us with no way to send assistance to my father and the others, so we had to go to someone for help. I chose Lord Engal to approach." She gave Kenar a dry look. "I hope I made the right choice."

He laughed, a soft huffing noise. "It's too late to change your mind now."

"Well, if I'd chosen Lord Ivers, I'm not sure Lord Engal would have sent men to harass us, shoot at us, and attack the ship before we left." She leaned back, her mouth set in an ironic line. "At least I don't think so."

"I don't think so, either," Emilie offered. "Lord Engal isn't subtle. He seems more the shouting-at-you-in-person type."

Miss Marlende gave her a quizzical expression. "An astute observation."

Emilie wasn't sure if she was being teased. She said, a little stiffly, "I'm used to dealing with people who shout."

"Who shouts at you?" Kenar asked.

"Oh, you know, my uncle." She made what she hoped was an offhand gesture, sorry she had brought it up.

"Is that why you ran away?" Miss Marlende asked, frowning a little.

"Mostly, yes." Emilie made the answer abrupt, hoping they wouldn't ask any more. "And my oldest brother Erin ran away to join the merchant navy and he did very well, so I was just following his example. Without the navy." He had been obsessed with going to sea and exploration, and used to make their other two brothers play his crew. Emilie had always been his second-in-command. Uncle Yeric had told Erin all his life that he meant him to stay at home and go into business with their cousins who lived in another town, and had never paid much attention to Erin's own aspirations. But in this new world, with all these new people, washed by a cool breeze on the deck of a ship sailing an alien sea, she didn't want to talk about her family. She asked Kenar, "Did our world seem very strange to you?"

"Yes." He smiled, the points of his teeth showing. "The cold weather was rather unpleasant."

"I'm afraid the whole thing was very unpleasant," Miss Marlende said, rubbing her forehead. "Lord Engal didn't trust Kenar's word. I'm not sure why. It's rather a large amount of trouble to go to for an elaborate hoax. And you know, Kenar's not human, and it's rather easy to prove his appearance isn't a sorcerous illusion or trick. We had to be very careful to conceal his appearance when we were in Meneport. You'd think that would have substantiated our story all by itself."

"It did." Kenar snorted amusement. "He thinks I'm luring you down here to kill you and take his engine."

Emilie pointed out, "If you had Dr. Marlende down here already, then you'd have his engine. Why would you need Lord Engal's too?"

"There's that," Kenar said dryly. "I don't want any engines."

"Logic didn't seem to enter into it." Miss Marlende sounded as if she was more than fed up with Lord Engal. "Every time I thought we had convinced him, he seemed to change his mind again."

Dr. Barshion, Emilie thought. He had been suspicious of Kenar, pressing Lord Engal about it even as the expedition prepared to leave. She debated mentioning it, but she didn't want to be seen as making trouble. *And probably they already know Dr. Barshion doesn't trust Kenar.* Yes, of course they did. Barshion had as much as said so when they were all waiting in the lounge together.

Miss Marlende was saying, "Lord Engal kept having Kenar locked in his cabin, if you'll believe it."

"Thank you for letting me out," Kenar told her.

She shrugged. "It was the least I could do."

*   *   *

After a time, Kenar and Miss Marlende went back inside, but Emilie spent the next couple of hours sitting in a chair on the glassed-in promenade, just watching the flooded city go by. She tried to stay awake, not wanting to miss anything, but found herself napping occasionally, drifting off in the mild sunlight and fresh air.

The towers and columns had been growing fewer, with more distance between them, for the last hour or so. Emilie thought it might be because there were smaller structures in this area, only a single story tall, covered completely by the flood. But even standing on a chair and craning her neck, she hadn't been able to see any sign of it below the clear water. She had caught glimpses of mosaics, blue and green and flecks of other colors, set in plazas between the towers.

Then a shrill whistle from the bow startled her. She heard footsteps pounding along the upper deck, and rushed to follow. She ducked inside, went up to the top deck, and ran around to the bow, to the open observation area just below the wheelhouse. A few crewmen were already there, and Emilie saw immediately what had caused the lookout to call the alarm.

Some distance ahead, just visible over the top of a half-sunken colonnade, was a ship's mast. "What is it?" Emilie said. From what she understood, they were still a long distance from where Dr. Marlende's airship waited, and this looked like a sailing vessel. "A Cirathi ship?" Maybe Kenar's people had come this way looking for help.

One of the crewmen gave her an odd look. "Don't know, miss. It looks like a wreck."

Kenar and Miss Marlende arrived a moment later, with Lord Engal striding up behind them. Miss Marlende was asking Kenar, "Is it your ship?"

He went to the rail, staring hard toward the mast. The crewmen moved away from him a little uneasily. As the *Sovereign* drew closer, two more masts were visible, but the ship seemed to be sitting at an odd angle. He said, "No, it isn't the *Lathi*. I don't recognize . . ."

The *Sovereign* was moving past the colonnade that had blocked their view, and now they could see the hull of the ship. It was a wreck, lodged partially atop one side of the pitched roof of a half-submerged structure. The hull was long, longer than the *Sovereign* or even the *Merry Bell*, but the steam-driven paddle wheel on its listing port side was smaller, as was the smokestack in the stern. Sails still clung in withered shards to the ruined masts, planking along the deck had rotted, and the metal hull was scraped and discolored by rust. "It's from our world," Miss Marlende said, her expression somewhere between appalled and fascinated. "But how—"

"It's the *Scarlet Star*, by God." Lord Engal lowered his spyglass. "You can still make out the name on the bow." He turned, waving up at the wheelhouse. He strode away, back toward the hatch that led inside.

"What's the *Scarlet Star*?" Miss Marlende asked, before Emilie could.

An older crewman said, "She was a cargo steamer, heading toward Meneport, when she went missing in a freak storm. This was about ten years ago. There was always something thought funny about it. There was no sighting from the Southern Light, no wreckage washed up anywhere ashore." He looked toward the battered wreck again, brow furrowed. "I guess this explains it."

"How is that possible?" Emilie asked. She hadn't heard the story of the *Scarlet Star* before, but it had happened a long time ago. She hadn't paid much attention to the shipping news when she was six years old. "It wouldn't have had an aetheric engine, would it?"

Everyone must have been wondering the same thing, because all the men were looking to Miss Marlende for the answer. Frowning, she said, "No, it couldn't have. But there is a theory that violent electrical storms do cause aetheric currents to act in very odd ways."

Kenar said slowly, "Very odd, meaning . . . snatch a ship from the surface world and bring it through the rift in the ocean floor and deposit it here?"

"But it wouldn't have the spell bubble, like we did," another crewman protested. "It would be crushed when it was dragged under, wouldn't it?" It was the young man who had been helping Abendle with the aetheric engine. He looked as if he had been working all night, his curly hair flat with sweat and his uniform rumpled.

"It wasn't crushed, and it got here somehow," Emilie pointed out.

"Yes, but Seaman Ricard is right." Miss Marlende leaned on the rail and studied the wreck thoughtfully. "There must have been some protection for it. Perhaps the storm caused a pocket of air to form, and that was what was pulled through the rift, with the ship brought along as part of the pocket."

Ricard looked at the wreck again. "So there could have been survivors?"

Kenar sounded grim. "For a time, maybe. There's no help out here, no fresh water, no food."

Emilie saw what he meant. This city must have been empty for decades, perhaps even before it flooded. And there was no land in sight.

It would be a rather bleak spot, if you were stuck without a ship or other means of transport.

An officer called from the upper deck, and the crewmen ran to obey. Emilie felt the engines change pitch as the ship began to slow. She said, "We're going to stop and search the wreck." She was torn between excitement at seeing a real shipwreck and feeling sorry for the crew. They must be dead, whatever had happened to them, whether they had drowned when the ship had been dragged into the aetheric current or died of hunger and thirst after being deposited here. She wasn't sure which was a better fate; both sounded painful and frightening.

"We're wasting valuable time." Miss Marlende gripped the rail, sounding as if she was struggling to control her temper.

"No," Kenar said. "It might tell us something about what we're to face in these waters." He added, "And we can use all the help we can get."

But the wreck provided no help at all.

The *Sovereign* slowed to a halt a little distance from it, and the launch was dispatched to investigate. Aboard were Kenar; Captain Belden's first officer, Oswin; and six armed crewmen. Emilie and Miss Marlende waited on the deck with Lord Engal and Dr. Barshion, who was taking a brief respite from working on the aetheric engine and had come out for some air. They watched tensely, but after a short time of climbing over the wreck, the boarding party returned with little news.

"Nothing there, my lord," Oswin reported to Lord Engal after they climbed back aboard the *Sovereign*. "I found the cover of the logbook but water had washed into the bridge and the pages had rotted away. There was no sign of the crew, alive or dead. I think they must have perished before the ship entered the rift."

"There was no sign of anything," Kenar added. "No supplies at all, in the hold or the cabins, no crates or casks, no blankets on the beds, no clothing, no pots in the cooking area. As if the ship was stripped."

"Yes, but it's been there ten years," Oswin said, before Lord Engal could reply. Emilie felt they had been arguing about this during the entire exploration of the wreck. "Everything that wasn't nailed down would have washed away."

"Not everything," Kenar said stubbornly.

"That aside," Lord Engal put in firmly. "If there's nothing more to learn here, we'll continue. At least we can reveal the solution to the mystery of the *Scarlet Star*'s disappearance when we return."

He went back up the stairs toward the wheelhouse, and the crew dispersed back to their duties. Miss Marlende lifted a brow at Dr. Barshion and said, "When we return?"

His mouth set in a grim line, he said, "We're working on it."

CHAPTER FOUR

When night fell, the sun didn't sink toward the horizon; the shape of the Dark Wanderer moved across it, causing an eclipse.

Emilie had seen an eclipse of the moon before, but never the sun. While it was impossible to look directly at even the Hollow World's smaller sun without going blind, they could see the eclipse coming by the line of darkness sweeping slowly across the sea toward the ship.

Once the sun was completely obscured, it was as dark as the most cloud-covered moonless night, with only the ship's running lights to guide them across the water. The *Sovereign* dropped its speed by half, chugging cautiously along, with lookouts in the bow to spot obstacles. Kenar said the darkness should last about eight hours by the ship's clock.

Except for the crewmen on watch, and the group still working on the aetheric engine, most people were going to take the opportunity to sleep. Miss Marlende offered Emilie the extra bed in her cabin, possibly in order to keep an eye on her. At the moment Emilie didn't care; she hadn't done anything but briefly nap for nearly two days, and was tired enough that she was ready to lie down to sleep on the deck.

The cabin was on the second deck above the hull, an interior one with no portholes. It was nicely appointed with two beds, roomy cabinets, a tap and small ceramic handbasin, a mirror, and a door leading to a small private water closet. Emilie expected to be given instructions to wash and change and attend to her hair, but Miss Marlende just sat down heavily on her bed to unlace her boots, and waved a vague hand toward the clothes cabinet and the basin. "There's water and things over there. Use whatever you need." Then she lay down on the bed fully clothed and was asleep in moments.

Emilie stared, bemused. It underscored the fact that Miss Marlende was an adventuress—not the romantic kind who got into trouble, but the intrepid kind who visited strange places and made philosophical discoveries and met new people. She thought of her friend Porcia, who had been training herself for adventures since Emilie could remember, and had already announced her intention of never marrying, and of traveling the world with several doughty female companions. One of the benefits that she and Porcia hadn't considered was that one could do what one liked and worry about comfort more than appearance. It made a nice change from Emilie's aunt, for whom appearance and what the neighbors thought was everything.

It was nice to be treated as an adult who could make her own decision about whether she should wash or not. Her aunt had never considered Emilie capable of it, seeing her as the same tomboy who had always come in covered with dirt and muck from the garden. *Well, that's what you thought, anyway.* Emilie looked at herself in the mirror, the memory of that last argument with her uncle making her cheeks heat with anger. It seemed obvious now that Aunt Helena had thought Emilie a great deal worse than just a tomboy. All because she had asked to go to Cousin Karthea's school.

She realized that the saltwater swim in the harbor hadn't done her hair any favors, and that her clothes were itchy in the most uncomfortable places. She sighed. It would be stupid to forgo washing just to spite her aunt, who, since Emilie had run away, was sure to be pretty well spited already. She ended up washing in the handbasin and rinsing out her underthings, taming her hair somewhat, and borrowing a thick cotton nightgown out of the cabinet to sleep in. Leaving one light on near the door, she tucked herself in and fell asleep almost as fast as Miss Marlende had.

She was jolted awake what felt like moments later by the ship's whistle. Miss Marlende sat bolt upright, gasping, "What the hell is that?"

"Ship's alarm!" Emilie realized the ship was slowing down even further, the low thrum of the engines changing in pitch. She struggled out of bed, squinting at the clock. They had been asleep about four hours; from what Kenar had said, the end of the eclipse was still some time away. She heard boots pounding out in the corridor and hurried to dress, scrambling into her still-damp underwear, bloomers, and one of Miss Marlende's shirts. Miss Marlende, older and slower to come to full consciousness, managed to struggle out of bed and get her boots back on. She reached the door only a moment ahead of Emilie.

Not bothering with her own boots, Emilie ran barefoot down the carpeted corridor after Miss Marlende. As they reached the hatch, Miss Marlende flung out an arm to stop her. "Careful," she said, low-voiced. "If there's something out there—"

"Right," Emilie said, making a mental note not to plunge headlong out of hatches at night while in strange worlds.

Miss Marlende peered through the glass window of the hatch, then twisted the handle and pushed it open. She stepped out, still cautious, and Emilie stood on tiptoes to see over her shoulder.

The night was lit only by the lamps along the deck, but someone up by the wheelhouse was shining the ship's spotlight down on the water ahead. "What is that?" Miss Marlende muttered.

"It looks like . . . seaweed?" Emilie followed her, trying to see in the uncertain light. The water was clotted with some sort of plant. The searchlight picked up vines growing thickly over the surface, with large lumps floating among them. It looked distressingly like a Sargasso Sea, which had featured in frightening detail in one of the Lord Rohiro novels.

Miss Marlende moved to the railing. "Emilie, you should go back to the cabin."

"Why? What is it?" Emilie still couldn't see anything in the searchlight beam but thick weeds. On the main deck below, sailors were moving around with lights, but it was too dark to see what they were doing.

"I don't know what it is," Miss Marlende replied with some annoyance. "That's why I think you should go back to the cabin." She gave Emilie a stern look. "Now go."

Fine, Emilie thought, annoyed herself. "I'm going," she said, with dignity. Moving as slowly as possible away from the rail, she heard voices raised in agitation and caught a glimpse of Kenar standing on the deck below with a lamp. He was talking to someone; she thought it might be the first officer, Oswin.

"Kenar!" Miss Marlende called softly. "Do we know what it is?"

Kenar and Oswin turned, looking up, and Oswin said, "It looks like—"

Something flipped up out of the water, a long narrow shape, as if one of the vines had suddenly stood straight up. Emilie pointed and gasped an incoherent warning. Old woodcut pictures of sea monsters flashed through her head; she thought she was looking at a giant tentacle. It swung toward the ship, slamming into the rail a bare three steps away from Emilie and Miss Marlende. Then something leapt off it and landed on the deck.

Miss Marlende yelled in alarm and Emilie jerked backward. The thing had two arms, two legs, and a slender body—for an instant Emilie thought it was a person, albeit a naked person with green skin. Then she got a better look at its head. It was eyeless, noseless, earless, its face a blank except for a wide slit for the mouth.

Miss Marlende lifted her hands, palm out, saying quickly, "We mean you no harm. If we came near your . . . your territory, it was an accident, we're only passing by—"

It hissed, opening its mouth to show a shockingly large rictus of fanged teeth. Then it lunged forward and grabbed for Miss Marlende.

Miss Marlende swung at it, hit it in the face with her fist, but it caught her arm and dragged her toward the railing. Emilie shrieked for help at the top of her lungs, then grabbed for Miss Marlende and wrapped her arms around the other woman's waist.

It dragged them inexorably to the rail, far stronger than a human of that size. But as they hit the rail Miss Marlende dropped to the deck, throwing the creature off-balance, then used the moment of distraction to wrap her legs around the lower strut of the rail. *Yes!* Emilie thought, letting go of Miss Marlende with one arm and wrapping it around the post below the strut. The creature pried at them, hissing, and the metal ground painfully into Emilie's arm. She wrapped a leg around the post and held on with grim determination.

A crewman ran up the deck, yelling. He struck at the creature and it let go of Miss Marlende long enough to backhand him. The blow was hard enough to send him flying back across the deck and slam him into the wall. Miss Marlende fell away from the rail, and Emilie sat down hard. The creature reached down and slapped at Emilie, sending her rolling away.

Emilie landed hard on the deck, reeling from the blow, and looked up in time to see the creature drag a fighting Miss Marlende to her feet. Emilie looked desperately around, saw something lying near the fallen crewman—it was a fire ax. She shoved to her feet, snatched it up, and darted forward.

She swung it at the creature and the blade bounced off its head, painfully jolting Emilie's arm. Apparently unhurt, it dropped Miss

Marlende and turned to Emilie. She lifted the ax again, for all the good it had done her, but she wasn't going to let it hit her again without a fight.

Then she saw Kenar behind it, climbing up over the railing from the deck blow. Emilie waved her ax, yelling "Yah! Yah! Yah!" to keep the creature's attention on her. It jerked back uncertainly. Then Kenar swung over the railing, grabbed the creature by the throat, and tossed it off the deck.

Emilie lunged to the rail, looking down in time to see the creature bounce off the lower deck and fall into the weed-choked water. But more slim green forms climbed the hull to the lower deck, tendrils of vine waving angrily in the mass of weed. Gunshots rang out as crewmen along the middle deck fired at the creatures. The ship's stack belched as the boilers built up steam for an escape.

Miss Marlende stumbled to her feet, saying hoarsely, "What was that thing? A plant?"

"Yes, it looked like part of the weeds." Kenar turned, reaching out to steady her.

Emilie couldn't tell if the gunfire was driving the creatures off or just startling them. "If they're plants, it can't do much good to shoot them," she said. It might be just as useless as shooting a tree. "Oh, there's Dr. Barshion!"

Dr. Barshion had stepped out onto the deck just below. He was coatless, his normally sleek hair mussed. He held a small book in one hand, his other hand clenched in a fist. Emilie thought he was reading aloud, but she couldn't catch the words. On the lower deck, a plant creature swung over the rail, grabbed a crewman, and tried to drag him over the side. But two other men drove it off with blows from their rifle butts. Emilie heard Lord Engal shouting orders. Kenar stepped up onto the rail, meaning to leap back down into the fray, but Miss Marlende caught his arm. "Wait!"

Below them, Dr. Barshion raised his voice, crying out something Emilie couldn't understand, then he made a throwing gesture with his free hand. Sparks of red light glittered along the hull; the plant creatures climbing the rails keened in alarm and fell back away from the ship. A moment later the stacks belched again and the ship angled away from the weeds, and a gap of dark water opened between it and the green mass.

"He manipulated the remnants of the aether bubble to repel physical objects," Miss Marlende murmured. "Finally. I was beginning to wonder how much good he was as a sorcerer." She swayed a little.

Kenar asked, "Are you all right?"

She waved him away, turning back to the deck. "I'm fine. But this man was injured . . ."

The crewman who had tried to help them was stirring and trying to stand. Kenar went to haul the man to his feet, and in the lamplight Emilie saw it was Ricard, the young assistant engineer.

The young man gasped, "That was—What was—"

"No one knows," Kenar told him. "But some of that weed was caught on the hull, we can have a closer look at it."

Miss Marlende told him, "Yes, but let's get Ricard inside first so I can check his head." Tugging her jacket back into place and pushing her disordered hair out of her eyes, she turned to Emilie and said formally, "Thank you, Emilie, your assistance was effective and timely."

"You're welcome," Emilie said automatically. She realized she had clasped the ax to her chest. She decided to keep holding it for a while; it was reassuring.

Her heart was still thumping. This had been very different from hitting the robber with the fire bucket. The worst she had thought would happen then was that the man would hit her back, knock her down. She had realized later that that might have been naive; those men were deadly serious and he might have shot her. But even that wasn't as bad as that creature, dragging her and Miss Marlende off the ship to be . . . *Drowned? Eaten?* It was possibly better not to know for certain, but her imagination was doing a good job of filling in the details.

They went back inside, and once Ricard stepped into the brighter light of the corridor, they saw he had a bloody gash on his temple. "I thought you were helping Abendle and Dr. Barshion with the aetheric engine?" Miss Marlende said, helping Kenar guide Ricard down the first set of stairs.

"It was my turn to take a break, miss," he explained, wincing. "I was walking around the ship for a bit before I turned in."

"Lucky for us," Emilie put in, following behind them. "You distracted it." *And brought me the ax,* she thought.

He glanced back, giving her a wan smile. "I think you did a better job of distracting it than me."

Emilie didn't know what to say. She wasn't used to compliments about actual accomplishments, just stupid things, like needlework and decorating hats.

They reached the main lounge, and Miss Marlende caught a steward's assistant and sent him running off to get the ship's medical kit. Kenar left them to head back out to the main deck, and after a moment of hesitation, Emilie followed him. She had decided that knowing what was out there was better than just imagining terrible things.

Out on the deck, Emilie was glad to see the men with rifles were still keeping watch. The searchlight swept back and forth across the water, showing they were some distance from the vine mat already and moving steadily away. But a small section of it had caught on the ship's hull, and the crew had dropped the launch's platform to get a closer look at it. Lord Engal was down there with a few crewmen carrying lights. Kenar started to climb down, and Emilie realized she would have to relinquish her ax to follow him. Curiosity won out, and Emilie set the ax down on a handy fire equipment box and followed Kenar down the ladder to the launch platform.

The first thing that struck her was the smell; it was more like rotting meat than any kind of plant. The men were poking cautiously at the mass of weeds with boathooks. One of them drew a lump in close to the platform, and another hacked it free of the weeds. "It's a broken cask," he reported. Looking up at Lord Engal, he added, "Could even be from the *Scarlet Star,* my lord."

"They seemed to try to take anything they could grab," someone said, and Emilie recognized Oswin's voice. "They got two of our life preservers and a coil of rope."

"It explains why the wreck was stripped of everything movable," Kenar added, stepping around Oswin for a closer look.

"At least they didn't get any of us," Lord Engal said. He glanced at Kenar. "Is Miss Marlende all right?"

"Yes. She's tending to the man who tried to help her." Kenar crouched down to get a better view of the weeds. Emilie felt she could see well enough where she was, and stayed near the ladder.

"Perhaps she'll be more cautious next time," Lord Engal said.

Emilie snorted quietly to herself. *Typical and unfair,* she thought. With some asperity, Kenar said, "She was cautious. She was two decks above the water. Sometimes caution doesn't help."

Lord Engal didn't reply to that.

"Look at this," another crewman said, holding up a clay sculpture in the shape of a bird.

Kenar stood up to examine it. "That's a net weight," he said. "The Lothlin hang them off the rails of their boats."

Lord Engal turned to him. "These plant creatures are called Lothlin?"

"No, no. The Lothlin are fisherfolk, peaceful. Nothing like those things." Kenar sounded disturbed. "If one of their boats was driven this far from their home territory, trapped in the mat—"

The first crewman said, grimly, "It looks like they didn't make it out."

Emilie stepped forward to look. Prodding at the mass of vines had released dozens of small objects that had been wound up in it. They bobbed free in the water, sticks, odd-shaped knobs, round things like smooth rocks. She tried to see them as wood, the debris of a wrecked ship, but the colors were bleached white, dull yellow, rotted brown . . . Then a round object floated closer, turned as the crewman poked it with the pole. It had a face, or what was left of one, with empty eye sockets, a hole for the nose, teeth, the lower jaw broken away.

Emilie pressed back against the ladder, cold shock washing over her. They were bones, all bones, wound up in the vines. Long bones, knobs of bone, fragments, skulls. She swallowed hard as a whole rib cage bobbed up out of the weeds. What was left of the sausage from this morning tried to exit her stomach and she took a deep breath, willing it back into place. *That's a lot of dead people. Pieces of dead people.* Emilie had seen the dead laid out decorously in coffins, but never anything like this.

Lord Engal stepped back, his grimace of distaste visible in the lamplight. "I think we've seen everything we need to see. Cut this mess free of the ship and draw up the platform."

Emilie realized she was in the way and turned to climb the ladder back up to the deck. She had to grip the ladder extra hard because her hands suddenly felt numb and chilled, as though it was freezing out here rather than only pleasantly cool. *Eaten, we definitely would have been eaten,* she thought. On reflection, it seemed obvious. Plant creatures with sharp teeth didn't try to pull people off ships in the middle of the night for a good reason.

She stood near the rail to watch the lights dance as the men hacked and prodded away at the mass. Bits of it broke off and swirled away, caught in the ship's bow wave, then the whole thing finally gave way. Kenar came to stand beside her as the launch platform was hauled up and Lord Engal gave muttered orders to Oswin and the other crewmen.

Dr. Barshion came out on the deck a little distance from them, and she heard Lord Engal congratulate him on driving off the creatures. But Barshion said, "Unfortunately, it's not something I can repeat. The aether in the remnants of the protective bubble is completely depleted now. I can't use it to drive off an attack unless I re-create the spell, and I won't be able to do that until we get the motile working again. The two are meant to work together."

That's not good, Emilie thought, hugging herself. It seemed a long time until the night eclipse would be over; the ship was like a bubble of light traveling through impenetrable darkness. Emilie said, "Do you think we'll run into anything else tonight?" She realized it was a stupid question as soon as the words were out. Kenar had told them over and over again, he had no more idea of what was in these waters than they did.

But he just put a hand on her shoulder and gave her a one-armed hug, saying absently, "I hope not."

* * *

Emilie would have thought there was no way she would be able to go back to sleep after everything that had happened. But the shock of seeing the bones had rather crushed the excitement right out of her, and she found herself so heavy with exhaustion that she could barely drag herself back to Miss Marlende's cabin. Without bothering to undress, she lay down on the bed. Her restive stomach found this position much more amenable, and she quickly slid into sleep.

She woke briefly when Miss Marlende came in, drifted off again, then roused herself to see what the clicking noise was. It was Miss Marlende, sitting on her bed, loading a revolver. Miss Marlende saw her watching, and said, "Obviously I should have taken this precaution earlier."

It was a little odd to see a woman with a gun, especially a pistol. But after what had happened, it seemed an excellent idea. Emilie asked, "May I have a pistol too?"

Miss Marlende frowned. "Have you ever used a pistol before?"

"No."

"Then you may not have one."

"Hmm." Emilie subsided, sinking back down onto the pillow to go back to sleep. She recalled accidentally stabbing herself with a penknife while trying to cut reeds for a fishing rod one summer, and decided Miss Marlende was probably right.

* * *

Emilie slept through the end of the night eclipse and three hours into daylight. She woke, blearily stared at the clock, and struggled out of bed. After a quick wash, she tied her hair back, laced her boots, and hurried out to see what was happening.

She stepped onto the deck into dim sunlight and a humid breeze. Dark gray clouds filled the sky, heavily bunched in the direction the ship was heading. It completely obscured the cloudy column of the Aerinterre aether current. They had left the remnants of the flooded city entirely behind, but the sea wasn't empty. The ship was steaming toward a series of small islands. *Odd islands,* Emilie thought, shading her eyes to see. They all stood high above the water, at least twenty or thirty feet, with trees and clumps of vegetation on top and sharp cliffs dropping down to the waves.

By going to the bow and looking over the rail, she found Miss Marlende and Kenar on the main deck. Miss Marlende was using a spyglass to study the islands. Emilie hurried down the nearest set of stairs to join them. "What's that?" she asked. "Are we nearly there?"

"Possibly," Kenar admitted. "These islands are similar to the ones near where the airship went down. I just hope we can navigate through them."

Miss Marlende lowered the spyglass. "The channels between them seem quite narrow in spots. We're going to have to go very slowly." She tapped her fingers on the rail in frustration.

"And hope nothing tries to grab us," Emilie added, thinking of the Sargasso creatures last night.

"There's that," Miss Marlende added wryly.

There seemed to be nothing more to do at the moment than watch the islands draw closer, and Emilie's stomach was growling. She went back inside, and found her way down to the crew's galley. Mrs. Verian wasn't there, but her young assistant was scrubbing the tables, and Emilie managed to get him to stop long enough to find her an egg sandwich, an apple, and a mug of very sweet tea. She was so hungry she ate the sandwich standing up at the serving counter, then put the apple in her pocket and carried the mug of tea out, meaning to head back up to the main deck.

But just down the corridor, at the base of the stairwell, she heard Dr. Barshion's voice and stopped to listen. "—I'm sorry, Abendle, I just don't believe that's the right method. We should be adjusting the axis slowly, not trying to reorient it completely."

Abendle. That was the older engineer who was working on the aetheric engine with Dr. Barshion and Ricard. *Dr. Barshion sounds exhausted,* Emilie thought. Sounding even worse, Abendle replied, "Yes, Doctor, you know more about it than I do, but I still think these figures don't show what they're supposed to. Maybe if Miss Marlende looked at them—"

"No, Abendle, she's not familiar with her father's work in that detail. I wish she was." Dr. Barshion laughed a little wryly. "No, you and I will have to try to puzzle it out."

Steps sounded on the metal stairs above and Emilie hurried away down the corridor, looking for the next stairwell. She made it before the two men reached the corridor, and escaped unseen up to the next deck. She wasn't sure why she had fled, except that Dr. Barshion already thought she was an eavesdropper and she didn't want to confirm that supposition by being caught at it again.

* * *

Emilie spent the morning out on the promenade deck, with Kenar and Miss Marlende. But Miss Marlende was too impatient to stay in one spot for long, and kept getting up to walk around the ship.

The scenery they were passing was endlessly fascinating. The islands were growing larger and closer together, so sometimes it was difficult to find a course through them. The ship kept having to stop and send out the launch to take soundings, which made Miss Marlende even more frustrated.

The trees were like the palm trees Emilie had seen drawings of, the ones that grew on the coasts far to the south of Meneport. But the fronds were much bigger, stretching out for ten or fifteen feet and then drooping at the ends. There were other trees like none she had ever seen before, squat with thick conical trunks, topped by sprays of feathery fern-like leaves. Beautifully colored birds, blue, yellow, green, flew away from the ship's passage, too quickly for Emilie to get a good look at them.

After the third time Miss Marlende excused herself to go up to the wheelhouse, Emilie said to Kenar, "You're not nervous."

"I'm less nervous." He smiled at her, a quick flash of pointed teeth. "My people are in an area that's foreign to them, but the ship was in good repair when I left, and they had plenty of supplies. And I know they can take care of themselves, and that they will watch over Dr. Marlende and his crew. Vale knows that too, but she's waited and worried a long time."

Emilie noted that he had used Miss Marlende's first name, then realized it probably didn't mean the same thing to him. Kenar seemed to have only one name, himself. Though after their shared trouble, he and Miss Marlende did seem to be good friends. And she thought he had been through a lot too, what with the dangerous trip to a strange world, and Lord Engal's suspicion and distrust. "Why did you go with Jerom to get help?" she asked. She had asked him that before, but he hadn't given her a very good answer. "I mean, it was very difficult."

He looked out at the channel again. "Dr. Marlende brought his ship and his people into danger to help us. We had anchored near a series of small islands and sandbars, and sent a small boat ashore to replenish our water supply. Rani, my partner, was aboard it."

Just the way he said the name "Rani" caught Emilie's attention. She wondered if "partner" was the correct word or if Kenar was perhaps translating it wrong.

Kenar continued, "The island we chose turned out to be a trap. A giant creature, bigger than this ship, lived on the seafloor beneath it, feeding on the fish and birds that came within range. When Rani, Beinar, and Sanith beached their boat on the sandbar, the creature raised folds of skin out of the water, swallowing the sandbar entirely, trapping them. We couldn't reach them, and we knew if we didn't, they would be eaten alive. But Dr. Marlende had seen our ship and been heading toward us already, meaning to try to speak to us. He saw what had happened and took his airship down low over the island, and fired weapons at the creature. When that didn't work, some of his men let themselves down with ropes and hacked at it with axes and burned it with fire. Finally it opened, and he dropped a ladder, and Rani and the others were able to escape with only minor injuries." He let out his breath, as if putting aside the frightening memory, and smiled down at Emilie. "We sailed together for a while, learning about each other, helping each other as we explored this territory. When his engine be-came damaged later, we felt it was our chance to repay the favor he had done us. And we're explorers. I couldn't let the opportunity to travel to the legendary outer world pass by." He gave her a thoughtful look. "You didn't explain why you left your home."

"Didn't I? Oh." Emilie realized uneasily that she had been asking him a lot of questions, and that he had perhaps noticed that she had been avoiding his inquiries. "I left home because when my mother was only two years older than me, she left home." Kenar frowned, not under-standing. Emilie added, "She became an actress. She could have come to a bad end." Kenar still didn't appear to understand. "It was very shocking," she said. "Some people think actresses are, you know . . ." He probably didn't know, and she found herself extremely reluctant to tell him that some people thought actresses were prostitutes. She was afraid he would ask her what a prostitute was. Kenar, after all, had learned Menaen from Dr. Marlende, and there were probably a lot of words that just hadn't ever come up in conversation. And she didn't like to put it into words, the idea that her aunt and uncle seemed to have, that any decision a woman made about her life was somehow a criminal act. Or at least any decision Emilie wanted to make about her life. "It's hard to explain."

"I'll take your word for it," he assured her gravely. "I still don't see what a parent's past actions have to do with you."

"Because I'm her daughter, my uncle and aunt always felt that I'd do the same. Only perhaps I wouldn't be lucky, and meet a man like my father, who would marry me anyway." Emilie tried to sound matter-of-fact, though it wasn't easy, and she could hear the anger that made her throat tight creep into her voice. She had been told over and over again, for what seemed like years on end, that she was destined to come to a bad end, even before she had had any idea what a bad end was. But deep down, she hadn't really thought that they believed it.

Emilie liked to read, liked to take off her shoes and stockings and wade in the creek, to explore the fields and copses around the village farms. She had only been interested in the local boys while they were all young enough to play at being pirates and highway robbers together; as she had gotten older, it was only the adventurous heroes in books who had caught her attention. She was certain she was the least likely girl in the village to come to a bad end because she lost her head over a boy. Or anyone, for that matter. If she was going to lose her head over someone, it would have been Porcia.

But you still could have died, she thought. *You could have gotten yourself murdered in an alley, crossing through Meneport, no matter how careful you thought you were being.* Uncle Yeric's prophecy might have become a self-fulfilling one on Emilie's part.

"Do you want to become an actress?" Kenar said, still puzzled by her attempt to explain.

"No. It sounds rather difficult to learn acting, and I can't sing well, and I'm not a good dancer." She tightened her hands on the railing. She had never had any specific ambition, except that she had wanted to travel, wanted to visit places that were just names in books in the lending library or on the maps in the village school's atlas. But that took money, and she had none of her own; she had known she needed a more realistic goal, if she didn't want to be stuck as her aunt's companion for the next twenty years. "I didn't really know what I wanted to do. But my friend Porcia Herinbogel was going off to school, to Shipands Academy." It was a real school, that taught things like mathematics, history, languages, agriculture, and even mechanics, and it was admitting young ladies for the first time. Porcia had been mad to go; she hadn't inherited her father's magical talent, but she was terribly clever, and wanted to take the courses necessary to be considered for a medical academy in Meneport that allowed women students. Emilie was certain that her uncle would not agree to pay for anything like that, but it had given her an idea. "I asked my aunt and uncle if I could go to my cousin Karthea's school, in Silk Harbor. She's my father's sister's daughter, and that side of the family isn't as . . . as my mother's side. I thought I could help with the work, look after the younger girls, maybe, while

I took some of the classes. It's a lot of work, running a school, Karthea talks about it in her letters. I know she needs help." She and Porcia had talked it all over, and her father had offered to bring Emilie along when he took Porcia to Shipands. They would be going through Silk Harbor anyway and could drop Emilie off on their way. It had seemed a modest goal and a perfectly respectable occupation. It had not seemed like much to ask.

Kenar still looked as if he wasn't certain he understood. "You ran away because your uncle and aunt forbade you to go?"

"Yes, partly. It was the way they did it." Porcia, Mr. Herinbogel, and two of her aunt's friends, Mrs. Rymple and Mrs. Fennan, had been invited for tea, and Emilie had chosen that moment to broach the subject. But Uncle Yeric had refused to listen and forbade her to even mention it again. Emilie had lost her temper and shouted. The argument had escalated to the point where her aunt had burst into angry tears and her uncle had accused her of using the school as a ruse to get out from under their watchful eye, where she could become a prostitute like her mother.

The memory of being shocked senseless with humiliation, sitting on the couch in the familiar parlor while the embarrassed visitors hastily took their leave, still made her cheeks burn. It had gotten worse once they were alone. That was when her uncle had added that he thought she meant to use the trip as a ruse to fix her interest with Mr. Herinbogel, a widower old enough to be Emilie's father.

Thinking about it still filled her with fury, made her pulse pound. She had known then that whatever she did, she would never see her aunt and uncle again, not if she had to run to the ends of the earth. And she really didn't want to tell any of this to Kenar. It was hard enough thinking about it, but she had to finish the story. "They thought I was lying about helping with the school. They thought I wanted to use it as an excuse to get away from home. They said if I persisted, they would send me away to a place to be locked up." She wasn't certain if Uncle Yeric had meant an asylum, or a prison. She had known that if he told the magistrates that she was a disobedient girl who wanted to run off and find men to sleep with, they would believe him and not her.

Kenar shook his head slowly. Emilie thought he was rather appalled, even at this mild version of the story. "Your mother is not here to . . . shield you from the rest of her family?"

"No. She and my father died, when I was very young. My oldest
brother hasn't come home since he ran away to join the merchant navy,
and my other two brothers like my uncle and agree to whatever he
says." They had agreed about her, too. She supposed she should have
expected it, but it had been just one more shameful blow on top of all
the others. She had been close to them once, but when they had been
sent off to boarding school, and no longer saw her every day, it was as
if the real her had been replaced in their minds by her uncle's version
of her. And when their older brother had run away, it had perhaps
been worse for them than Emilie. He had confided in Emilie more, so
she had been more prepared when he left, though it had still hurt her.
To them it had been a bigger shock, and maybe they had turned to
her uncle for reassurance, and it made them more susceptible to being
swayed by his opinions. It had occurred to her later that she might
have been more helpful to them at the time, but she had been so upset
and so resentful herself that she hadn't been thinking about anyone
else's feelings.

Kenar said, "I see. You could not join your older brother?"

"No. He's on a ship, now." She added, in case Kenar didn't realize,
"They don't let women join the navy in Menae."

"That's seems an odd thing to forbid. You would make a good
sailor."

"Thank you." Emilie felt a huge relief at leaving the subject. She
took a deep breath, and felt the breeze cool her flushed face. "If I was a
Cirathi, I could be a sailor?"

"Of course. My partner, Rani, is a woman and is captain of our
ship."

Emilie lifted her brows, intrigued. "Really?" She wanted to ask
more, but Oswin came to tell Kenar that Lord Engal wanted to speak
to him, and he went up to the wheelhouse. She stood on the deck for a
long time after that, though, thinking about being the captain of a ship,
and mentally rewriting the Lord Rohiro novels with someone like Miss
Marlende as the main character.

* * *

It was late in the day when the ship's alarm sounded and someone
shouted, "There it is!"

Emilie ran out to the rail, where Miss Marlende, Kenar, Lord Engal, and some of the crew were gathered. They were approaching a sizable island, ringed by cliffs like the others. At the base, anchored next to a narrow stretch of beach, was a large wooden sailing ship. It had three masts, with faded purple sails furled around the lower spars. Cabins with round windows were built all along the main deck, and they were painted various bright colors, now faded by sun and weather. Flowering vines were painted below the railings on the hull. "It's such a lovely ship," Emilie said, before she realized what was wrong, why everyone was so silent.

The sailing ship's deck was empty. There was no sign of life aboard, no one coming out to investigate the chugging sound that signaled the *Sovereign*'s approach. Emilie looked at Kenar, stricken.

His expression was closed, opaque. But she felt it was hiding a good deal of fear.

Miss Marlende said, "Perhaps they had to retreat into the interior of the island for some reason." Emilie looked at the cliffs above the beach, but there was no sign of life or movement there, either.

Miss Marlende lifted the spyglass, studying the trees. "Perhaps they're at the airship, with—"

"We should be able to see your father's airship from here," Kenar interrupted, an edge to his voice. "It's gone."

She turned to stare at him, startled. "Are you certain?"

At her expression, he shook his head, avoiding her eyes. "Maybe they had to move it."

Lord Engal looked from one to the other, frowning. Emilie thought he might say something to make it worse, but instead he just said briskly, "Now then, you can't expect them all to be standing out here waiting for us. They've probably been quite busy in our absence." He turned to Oswin. "Make ready to lower the launch. We'll soon get to the bottom of this."

* * *

Kenar and Miss Marlende boarded the launch with Lord Engal, Oswin, and six armed crewmen. Emilie slid into a seat next to Miss Marlende, and no one objected.

Emilie had managed to add herself to the landing party simply by staying close to Miss Marlende and Kenar, who were too distracted to notice her. If they had noticed her, each probably assumed the other had asked her to come along. She was sure Lord Engal, Oswin, and the other sailors noticed her, but they must have assumed that Miss Marlende had given her permission. Emilie thought Lord Engal must be making sure to be more polite to Miss Marlende, after their earlier disagreements, and the fact that . . .

That they might find her father, his crew, and all of Kenar's crew dead on the island somewhere.

The launch puttered across to the island, its engine sounding very loud in the silence of calm wind and water. The strip of beach was narrow, the rocky bluff above it draped with flowering vines. Two crewmen climbed out to help push the boat up onto the beach, and they all clambered out, splashing in the shallow water. Leaving a crewman to watch the boat, they approached the Cirathi ship cautiously.

Kenar went first, the others following, Emilie bringing up the rear. The soft sand crumbled underfoot, the scent of green plants and sweet flowers was heavy in the air. It would have been a lovely place, except for the silent ship. Kenar headed for the bow, and the crewmen spread out to search along the bluff. The wooden hull was covered with tar, or whatever the Hollow World equivalent was, and from this angle only the decorative painting made it different from a Menaen ship.

They circled around to the port side, the side facing the island that they hadn't been able to see from the Sovereign. A rope ladder hung over the rail there, dangling down to the sand. "Was that here before?" Miss Marlende asked tensely.

"Yes." Kenar started to climb.

"No sign of tracks on this sand, but wind or water may have worn them away," Lord Engal said, mostly to himself.

A crewman called out, "There's a way up the bluff, here, my lord. Steps cut into the dirt."

"We did that, to get up to the airship," Kenar said, already vanishing over the rail.

Lord Engal turned to follow him, telling the crewmen, "Two of you climb up there, look for signs of the airship. Stay within shouting distance."

Oswin picked out two more men to remain on guard on the beach, then followed Lord Engal up the ladder with the others. Emilie followed them. She looked back to see Miss Marlende hesitating, torn between the ship and joining the search for the airship atop the bluff. Then she turned to follow them up the ladder.

Emilie climbed awkwardly over the solid rail onto the deck. She had been afraid to see the place strewn with bodies, but there was no sign of that. *Yet,* she thought, a little sick.

Kenar did a quick circuit of the deck, which to Emilie's untutored eye seemed undisturbed. There was nothing broken, no loose lines in the rigging, the casks and barrels of supplies—as gaily painted with vines and flowers as the rest of the ship—were still lashed into place. Kenar opened the door into the long series of cabins along the deck, moving quickly through.

Emilie followed behind Lord Engal and Oswin. The windows were all shuttered, but the slats were tilted to allow in light and air but deflect rain. They moved quickly along, and she got only fast glimpses of bunks and seats built into the walls with brightly colored cushions, blue and gold pottery jars, a cabinet stacked with scrolls of paper. One scroll had been left unrolled on a stool, and Emilie stopped to look at it. It wasn't a map, as she had thought at first—she remembered that the map Kenar had carried had been drawn on a square of fabric—but a long list of notes handwritten in an oddly square script. She wondered if it was a chronicle of the voyage. *Maybe someone left a log entry, a note about where they went, what happened to the airship,* she thought. *And why they didn't take their ship, even though it doesn't look like there's anything wrong with it.* She suspected she was being optimistic again.

She hurried to catch up with the others, who were just going down the open hatch into the hold. It was warm down there, and crowded with supplies, mostly casks and more of the pottery containers, so Emilie stayed on deck with Miss Marlende. There was another separate cabin back here, and Emilie stepped inside to see it was a small galley. There was no place to eat inside, but there was a small squat metal stove with a flat cooktop, and pots and jars were stored on shelves against the walls, with rope webbing to hold them in place against the ship's motion. The room smelled of herbs, wilted greens. There was a pot beside the stove, still half full of stale water, a wooden spoon with a carved flower handle standing in it. Emilie took the spoon out, so it wouldn't be ruined by soaking too long in the water, and hung it on an empty wall hook.

Miss Marlende was shielding her eyes, looking toward the bluff. From here there was a better view of the top, and Emilie could see the two crewmen moving through tall grass, in a big clearing half surrounded by the tall palm trees. They were scuffing at the ground with their boots, poking through the ferny bushes. It didn't look as if they were finding anything. Not anything terrible, anyway. Emilie said, "Maybe they fixed the airship's aetheric engine." It was a stupid thing to say, but she was finding it hard to just stand here silently, as if they were at a funeral. She could hear wood creak as the men below searched through the holds, but she bet they weren't finding anything, either.

Miss Marlende bit her lip. "The Cirathi would leave someone behind to guard their ship. Unless something attacked them and they all had to escape."

The ladder creaked as Lord Engal climbed back up, followed by Kenar, Oswin, and the other crewmen. Kenar moved away immediately to the railing, knotting his fists on it and looking across at the island. Lord Engal cleared his throat. He was sweating in the damp air, and had pulled his shirt collar open. He said, "There's no sign of violence, but there's no sign they took any of the supplies they would need to leave the ship for any length of time." He frowned at the island, the men still searching the top of the bluff. "Hmm. A closer look at the airship's landing site may tell us more." He focused on Miss Marlende and said, "We'll find them. Obviously they had a compelling reason to leave this spot, even if it isn't obvious to us."

Miss Marlende nodded tightly. "We took too long to get here."

Lord Engal's brows lowered, but he kept a hold on his temper. He said, "I apologize for the delay but I assure you—"

"No, not you." Her voice was thick with the effort to control her emotion. "I should have acted more quickly. As soon as Kenar arrived with the news of what had happened, I should have . . . had plans already in place, I should have . . ." She shook her head, and turned away.

Emilie unobtrusively pressed her sleeve to her eyes. It was obviously taking a great deal for Miss Marlende not to give way, and she didn't want to add to the burden by succumbing to sympathetic and completely useless tears herself. She wasn't sure if Miss Marlende wanted to be comforted, or how to go about it, or if the attempt would just make things worse. Kenar, still standing at the rail and lost in his own grim thoughts, clearly wanted to be left alone.

Lord Engal seemed to be facing a similar dilemma. He hesitated, then finally said gruffly, "Not much opportunity to plan for this sort of eventuality, when one had no idea what Dr. Marlende was going to discover, if anything. Seems to me we've all been simply doing our best with what little we know." He cleared his throat. "Now let's have a better look at this landing site and see what it tells us."

Miss Marlende pressed a hand to her temple for a moment, then said, in a steadier voice, "Yes, of course."

*   *   *

They went up the dirt-cut steps to the top of the bluff. It was warmer up there than down by the water, and Emilie was glad she was wearing one of Miss Marlende's lighter cotton shirts. The large grassy clearing looked bare of clues at first, but as soon as Kenar and the others began to point things out, Emilie could see the signs that a great many people had been here.

There were footmarks in the dirt, tufts of grass that had been ripped up, divots in the ground and spots of flattened vegetation where large heavy things had rested. Back under the shade of the trees, they found a rock hearth where someone had made a campfire, places where food garbage had been buried, a dropped handkerchief stained with engine oil, a wrench that had been accidentally kicked into a bush. Oswin pointed out that there was only a little rust on it, that it couldn't have been there for more than a few days.

They could see the marks on the nearby palm trees where heavy ropes had been tied, that must have been the anchor lines for the airship. And there was a big square spot in the dirt where Kenar said the main cabin had rested, when Dr. Marlende had lowered the craft all the way down to try to repair the aetheric engine. "It looks as if they moved it, at least twice," Oswin said, poking at a tuft with the toe of his boot. He looked at Kenar inquiringly.

Kenar spread a hand, shaking his head. "They may have. When Jerom and I left, Dr. Marlende still hadn't given up on the idea that he could fix the engine himself."

"It was only the aetheric engine that was damaged, correct?" Oswin said. "Not the smaller oil-fueled engine that would allow the airship to maneuver."

Kenar nodded, glancing at Miss Marlende. "But Dr. Marlende

didn't want to move the airship too far without the aetheric engine. He was afraid he would run out of fuel for the other one. That's why we took the balloon to the aetheric air current on the *Lathi*."

"And obviously the ship returned here safely," Lord Engal muttered, walking past them. "We need to search the rest of the island."

But they found nothing, just trees, flowers, and bird nests.

CHAPTER FIVE

When they finally finished the search of the island, it was time for dinner, though there were several hours of daylight left before the next eclipse. Emilie ate with the others in the passenger lounge this time, since she knew they would be discussing what to do next and she didn't want to miss anything.

She sat in the back, eating a potted chicken sandwich, trying to stay unobtrusive. Captain Belden was here, as well as Dr. Barshion, Ricard, and Abendle, the engineer. The last three men looked terribly weary; they must have been working almost nonstop on the aetheric engine. Ricard's head was still bandaged from his encounter with the Sargasso creature.

"They could have taken the airship to the aetheric current, to test their repairs," Lord Engal said, thinking aloud. "But why abandon the Cirathi ship?" He turned to Kenar, eyeing him uncertainly. "Your crew wasn't eager to travel to our world, were they?"

Kenar rubbed his eyes. With the scales and the fur, it was hard to see how affected he was, but Emilie thought his shoulders were tense and his usual calm self-possession was gone. Sounding a little exasperated, he said, "Not at all. Until we met Dr. Marlende and his crew, we thought your world a legend. We have our own concerns here. They could spare me for a brief visit, to help pay our debt to Marlende, but there is just no reason the others would make the trip."

Captain Belden said, "Dr. Marlende could have left with the airship, and something attacked the ship's crew before they could leave the island."

Emilie saw Kenar's jaw tighten at the thought. Miss Marlende sat forward impatiently. "This kind of speculation is useless. Our assumption must be that someone or something attacked the island, and both crews were forced to flee in the airship."

Kenar looked up, his expression thoughtful, and Emilie found herself nodding. If something like the Sargasso creatures, or worse, had attacked, the airship would be the quickest way to escape. "The airship might have run out of fuel then, and be stuck on another island," she said.

Captain Belden frowned at her, as if he didn't think she should be giving her opinion, but Miss Marlende said, "Yes, that could very well be it. The question is, how do we find them?"

"There hasn't been a peep out of the wireless, not that it's supposed to be much use down here," Oswin said, sounding glum. "We can't track them through the air or the water. It's not as if they'll have left tracks."

Abendle cleared his throat. "They might have."

Intrigued, Lord Engal twisted around to stare at him. "Yes? Speak up, man."

Abendle stepped forward, seeming uneasy with all the sudden attention, but he said, "Aetheric engines do leave tracks, my lord, when they aren't traveling through aetheric currents."

"But the airship's aetheric engine was damaged." Miss Marlende looked uncertainly from Abendle to Dr. Barshion. "They shut it down to use the airship's conventional engine."

"If it's even them still running the airship," Oswin said. "If something didn't attack both crews to steal it." Captain Belden nudged his shoulder in silent remonstrance.

Emilie didn't think Oswin was speaking out of turn. There was surely no one on the ship who hadn't considered the possibility that the Cirathi crew, and Dr. Marlende and all his men, might be dead or captured by something. It was an awful possibility, but it was still a likely one.

"Aetheric engines can't ever really be shut down, once they're started up," Abendle explained. "The aether that powers them is still active, still producing power, and connecting with the aether in the air, if you see what I mean, even if the motile itself is not being used to draw the vehicle along an aetheric current. It's as if it pulls bits of aether into itself, and leaks bits out as it moves along. Like a normal engine will leak oil. Those bits will be clumped up, so to speak, much thicker than the normal concentrations of aether in the air." He appealed to Dr. Barshion. "Isn't that true, sir?"

Everyone turned to Barshion. "Well, yes," he admitted reluctantly. "It's a possibility. But I'm not sure how an aetheric engine would behave here, in this world. Its aetheric composition is different from our own, you know."

Kenar was sitting up straight, listening intently. He looked hopeful for the first time since they had seen the empty Cirathi ship. Miss Marlende said, "We can try, surely."

Emilie eyed Barshion, not sure why he was so reluctant. *It's not as if we have a lot of other pressing things to do while we wait for him to fix our aetheric engine,* she thought. Everyone else, even Lord Engal, seemed game to go on with the search.

"Yes, how would this be accomplished, Barshion?" Lord Engal said. "There should be some way to detect the traces of aether left behind . . ." He snapped his fingers. "The aether navigator!" He jumped to his feet, forgetting he still had a sandwich plate in his lap. He caught it agilely before it fell onto anyone's head, and handed it off to Captain Belden. "It should detect the presence of aether, any aether, even a small fragment in the air!"

Lord Engal dashed off down the corridor to the stairwell, apparently intending to test this immediately. Everyone set plates and cups aside as they hurried to follow.

In the wheelhouse, Lord Engal, with Dr. Barshion and Captain Belden, poked at the aetheric navigator, making minute adjustments to its silver wheel, and turning it this way and that. Miss Marlende stood nearby, managing to look over the shorter Dr. Barshion's shoulder, but Kenar stood back at the port, looking toward the abandoned ship.

Emilie angled around, trying to get a good view without getting in the way or jolting anybody's arm. She finally found a spot where she could look under Lord Engal's elbow.

Emilie had read descriptions of aether navigators in her favorite sea adventures, but never seen one in person. The aether navigator had a flat silver plate, etched around with the symbols and degrees of the compass directions. Two silver rings could be rotated around it, apparently to help figure longitude and latitude, though Emilie couldn't quite follow how. On the plate itself, in a shallow dish, was a silvery substance that looked like mercury but was actually drops of clarified, stable aether. It would roll around as the plate was turned and rotated, pointing the way toward aether currents in the air and water.

Then Dr. Barshion said quietly, "Wait, wait. I think that's it."

"Yes, it's reacting to a concentration of aether somewhere nearby." Captain Belden carefully marked a spot on the outer ring. "But could it be traces from the airship's earlier movements, when it first arrived at the island?"

Tilting the navigator's wheel slightly, Dr. Barshion muttered, "I don't think it would remain that long . . . aether outside a current dissipates relatively quickly. And we know they were here for some time, preparing the balloon to make the attempt to get help from the surface . . ." The base plate tilted, sending the stable aether skittering around its shallow bowl. He stepped back, shaking his head, grimacing. "I'm sorry, I've pushed it out of alignment."

"No, no." Lord Engal frowned, catching the plate, his big hands unexpectedly gentle as he turned and angled it slightly. "Look at this, it's picking up something on the lower strata. Belden, you know more about surface aether navigation, is that what it looks like . . . ?"

Belden leaned forward, reading the marks. "Faint traces in the water. Yes, my lord. It's definitely there. That's going toward the east . . ." He glanced up at Miss Marlende. "Could the airship float?"

"Float?" She glanced at Kenar, brows lifted. "I suppose the main cabin might be somewhat buoyant, but I can't imagine that they would try to turn it into a boat. If they had all needed to leave by water, surely they would have taken the Cirathi ship."

Kenar came forward, his scaly brow furrowed. "No, there was no plan for that . . . Perhaps another ship arrived, placed the airship on board, and carried it away."

"It would have to be a large ship." Miss Marlende paced away, shaking her head as she thought it over. "But it would be possible."

"Did your people encounter anything like that in this area?" Belden asked Kenar, apparently forgetting how much he disliked him under the excitement of the mystery. "A vessel large enough to transport the airship? Or a settlement capable of building one?"

"No. In fact, we thought this area was mostly uninhabited." Kenar pulled the folded square map out of a pocket inside his shirt and moved over to the chart table to spread it out.

Oswin put in, "That empty city we passed, whoever built that must have had a fleet of ships."

Lord Engal followed Kenar to the chart table. "Yes, of course, but it must have been abandoned for a century or more, long enough for the sea to shift."

"Unless it was built in the sea originally," Emilie said. If there were creatures here as strange as the Sargasso people, she didn't think mermen who lived half underwater and half above it were too far beyond the realm of possibility.

The others hadn't heard, but Miss Marlende stopped and stared at her for a moment. Long enough for Emilie to realize she had possibly said something very stupid. But Miss Marlende just pointed at her and said, "Keep that in mind."

Tracing routes on the map, Kenar was saying, "One of the reasons we wanted to explore in this region is because so little was known about it. We know a great deal about far-flung areas of our world because of traders passing along maps and information. But no maps exist of this place, as far as we know. Except this one, that we were drawing up as we went along."

"You hadn't explored in this direction?" Lord Engal tapped a spot on the map.

"Due east from this island? Not yet. Dr. Marlende hadn't ventured that way either. But we did see signs of ancient occupation, the remnants of very old buildings, similar to the flooded city we surfaced near. That was here, here, and here." Kenar marked the points on the map. "Nothing we saw was anywhere near as large or as extensive as that city. But if these people once spread throughout this area, there may still be remnants of them living now."

Lord Engal nodded thoughtfully. "The question is, why would Dr. Marlende accompany these people? Could they have promised him help with the airship? Their old city was nearly right atop an aetheric fissure; they may have had their own knowledge of aetheric engines."

"That might be true," Miss Marlende said. "If the Cirathi weren't missing. There might have been a reason for my father to leave with these hypothetical people, but not the Cirathi."

"Yes." Kenar frowned down at the map, still lost in thought. "My people wouldn't have abandoned their ship. Not unless it was a choice between that and death."

Which really, Emilie thought, *is what we all thought as soon as we saw the empty island.* She just hoped they were all still alive, wherever they were.

* * *

After some discussion, they decided to tow the Cirathi ship behind them. Rigging this up took some time, but the sailing ship was light compared to the *Sovereign's* bulk, and it didn't seem to slow their pace. Emilie thought it seemed optimistic, too, implying that they were going to find the missing crews. They also topped off the *Sovereign's* water supply from the freshwater spring on the island, refilled the casks aboard the Cirathi ship, and replenished the food stores with some fruit and wild melons that Kenar said were good to eat.

The *Sovereign* turned east, following the tiny traces of aether. They had to go slowly, to give Captain Belden and Lord Engal time to adjust the navigator.

Steaming down a wide channel between scattered islands, they had come some distance by the time the Dark Wanderer started to move over the sun. These islands were different from the others, flat and low, with wide beaches, green reeds growing thickly out into the water, and shorter brushier trees. Up on the second deck, Miss Marlende lowered her spyglass and said to Kenar and Emilie, "Does this channel look man-made to you?"

Emilie nodded. From up here, she could see how the shape of the islands lining the channel seemed oddly regular. They might have been naturally sculpted by the water, but still, it was strange. "It does. It looks like a big canal, like someone chopped out whatever was in the middle and left the edges." The light wind moved the reeds, and the air smelled of sun and sand and a little like the jasmine toilet water her aunt had been sent as a gift from relatives in Coress. Except this wasn't cloying, it was clean and fresh.

"I agree." Kenar leaned on the rail. "Which implies that this channel leads somewhere." He seemed outwardly relaxed, but Emilie looked at his hands, so tight on the railing it was stretching the scaly skin over his knuckles.

"We'll find them," Emilie told him impulsively, though she was well aware that she was in no position to make promises. "All of them."

"I know. I won't give up hope until we—" Kenar broke it off, shook his head, and smiled down at her, though the smile was a little wry. "When you get back to your own world, will you really be content to sit meekly in a school after all this?"

Miss Marlende, engrossed with her spyglass again, snorted. "Whatever she does, I doubt she'll do it meekly."

"I don't know," Emilie said, looking out over the sun-drenched islands. Though inwardly she was a little pleased by Miss Marlende's comment, she wasn't sure how she felt about all this yet. As if all her life she had thought her world was one thing, closed-in and solid with carefully defined boundaries, so much so that running away to a relative with a respectable girls' school in Silk Harbor was almost unimaginably daring. Now the boundaries had fallen away, leaving a broad vista that was stranger than anything she had read in a gothic novel.

Going back behind the walls would be very hard.

* * *

As the eclipse's line of darkness swept across the sea and the sandbars and islands, more crewmen were posted outside on the decks, and the ship's lamps were lit. Emilie wanted to see how things were going in the wheelhouse without being labeled a snoop, so she managed to be on the spot when Mrs. Verian needed to send a tray of tea mugs and buns up to the men working there. Emilie hurried to volunteer herself.

She carried it up to the wheelhouse, where a young crewman directed her to set the tray on the chart table. As the other crewmen stationed there helped themselves, she lingered to watch Captain Belden and Lord Engal making minute adjustments to the navigator, and hastily scribbling notes on pads of paper. Sometimes they told the crewman manning the wheel to adjust their course slightly.

It surprised her to see that Lord Engal was so adept at this. She knew he wasn't one of those very rich men who did nothing with his time but hunt and buy horses. Emilie had read about lords who were members of the Philosophical Society and spent all their time and money hiring philosophers and sorcerers to discover things and form theories and write books, and she knew Lord Engal must be one of them. But she hadn't expected him to be someone who could do some of the work himself.

Captain Belden yawned, quickly covering his mouth with his sleeve. "Excuse me, my lord."

"You're excused," Lord Engal said absently. "Do you think we should travel through the night, again? We survived our previous experience, but I'd hate to run out of luck."

Belden glanced out the big window, thinking it over. The line of darkness was nearly upon them, coming at an angle toward the long narrow island on their port side. "I'd rather not run up on whatever it was that took the airship, without some sort of warning. But I'm not sure we can afford to lose a full eight hours."

Lord Engal turned the navigator's wheel and made another note. "I'm not either. Finding Dr. Marlende has become less an act of charity and more of a necessity, since we need him to repair our aetheric engine." Captain Belden snorted, startled and amused. Lord Engal cocked an eyebrow at Emilie and added, "You didn't hear me say that, young lady."

"No, sir. My lord." Emilie was startled, both because she hadn't thought he had noticed she was here, and because she hadn't thought anyone else was worried by the lack of progress in repairing the engine. That was probably silly; they must have all noticed it, all been worried by it, even if they weren't speaking of it. *They aren't speaking of it where you can hear,* she amended. She would bet the crew had some choice words about it. She blurted, "Mr. Abendle thinks Miss Marlende should look at the numbers. Not the numbers, the figures. Something like that, to do with trying to fix the motile."

Lord Engal, caught making a minute adjustment to the ring, didn't look up, but she could tell he was listening. Captain Belden stared at her, frowning slowly. "What's this?"

Emilie took a deep breath. It was a little late to reconsider now. "I overheard Mr. Abendle ask Dr. Barshion to show something, some calculations, to Miss Marlende, to get her opinion, but Dr. Barshion didn't want to. He didn't think it would help."

Lord Engal finished the adjustment and cocked his head at her. "When was this?"

"A bit after breakfast, yesterday."

Captain Belden seemed concerned. "Perhaps you should have a look at these calculations, my lord."

Lord Engal looked thoughtful, tapping his pencil on the pad of paper. "Perhaps I shall."

Captain Belden nodded to Emilie, a clear dismissal, and she walked out of the wheelhouse, taking the stairs back down. She wasn't sure if he was going to listen to her or not. *If he does,* she realized a little bit-terly, *it would be a first for me.* She just wasn't used to having things she said be taken seriously, especially by men.

But an hour or so later, when the complete darkness of the eclipse surrounded them and the ship had to slow to half speed, a message went around through the ship's speaking tube, calling everyone to the passenger lounge. Emilie wasn't called, but she went anyway.

Miss Marlende, Kenar, and Oswin came to the lounge, and even Dr. Barshion and Abendle appeared. Both men looked even more exhausted. Dr. Barshion was in his shirtsleeves, his hair mussed, his face lined with lack of sleep.

Lord Engal walked in and said without preamble, "We have a problem. We've lost the trail of aetheric traces."

Kenar looked away, his shoulders slumping. Miss Marlende sank down on the couch, disappointed. "We were too late?" she asked. "The traces have faded?"

Engal shook his head. "No, it's that we're too close to the Aerinterre aether current. It's so powerful it overshadows any other aetheric traces in the air, and the navigator points only toward it."

"What now?" Kenar asked. Emilie stared at him, struck by a sudden realization: if they didn't find Kenar's crew, he had nowhere to go. Not only had he lost his friends, but he couldn't sail the big Cirathi ship by himself. He would have no way to get back home.

Engal said, "We'll keep our present course. We know the airship at least went in this direction. We can only hope we can see some evidence of it, some sign to point us toward it." He scratched his beard absently, and added, "And in the meantime, Miss Marlende, I'd like you to give your assistance to Dr. Barshion and Mr. Abendle. Perhaps your familiarity with your father's work can aid them."

Abendle brightened, and Dr. Barshion looked startled. "Oh yes," he said, as if he hadn't heard of the idea before. "Her assistance would be welcome."

* * *

Emilie tried to sleep, but managed only a brief nap in Miss Marlende's cabin. She was tired, but whenever she lay down, all she could think about was Kenar, and Dr. Marlende, and all the other lost people. And the fact that if Barshion didn't fix the aetheric engine, the *Sovereign* might join them. *This place is lovely and strange and exciting,* she thought, *but I'm not keen to live here forever.*

She got up, washed and dressed, and went up on the second deck above the bow, where Kenar was keeping watch. The night was cool but not uncomfortably so, and the ship's spotlight swept back and forth over the dark water, catching glimpses of the high stands of reeds and the white sand beaches of the nearest island. She saw Kenar standing at the railing with another dark shape. It wasn't until it spoke that she realized it was Oswin. He was saying, "Yes, we've spoken about it, though no one's mentioned it to Lord Engal."

As Emilie approached, Oswin said, "I'd better get back to my duties," and walked back up the deck, giving her a nod as he passed.

She leaned on the railing next to Kenar. He was watching the lights of the launch a hundred yards or so ahead of them. It was taking soundings to make sure the *Sovereign* didn't run aground. She said, "What was that about?" She thought Oswin had left the conversation because he didn't want to frighten her.

Kenar had a better opinion of her nerves. He said, "They're worried about the coal and oil store. This ship carries enough for long ocean voyages, but they were also planning on staying in the aether current for a longer period of time. I pointed out that if they wanted to remain longer, we could find a safe spot to anchor this ship, leave men to guard it, and continue the search with the *Lathi.*" He added wryly, "I'd have to teach most of them to sail first, of course."

"That makes sense." Emilie propped her chin on her folded arms. "It would give us more time to search." She thought about asking Kenar what he would do if Lord Engal decided to call off the search and leave. *But then we can't leave until they fix the aetheric engine, so right now we're all in the same boat. Literally.* So there was no point in asking painful questions yet.

"What's this?" Kenar said suddenly.

Emilie looked up. She could see the launch's running lights on the bow and stern. It had stopped and turned sideways. That was odd. "Is it coming back?" she said. "Maybe it's too shallow up ahead." If it was too shallow for the *Sovereign* and the *Lathi,* it had surely been too shallow for the vessel which had carried away the airship. *I hope we haven't taken a wrong turn already,* she thought.

"Perhaps, but—" Suddenly gunshots rang out over the water. "It's under attack!" Kenar pushed away from the rail and ran back toward the stairs to the lower deck.

Emilie leaned forward over the rail, as if that would help her see better. The ship's spotlight swung around, illuminating the water just past the launch, and she gasped. There were other boats in the water, low flat rafts, as if they had popped up out of nowhere. She caught glimpses of slim figures, tossing ropes at the launch trying to catch it and pull it in. And they were throwing things, that reflected silver in the light—Emilie jerked back as a short javelin bounced off the railing just below her. "Uh-oh," she gasped, and bolted for the hatch.

She ducked inside and took the first set of stairs down. Coming out on the main-deck cross corridor, she dodged a sailor with a rifle running for the outer starboard hatch. She fell in behind him.

As they neared the hatch Emilie heard yells and a series of thunks. *They're boarding us,* she thought in alarm. The sailor burst out of the hatch ahead of her, then staggered back, dropping his rifle. He turned toward her, his eyes wide with shock; a narrow metal bolt pierced his shoulder.

Emilie lunged forward and grabbed his other arm, supporting him. He sagged against her, and she stumbled, took a breath to shout for help. Then over his shoulder she saw three silvery forms climbing over the railing.

They looked like people, but their skin was iridescent, glinting in the ship's lamps. And they were carrying short spears. *Oh no.* Panic gave Emilie strength and she pulled the wounded man back through the hatch, half dragging him over the rim.

She couldn't run with him, and there was no one else in the corridor. She shoved him against the nearest wall and turned back to the hatch. The three men, creatures, whatever they were had seen the open hatchway and started toward her. Emilie grabbed the handle and swung it closed, just as they reached it. She slammed the bolt home, feeling a violent tug from the other side that told her she was just in time.

Emilie caught a glimpse of a smooth silvery face peering through the porthole, and stumbled back. She shook her head, looking down at the wounded sailor. He was slumped against the wall, his face ashy with shock, blood staining his uniform around the bolt. She leaned over him, but he gasped, "The other hatch, check the—"

"Oh hell!" Emilie shoved to her feet and ran down the outer corridor. There was another hatch barely thirty feet down the length of the ship, she could see it standing open, the light from the nearest sconce falling through it out onto the deck. The intruders would surely notice it.

When she was almost to the door, a silvery form stepped through, spear-first. Emilie slid to an abrupt halt. *Oh, oh, no.* It stared at her and she stared at it. Its face was smooth and oddly textured, but more human than the Sargasso creatures', with dark eyes, a small nose, and a thin-lipped mouth. She looked around wildly, but the corridor was horribly bare of potential weapons. There wasn't even a vase to throw.

Then gunshots sounded from the deck, close enough to make Emilie's ears ring, and the intruder jerked back out of the hatch.

Emilie gasped, realizing she had been holding her breath. She went to the hatch, reaching it in time to see Kenar, Miss Marlende, and several sailors running up the deck. The sailors were armed with rifles and Miss Marlende had her pistol.

Kenar flung up a hand, shouting for them to stop. As they halted, Emilie looked down the deck to see there were now perhaps ten of the silvery intruders ranged down near the other hatch. They had the spears, and long tubes that might be projectile weapons. Emilie thought of closing and locking the hatch, but if Kenar and Miss Marlende and the others had to take cover, it was the closest way to reach safety.

Kenar called something to them in a language Emilie didn't understand; whatever it was, it sounded angry. They didn't answer. Miss Marlende said, "Tell them we'll fire unless they get off the ship."

"I don't think they can understand me," Kenar told her. "Try firing over their heads—"

He was interrupted by a strange loud sound, like someone trying to blow a badly damaged horn, coming from somewhere out in the water. Abruptly, the intruders bolted for the railing, leapt it, and landed with huge splashes below.

"What?" Emilie said aloud. She didn't see any reason for the sudden retreat. Kenar, Miss Marlende, and the sailors cautiously approached the railing, but it didn't appear to be a trick.

Emilie shut the hatch and went back down the corridor, worried about the wounded sailor, but Mrs. Verian and another crewman had already found him. They had stretched him out on the corridor floor, and Mrs. Verian was pressing a towel around the base of the bolt still sticking out of his shoulder. Blood soaked the towel and stained her hands, and the man's eyes were tightly shut, his face taut with pain. Emilie steadied herself on the wall, suddenly light-headed, with an odd heavy darkness trying to creep in around the edges of her vision. She looked away hastily, taking deep breaths. *That's right, people faint at blood.* She had never fainted at blood before, but then she had never seen anyone lose what looked like a bucket of it at one time. She couldn't faint; Mrs. Verian certainly didn't have time to deal with her, and the crewmen would think she was a weak ninny. "Will he be all right?" she asked thickly.

"I don't think it hit anything vital, lucky man," Mrs. Verian said, distracted. "Can you find Miss Marlende?"

Relieved to have a reason to escape, Emilie took a quick look out the porthole to make sure the deck was still clear, then opened the hatch. The others were at the railing, looking out into the dark as the spotlight swept the water. The cool air cleared her head, and she called out, "Miss Marlende? There's a wounded man!"

"Is there? Thank you, Emilie." Miss Marlende hurried past her through the hatch.

Emilie went to the railing to stand beside Kenar. The slight breeze smelled of gunpowder. She saw the faint flickers of light as the small skiffs fled. "They all left?" she asked hopefully.

"Something drove them off, and it wasn't us," Kenar said, staring into the darkness. "There's another ship out there, a big one."

"Another ship?" Emilie squinted, but the darkness beyond the ship's lights was impenetrable. *No, wait.* There was something out there, more glowing spots of lamplight, marking a large shape riding low on the water, perhaps a couple hundred yards away. "I see it. Is there light in the water below it, or is that a reflection?"

Kenar said, "No, it's a smaller boat." A single flicker of light had broken off from the larger shape, and was coming toward them. "They're sending a launch to us." He started along the deck and Emilie hurried after him.

They met Lord Engal and Oswin above the launch platform. Several crewmen with rifles were scattered around the deck and two wounded men were being helped inside. The silver people had obviously tried to board this side of the ship as well. "Do you know who they were?" Lord Engal asked Kenar.

Kenar shook his head, watching tensely as the *Sovereign's* launch puttered up to the platform. The engine cut and it slowed, and the crewman waiting below tossed a line to the man in the bow.

"What happened, sailor?" Lord Engal called down. "Where did they come from?"

The sailor started up the ladder from the launch platform, saying, "I'm not sure, my lord. They were in the reeds, waiting for us. Then that larger ship drove them off. It tried to hail us but we couldn't understand them." He stepped onto the deck and hesitated, suddenly sounding self-conscious. "My lord, after the attack, I thought it was best to return to the ship. I hope—"

"No, no, Feran, you've done right," Engal said, moving forward, looking toward the approaching light. "They seem to have helped us by driving off the attack, but we've got to be very careful here. Any advice, Kenar?"

"Don't shine the big lamp on them," Kenar said immediately. "If the night is their natural time, the light might hurt their eyes. They might think it an attack."

"Good point." Engal waved at Oswin, who bolted for the nearest stairwell, heading for the wheelhouse to pass along the order.

They waited, the air thick with tension. Miss Marlende arrived, a little breathless and with bloodstains on her sleeves. "Three wounded," she reported to Lord Engal. "They're all right for the moment, but it would be better if Dr. Barshion could take a look at them. A healing spell to prevent infection might make all the difference."

"I'll make certain he does," Lord Engal said, his eyes on the approaching boat.

It was drawing steadily closer and Emilie could make out the shape of it a little better now. A lamp hung on the prow, a few bare inches above the black glassy surface of the water. The boat itself was very broad, made of some kind of light wood, and looked more like a raft with a raised edge. But it moved swiftly and easily for a raft, and the people paddling it so skillfully were balanced on the very edges, one leg in the water.

Closer, and she could tell they weren't human people, either. One of the sailors said, "My lord, they're the same as the ones who attacked—"

"I know," Lord Engal said. "Steady."

The lamps reflected off iridescent skin, that rippled and changed with every movement and shift of the light. "Look, they have fins," Miss Marlende whispered, sounding fascinated. "I didn't notice that before." She was right, they had long feathery fins along their arms and legs, with a similar crest on their hairless heads. "Kenar, have you ever seen anything like them before?"

He moved along the rail toward them, keeping his voice low. "I've seen water dwellers who looked something like this, but they can't live in the air for more than a few moments. These seem to be made for both."

One of the merpeople lifted a hand, and called out in a language Emilie couldn't understand. The voice was light and soft; it was impossible to tell if it was male or female.

Lord Engal lifted his hand in response. Oswin had returned, and he said, "We've got men posted around the ship, to make sure this isn't a diversion."

Emilie looked around; more crewmen armed with rifles had come out onto the deck. Lord Engal said, "Good. But if anyone fires on this raft without a direct order from me, I'll fling him off this boat. Understood?"

There were muted "yes, my lord"s in response.

Dr. Barshion stepped out of the hatchway, moving up beside Lord Engal. "My God," he said softly. "Do we know what they are?" Lord Engal shook his head.

With expert paddling, the raft came smoothly to a halt a few yards from the *Sovereign*. There were square openings in the bottom of the raft, presumably so the occupants could slip in and out of the water. *A boat for people who are as at home in the water as out of it,* Emilie thought, fascinated.

"Half in, half out of the water," Miss Marlende said to herself. She caught Emilie's arm. "You could be right about that abandoned city. If people like this built it, merpeople . . ."

One of the merpeople waved a hand, speaking again. This close, in the yellow reflected light from the ship's lamps, Emilie was fairly sure it was a woman. Kenar shook his head, tapping his ear to show he didn't understand. He spoke to her in a language that was all breathy growls and clicks; Emilie thought it must be the Cirathi language. But the merpeople didn't appear to understand that, either. Two of them shifted around, taking a box out of a net bag that hung down in the water.

One of the crewmen shifted uneasily, and Lord Engal said, "Steady, men. They seem peaceable and they want to talk, and for all we know they're about to produce a Cirathi phrasebook."

Emilie still had her reservations about Lord Engal, but she had to admit she thought he was handling this well. She leaned on the railing, finding herself barely five feet away from the merpeople as their boat drifted closer. The one nearest was staring curiously at her, and Emilie stared back. This one might be female too, just from the shape of the slim body. The hands curled around the light wooden paddle were webbed, and the nails were small and neat, not claws. Emilie distinctly remembered the plant people from the Sargasso as having claws. The merwoman was wearing silvery bangles around one wrist, and little silver beads were woven into the feathery crest on her head. Emilie realized suddenly that the merwoman, all the merpeople on the boat, were naked except for skimpy wraps of metallic cloth around their waists; she felt her cheeks flush with embarrassment. She hadn't noticed before because their iridescent skin seemed almost like clothing, or a protective outer covering. *They don't have breasts,* she thought, still curious despite the awkwardness of looking at naked people. *Maybe that means they lay eggs.*

The merwoman who seemed to be the leader took something out of the box, something that looked like an elaborately curving shell, the kind that washed up on beaches at Liscae and the other southern ports. She spoke into it, and projected from it, her soft voice said, "Do you understand me?"

It was one more astonishment on top of everything else. Lord Engal moved up beside Kenar, and said, "Yes, we understand you. How can you speak our language? Have you met our people before?"

The merwoman held the shell to her ear, listening to his voice through it.

"The shell is some sort of translation device," Kenar said softly. "I've heard of such things before, but none that worked this well."

Keeping his voice low, Dr. Barshion said, "Yes, it must be a spell. A complicated one."

The merwoman tapped the shell. "This device translates. I am Yesa,

I speak for the queen of the Sealands." She looked from Kenar to Lord Engal. "You are not hurt?"

Lord Engal replied carefully, "We have three men wounded, but other than that, we're quite well, thanks to your intervention. Can you tell us why we were attacked?" Emilie thought he had picked a delicate way to ask that question.

"They were the Darkward Nomads," Yesa said. "They attack all shipping in these seas."

The Darkward Nomads. Emilie remembered "darkward" was the Hollow World term for the direction to the west, where the Dark Wanderer came from, so it wasn't quite as intimidating a name as it seemed at first. *But still . . .*

Miss Marlende looked at Kenar for information, and he shook his head slightly to show he had never heard the name before. Then Yesa asked, "You are perhaps looking for missing people?"

"Yes, yes we are!" Miss Marlende called out, then whispered, "Sorry, spoke out of turn," to Lord Engal.

"Quite all right, but try to contain yourself," he said to her. He turned back to the merpeople and said to Yesa, "You have news of them, of people like us?"

"Yes. We have heard of them. You will follow us, speak to our queen?"

Lord Engal exchanged a guarded look with Kenar, and said, "Yes, but can't you tell us what happened to them? Where they are, if they're well?"

"I don't know if they are well." Yesa hesitated, lifting her elegant webbed hands in a helpless gesture. Emilie got the sudden sense that Yesa didn't know much at all, that she was possibly as nervous about this encounter as they were. *If I was her, I'd be nervous too.* Sent out in a little boat, to talk to people in a strange big noisy ship, and without the information to answer their questions. Yesa said, "My queen wants to speak of all this with you herself. If you follow us to our city, all will be explained."

Lord Engal looked at Kenar and Oswin, then turned to glance at Dr. Barshion. "Gentlemen, I don't think we have a choice."

CHAPTER SIX

The *Sovereign*, moving at its slowest speed, followed Yesa's boat through the darkness. Emilie watched from the bow with Kenar and Miss Marlende as the boat led them through the island channels. As the *Sovereign*'s spotlight swept back and forth, they began to catch glimpses of white stone structures on the islands or near them, lapped by the waves from their passage. It was hard to tell in the dark, but they all seemed ruined, or empty, with stones tumbling down or lightless windows.

"The Sealands, she called it," Miss Marlende said thoughtfully. "If their civilization once spread through this entire area, all the way to that ruined city we passed, they must have been very powerful."

"They might still be." Kenar was pacing the deck behind them. He had been restless and uneasy for the past hour, and Emilie wasn't certain it was due to the slow pace of the ship. "I'm wondering how they knew we were out here, in time to intervene during the attack."

Miss Marlende rested her elbows on the railing. "Sentries, perhaps. Hidden on one of these islands. They might have some form of distance communication, like a telegraph."

"Or they might have magic." Kenar didn't sound pleased at the prospect. "That could put us at a great disadvantage, if they carried off our people against their will."

It wasn't an encouraging thought, that the merpeople might be leading them into a trap. Emilie squinted to see the little boat. The larger craft it had come from was just ahead, the spotlight catching occasional glimpses of it. It was big, flat, and barge-like, easily the size of the *Lathi*. But instead of sails it had rows of oars, moving smoothly and steadily against the low sides.

Emilie thought Yesa had been telling the truth. *But then maybe the person who sent Yesa didn't tell her it was a trap.* Or maybe Emilie was no good at reading the expression and intent of people who weren't human.

She didn't seem to have any trouble reading Kenar's expressions and understanding his intent. But the Cirathi weren't merpeople; from what Emilie could tell, there weren't many differences between Kenar and a human, besides his appearance. Meeting him had been more like meeting someone from a distant country than from another species. It was probably why the crew of the *Lathi* had gotten on so well with Dr. Marlende's crew. And as explorers and traders, they had more in common with Menaens than not. *Just be careful,* she reminded herself. She didn't like judging other people, having had more than her fill of being judged herself. But she didn't want herself or any of the others to be hurt or killed.

"We've got Dr. Barshion," Miss Marlende was saying. "He does seem to be quite a decent sorcerer, even if he's not as expert with aetheric engines as he thought."

"Has there been any progress?" Emilie asked her. "Did you look at the figures Abendle wanted you to see?"

"Yes, and Abendle's right, the problem isn't in the way the motile is calibrated." Miss Marlende didn't quite sound defeated, but she didn't sound enthused by their prospects, either. "It should be working. I suggested they try to dismantle the aether navigator and make certain there's nothing wrong with it. If one of the rings had been jostled during our descent, that might cause the engine instability."

"The navigator?" Emilie had thought it was working fine, from what she had seen in the wheelhouse. "The one we were using to follow the aether traces?"

"No, that's the standard ship's navigator, used for surface vessels. The motile has a separate aether navigator built inside it, that allows it to stay within the boundaries of the aether currents."

"Oh, I see." Emilie wasn't sure she did see, but at least now Dr. Barshion and Abendle would know what was specifically wrong with the motile.

* * *

They traveled for the rest of the night, and finally reached their destination as the eclipse ended, the wall of light moving slowly across the islands and the sea. As it advanced, it revealed the city spread out before them.

It was made of white stone and stretched for miles. Bridges and open-air plazas and pillared walkways marched across the low-lying islands, to towers and large buildings with pitched roofs standing in the broad channels between. For such a vast city, the buildings weren't very tall, not even the towers standing more than a few stories above the water. *But then, they're resting on the bottom, so they're taller than they look,* Emilie thought, fascinated. Borrowing Miss Marlende's spyglass, she could see people out on the walkways, the sun glinting off their iridescent skin, casting back rippling reflections of blue and green. They wore jewelry of silver chains and pieces of polished shell, and very little clothes, mostly just kilts or drapes around their waists. It still wasn't as disturbing as it should be. Perhaps because it was natural for them, and they were all doing it. As she watched, she saw a merperson leading a merchild down a set of steps into the water, vanishing under the surface. Another walked up the steps, shaking his head to get the water out of his feathery head fins. There were more merpeople on the islands to either side of the channel, some in boats and some in the water, fishing in the reeds with nets and small spears. They stopped to stare at the *Sovereign* and the *Lathi,* pointing at them, clearly amazed by the two ships' appearance.

"They've never seen anything like this vessel before," Kenar said under his breath. "It doesn't mean they haven't seen the airship."

"They must have seen it," Miss Marlende murmured, her eyes on the city ahead. "The trail was leading us here."

Yesa's boat conducted them into a harbor at the edge of the city, where the channel broadened into a large lagoon. A long building with two stories of pillared galleries stood at its edge, with piers stretching out across the water. The piers stood only inches above the surface, so they were constantly awash, which didn't seem to bother the merpeople at all. Dozens of boats were tied up along them, of all sizes. Their large escort ship broke away to head toward the other end of the harbor, where several larger barges of a similar design were anchored, some bigger than the *Lathi* and even the *Sovereign.* From what Miss Marlende and Kenar had said, one of them should be more than large enough to carry the airship. *But it's not here,* Emilie thought, studying the farther docks. *At least not where we can see it.*

The *Sovereign* slowed to a crawl, then dropped anchor near the end of a pier. Yesa's small boat came around to speak to them again, and Emilie followed Miss Marlende and Kenar back to the port side.

Lord Engal, Captain Belden, and Oswin were already waiting there. The boat drew up next to the *Sovereign*'s launch platform, and Yesa took out her talking shell to say, "You will come in your small boat and speak to our queen now?"

Everyone looked at Lord Engal. He let out his breath, and said, "Give us a moment to ready ourselves, please."

Yesa nodded and lowered the shell. The other merpeople were taking the chance to get a better look at the *Sovereign* and her crew in the daylight, pointing and talking among themselves.

They moved back from the railing. Lord Engal scratched his chin and said thoughtfully, "We'll have to go. It would be the height of rudeness to ask her to come out here to speak to us."

Captain Belden said, "You shouldn't go, my lord."

"I'll go," Kenar said. "I've met with stranger people than this, believe it or not."

"And I," Miss Marlende added. "Kenar and I have the most at stake, after all. We should take the risk. If there is any."

With some asperity, Captain Belden said, "I appreciate your confidence, Miss Marlende, but all we know about these people is that they might have made off with an airship and kidnapped a number of people, and then lied about it. If you—"

"That's enough," Lord Engal said. He told Belden, "Of course I'm going, it's a foreign monarch, I can't risk insulting her. If Menae develops any sort of trade and diplomatic relations with this world, we'll have to deal with these people as they're the closest to the aetheric current outlets and they clearly claim this territory. I'm not going down in history as the man who started off on the wrong foot."

Captain Belden pressed his lips together, clearly unhappy. "I'm not keen on going down in history as the man who stood by while Lord Engal was killed, my lord."

"Well, that's just a chance you'll have to take." Lord Engal added, "I'll take Kenar with me, and Oswin, and two sailors. Sidearms, but no rifles. If we don't reappear or send a message within—" He checked his pocket watch. "—two hours, leave the harbor, and do what is necessary to get the ship back to the surface world."

"The queen sent a woman as her emissary," Miss Marlende said pointedly. "It would only be sensible to send a woman to speak with her—"

Lord Engal cut her off. "Sensible, but not absolutely necessary, and I'm not risking anyone else on a whim." He stepped to the railing and told Yesa, "We'll be ready to leave in a moment."

Yesa waved an acknowledgment, and signaled her boat to withdraw, taking it toward the nearest dock to speak to some merpeople waiting there. Oswin called for sailors to lower the launch, and everyone scrambled to get ready. Emilie stood aside with Miss Marlende, who fumed silently, her jaw set. Emilie sympathized. There hadn't been a hope in hell of getting herself included in the party, but she had thought Miss Marlende would surely have a chance to go. She said, "At least he didn't say it was because you were a woman."

Miss Marlende folded her arms and muttered something grim about stiff-necked blowhards.

But when the launch was lowered into the water, and the landing party started to climb aboard, Yesa's boat returned to hail them again. Using the shell, she said, "I apologize, I should have told you, our queen will wish to meet your female leaders, also. This is our custom."

Lord Engal, one foot in the launch, stopped and said, "Oh, is it?" He was clearly scrambling for a polite way to decline. "Ah, our custom is not quite so—"

Yesa pointed up at Miss Marlende and Emilie, standing at the rail. "Perhaps they would accompany you?"

Miss Marlende said immediately, "I would be happy to go, but Emilie is rather young—"

Lord Engal stared up at them, disconcerted. "Miss Marlende, yes, I suppose, but I don't think the girl can possibly want—"

Emilie bit her lip, trying to control herself. Jumping up and down like a little girl and begging *Please! I want to see the queen of the merpeople too!* was hardly likely to engender confidence. She knew that it could be dangerous, that they had been attacked once already, that human people could be violent for no sensible reason at all and there was nothing to say that these merpeople weren't the same. But that didn't matter. She said, a little too loudly, "I'll go. I don't mind. I mean, I'd love to."

Miss Marlende frowned at her. She had one hand on the ladder, clearly torn between establishing herself in the launch before anybody raised more objections and a need to dissuade Emilie. Keeping her voice low, she said, "Emilie, I don't think it's wise. It is a risk; after the past few days you have to realize how big a risk it might be."

From the platform, Lord Engal said, "Yes, I'd better ask Mrs. Verian to accompany you instead." He waved to one of the sailors up on deck. "Send someone to find her."

Seeing her chance slip away, Emilie hastily whispered to Miss Marlende, "It's pretty risky to be on this ship at all, with a sorcerer who can't make his aetheric engine work. We might have to live here."

"Emilie!" Miss Marlende glanced around to make certain no one had heard. "I thought the crew was gloomy, but you're the biggest pessimist on this ship."

Emilie didn't think it was pessimism, just the result of having her expectations continually stamped on while growing up. She said, "Are you really going to let him ask Mrs. Verian to go? She won't want to at all, and Mr. Verian won't want her to go either, but they'll think they don't have any choice, since they work for Lord Engal. I've got a choice, I'm a volunteer."

From Miss Marlende's expression, the point about Mrs. Verian must have hit home. She said, reluctantly, "You're right. If we drag the poor woman along against her will . . . But if—when we get back home, don't let any word of this get back to your uncle. I don't want him trying to have me taken in charge, or dragged into court for God knows what."

Just in time, Emilie reminded herself not to jump up and down. "Thank you," she breathed.

Miss Marlende called to Lord Engal, "It's not necessary to send for Mrs. Verian. Emilie can accompany us." She started down the ladder, Emilie right behind her.

Lord Engal frowned at Emilie, but he glanced at Yesa, still waiting in her boat well within earshot, her translator shell held up to listen. He appeared to swallow a more forceful objection and only asked Miss Marlende, "Is this wise?"

"I think so," Miss Marlende said. Kenar gave her a hand to steady her as she stepped into the launch. "If it's safe enough for you, it's safe enough for her."

"I hope you're right," Lord Engal said, and helped Emilie into the boat himself.

The sailors cast off from the platform, and started the launch's small engine. Yesa waved for them to follow, her boat leading them between the piers toward the big open structure fronting the harbor. Merpeople in other boats and working along the piers stopped to stare at them; Emilie resisted the urge to wave, feeling it might not be entirely appropriate. Miss Marlende, leaning out to look down over the side, tapped her arm. Emilie looked too, and saw slender iridescent shapes flickering in the water below them: merpeople swimming along the harbor's shallow sandy floor.

The big structure was made of white stone, and stood three tall stories above the harbor. Broad pillared galleries along the front were open to the sea breezes. It looked like part of the second level might be a market, where goods were piled up for sale. From the clay jars and bundles stacked in the lower level, it could be for storing or selling cargos. Emilie noticed the place didn't smell like a harbor; it smelled fresh and clean, with no stench of dead fish or tar. *They live in the water at least some of the time, so they have a much bigger stake in keeping it clean,* she thought.

Yesa was leading them toward a tall archway where a water channel cut through the lower floor of the building. Her boat turned down the channel, passing inside.

At the tiller, Oswin asked Lord Engal, "My lord, do we follow?"

Lord Engal didn't hesitate. "Go on."

Kenar said, low-voiced, "It would have been better if they met with us on the docks. But I can see why they want a demonstration of trust."

"On our part and theirs," Miss Marlende said.

The launch turned down the channel, passing under the arch and between the high stone walls, the putter of its motor suddenly much louder. The walls were carved with tall figures of merpeople, fighting with some large tentacled creature. Very large, perhaps big enough to wrap around the *Sovereign* and pull it under. Emilie leaned forward to ask Kenar, "Is that like the creature that Dr. Marlende fought off?"

He turned his head to tell her. "Very similar, but it seemed much bigger at the time."

Emilie sat back, impressed.

They passed out from under the archway into the open again, the channel leading through a plaza surrounded by towers with balconies. A bridge arched above them, and they passed pillars with water pouring down the sides. Looking up at the bridge, Emilie caught sight of startled iridescent faces looking down at them.

Then they were moving into another building, small but with a vaulted ceiling and an elaborate waterfall grotto to one side. Merpeople were gathered waiting, but they wore more jewelry than the people working in the harbor, polished shells and more silver chains woven through their head fins, and drapes of metallic fabric that caught the light in different colors. There was a short dock extending into the channel and Yesa was guiding her boat toward it.

"I think we're in a palace," Miss Marlende muttered to Emilie. "It certainly looks like the right spot to meet with a queen."

The launch bumped the dock and Yesa's crew moved hurriedly to help the sailors tie it up. Stepping out of the launch down onto a stone surface that was level with the water was awkward for Emilie, mostly because she had shorter legs than the others. She found herself having to cling to Kenar's arm to manage it without falling. Miss Marlende and Lord Engal were more graceful.

"This way, please," Yesa said through the shell, leading them toward the grotto. Emilie walked beside Kenar, following Lord Engal and Miss Marlende, with Oswin and the two sailors bringing up the rear. The merpeople were all staring, murmuring to each other, and Emilie felt her face heat. The startled stares from the harbor people and those on the bridge hadn't bothered her; the curiosity had been mutual. But at close range, it was harder to ignore.

As they got closer to the grotto, Emilie saw the rocks had been shaped by the water into formations like giant swaths of lace. The floor they were walking across was set with medallions that looked like mother-of-pearl. At the foot of the grotto, a woman sat in a carved stone chair, the water lapping at her feet. She wore a headdress of polished shell and pearl, more pearls draping her body, wound around a dark blue stole shot with metallic streaks.

The queen, Emilie thought, her heart pumping. It was hard to tell how old she was; unlike Yesa, there was a faint darkening of the smooth skin at the corners of her eyes and mouth. Other merpeople, men and women, sat in the water at her feet or stood behind her.

Yesa said, "This is my lady, Queen Tath-alare." She bowed her head.

One of the queen's attendants lifted another translation shell, holding it up for the queen. She said, "You are from the upper world." Her voice was deeper than Yesa's, but still soft.

Lord Engal gave her a formal half bow. "Yes, Your Majesty. All but our friend Kenar, who is of the Cirathi, and has graciously agreed to guide us through your waters."

The queen inclined her head. Emilie got the impression that she was pleased with Lord Engal's manner. It was probably handy to have someone with them who was used to speaking to royalty. Though speaking to the king of Menae must be vastly different from greeting the queen of the Sealands. The queen said, "Your world is a legend to us. I had never thought before that it might be real."

Lord Engal said, "This is what we thought of your own world, Your Majesty." Emilie hadn't heard any of those legends; she suspected he was just being polite. "I am Lord Engal, and this is Miss Vale Marlende." As he introduced the others, Emilie watched the queen's face. Had she reacted to the name "Marlende"? It was hard to tell. He continued, "We came here to search for missing companions. Your emissary Yesa said that you wish to speak to us of this."

The queen nodded, her eyes thoughtful. "I did. Your lost companions came in a ship that flew through the air. We have seen it."

"Where?" Lord Engal managed to look as though he was only politely interested in this information.

"The ship was seen being carried on a barge, belonging to the Darkward Nomads, who also attacked your ship. They live in the outskirts of our empire, in the cities and other parts of the Sealands that have fallen to time, and been abandoned."

Brow furrowed, Lord Engal said, "Why would they have taken the airship? And attacked us, without provocation?"

"They take things," the queen said simply. "Small boats, cargos, fisherfolk who live on isolated shallows, ships, if they can get them."

Oh, that doesn't sound good, Emilie thought. Lord Engal said, "For what purpose?"

The queen made an open-handed gesture, as if the answer was obvious. "This is how they make their living, rather than fishing or farming. Perhaps they take the people as slaves, or perhaps there is a darker reason. We do not know."

There was an uneasy stirring from the assembled courtiers. Emilie felt uneasy herself. "A darker reason" suggested all sorts of terrible things.

Miss Marlende cleared her throat, and said, "Your Majesty, has no one ever escaped the nomads, to explain why they were taken?"

"No, never, that we have heard of," the queen replied. She said to Engal, "You wish to secure the return of your people and property?"

"Yes, Your Majesty." He watched her carefully. "You have a suggestion?"

"We are planning a raid, to drive the nomads away from our borders, to protect the fisherfolk who ply those waters." The queen tilted her head. "You could join us, add your might to ours, and we would help you search for your people."

Emilie was standing a little behind Kenar, so she saw the reptilian folds of skin at the back of his neck twitch. He exchanged a look with Miss Marlende, whose expression was close to horrified. *The queen just asked us to go to war with her, against people of her own country,* Emilie thought, feeling a wary sickness in the pit of her stomach. It happened all the time in books about explorers venturing in far countries. *And it never ends well.*

Lord Engal gave the queen a polite half bow. "If we could have a moment to speak of this in private, Your Majesty?"

* * *

The room they were taken to was above the grotto, with one wall open to the outside. A balcony extended out from it, looking down on a little submerged courtyard filled with richly flowering water plants. Lord Engal had sent one of the sailors back to check in with Captain Belden and tell him that all was well so far.

"We're not here to fight a war," Miss Marlende said, as soon as they had privacy.

With some impatience, Lord Engal said, "I agree completely, but that may be our only way to free our people."

Miss Marlende lowered her voice. "If we believe her." She looked at Kenar. "What do you think?"

He folded his arms, and Emilie thought he looked deeply troubled. "I don't know. It isn't . . ." He shook his head, frustrated. "It's possible, but our appearance here seems very convenient for the queen."

"You believe the woman has constructed some sort of plot to deceive us?" Lord Engal sounded almost amused.

Looking down into the courtyard, Emilie recognized the superior tone in his voice and rolled her eyes.

"You don't think it's possible?" Miss Marlende challenged. "Because she's too naive and simple, perhaps?" She waved a hand toward the city. "Look at this place! It's the capital for a fallen empire that must be hundreds of years old; their monarchy must go back for generations. If there's anyone who could engage in intrigue and deception, it's her."

Emilie watched them worriedly. She suspected Miss Marlende was right. There was no reason to discount the merpeople's intelligence or their desire to pursue their own motives. *We haven't helped them, saved lives, like Dr. Marlende did for the Cirathi. We haven't become their friends.* The merpeople had no reason to be kindly disposed toward them.

"I will take it under advisement," Lord Engal said, which caused Miss Marlende to flush with fury, "but I don't see that they have any reason to lie to us—"

"Unless they want to use us as living shields against these nomads—" Miss Marlende supplied.

"Do you have any other suggestion as to how we're to find your father and the others?" Lord Engal said. "Because I'd like to hear it."

That gave Miss Marlende pause. She pushed her hair back in frustration. "No. I wish I did."

"These marshy islands seem to go on forever," Kenar pointed out. He didn't look happy, either. "Unless we have some idea of where these nomads camp, we'll have no way to find them."

Miss Marlende said wearily, "Yes, I see the problem. I just wish there was another solution."

Lord Engal eyed her, apparently unsatisfied with that admission. "I'd like you to stay here while I continue our conference with the queen."

Miss Marlende frowned at him. "So I don't interrupt you with valid objections? Yesa did request my presence."

"Exactly. And if she asks for you to return, I'll send for you." He set his jaw. "Or would you prefer to wait on the ship?"

Miss Marlende smiled thinly. "I'll wait here."

Lord Engal walked out, collecting Oswin and the sailor on the way.

Kenar touched Miss Marlende's shoulder and said, resigned, "At least he knows that this might be a trap."

As Kenar followed the others, she muttered, "Does he? I'm not so sure."

"He's awfully stubborn, and he likes to be right," Emilie said. Everybody liked to be right, of course, but some people were so invested in it that it blinded them to common sense. Though she was mostly thinking of Uncle Yeric and her brothers; she didn't think Lord Engal was quite as bad as they were.

Miss Marlende jumped, as if she had forgotten Emilie was there. She sighed and came to stand beside her. "If it was just his ego at stake . . ."

Emilie frowned, considering. "Do you think it would help if we took a look around? Maybe, if it was these merpeople who took the airship and the Cirathi, and not the nomads, we could see some sign of it." She didn't really think they would be that lucky, or the merpeople so careless, but maybe they could see something that would help make their decision easier.

Miss Marlende stared at her. "Surely the merpeople would object . . . They wouldn't want us to wander their city unescorted."

"Yes, but we could be ignorant people who don't know any better," Emilie said. Even her vigilant aunt had fallen for that one a time or two. It was how Emilie had gotten to see the Philosophical Society exhibit at Starling Hall in Meneport one year, by wandering off from a shopping trip in apparent innocence. Of course, it had probably just been more fodder for her aunt's belief that Emilie was actively looking for opportunities to disgrace herself in some way, but she hadn't known that at the time. "No one said specifically that we had to stay here. I mean, Lord Engal did, but really, he meant you weren't to come with him—"

Miss Marlende was already heading for the door. She stopped just inside, looking out to the gallery that overhung the grotto room. She came back to Emilie. "I don't know that we can slip out that way. There are some merpeople standing by the stairs."

Emilie stepped out to the balcony. There was no railing, just a low curb around the edge, barely a foot high. The drop wasn't far, and they could jump down into the water filling the court below, but that was bound to be noticed. And the water was thick with reeds and flowering plants, and the big blue-green pads of something similar to water lilies;

it would be hard to explain how they had thought jumping off the balcony into a garden was a sensible thing to do.

But the wall of the palace had heavy carving, wide ridges of it, curved out like a narrow steep stairway. It led down the wall to a little platform even with the surface of the water.

Emilie braced a hand on the wall to steady herself and leaned out. She thought it was a stairway, but meant for people who normally went barefoot, with no large clunky shoes or boots. The platform below it had bigger stairs leading down into the water, but it also led to a colonnaded walkway, stretching along the side of the building. "If we go down this way, we can get to that walkway. It has to go somewhere."

Miss Marlende stepped past Emilie, craning her neck to see down. She said, "Yes, that waterfall inside the audience room was against this wall, so there aren't any windows down there where they could see us." She gripped a piece of the carving, and carefully stepped out onto the first narrow step.

Emilie followed her carefully, one hand on the gritty stone wall to steady herself. She reached the platform, which was a colonnade running along the side of the building. Miss Marlende led the way down it. The paving was set with shells and vines growing up out of the water twined around the columns, and small brilliantly colored fish darted among the floating pads.

They came to the corner of the court, and Emilie was relieved to see an arch leading through a small passageway, with a smooth stone stairway. They climbed up to a roof terrace, the upper galleries of the palace looking down on it. The terrace faced toward the city, with a beautiful view of the bridges, tiled rooftops, and towers surrounding a big open plaza. But the terrace wasn't unoccupied. There was a big square pool in the center, with several merwomen seated in it talking. They had seen Emilie and Miss Marlende, and were staring curiously.

"Uh-oh," Emilie said under her breath. She knew they would be spotted, but she didn't think they would be spotted so soon. Someone was bound to ask about them and carry the word back to the audience room. "Sorry," she told Miss Marlende. "I thought it would work better than this."

"It's all right," Miss Marlende told her. She walked to the edge of the terrace, where it looked out over the city. Emilie followed her, standing at the low balustrade. The plaza below was filled with water, but there was a blue and green mosaic set into it, and merpeople swimming past. Miss Marlende added, "It was a long shot, at best."

The sun sparkled off the clear water and the breeze was cool and fresh. Merpeople moved along the bridge at the far side of the plaza, and small boats plied the waters of the canals beyond. "I'm glad we did it, anyway," Emilie said. She wouldn't have missed this view for anything.

Miss Marlende turned back to face the palace, muttering, "This place is larger than I thought. They could have the airship anywhere, even outside the city. If they have it at all. What we need is a small portable aether navigator."

"Do those exist?" Emilie asked. All the aether navigators she had read about were fairly large and cumbersome.

"Unfortunately not." Miss Marlende turned and started for the far side of the terrace. "Let's try to see as much as we can before we're stopped."

They made it almost to the steps leading up to a short bridge before Yesa came hurrying out of the lower gallery. Obviously startled to see them, she fumbled for the shell around her neck to ask, "What are you doing here?"

Miss Marlende smiled as if she had been hoping to see Yesa all along. "We wanted to see more of your beautiful city. I hope that's all right."

Yesa hesitated, taken aback. Emilie kept the smile on her face, imitating Miss Marlende, but she felt all the weight of her presumption. Being rude to possibly innocent strangers was much worse than being rude to relatives. Yesa said, "Oh, I see. I will come with you."

"We would be honored," Miss Marlende said. As Yesa turned to lead the way, Miss Marlende gave Emilie a frustrated look. Emilie agreed. Yesa was hardly likely to lead them on a tour of the city's secrets. And they had to hope that whoever had alerted Yesa to their excursion hadn't passed word along to the queen and Lord Engal.

Yesa looked out over the terrace thoughtfully, deciding where to take them. Then she turned toward the steps, leading them up toward the bridge. Emilie felt depressed; if Yesa was willing to take them there, then there couldn't be anything that shocking to see.

The bridge led them over more courts filled with flowers, to a gallery that provided another view of the city. Miss Marlende let Yesa give them the tourist's tour for a time, making polite interested comments as Yesa pointed out views, public buildings, the major waterways. Emilie didn't have to pretend to polite interest; everything was new, strange, and fascinating.

Then, as they were walking over a bridge, Miss Marlende said thoughtfully, "The queen told us about the problems with the nomads. How long has that been going on?"

"As long as I can remember," Yesa said. "We are told that they were from one of the outer kingdoms, to the darkward side of the empire. That when the old wars started and the empire fell, the central Sea-lands lost touch with many of the far-flung territories. When embassies were sent many years later, they found only empty cities, abandoned."

Miss Marlende said, "We saw one of those, to the . . . antidarkward, where we entered this world."

Yesa nodded. "Just so. We think the nomads are the survivors of those cities, forced to leave to find better fishing grounds."

"Did they find them?" Emilie asked, shading her eyes to look out over the view. There was a plaza just visible that seemed to be a market, with all the goods displayed in the vendors' boats.

"Yes. It was only fishing grounds around the cities that had begun to fail, which is one of the things that caused the wars. There were plenty of others among the archipelagos, and islands to farm."

"So why do they steal, then?" Emilie turned back to Yesa. "If they like moving around, they should have more food than they know what to do with."

"I don't know," Yesa said. It was hard to tell through the translation, but she sounded a little troubled. "It is one of the frightening things about them, that we don't know why they do such things."

Miss Marlende was frowning in thought. "Have you ever known anyone who was kidnapped—stolen—by them? Or seen a farm or a fishing area that was raided?"

"I've seen places that were raided, within the past season. It has been getting worse. I don't know anyone who was stolen—" Yesa made a little throwing away gesture, which Emilie thought might be some-thing to avert bad luck, like knocking on wood. "—but I have seen the empty settlements in the darkward shallows and the archipelago." She looked at Miss Marlende, her delicate brows arched. "Did you doubt that the stories about the nomads were true?"

"I'm sorry, but yes," Miss Marlende admitted. "We're strangers here, and we know nothing about this situation."

"I understand. I will say, I do not like this plan of going to fight the nomads." Yesa turned back, heading out of the bright sunlight into the shaded gallery behind them. "I will take you back through this part of the palace."

They passed inside, into a wide passage, and Emilie blinked, temporarily blinded by the transition from sunlight to interior shadow. Yesa turned left abruptly, through a small grotto room with an elaborate stone waterfall, surrounded by deep blue flowering plants. Emilie stopped, waiting for her eyes to adjust, wanting a better look at it.

Miss Marlende and Yesa passed into the next room. Suddenly Miss Marlende shouted a warning. Startled, Emilie stared. There were three men in the next room, human men, two Northern Menaen and one Southern. For an instant she tried to recognize them as crew members from the *Sovereign*. Then she saw the blue uniforms, that these men were rougher, unshaven. Like the men who had attacked the *Sovereign* when it was docked at Meneport. *Lord Ivers' men.* Emilie moved forward, her first impulse to help Miss Marlende. But one of the men grabbed Miss Marlende's arm and yanked her out of sight, and the other two started forward. *Get help,* Emilie thought wildly, and whirled around and bolted.

Right into the two men coming out of the passage behind her. She bounced off one's chest and he grabbed her arms. Emilie struggled furiously, kicked him, bit at his hands, but the other one forced a sack over her head. Then the first one flipped her upside down, trapping her arms in the sack and making her head swim.

Distantly, muffled by the heavy coarse material, she heard Yesa say, "I don't like the plan. But I have no choice but to participate."

CHAPTER SEVEN

Trapped in the sack, Emilie fought in a panic, struggling furiously, until her lungs ached from lack of air. She sagged limply and tried to breathe through the rough material.

"She's out," one of them said, his voice muffled by the blood pounding in her ears, and the other grunted an acknowledgment.

They thought she had fainted. *That . . . isn't a bad idea*, Emilie thought. She would rather like to faint and not experience this, but as a long-term solution it was impractical at best. *Solution, think of a solution.* They hadn't strangled her or drowned her immediately, and they seemed to be taking her somewhere in a very purposeful way. She could try to question them about where they were going, or keep pretending to be unconscious. The pretend-unconsciousness seemed to offer the best chance of escape; if they put her down to rest, she might be able to wriggle away before they noticed. She admitted that that was probably not likely, but at least it gave her something to think about besides being strangled or drowned or shot.

They carried Emilie for some distance, hauling her like a sack of potatoes. She concentrated on breathing and trying to listen for any indication of where they were going. She heard water lapping and the occasional distant voices of merpeople. Sometimes the men spoke to each other, gruff instructions to turn right or left or go that way; it didn't tell her anything except that there were at least two of them. And she couldn't hear any hint that Miss Marlende was anywhere nearby. *Though I bet they meant to capture her all along*, Emilie realized suddenly. *That's why Yesa came back and asked for us to come with the others to speak to the queen.* Someone had perhaps passed along a description of Miss Marlende, but what was obvious to another Menaen wasn't obvious to Yesa, and she had asked for both of them as the only two women in view.

Sometimes they walked outside and sometimes through buildings; she could tell by the light working its way through the sackcloth and the feel of the sun on her legs. It seemed to take a long time, but the sack was hot and her arms ached from where the men had grabbed her, and she suspected discomfort was making the trip seem much longer.

Finally they went into a cool shadow that meant they were inside a building, and started to go upstairs, up a lot of stairs. Emilie tensed, her heart pounding again, knowing they must be nearly at their destination. *Whatever that is.* Maybe she would find herself facing Lord Ivers himself. *An evil nobleman,* she thought. It was just like something out of her favorite adventure novels. Only very real, very uncomfortable, and very frightening.

The men reached a landing and started down a corridor. Ahead she heard keys rattle and what sounded like a heavy metal door creak open. There was some shuffling around, and a gruff voice said, "Don't move, or I'll blow your head off."

Emilie caught her breath, wondering if he was talking to her. Then she was dumped on a cool stone floor. She lay like an unstrung puppet, keeping her breathing even, listening to footsteps walk away, the metal door shut. They hadn't deposited a second person, so Miss Marlende wasn't with her. She waited a moment, and then was glad she had; there was something else alive in the room. She could hear breathing, a scrape against the floor as something moved.

"You can get up now, I know you're awake. Though don't misunderstand me, it's very convincing."

The voice had a thick accent Emilie thought she recognized. She dragged the sack off her head, taking a deep breath of the cool damp air. She was in a small bare stone room, light coming in from a little round window high in the wall. The only furnishings were a couple of wooden buckets, and a blanket. The door was made out of silver metal, showing streaks of rust in the damp. She sat up, twisting around to stare at the other person.

He—she—sat back in the corner, watching Emilie with a quizzical smile. It was a Cirathi.

Her face was fuller than Kenar's, though it was coated with the same tiny black scales instead of soft skin. Her dark eyes were wide-set under brows of feathery fur, her lips full. Her dark hair was braided with strings of beads, hanging down over the folds of reptilian skin at the back of her neck. She wore dark leather trousers tucked into low boots, armbands and bracelets and rings of gold metal, and a stretchy blue camisole that made it easy to see she was female. Emilie didn't know whether to be shocked or admiring; on her the skimpy clothing was somehow more obvious than on the merpeople, maybe because the Cirathi seemed so much closer to human. "Who are you?" Emilie demanded.

She smiled. "I asked you first."

"You did not," Emilie pointed out. "But I think I know who you are. Are you from the ship *Lathi*?"

"Yes." She cocked her head, still smiling, but with a trace of skepticism. "But you would know that."

"If I was one of Lord Ivers' crew?" Emilie saw the difficulty; the woman thought she was a spy. "But does Lord Ivers know Kenar, and how he and Jerom went into the aether current to bring help for Dr. Marlende's airship?" Of course, if the Cirathi woman was a spy, Emilie was giving the game away, but she thought that was so unlikely as to be worth the risk.

The woman eyed her sharply, all the teasing forgotten. "You know of Kenar?"

"Yes. Do you know Rani? She's his . . . friend." Emilie wasn't quite sure what to call their relationship and didn't want to make a hideous social gaffe.

"I am Rani." She sat bolt upright, new delighted energy in her face, her voice. "Kenar brought you here? He's alive?"

"Yes, he is! He's here in the city, with Lord Engal, who brought us here in his ship, with Miss Marlende, Dr. Marlende's daughter. But then they caught us, Lord Ivers' men, Miss Marlende and I, so I don't know if the others are still free or not." It sounded very confusing put that way, but the Cirathi woman seemed to be following it. "I'm Emilie."

"I am very happy to see you, Emilie." Rani pushed to her feet, reaching to give Emilie a hand. Emilie took it, finding the blunt claws and the calloused palm of Rani's hand a strange contrast with the softness of the fur on her knuckles. Rani pulled Emilie to her feet, so energetically that Emilie bounced. "I haven't been able to reach that window by myself, but if you stand on my shoulders I think you might."

"Yes, I think so," Emilie said, and sat down to quickly take off her boots and stockings. Facing the wall with the window, Rani crouched down and Emilie clambered onto her shoulders, being familiar with this process from rampaging around the village with the neighboring children.

Rani straightened up slowly, and Emilie held her clawed hands to help her balance as she put first one foot, then the other, on Rani's strong shoulders. Emilie pushed herself upright, let go of Rani's hands to lean against the wall and guide herself the rest of the way up. They did it as smoothly as a pair of acrobats at a fete, and Emilie was rather proud of them. She gripped the smooth edge of the window to steady herself, though there wasn't much purchase. By stretching and craning her neck, she could just see out.

The view was of a huge open court surrounded by sizable buildings. Floating in it was the curve of a large dull gray-white object, almost filling the big space. There was some sort of netting over it, perhaps to hold it down . . . "It's an airship!" Emilie said, startled. "Is it Dr. Marlende's?"

"No, that one isn't here. At least I hope not. That belongs to our meddlesome Lord Ivers." Rani lifted her a little higher. "Can you see anything else?"

"No, it's a bad angle." Emilie peered down at her. She thought Rani was quite strong, as strong as a real acrobat. "Can I stand on your hands?"

Emilie almost fell once, but after a moment they managed it, and Rani was able to lift her so Emilie's head was level with the top of the window.

Now she could see the rest of the airship, and more of the court. They were about four stories up. The balloon wasn't round, as she had been half expecting, but long and bullet-shaped, coming nearly to a point in the front, stretched over a rigid framework. Below the huge swell of it and running nearly half the length, there was a long cabin with curving wooden walls and big round windows. It looked large enough to have at least two decks, which surprised Emilie. She had thought it would be smaller, more like the hot-air balloons that sometimes came to holiday fairs. The buildings lining the court had the open galleries that were usual for the city, but she didn't see any sign of life on them. And the walls and pillars looked dingy compared to the buildings around the palace, as if these structures weren't much occupied or cared for. She said, "These buildings look empty. I wonder how many merpeople know Lord Ivers is here. Is Dr. Marlende's airship that large?"

A little breathless, Rani said, "Less sightseeing, more cogent information."

"Sorry!" Emilie reached through the window and grabbed the outer edge, chinning herself on it. Now she could see the platform dock just below the airship's cabin. The airship itself was floating over the water filling the court, but it was tethered to the stone pillars of the lowest level with thick cables. A gangplank had been stretched over the water, between the open cabin hatch and the dock. She saw three men dressed in dark blue uniforms carrying supplies aboard, small metal casks, boxes. "They're loading it. They might be getting ready to leave. I don't see anyone who might be Lord Ivers."

"Oof, all right, come down." Rani lowered her partway, until Emilie could jump down.

They faced each other. "What happened?" Emilie asked. "We found the island where you were supposed to be, and your ship."

"These people, the same sort of sea people who live in this city, arrived one night, slipped past our watchmen, and captured us. Then they threatened us, and forced Marlende and his men to surrender." Rani made an elegant gesture. "It was not our finest moment as a crew of intrepid explorers."

"Were these the nomads? The queen of the merpeople told us you and Dr. Marlende's crew had been captured by nomads," Emilie said, and had a moment to wonder at what an odd turn her life had taken that it made sense for her to say something like that.

"Yes, they took the airship, and accused Marlende of being in league with this queen to destroy them. He was trying to persuade them otherwise, but without much luck. We still hoped help would come to the island, so on the third night of our journey, the others contrived a distraction, and I slipped over the side of the nomads' ship. Then I returned to the island, hoping Kenar and Jerom would show up soon."

Emilie nodded. "How did you get back? Did you steal a boat?"

Rani said, "I swam, from island to island." Emilie stared, and Rani added, "I didn't say it was easy." She continued, "But I had only been there a day or so, when another airship arrived."

Emilie suddenly saw what had happened in disheartening detail. "Oh. Lord Ivers. But you thought it was us."

"Yes, another of those not finest moments," Rani said, her voice dry. "Marlende had not made clear that he had enemies who would follow him here."

"I don't think he knew. Miss Marlende knew he had rivals, but I think it was a surprise to everyone just how . . ." Emilie waved her hands. ". . . big a rivalry it was. Lord Ivers' men boarded our ship and shot at us while we were leaving the port, but I don't think Lord Engal knew that Lord Ivers had already come down here."

"I see." Frustrated, Rani turned to pace the cell, like a big cat in a cage. She tugged on the door handle, apparently just to see if their captors had forgotten to lock it, but it didn't budge. "Now which one is Lord Engal?"

"He's the one Miss Marlende asked to come down here to help her father. Well, not asked, but bribed him with her father's work. He's here with his ship, but he and the others don't know Lord Ivers is here too. The queen told them the nomads had captured you, but she didn't say anything about the rest. Do you know what Lord Ivers is planning?"

"He has not been forthcoming on that point," Rani said with considerable irony. "But I think it is the queen who has the plan. The nomads were convinced she meant to destroy them with the help of some foreign weapon."

"Lord Ivers' airship," Emilie said, feeling a sinking sensation. But Lord Ivers shouldn't want to get into a war, particularly a war in the Hollow World. He was an explorer, a scientist like Lord Engal, if more violent and ruthless. If he helped the queen fight the nomads, he would just waste time . . . *Oh, that has to be it.* "It was a trade!"

Rani stopped, startled. "What was a trade?"

"Lord Ivers wants to get back home before Dr. Marlende and Lord Engal, so he can take the credit for the discovery. He must have got mixed up with the queen somehow, and promised her he would help her fight the nomads. Somehow the nomads learned about it, maybe they have spies in the city, and that's why they went after Dr. Marlende's airship. But Lord Ivers doesn't want to keep his promise, so he's gotten the queen to get Lord Engal to take his place." Emilie turned to look up at the window, frowning. "I bet they are leaving. They're getting ready to go back up the aether current to home."

Rani stared, appalled. "That is what this is all about? Who claims credit?"

"Yes." Emilie admitted, "It's stupid."

"That is one word for it." Rani shook her head, her beaded braids flying. "I don't want my crew mixed up in a war. No good can come of it."

She was right about that. "Lord Engal will know something is wrong. He'll want to know what happened to Miss Marlende and me."

"The queen can hold you hostage, force him to do as she says." Rani looked down at Emilie, her brow furrowed in consternation. "Would he do that?"

"I think he might." Emilie looked up at the round window again. It looked small from this angle, but when she had pulled herself up into it, it had been an inch or so wider than her shoulders. "I can climb out that window."

"What?" Rani looked from Emilie to the window. "And then what, fly?"

"I can climb down. Then I could warn Lord Engal." Emilie felt the need to swallow in a suddenly very dry throat. This was much higher than the balcony over the water garden. But she had to be the one to do it. Rani, who was at least as big and strong as Kenar, would never fit through the narrow space, never mind that Emilie could never lift her high enough to reach it. "I saw on the opposite wall, there's an open gallery on the level just below this one. If this side matches it—"

"That's a lot to place on an 'if.'" Rani eyed her worriedly. "Are you sure?"

"Yes." Emilie made her voice firm. Rani lifted a skeptical brow and Emilie amended, "Mostly. We've got to try something."

"That we do." Rani looked at the window and winced. "But I hate to throw you out a window on such short acquaintance." She crouched down for Emilie to climb on her back again.

It wasn't any easier than it looked. Once Emilie got up to the window, she made sure there was still no sign of anyone on the galleries opposite, and that the men below loading supplies onto the airship didn't seem inclined to look up. Then she pulled herself halfway through the little opening, with Rani hanging on to her ankles to keep her from falling. That way, Emilie was able to lean out and look straight down the wall.

Dangling, the cool breeze in her hair, she could see the low balustrade of a gallery on the floor just below this one. The wall was rough and ridged, but instead of water below, there was a stone platform with a pretty shell pattern, extending out from the lowest level. So if Emilie fell, there would be no chance of survival. Or not pleasant survival, anyway. "All right, I think I can do this," Emilie muttered.

"Be certain," Rani said from below.

"I'm certain." Emilie gritted her teeth. *I am certain. I can do this.* She edged around until she was braced across the windowsill on her back. Gripping the ridge just above the opening, she wriggled forward out over empty space.

The moment when Rani had to let go of her ankles was not an easy one, and Emilie had to take a deep breath. She hadn't known how reassuring the feeling of having someone very strong hold on to you was until it had suddenly gone. Rani whispered, "Careful, little one. Go straight to your Lord Engal."

"I will." Emilie eased one leg out, straddling the window and finding purchase on the ridge below it, then did the same with the other leg. Still gripping the window opening, she took one glance down to make sure Lord Ivers' men hadn't looked up. It made her dizzy, and she decided that all the dramatic adventure stories she had read were right: it was better not to look down.

Feeling for hand- and toeholds in the ridges, she started to climb down. It went well enough, until her right foot reached for a toehold in empty space. Her stomach lurched, her head swam, and she nearly lost her grip. *Deep breaths, deep breaths,* Emilie chanted to herself, fighting down the fear. She lifted her foot again, found purchase, and started to edge sideways. After about a foot, she gingerly tried again. Still nothing. *Keep going.*

On the fourth try she found purchase, the rough surface of a column. A little fumbling, and her foot found a decorative finial on it. Carefully, she eased herself down, one ridge at a time.

Finally she could wrap her legs around the column and edge down it, until she could swing over onto the gallery floor. As soon as her feet touched the firm stone surface, her legs gave out and she sank down into a huddle. Shaking in relief, she thought, *If I'd known it was going to be that hard, I'd never have tried.* Her hands and feet were scraped, her fingers sore, her arms trembling from the effort. *So it was a good thing*

I didn't know. She couldn't believe she had actually done it. The idea of getting caught after that effort was horrific.

If you can do that, a voice in her head whispered, *you can do anything.* Anything she had to do to get herself and Rani and Miss Marlende out of here. Huddled trembling on the stone, she suddenly felt a hundred times stronger.

Now get on with it, Emilie told herself, and eased forward to take a careful peek between the balusters. The men had stopped loading the airship, and were standing on the platform, talking to a man dressed in ordinary clothes rather than a uniform. He was in his shirtsleeves, no coat. Lord Ivers, maybe, or someone else of high rank in the crew. He was tall and slim, with the blond hair and light skin of someone of Northern Menaen descent. That would be a good clue, if she had ever heard a description or seen a photograph of Lord Ivers, which she hadn't. She couldn't hear what they were saying either, just snatches of words carried on the breeze.

She crawled back from the edge and stood, padding barefoot toward the nearest door, the tile cool under her feet. It was an open arch, leading in to a big empty room with a blue and green mosaic floor. It had a lonely air of long disuse, and there was even a patch of mold on one wall. She slipped through it and two other similar empty chambers, and found an open door out to a corridor. It was empty and shadowy too, no lamps in the niches, the figures of merpeople painted on the walls faded and blotched. She couldn't hear any voices or movement. As Emilie stepped out into it, she spotted a large curving stair at the end.

She knew what she should do; she should run immediately back toward the harbor and swim out to the *Sovereign.* The problem was, she had no idea where she was or how to get to the harbor from here. She didn't know the language or have a translator shell to ask for directions, and she had no way to tell which merpeople were involved in the plot or which were innocent bystanders, so she couldn't risk approaching anyone for help. And if she did somehow make it to the *Sovereign,* the queen could still hold Miss Marlende and Rani hostage against Lord Engal's cooperation. *If he and Kenar aren't hostages now, too, to force Captain Belden to attack the nomads.*

The obvious conclusion was to rescue Miss Marlende and Rani before proceeding. Rani first, since Emilie knew where she was.

Emilie started toward the stairs. Just as she reached the stairwell, she heard voices echoing up from below, and she froze like a startled rabbit. It was Miss Marlende, and a male voice with a Menaen accent that she didn't recognize.

Miss Marlende was saying, "I think you must be mad."

The man laughed, not sounding offended. "No more mad than your father or Engal."

Lord Ivers, Emilie thought. Funny, he didn't sound evil.

Fury in her voice, Miss Marlende said, "My father and Lord Engal aren't causing a war simply for their own gain!"

"I'm not causing this war, young lady. The queen would still be fighting the nomads even if none of us had found our way down to this world. She's considerably more cunning and more determined than she looks, believe me." With a laugh, he added, "Those were her men who attacked the *Sovereign* during the last eclipse, not the nomads. Didn't you think the arrival of Yesa and her warship was excessively fortuitous?"

Miss Marlende said, startled, "She didn't—" After a moment, sounding more thoughtful, she said, "Of course, I see."

Emilie shook her head, but it did make sense. She remembered what Miss Marlende had said about the size and age of the city, as a relic of a disintegrating empire, and what the rulers of such a place must be like. Miss Marlende must have remembered it too. Sounding less certain, she said, "Why is she so determined to fight the nomads, then?"

"Because they are the future," Lord Ivers said, as if he were giving a lecture. "If what she and the others have told me is true, the Sealands have been changing for generations. The weather has grown warmer, and it's affecting the water depth, the way the fish run, how the plants grow, the way the islands form. These shallow seas can no longer sustain cities this size, the way they could in the empire's golden age. Now the fishers and gleaners and growers have to go further and further afield to bring in enough food for the rest of the population." Lord Ivers' voice warmed with his enthusiasm for the subject, and Emilie leaned on the stone banister, listening intently. The footsteps she could hear sounded as if they were made by more than two people, so Lord Ivers must have one or more of his men with him. "The nomads' ancestors saw the writing on the wall a long time ago, and changed their way of living and their way of governing themselves. They left the cities, broke up into smaller groups, and now travel to different fishing and farming grounds throughout the year, giving the sea and the land time to replenish itself. They've succeeded marvelously. So marvelously, the outlying farmers and fishers of this city, the greatest and possibly last outpost of the old empire, often desert their posts to join them."

Ah, Emilie thought. *The merpeople aren't being stolen away. They're deserting to the other side.* No wonder the queen was angry.

Miss Marlende must have come to the same conclusion. In a different tone, she said, "I see."

"Of course you do. There's nothing I could do to stop this," Lord Ivers concluded. "There's no place for the queen or her nobles or their way of life in this new style of living. If the queen was a forward thinker, she would form her people into their own groups of nomads and send them off to look for new fishing grounds. She isn't, and she won't. She's determined to preserve her control over this dying city for the rest of her generation."

"But you're using her for your own purposes—" Miss Marlende protested loudly. Then Emilie realized her voice wasn't getting louder, it was getting closer—Lord Ivers and Miss Marlende were coming up the stairs to this floor.

Oh, hell. Emilie bolted up the stairs, trying to keep her steps quiet. She reached the upper floor, where the stairwell foyer had two arched doorways opening into corridors, one to the left and one to the right. The room Emilie and Rani had been locked into should be on the right, facing out into the court. And Emilie didn't think it would be unguarded. Mindful that Lord Ivers would be here in a moment, she stepped silently to the right-hand archway and took a cautious peek.

The hall was lined with doorways, all with heavy metal doors, and midway down it there was a man in a blue uniform, sitting on a camp stool. The door nearest him had a big padlock through the metal handles. Emilie drew back, thinking, *Damn, I was afraid of that.* She had no idea how she was going to get Rani out of there.

Movement and voices drawing closer from the stairs made her dart across the foyer and through the archway on the left. Fortunately, that corridor was empty, leading out to a long room of open galleries. She crouched behind a pillar, trying to make herself small, and hoped they went the other way.

She heard them reach the landing and turn down the right-hand corridor. There was a scrape and shuffle as the guard got hastily to his feet and greeted Lord Ivers respectfully. Then Lord Ivers said, "Open the door, Cavin."

Uh-oh, Emilie thought. She heard the jingle of keys, clicks as the man fumbled with the padlock, then the door creak open. Rani said, "Finally. I was wondering if you had planned to settle here permanently, perhaps take up reed farming or some other useful occupation."

There was a moment of fraught silence, then Lord Ivers demanded, "Where is the girl?"

"What girl?" Rani said, sounding completely unperturbed. Emilie wondered where Rani had hidden her boots and the sack, the only evidence that she had really been in the cell.

Lord Ivers must have looked at Cavin for confirmation, because the man said, a little desperately, "Semeuls, Rail, and I put her in there, my lord. They can vouch for it."

Rani said, complacently, "He is lying. You should hire better henchmen."

"Perhaps you're right." Lord Ivers' voice was tight with fury. "Let's go."

More footsteps. Emilie risked a peek around the pillar and caught a glimpse of Miss Marlende, Rani, Lord Ivers, and three uniformed men with rifles, two who must have come up the stairs with Lord Ivers and one the unfortunate Cavin.

"And where are we going?" Miss Marlende asked.

"Back to the surface." Lord Ivers' voice sounded more distant as he started down the stairs. "I've persuaded the queen to accept Lord Engal's help instead of mine, and I have no reason now to linger."

"Ah, you will be dropping me off on the way, then?" Rani said, still sounding as calm as if she were having this conversation at a garden party, or the Cirathi equivalent.

"No, you'll be coming with me," Lord Ivers said. "You'll provide incontrovertible evidence of my achievement."

Emilie gasped in outrage. Rani's reply was drowned out by Miss Marlende's angry protests as the group continued down the stairs. *I can't let them get on the airship.* Emilie stood and ran to the archway, then to the top of the stairs. The group was about two floors down. She needed a weapon. She didn't even have anything to throw.

She went to the archway to the other corridor and looked down it just to see if there was anything helpful left behind. The metal camp stool still sat beside the wall. It was better than nothing. Emilie hurriedly retrieved it, then started down the stairs, her bare feet noiseless on the smooth steps.

She reached the third-floor landing, and looked over the open banister to see Lord Ivers and the others on the second, just turning to go down. The bottom level of the structure was an open area two floors high, with no floor, just narrow walkways level with the water and big pillars supporting the upper structure. One more stairway down and they would be out on the platform next to the airship, with the rest of Lord Ivers' men. Miss Marlende was still protesting loudly with occasional profanities, and one of the men had her arm, dragging her along. Rani's shoulders looked tense, and the other two guards watched her warily.

Emilie went to the top of the stairs, aimed at the man on Rani's right, and slung the camp stool at the back of his head. "Rani! Run!" she yelled.

The stool hit the man right between the shoulders and sent him jolting forward to tumble down the last set of stairs. It was poor Cavin, Emilie noted. Lord Ivers was knocked into the banister, and Miss Marlende shoved against the man who held her, knocking him off-balance. Rani moved like lightning. She grabbed the rifle of the man on her left, slammed the barrel into his face, twisted it away, and vaulted the railing to land with a splash in the water below.

Struggling with her guard, Miss Marlende yelled frantically, "Run, Emilie, run!," and Emilie realized she really should be running. Lord Ivers turned toward her, and Miss Marlende's guard tried to get his arms free to shoot at her. She turned and bolted back along the corridor, hoping there was another way down. *It's a big building,* she told herself, panting more from fear than exertion, *surely there's more than one stair!*

There wasn't, at least not off this corridor. The guards shouted behind her and a bullet rang off the stone wall. Emilie yelped and ducked into the room at the far end, praying that there would be a window. There was, a big one, that looked out over an open waterway at the far end of the building. She scrambled up onto the sill, glanced back to see a guard just behind her. As he lunged for her, she jumped.

By pure luck she missed the stone dock platform and plunged into the water. She floundered to the surface, coughing and gasping, heard someone yell about shooting at her, and flailed away, swimming frantically.

She managed to get headed down the waterway, away from the window, but another gunshot rang out behind her. Then something grabbed her ankle and jerked her under water.

Emilie struggled wildly, until she realized whatever had ahold of her was both furry and scaly. It had to be Rani. She hoped very hard that it was Rani. They passed through a dark section of water and she thought they were going under a solid object. Right at the point where Emilie thought her lungs would burst, they surfaced abruptly.

Emilie coughed and spit up water as Rani pulled her up onto wet stone. Emilie sputtered and managed to get a full breath. "You all right?" Rani asked.

Emilie nodded weakly. They were inside a building, perhaps next door to the one the airship was docked in. The ceiling was low and arched, cracked and stained with mold. There was more floor space between the pools of water.

"I had to stuff your boots and the sack they brought you in into the slop bucket," Rani said. "Sorry. I saved these." She pulled Emilie's dripping stockings out of the front of her shirt.

"That's all right." Emilie took the stockings, though she wasn't sure what good they would do her at the moment. "I don't think Miss Marlende got away." She coughed again.

"No, but she was very helpful, your friend. I would not have gotten away without her. And you," Rani added, giving Emilie a friendly nudge to the shoulder that almost pushed her over. "You are one brave little person."

"Thank you." Emilie was too worried to be flustered by the compliment. "We have to rescue Miss Marlende."

"That we do." Rani got to her feet, giving Emilie a hand up. "This way."

They made their way through the long building. It was quiet except for the water lapping in the pools, and Emilie saw cracks in the pillars and more splotches of mold; it had clearly been abandoned for some time. She wondered how many empty structures there were in this section of the city. Probably many, since the queen had chosen this area to dock Lord Ivers' airship. This city was not as prosperous as it had looked at first, more evidence that what Lord Ivers had said was the truth.

They came to a doorway on the far end, opening out to a narrow canal, with steps and platforms for merpeople to enter the water. It was lined with three- and four-story buildings, with large windows and balcony platforms. There was no sign of life or movement. Rani turned back toward the airship building, and Emilie kept close to the wall. Being shot at was not an experience she wanted to repeat. *We need to steal a gun,* she thought. The rifle Rani had jerked out of the guard's hands had fallen into the water, and Emilie wondered if they could retrieve it, if it would still work. She rather thought it wouldn't.

They reached a doorway leading into the airship building, and Rani stopped abruptly, holding up a hand. Emilie froze, and realized she could hear a low metallic buzz. "You hear that?" Rani whispered, then she said something in Cirathi that was probably a very bad word, adding, "The engine!"

Rani ducked through the doorway and Emilie hurried after her. They went through a wide shadowy passage with a shallow stream of water running down the center, toward an archway that opened into daylight. *That must be the courtyard.* Emilie's heart was pounding. If they had already started the airship's engine . . .

Rani stopped at the edge of the archway, taking a cautious peek through it. She cursed again and said, "We are too late, Emilie."

Emilie looked, in time to see the cabin of the airship clearing the top floor of the building, the enormous balloon throwing a huge shadow over the water court. *Damn it, no!* Desperate for it not to be true, she said, "Maybe they left her behind."

Rani ruffled Emilie's hair sympathetically, but said, "We'll search."

Cautiously, they looked through the lower floor, then worked their way back up, all the way to the cell level. There was no sign of Miss Marlende, but they could see the place had been occupied. In one room they found fruit rinds and crumbs, and bits of food trash that had clearly come from Menae: a couple of brown bottles that had probably held beer, and a wrapper for a cracker packet. There were some bits of crumpled paper and a blue uniform cap someone had dropped.

Emilie rescued her boots from the slop bucket in their cell, and admitted bleakly, "They didn't leave her behind."

Rani turned back toward the stairs, asking, "Do you know what they will do with her?"

"I don't know." Emilie hadn't thought Lord Ivers had seemed like the type to murder people, until his men started shooting at her. "If he just takes her back to the surface, to Menae . . . If he doesn't hurt her, when Lord Engal gets back he can tell the magistrates what happened. They'll arrest Lord Ivers if he doesn't let her go." Lord Engal must have just as much influence as Lord Ivers, and the magistrates would have to believe him and take action. *If Lord Engal can get back to Menae. If we can all get back.* "What do we do now? Try to get to the harbor and find Lord Engal and the others?" If he wasn't a hostage too.

"Yes, I think it must be your Lord Engal, for now," Rani said, thinking it over. "If he has no solutions, we'll have to think of one for ourselves. And I wish to retrieve Kenar as soon as possible." She paused on the landing to confide to Emilie, "Men are not good left on their own, you know. They pine."

Emilie had never heard that before and the thought kept her occupied all the way down the stairs.

* * *

Getting to the harbor was just as difficult as Emilie had suspected it might be, even with Rani's help.

Rani knew what direction they had to go in, but when they came to the edge of the empty area, there were too many merpeople between them and the waters of the harbor. Merpeople swimming in the waterways, towing little rafts piled with bundled goods, merpeople walking along the bridges and the galleries. The light was starting to get that edged quality that meant the Dark Wanderer was bringing the night eclipse, and Emilie thought this might be the rush to get home before dark, or to get the last things done for the end of the working day.

She was glad she had decided to try to rescue Rani and Miss Marlende, and hadn't fled alone toward the harbor for help; not only would Lord Ivers have been able to leave with both of them in his airship, but Emilie would have become hopelessly lost and recaptured by the merpeople.

Rani left Emilie to hide in an enclosed passage in the last empty building, and made several forays to check on different possible routes.

Emilie sat on the cool smooth floor, washed her boots off in a little pool, and worried. Her stomach was also starting to growl; it had been a long time since breakfast. She had also had time to feel her bruises from being manhandled into the sack; her arms looked like she had put them into a vise.

Rani returned finally, surfacing in the pool suddenly and giving Emilie a start. "It's not good news," Rani reported, and slung herself out of the water to sit on the platform. "The harbor area must be the most crowded part of the city. I think we must wait until dark before we try to make it to the docks."

"That's not long, though, is it?" Emilie asked, trying not to sound as weary and anxious as she actually was. "Maybe another hour?"

"Not long." Rani absently wrung out her long braids. "Your Lord Engal's ship would not travel at night, would it?"

"Um, yes. It has spotlights. We've been traveling at night all along, because we wanted to find Dr. Marlende and you all as quickly as possible." Emilie bit her lip. "You think the queen might have made them leave already?"

"Ah." Rani frowned, preoccupied, but she said reassuringly, "We'll see. Perhaps we'll be lucky."

Emilie thought Rani was probably an optimist.

* * *

About an hour later, the complete darkness of the eclipse settled in, and they crept out of hiding. Lamps, burning oil that smelled vaguely fishy, had been lit along some of the waterways and bridges, but most of the byways were dark. Rani moved silently over the walkways, giving wide berth to the lighted areas, leading them toward the docks.

Emilie was relieved to be moving. The wait for darkness had worn on her nerves, though at least the anxiety had kept her awake. It had been a long time since her last good night's sleep, as well as a long time since breakfast. At one point Rani had demanded, "What is that noise? Is that you?"

"It's my stomach," Emilie had replied defensively. She had noticed that Rani didn't speak Menaen as readily as Kenar; she thought that was because Kenar had been with Miss Marlende, probably talking himself hoarse to help her convince Lord Engal of what had to be done to come to Dr. Marlende's rescue, while Rani had been locked up with not much of anyone to speak with. "Doesn't your stomach grumble when you're hungry?"

"Yes, but not that loud. No one's stomach is that loud."

Now Emilie was almost willing to believe she was right, and hoped her stomach didn't alert any merpeople swimming through the dark water below them. She had kept her boots off in case they had to swim, tying them together and looping them around her neck, and the smooth stone was cool underfoot.

They came down a narrow walkway above a deep canal, and out onto the docks, under the shelter of the lower level of the big gallery. It was quiet except for the breeze on the water, and this part of the gallery smelled of the bundles of wet reeds stacked and piled everywhere. There were more lamps lit here, illuminating the piers that ran out into the water. Rani drew Emilie forward, using the reed bundles as cover, to where they could look out over the ships.

Emilie's heart sank immediately, but she still squinted, studying the piers, the place she was sure the *Sovereign* had been anchored. But the *Sovereign* would have been the most obvious thing in the crowded harbor, with all its running lights lit. "Not there?" Rani asked quietly.

Emilie shook her head, unexpectedly and stupidly feeling tears well up. They had known this was a possibility. She swallowed hard and managed to say, "No, it's gone."

"Hmm. Then we go with the other plan. Wait here." Rani ghosted away down the gallery before Emilie could say, "What other plan?"

Emilie crouched on the cool stone, waiting. She heard merpeople talking somewhere nearby and flinched, but after a moment it was obvious they were on the gallery a level or two above, and walking away. She realized she was trying not to bite her nails, recalled that her aunt was not here to remonstrate with her about it, and that she could bite them as much as she liked. It was a relief to her abused nerves.

Rani finally returned with a net bag slung over her shoulder. "This way," she whispered, and they went the other way down the gallery, away from the lighted piers. Emilie wanted to ask where they were going, but was afraid their voices might carry over the water. If one of the merpeople in the gallery heard a conversation of more than a few words, they might realize they were hearing a strange language and give the alarm.

They left the shelter of the gallery and headed toward the far side of the harbor. It was so dark, Emilie couldn't make out much, but when she tripped over a coil of rope and stumbled on a ramp, she realized they were passing the taller piers where the big barges had been docked. *Had been docked.* Now that she looked, she could see the empty water glinting faintly between the dark shapes of the piers. She tapped Rani on the back, and whispered as softly as possible, "The barges are gone."

Rani stopped, leaned back to cup her hand around Emilie's ear and say softly, "They've gone with your ship, after the nomads."

Oh, no, Emilie thought. They must have left when the *Sovereign* was forced to go, sometime this afternoon. When Rani started to pull away, she caught her arm and whispered, "Where are we going?"

"After them," Rani replied.

Oh. Startled, Emilie followed Rani through the dark. *Good.*

CHAPTER EIGHT

Past the big barge piers, Rani turned and stepped down onto a platform at the water level. From the dim glow of the lights on the gallery, Emilie could just make out the shapes of small boats, no bigger than the rowboats that plied the village pond at home, tied up along it. Rani selected one, motioned for Emilie to climb in, and began to untie it.

Emilie managed to clamber in and sit down on the narrow seat running down the center without flipping the boat over, though it was a near thing. The hull was made of something as light as straw; it must be dried reeds. Rani cast off, and stepped in to push away from the pier. She took a seat in the back, dumping her net bag in the bottom of the boat. Something poked Emilie in the back, and she twisted around to take the paddle Rani was handing her.

They paddled as quietly as possible, Rani guiding them out of the harbor, away from the city. The dark was so complete they had to navigate by brushing against the stands of reeds that bordered the outlying islands. After a time Emilie made out isolated lights that must be burning in the windows of the occasional settlements; she hoped that Rani knew where they were going, because Emilie was completely lost.

Finally, when the lights of the city were a good distance behind them, Rani said, "We must stop for a moment."

Relieved, Emilie pulled her paddle in, and stretched her neck and back. She turned around, listening to Rani rummage in the net bag. Then Rani handed her a heavy soft object. It felt like a big peach. Emilie said hopefully, "Fruit?"

"Yes. You can eat the peel." She crunched into one herself, and Emilie hastily followed suit. It was sweet, with the texture of an apple, but the inside was thicker and more filling. She hoped the sack was full to bursting.

Rani rummaged in the bag again, and Emilie heard a faint clank of metal. Then a small flame sparked and she saw Rani lighting a lamp with a big matchstick. Or it looked like a matchstick, except that it sparked blue and didn't smell of sulfur. "There, that will make our journey a little easier." She handed Emilie the lamp.

Emilie took it and stretched forward to hang it on the hook above the bow. Swallowing the last bite of fruit, she asked, "How do we know where the nomads are?" She remembered that Rani had escaped before the nomads had reached their final destination.

"This." Rani pulled off one of her necklaces, and handed it to Emilie. She couldn't see detail in the dark, but it felt like a piece of soft round stone. Rani said, "Spit on it and rub your thumb over it."

Emilie followed instructions. After a moment, light gleamed inside the stone, forming an arrow. It swung around like a compass, pointing toward Emilie's right. She looked up, smiling, and handed it back. "A magic compass?"

Rani looped it around her neck again. "Dr. Marlende made it, and gave it to me in case our ships became separated. It shows the way to find him, wherever he is." She leaned over to feel along the side of the boat, where a long reed wrapped in cloth was clipped to the hull. She lifted it up, and Emilie realized it was a sail. "The queen's ships will have to search around for the nomads, even if her spies know roughly where they have taken our friends. With the compass, we can beat them there." She added more quietly, "I hope."

Emilie shifted around on the seat to help her hold the pole steady while Rani got it fixed into the base mounted to the bottom of the boat. She had almost forgotten that Dr. Marlende was a sorcerer, like Dr. Barshion. Except better, apparently. "I wish he'd given one to Kenar. At least then we could have dealt with the nomads and skipped the queen."

Rani tossed Emilie another piece of fruit. "He didn't have to. Jerom had the magic of his own, to find us." She hesitated. "Jerom is not with your ship?"

Emilie hesitated. She hadn't told Rani that part yet. "No, he died, I'm sorry. It was more dangerous than they thought it would be. But Kenar got through it all right."

"I see." Rani sounded pensive. She was silent for a time, finishing her second piece of fruit and tossing the hard rind into the water. She said finally, "I think your people are a little more delicate than us. And

perhaps the ease of their journey down here made Marlende and Jerom incautious."

Emilie thought that was very likely. "Our journey was easy up to
the point where the engine stopped working and we would have been
crushed to death if we hadn't been so close to the Hollow World already."

Rani snorted with wry amusement. "That sounds typical. Now . . ."
She stretched out the light fabric of the sail, fixing it to the lower reed.
"If we can get this to work the way it's supposed to, we can make better
time."

With Emilie to hold things and help tie the light seaweed-braided
ropes, Rani got the sail rigged. It caught the breeze and they began to
move, skimming lightly over the water.

They sailed through the night, sometimes having to stop and use
the paddles to get the boat through a narrow island channel, or through
stands of tall reeds. Emilie knew she was lucky the boat was light and
easy to paddle, and that there seemed to be no strong current to fight.
The wind was light but steady, full of the scent of the sea, and the
jasmine-like fragrance of the reeds. When Emilie's stomach started to
growl again, Rani passed out more food from her bag, including some
pieces of dried fish that tasted salty-sweet. It wasn't entirely pleasant,
but it gave Emilie the energy to carry on.

For a while, at least. They had been passing through an empty
stretch of water for some time, with no islands or obstructions that
required them to use the paddles. Emilie caught herself slumping
forward. The second time, her forehead banged her knees before she
woke up. Behind her, Rani said, "Sleep, before you fall out of the boat."

Groggy, Emilie rubbed her eyes. "What about you?"

Rani chuckled. "After too many days as Lord Ivers' prisoner, with
nothing to do but sit or sleep, I could go on forever."

Emilie was sure not even Rani could go on forever, but she appreciated the chance to rest. She shifted around in the bow, easing down
to the bottom of the boat, and put her head down on the seat. She was
asleep instantly.

* * *

It took them a day and a night of sailing, just Emilie and Rani, out on
the sea. When daylight returned, they stopped at a small island with

a spring, so Rani could refill the clay water jug in the bottom of the boat. Rani gave Emilie a small knife she had managed to find along the dock, and Emilie used it to cut some dried reeds. Once they were underway again, she wove sun hats for them both.

The hats made the glare off the water bearable, though at least the wind was cool and the sun down here in the Hollow World didn't seem as bright or as hot as the one above the surface. Emilie would never have thought that weaving sun hats, a skill gained during long summer afternoons at her aunt's sedate garden parties, would come in this handy.

They passed islands with strange spiny trees, which rustled with all sorts of animal life, and long-legged bright blue water birds standing amid the reeds in the shallows. They saw crumbling towers and halls and other remnants of the old Sealands empire. And sometimes there were waterspouts in the distance, which Rani said might be caused by some sort of large sea life.

At one point, after they had to use the paddles to guide the boat through a maze of sandbars, Rani said thoughtfully, "You know, I think this thing is even better than I thought."

Emilie twisted around to see her examining the compass. She lifted her hat to wipe the sweat off her forehead. "Why?"

"I noticed it was taking us on a route through the islands that was too quick to be luck. Then it led us on the best path through these sandbars; if I had used my own judgment, we'd have run aground and had to go all the way around the other end of the island to get here." Rani slipped the thong around her neck again. "I think it shows the way, the best turns and twists, to get to Dr. Marlende, and not just the direction toward him."

It made sense. "It's the aether," Emilie said. "Aether's in everything, air, land, water. I bet that's a bit like an aether navigator, only it's using the aether currents to find Dr. Marlende."

Rani lifted her brows. "You study this stuff too?"

"No, not really. I just read about it, in the Lord Rohiro novels."

"Now which one is Lord Rohiro?"

So Emilie told her about Lord Rohiro's adventures, which occupied the next few hours.

Rani was more talkative than Kenar, and Emilie learned a lot about their past adventures, too. They had been traveling for a long time, and had been crew together on Rani's mother's ship before Rani had grown up and acquired the *Lathi*. They had gone to some exceedingly strange places, and the stories about the sinking islands and the people who lived inside giant dead sea creatures would have sounded made-up, if Emilie hadn't known better.

Rani also taught Emilie how to hold the tiller and the sail to keep them on course, so they could keep going while Rani slept. Emilie would never have thought she would do something like this, sailing a small boat, let alone voyaging over an otherworldly sea, guiding it with a sorcerer's compass. Being so close to the water, dependent only on herself and Rani, mostly Rani, for safety, was very different from being aboard the *Sovereign*.

In all, she was enjoying the trip immensely, except for the fact that all their friends were in danger. Emilie knew she should feel guilty about that. But she had never done anything like this before, and the sea and sky and the islands were endlessly diverting, providing a constant distraction from their predicament.

They were both awake by the time the next eclipse passed on, and Emilie, squinting at the horizon in the gradually brightening light, was the first to say, "Land!"

"I see," Rani said thoughtfully. "I think we are there, Emilie."

Emilie hoped so. The island ahead stretched for some distance, and was higher than the others in this region. From this vantage point, it looked like the shore was lined with rocky cliffs, topped with tall dark green vegetation. If this wasn't their destination, Emilie didn't know how they were going to get their little boat around it. "How do you know?"

Rani, her hands occupied with the sail and the tiller, jerked her chin toward the starboard side. "Because I think that is one of the queen's barges, over there. We did not beat them here, after all."

Emilie looked, staring hard, knowing by now that Rani's eyes were sharper than hers. After a moment, she made out the dim gray-blue shapes, long and low, in the water toward the far end of the island. She could barely see them, but the good thing was, she didn't think anyone aboard would be able to spot their tiny boat. She thought she saw the sun glinting off something metallic, and said, "Can you see the *Sovereign*?"

"I see something big and coppery, I think that must be it." Rani grimaced, tipping her straw hat back. "But it is surrounded by the barges, so that's one of our plans in the crap hole."

Rani's language was also a bit more earthy than Kenar's, something else Emilie liked about her. They had talked about possibly sneaking aboard the *Sovereign*, once they located it, and joining forces with Lord Engal and Kenar and the others. They could warn them about Lord Ivers, and tell them that Miss Marlende was aboard his airship, heading toward the surface, and not a hostage to the queen. "You don't think we could sneak aboard it?"

"No, we would have to swim underwater, amid a small fleet of people who live underwater part of the time; I think we would be as obvious as if we painted our boat red and beat a drum as we sailed right up to them."

She was probably right. "So we're going to try the island?" The other plan was to locate Dr. Marlende and the Cirathi, and try to rescue them. It was a broad, vague plan, at best. "And hope the queen hasn't attacked the nomads yet?"

"We try the island," Rani agreed, as their little boat sped toward it. "And hope."

* * *

Several hours later, they dragged their boat up onto the narrow strip of beach below the short sandy cliff. Emilie stumbled a little and had to stop and stretch. They had been stopping briefly on the low islands, sometimes to look for springs, sometimes just to answer calls of nature and stretch their legs. Last night was the longest interval they had gone without stopping. She helped Rani take down the sail and clip the poles to the side again, and they pulled the boat up behind some rocks to hide it if any Sealands or nomad ships patrolled past this shore. The sand was soft, and their feet and the boat kept sinking into it. Emilie fell down a few times, but they managed it.

They left their straw hats in the boat, but Rani took the bag with their dwindling supply of food, and filled a waterskin from the clay jar in the boat. She also had a knife to tuck into her sash, a long one made from bone that she had picked up along the city's dock with the rest of their supplies. It was a good weapon, though Emilie still wished they had been able to get one of the rifles.

Getting up the cliff was easier. It was about twenty-five feet high, with tall trees that had large palm leaves below crowns of red spiny clumps, and tall grassy bushes. Rani found a spot with lots of rocks and weeds, and told Emilie to climb onto her back. Then she dug her hard claw-like nails into the clumps of weed and scaled the cliff.

Emilie had brought her boots, tied together and slung over one shoulder. When they reached the top, she sat down to hastily put them on as Rani scouted around. As Emilie was tying the laces, she noticed the ground was unexpectedly hard. It was sandy, with clumps of green-yellow grass between the thick ropy tree roots. She scraped at a bare patch, and after only a half inch or so, encountered stone. It was flat and smooth, and there was a straight groove through it, too straight to be natural.

She looked at the nearest tree, feeling the roots, and saw they had burrowed down right through the stone. *Like weeds,* she thought. *Very big weeds.* As if sand from the other islands washed up here over the years, the seeds for the grass and trees carried with it or blown here by strong winds.

Rani returned, saying, "No one around here, at least. What are you looking at?"

Emilie pushed to her feet, dusting her hands off on her shirt. "I think we're on top of a wall, or a roof, or a plaza or something. Part of one of the old Sealands cities."

A thoughtful "Hmm" was Rani's only comment.

They made their way forward through the trees and tall bushes. There were birdcalls, the hum of insects, the rush of waves and the wind, but no sound of voices. Keeping her own voice low, Emilie said, "If the queen's ships came straight here, they would have started fighting already, wouldn't they? Maybe they've already defeated the nomads."

"Maybe. If not, I wonder what they are waiting for." Rani was distracted, listening. "Do you hear that water?"

Emilie had heard it, but she had thought it was the sea. Now that she thought about it, the waves hadn't been that loud down on the beach itself. "A waterfall?" But she had trouble imagining a big water-fall on this island. She couldn't see any sign of rocky cliffs or hills above the trees.

With a frustrated grimace, Rani shook her head. "This place gets odder and odder."

They pushed forward for a time, and Emilie began to see more light through the trees ahead, as if they were coming to an open area. *Or the other side of the island,* she thought. The sound of rushing, falling water grew steadily louder as they walked.

Rani was just ahead of her, pushing through the last stand of bushes, when she made a soft exclamation of surprise and stopped abruptly. Emilie bounced with impatience, then Rani reached back and drew her forward.

They were standing not far from the edge of a cliff, looking out over a giant canyon. It was at least two hundred feet deep, and surely more than a mile across. Past the drifts of mist that laced the air, Emilie saw the far side had the waterfall, running the entire length of the cliff. It didn't come from a river, but from a slot in the cliff rock itself, about twenty feet below the top, which was lined with a forest similar to the one they were standing in. "That's not possible," Emilie said, baffled. She had to raise her voice to be heard over the din. "It's deeper than the island is tall."

"I know." Rani pulled her down and they crawled toward the edge. Peering over, Emilie saw a waterfall ran down this side too, and the air was heavy with its spray. It fell down the rock wall to a canal far below, running all along the base of the cliff. The canyon was a huge oval, and must take up the whole center of the island. The mist obscured much of the view below, but what Emilie could see was a green forest, more lush than the one up here, dotted with streams and ponds.

Rani scraped at the dirt and grass on the edge, sending it crumbling down into the rush of water. "You were right, Emilie." She tapped the hard gray-white surface under the dirt. "This place was built, ages ago."

"The water is coming from the sea?" Emilie wondered. "If we fell off the boat in the water around the island, would we be sucked under into this waterfall?"

Rani gave her a dry look. "You have a very interesting imagination, but this water is fresh. Maybe it comes from underground."

"Or the surface? My surface, I mean." She imagined a subterranean river, wending its way down through the earth, until it was tapped by the ancient builders of the Sealands.

"At the moment anything is a possibility..." Rani sat up a little, saying with satisfaction, "Ah-ha, there's our airship!"

Emilie craned her neck, trying to see. "Where?" Rani pointed. A drift of mist was shifting with the wind, and as it cleared, the gray bullet shape of an airship's balloon was visible above the trees. The shape and color were just different enough from Lord Ivers' balloon to make this one distinct. There might be some buildings near it, obscured by leaves and branches. It certainly wasn't a city, unless it was buried underground, which seemed very unlike the merpeople. She bet the nomads used this place as a temporary refuge, or meeting place. "This is why the nomads were so suspicious of the airship, so afraid the queen would use it. If this is their fortress, it would be a perfect way to attack it."

"So perfect, I wonder why she let Lord Ivers go," Rani said, with wry emphasis.

Emilie blinked, thinking it over. It was an excellent point. "You think it was a trick, that she stopped him somehow, after he left the city?"

"It's a possibility, though I'm not sure how she would do it. At least we haven't seen him around here yet." Rani crawled back from the cliff edge, withdrawing into the stands of grass, and Emilie followed her.

They sat in the shelter of the brush, and Emilie said, "There has to be a way down there, besides airships. Maybe stairs under the waterfalls, or a ladder—Ooh, that's a good idea."

Rani was holding Dr. Marlende's compass, rubbing her thumb over the smooth surface. "Yes, I hope it works the way we think it does."

Meaning it would lead them to the way to find Dr. Marlende, not just point directly toward the airship. Emilie held her breath.

The arrow pointed not toward the canyon, but parallel to it, in the antidarkward direction. "Ha," Rani muttered in satisfaction, pushing to her feet.

They followed the arrow through the spiny palm forest, having to stop frequently and rub spit on the stone again, then adjust their course. Emilie expected to find something right away, but after about an hour of walking on the hard sandy ground, finding their way among the tall curving trunks and the clinging grass-bushes, the excitement started to pall.

They stopped briefly to eat the last of the fruit, and a little dried fish, and drink some water. As they started again, Rani admitted, "I hope this thing isn't confused, and is not just telling us to circumnavigate this island."

Emilie hoped not, too. If it was, she didn't know what they were going to do next, except perhaps try to get past the merpeople to the *Sovereign*. Somehow.

But after another long time of walking, the compass suddenly pointed away from the canyon wall, back toward the beach. They exchanged a look, and Rani cautioned, "Don't get too excited. It could be telling us to go jump in the sea and stop bothering it."

Emilie couldn't take that advice. Forgetting all about her sore feet, she hurried after Rani.

They had just passed a big mound of grass-bushes when the compass abruptly started to point back the other way. "It means in here!" Emilie plunged into the bushes, stopping just as abruptly when Rani grabbed her belt and hauled her back.

"Me first," Rani said, "And remember, we're looking for a way down, so watch the ground and don't fall in any holes."

"Oh, good point," Emilie muttered, and went more carefully, testing the ground first with each step, the way Rani did.

A moment later Rani jolted forward, flailing an arm for balance. Emilie grabbed her arm to steady her. Looking down, she saw Rani's foot had broken through a crust of dirt over a perfectly round hole. "I meant that to happen," Rani said breathlessly, freed her foot, then crouched down to knock away the rest of the dirt. Emilie hurried to help, beating at the hardened dirt until it fell away.

Her scaly brow furrowed, Rani said, "This is clearly not the way the nomads use to get down there. That worries me."

She was right, this wasn't a disguised entrance. The dirt plug had been formed by time and weather. "But the compass did point to it," Emilie said.

"I wonder at the compass's judgment," Rani said wryly.

Soon they had the hole clear. It plunged straight down through the earth, a dark stone-lined pipe. Steps had been cut into it, like the rungs of a ladder, a good indication that it led somewhere. And cool air flowed up from it, a sign that the bottom, wherever it was, wasn't blocked up. It smelled of dirt and damp stone.

Rani muttered a Cirathi curse. "I should have brought the boat lamp."

"It was bright daylight and we certainly didn't know there'd be any caves or tunnels," Emilie said. It would be too long a walk back to get it. "But you've got the matches?"

"Yes, that will have to do." Rani checked her bag, making sure they were still there. "Here, take some in case we are separated."

Emilie took the matches, tucking them into the pocket of her bloomers. Though the idea of being separated from Rani down in that underground space was frankly terrifying.

Rani leaned down, running her hand around the inside of the pipe. "Emilie, can your little claws manage this? I think you must stay here."

"No, I can manage it." The ladder looked sturdy and she could get her hands all the way around the rungs, which would make it easier to climb. It was the dark she was rather more worried about. The open dark of a moonless night, or the Hollow World's eclipse, didn't bother her. This enclosed darkness was different.

Rani leaned down, trying to get a better view of Emilie's expression. "Are you sure?"

Emilie made her chin firm and nodded. "Yes."

Rani sighed. "I wonder about both of us." She eased down, got a foot on a lower rung, then started to climb down. Emilie gathered her courage and followed.

The rungs were roughened slightly, in a way Emilie thought was deliberate, to help keep your hands from slipping off. As they climbed farther and farther down, she was very glad of the light from the opening overhead. Below them the pipe was utterly black. At least she could still look up at the sky and know it was there.

The circle of light that marked the opening was much smaller when Rani said suddenly, "Oof! I think we're there."

Emilie stopped, wiping sweat off her face onto her sleeve. "What?"

"There's a floor here." Rani's hand patted her ankle. "Come on down."

Emilie climbed down, and even though she was prepared for it, it was still a jolt when her foot hit the solid stone floor. She leaned against the ladder in relief, taking a deep breath. Now that she had stopped, her shoulders were shaking, her hands ached, and her stomach felt loopy. It was from pure nerves, and from gripping the ladder rungs too tightly, but knowing that didn't help.

The darkness was nearly absolute, but she could hear Rani running her claws over the walls. "Doorway here," Rani reported. "A passage. Here is where it gets interesting."

"Actually I haven't been at all bored up to now." Emilie stepped over to her, hands out, and bumped into Rani, who steered her to the wall. She felt the slightly rough stone walls, finding it was a good-sized doorway, stretching up above her head and about three feet wide.

Rani said, "Here, Emilie, keep your hand on my back so we stay together. I don't want to use the matches unless it gets worse."

Emilie wondered how the intrepid Rani was going to define "worse." After some fumbling, she took a firm grip of the strap of the supply bag. "Ready."

They made their way along, stumbling a little, leaving the faint light from the opening at the top of the pipe behind. Emilie forced herself not to think about walls closing in. The air was still flowing down the passage, heavily scented with earth and water, and she tried to imagine they were passing down a wide open road over a dark plateau. It almost worked.

But then Emilie began to hear the rush of the waterfall, vibrating through the stone, and the sense that they were close to their goal made the enclosed darkness easier to bear. *We're so close,* she thought. She just hoped the way wasn't blocked somewhere. She hoped the compass knew the difference between a tiny gap that aether could pass through and an opening big enough for people.

Not long later, Rani stopped suddenly. As Emilie bumped into her, she said, "Light ahead."

"Oh, good," Emilie breathed.

As they moved on, Emilie started to see it too, a faint lightening at the end of the passage. It grew gradually lighter, and she was able to let go of Rani and walk beside her. The rush of the waterfall grew louder, until she could almost taste the spray in the air.

They reached the opening, a narrow slot about two feet wide, lined with flat smooth stones. Past it they could see a curtain of falling water. Cautiously poking their heads out, they saw the doorway opened onto a narrow stone walkway that ran along the base of the cliff, behind the waterfall. The water itself was falling into a stone channel, far too regular to be natural.

Emilie followed Rani out onto the walkway. The din was too loud to hear anything, including each other's attempts to talk, and the walkway seemed empty as far as they could see. The curtain of falling water extended as far as they could see as well. Emilie couldn't make out much of what lay past it, except for glimpses of rich green vegetation.

Rani checked the compass again. Emilie stood on tiptoes to see; it pointed straight through the water. Rani looked up and down the walkway, her expression vexed. Emilie thought she understood; the nomads must not know about this way down, or the top of the pipe wouldn't have been blocked with dirt. But they had to know about this walkway, and if the queen's forces hadn't found a way down here yet, they would surely be patrolling it. Rani made her decision and motioned for Emilie to follow her.

They climbed down to the flat stone edge of the channel, and Rani paced along it a short distance. She stopped at a spot where the water seemed to be falling less heavily; at least, Emilie could see a bit more of what was on the other side: the opposite edge of the channel, and another walkway. Rani, with waving gestures and pointing, managed to communicate that they were going to swim under it, and that Emilie should hold on to her very tightly. Emilie nodded, and sat down to pull her boots off.

Rani took off her own boots, tucked them and Emilie's into the bag and tied up the neck of it tightly, took off the thong holding the compass and tied it tightly to her wrist. Then she mouthed, "Ready?"

Emilie wrapped her arms around Rani's waist, and took a deep breath. They jumped, and Rani pulled them under, swimming strongly.

Emilie helped her kick against the rough current, thinking it would be easy because Rani was so strong. Then they hit the water under the fall, and suddenly they were in a pounding, churning void. She tightened her hold on Rani, knowing she was holding on for her life. The force of it was like blows raining down, Emilie lost her last breath and inhaled water, choked, and thought they would both die.

They surfaced, Emilie choking and gasping. Then she realized Rani was limp, barely moving, starting to slip under again. Panicked, Emilie kicked out, letting go with one arm so she could paddle, dragging her toward the edge, saying, "Rani, Rani, wake up!"

Fortunately the water came right up to the flat rim of the channel, spilling over it, so Emilie was able to heave Rani and herself partially up onto the edge. She pounded Rani on the back, until Rani choked, pushed her off, and spit up water. Rani collapsed over the edge, but she was breathing, and groggily conscious.

Emilie sank against the stone, relieved and too exhausted to move. But they were out in the open, there was a wide area of low moss-like grass between the channel and the forest. A white stone path ran through it, and anyone coming along it could see them. "Rani, we have to get into the forest." The trees were tall and slender, with green trunks and darker green leaves sprouting out in big fan shapes. Tall ferns grew between them. It would provide good cover, if they could just get there.

Rani managed a nod, and started to push herself up. Emilie got a toehold in the side of the channel wall, and dragged herself up all the way onto the rim. Once there, she took Rani's arm, helping to pull her the rest of the way out. Some of the water dripping onto the stone was tinged with red. "Are you all right?" Emilie asked Rani, peering at her in new alarm. "I think you're bleeding."

"I think I'm not as waterproof as I thought," Rani admitted. She probed at her forehead, just at her hairline, and her fingers came away bloody. "And possibly hit my head on the bottom."

"We were that far down?" Appalled, Emilie glanced back at the water. She couldn't see the bottom.

"Yes." Rani staggered upright with Emilie's help, leaning on her. "This was perhaps not the best idea."

"I don't know what else we could have done." Emilie stumbled a little on the grass as they headed for the concealment of the trees. "The merpeople must be—"

She meant to say the merpeople must be guarding every entrance they knew about. But she caught movement out of the corner of her eye. She turned her head, and gasped, "They're here!"

Some distance down the open pathway, several silvery gray shapes were emerging from the forest—merpeople.

Rani looked, and snarled a curse. She pulled away from Emilie, stumbling, and ripped the thong with the compass off her wrist. She pressed it into Emilie's hand, and said, "Run."

Emilie darted a look at the merpeople. They pelted toward them over the mossy grass, carrying the short fishing spears they used as weapons. Rani gave her a push, her eyes on the merpeople, and shouted, "Run, I'll catch up with you!"

Emilie choked back a sob, and ran.

CHAPTER NINE

Emilie bolted through the forest, crashing through ferns, dodging past the slender green trunks. Instinct told her to run in a diagonal and not a straight line. Half-forgotten memories of hide-and-seek games with her brothers, back when they had been young enough to still want to play, came back to aid her. She stopped careening through the brush, running more slowly but taking care not to make noise and leave obvious signs of her passage.

She made herself stop and listen, holding her breath and trying to hear past her pounding heart. Bodies smashed through the vegetation not far away, and she knew Rani would never have made that much noise. Grimacing, Emilie fled off to the right and ducked between the bushes. Her boots were with Rani in their supply bag, but the ground was covered with a spongy moss that was soft on her feet and made no sound when she stepped on it.

The forest was cloaked in deep green shadows, the air damp and thick with earthy scents. The soft birdcalls and the occasional darting insect seemed different from the drier forest up on the island. *This place is below the sea level*, Emilie remembered. Maybe it was different, an artifact of the old Sealands empire, like the flooded cities.

She stopped three more times, and the third time she couldn't hear any sound of pursuit. Breathing hard, she kept moving but slowed her pace to a walk. *They must have captured Rani*, she thought, sick. *Because I abandoned her.* They would have both been caught if she hadn't, but it still felt like cowardice. Smart cowardice, but still cowardice.

Emilie was sick of being compelled to abandon people. First Miss Marlende, then Rani. *And your aunt and uncle, your brothers, and the rest of your family*, a traitor voice whispered. *That was different*, she told herself desperately. *That was a daring bid for freedom.* But her family wouldn't see it that way, and now she might be trapped here and never able to send word to anyone. Her aunt and uncle would probably assume she had gone off to become a prostitute, but there were others—her oldest brother, Porcia and Mr. Herinbogel, Karthea, other friends—who would worry, who would think something terrible had happened to her.

And they would be right.

Emilie stopped, crouched down behind a tree, and gave way to tears. Once the first hard sobs were out, it was a relief, and she felt as if she could think more clearly. Still dripping tears, she licked her thumb and rubbed the surface of the compass. The arrow formed, pointing the way through the forest toward Dr. Marlende. If he was dead, would this still work? she wondered suddenly. Surely aether navigators still worked if the sorcerer who had made them died, otherwise they wouldn't be very practical. But maybe spells like this were different. She hoped so, because if the nomads hadn't hurt any of their prisoners, maybe they wouldn't hurt Rani.

Emilie wiped her face on her sleeve, looped the compass's cord over her head, and took quick stock of her resources. The matches and the knife Rani had given her were still in her pockets, though the matches would have to dry out before she could use them. Other than that, she had nothing. Just herself. *You can do this,* she thought, still sniffling. *Whatever you have to do, you can do it. You aren't Emilie, runaway girl from the country. You're Emilie, the adventuress. Now get on your feet and find Dr. Marlende.*

She stood up and followed the compass through the shadowy forest.

* * *

Emilie made her way through the trees and brush for perhaps two hours, though it was hard to judge the time. Water wasn't a problem—she had crossed three shallow clear streams cutting through the mossy floor—but she knew she was going to be pretty hungry by the time of the next eclipse. The texture of the moss kept her bare feet from getting too sore, but she was collecting an impressive array of bruises and scratches. She stopped at one point to climb a tree, finding handholds and footholds in the hard ridges that circled the trunk. It was a dauntingly tall tree, but she climbed just high enough to catch a glimpse of the airship's balloon through the heavy screen of palm leaves.

Her first indication that she was nearing her destination was when she stubbed her toes on a rock. Hopping and muttering curses she had heard the *Sovereign*'s sailors use, she realized it was a line of paving stones, half buried in the moss. *I bet I'm close,* she thought, stepping over the paving and moving more carefully. There must be an old Sealands city or fort or something down here, that the nomads had taken over.

After a short time, the ground started to slope up, and she could see the trees and ferns thinned out ahead. She ducked down to creep close to the ground, and pressed on. As she got closer to the edge of the forest, the ground dropped away into a bowl-shaped depression, and above it rose the silver-gray curve of the airship's balloon. Near it was a collection of conical white stone roofs. Emilie flattened herself down in the moss in the shadows under the last clump of ferns, and crept as close as she dared.

Now she had a better view. Down in the shallow valley was a small city, much bigger than it had looked from the top of the waterfall cliffs when it had been concealed by the trees and mist. There were round towers, each a few stories tall, and between them short squat single-story buildings of smooth white stone. Unlike those in the queen's city, they were round with bulbous curving sides. The floor of the little valley was dotted with large pools, all perfectly circular. She could see the airship where it was anchored near this end of the valley, the cabin hanging level with the roof of the nearest round bulgy tower.

She could also see merpeople. Several moved purposefully out of one tower and toward another. There were three standing in front of the doorway of the tower nearest the airship, clearly on guard. All were armed with the short fishing spears. As she watched, another two merpeople surfaced in a pool, walking up the steps and out onto the mossy ground. The pools must be connected, to each other and maybe to the buildings. *And maybe to the channel that circles the canyon?* Emilie wasn't sure that would help her, if it was true. But there had to be a hidden harbor somewhere, where the nomads kept their boats, and it would make sense if it was reached via underwater tunnels. She thought this place must be used as a fortress, rather than a permanent settlement; she didn't see any children, just adults.

She looked harder at the airship, trying to see if anyone was aboard it. Like Lord Ivers' ship, the cabin was tucked up below the oblong balloon, and ran more than half the length of it. Unlike his, the cabin looked like it was made of some light coppery metal, and had a narrow walkway with a single railing running all the way around. She didn't think it was large enough to have two decks. The oblong windows were larger, but she couldn't see anyone moving around inside. The compass pointed toward the airship, or at least toward that end of the compound.

A plank bridge ran from the flat roof of the tower up to the closed door of the airship. *The prisoners could be inside there,* Emilie thought.

There were no windows in the top of the tower, but there were big trees along the ridge of the valley, and the bottom of the cabin, and the metal catwalk, was just above their heavy branches. It looked like a possibility to Emilie. Maybe the only possibility. The plank bridge suggested that there must be a trapdoor in the roof to allow access to the airship. But surely that door would be guarded too. *Maybe not, if the prisoners are locked up in rooms inside the tower.*

Emilie settled back into the ferns to think about it, knowing this was no time to act rashly. And that she had a few hours left until the next eclipse, so she might as well spend it resting, spying, and trying to think of a less mad plan.

But by the time the eclipse fell, she was fairly certain a mad plan was the best way to go.

* * *

Sometime after darkness fell, Emilie crouched on the edge of the valley, in the stand of big trees that overhung the airship, impatiently waiting for someone to notice her distraction.

The nomads had lit their encampment with lamps made from big curving shells, burning fish oil. The lamps lit the paths between the buildings and the pools, but the light didn't quite reach the airship, which was now just a big shape in the dark. While that would prove helpful, Emilie was afraid it was too dark to see her distraction.

Maybe I should just go ahead. She chewed her lower lip, considering it. The problem was, she wasn't sure she could do this at all, let alone do it in complete silence. *But you can't just sit here,* she thought in frustration. She couldn't come this close and stop.

Then below, a merperson came running from the opposite end of the compound, calling out to the others, pointing back over his shoulder. Emilie sat up, relieved. *Finally.*

Earlier, as the eclipse had been about to descend, she had crept around to the opposite end of the valley from the airship, and heaped up a big pile of dead brush and fallen palm fronds. The wood was green and damp, so setting it on fire had taken most of the Cirathi matches that Emilie had tucked into her pocket. But it had finally started to smolder and then burn.

She still couldn't see the smoke, but a moment later the breeze brought her the scent of it, which must have alerted the merpeople. Many ran toward that end of the compound, calling out to each other. Several dived into one of the pools, disappearing under the surface, presumably to carry the word or get reinforcements. The three men who were guarding the door of the tower moved away from the open doorway, facing down the valley, trying to see what was happening.

Emilie took a sharp breath; she had hoped they would leave, but had known that was a little much to expect. *All right, here goes,* she thought, and stood and turned to the tree she had picked out.

She started to climb, gritting her teeth as the ridges around the trunk dug into her fingers and toes. This tree was older and pointier than the one she had climbed earlier, but the trunk was also bigger around, giving her more room to climb. It was so dark she couldn't see her hands on the trunk, and the merpeople were all still occupied trying to decide if the fire meant an attack by the queen's forces. But it was still a relief when she reached the shelter of the screen of drooping palm leaves.

Emilie was sweating by the time she reached the gentle bend where the trunk broke up into individual branches, extending in curves out toward the airship. She shook the sweat out of her eyes and peered ahead. *So far so good.* The balloon and the cabin now blocked her view of the tower and the guards, but also their potential view of her.

She gripped the trunk with her legs and scooted awkwardly forward, out onto the highest branch. She climbed along it, closer and closer to the dark bulk of the airship. The branch was getting more slender, and Emilie winced when it creaked under her. She tried to tell herself it wasn't as bad as climbing out the prison window, but she wasn't so sure. Those ledges seemed quite wide and safe compared to this tree. She couldn't think what was worse, falling and dying or falling and breaking a leg or an arm or both, and being at the nomads' mercy. *Neither,* she thought, *please let it be neither.*

She edged farther and farther forward, until finally the airship's catwalk was just above her. About five feet above her. *Hell, it didn't look that far from across the valley.* Emilie tried to ease up slowly, felt herself start to slip, and dropped back to grip the branch tightly. She held back a sob of terror. *This won't work,* she thought, feeling the branch sway beneath her. It had to work. She couldn't go back.

She looked up again. She couldn't do it slowly, so she would have to do it fast. She pushed herself up into a crouch without letting go with her hands. Then she braced herself, and shoved upright in one quick motion, making a wild grab.

Her right hand brushed metal, she gripped the slim post of a railing, just as her feet slipped off the branch. She hung for a moment, her arm straining, then found the edge of the catwalk with her other hand. She hauled herself up as far as she could, her heart pounding with the effort, then managed to pull a leg up and hook her foot onto a supporting strut for the catwalk. Pushing from there let her drag her weight up onto the metal walkway. She huddled for a moment, breathing hard, astonished to be still alive. *That was a lot harder than I thought it was going to be,* Emilie thought, and scrubbed sweat off her forehead.

She eased to her feet, gripping the railing because her legs were still shaking and her arms hurt. She felt the airship move slightly under her, pushed by the wind. She realized belatedly that it might have moved when she had been hanging off the railing, but it was far too big to tip or shudder with her weight. If the nomads had noticed anything, they would think it was just the wind.

Emilie crept around the catwalk, stopping to peer into the darkened windows, but she couldn't make out anything inside. As she came around the bow of the cabin, she had a good view of the compound, while still being in the shadows above the reach of their lamps. There was still activity at the far end, toward where she had set the fire. She bet the darkness in the woods was helping her; the fire had been slowly smoldering rather than burning brightly. The nomads were probably having trouble locating it. The three door guards were still looking off that way, and there weren't any other merpeople around, at least that she could see.

Keeping her steps as quiet as possible, Emilie moved along the catwalk down the airship's side, to the narrow plank bridge that led from it down to the round roof of the tower. *Ha, I was right.* There was a circular opening in the roof, dimly illuminated by a light somewhere inside. It would have been disappointing, to say the least, to discover that there was no way inside the tower from here and that they had reached the airship with ladders up the outside or some other unusable method.

Emilie reached the catwalk and started across, moving slowly to keep the light wood from creaking. It was too dark to see the ground below her, and the bulk of the tower blocked her view of the guards.

She stepped down onto the smooth material of the roof, reflecting that the good thing about this stone was that it didn't creak. No one below would hear her moving around up here. She went to the opening and cautiously peered down.

All she could see at first was a white stone stairway with shallow steps, spiraling down the center of the tower. Emilie crouched on the edge and listened, but couldn't hear any movement or voices inside. She circled the opening, angling for a better view; she could see some bare floor in the room below, but that was all.

Nervously, Emilie leaned down far enough to get a good look, ready to dart away if the room was occupied. But it was just an empty room, at least from this angle. She stepped cautiously down the stairs, until she could see the rest of the room. It was empty, except for an old pile of ropes and nets in the corner. It took up the whole floor of the tower, too, no doorways.

She kept going down, and repeated this process at the next opening in the floor, that led down into the room below. It was empty except for a few clay storage jars, and a bowl-shaped lamp hanging from a ceiling hook, providing the wan light. *All right, this isn't good,* Emilie thought, moving quietly down the stairs. This place wasn't big to start with and she was running out of room to discover prisoners. *What if those men outside are just guarding the airship? What if the prisoners are all locked up in another building nearby?* She suppressed a groan, and checked the compass quickly.

The arrow now formed a circle. Emilie's brow furrowed. *It wasn't doing that earlier.* It looked like it meant for her to go down. *All right, then.*

Emilie went down to the next opening, the one that looked down into the ground level. She lay flat on the floor, angling her head so she could see toward the open doorway that looked out into the compound. She couldn't see the guards from here . . . *No, wait, there's one.* She could just see his leg and part of his back, as he was facing away from the door. She leaned down a little farther for a peek at the room, and grimaced in disappointment. It was empty, too, bare of anything except a round medallion on the floor, a few steps from the end of the stairway, on the farthest side from the outer door. Emilie blinked. *A medallion with a handle, and a bolt.* That had to be it. *There's an underground room. And it's locked from the outside.*

Emilie threw another look at what was visible of the guard, then ghosted silently down the stairs. At the bottom she stepped quickly to the trapdoor; the solid stairs blocked a little of the view from the doorway, but if anyone walked past . . . She knelt, slid the bolt back, and carefully pulled at the door. It lifted on slightly rusty metal hinges; it was heavy, and didn't creak.

Below was a stairwell with steps spiraling down, and a flickering lamp set into a niche. There was a door at the bottom, about twelve feet down, with light shining through it. Emilie swallowed in a dry throat, hesitating. There could be more guards down there, she could be trapping herself, this might be the stupidest thing she had done yet—Then she heard voices from somewhere outside, coming closer; she slipped down through the opening, carefully pulling the door down into place above her.

Emilie sank back against the cool wall, letting her breath out in a silent sigh. There wasn't anything to do now but go forward.

She went down the stairs to the doorway, and cautiously peeked around the edge. *Yes! I was right!*

It was a big lamplit room, much larger than the tower rooms above her. Stretched across a portion of it was a wall of metal bars, forming a jail cell, and on the other side, sleeping on worn blankets, were five Menaen men. They were all disheveled, dressed not in uniforms but in sturdy jackets and trousers meant for rough outdoor work. The cell was bare of necessities except for the blankets and a couple of covered jars that must serve as the water closet; it smelled like they had been imprisoned here for a while.

There was no guard, just another door on the far side of the room, and a pool of water across from the cell. Emilie tiptoed to the pool first, looking down into it to make sure there weren't any merpeople lurking there. The water was clear enough to tell the pool was empty, but there was a dark shape low on one side: an opening to some sort of water-filled underground passage. *I bet this is connected to the pools in the compound,* she thought, moving back to the cell. Which meant merpeople might appear in it any moment.

She went to the bars and, keeping her voice low, said, "Hey! Wake up! You're being rescued!"

One man flinched awake, then sat up and stared at her. He had dark weathered skin and dark hair peppered with gray. He demanded, "Are you a dream?"

"No, I'm Emilie." She realized she must look somewhat disheveled herself, covered with scratches, her hair wild and probably ornamented with twigs and leaves, barefoot with stains and tears on her bloomers and shirt. Not very much like a rescuer, probably, but they would just have to settle for her. Impatiently, she added, "Miss Marlende sent me." While not strictly true, it was close enough.

And it did the trick. The man scrambled to his feet, stooped to shake the others awake. "Come on, boys, we're getting out of here."

Emilie hoped they were getting out of here; she had just realized that the cell didn't seem to have a door. She tried to shake the bars, but they didn't budge. "How does this thing open?"

The older man pointed across the room behind her. "There. That lever. It cranks the whole thing down into the floor."

It was on the far side of the room, a metal lever sticking out of a slot in the wall. Emilie hurried over and grabbed it, and tried to push it down. "Oof." It was stiff, and she leaned on it with her full weight. The lever moved slowly, all the way down, but when she glanced at the bars, she saw they had only lowered a few inches. *Oh, come on,* she thought in exasperation.

"Let it come back up and then push it down again, like a pump," the older man told her. To the others, he said, "Here, grab on to the bars and put your weight on them when she pushes the lever down."

"Right." Emilie let the lever come up to its original position, then forced it down again. With the men adding their weight to the bars, it was much easier, and got them nearly a foot of clearance. "You're not Dr. Marlende, are you?" she asked the older man. There wasn't any resemblance between him and Miss Marlende, and despite his gray hair, she didn't think he was quite old enough. The other four men were all too young. Three were dark Southern Menaen, one pale Northern, all very scruffy. Though now that she had a chance to look at them, they all seemed more the scholarly type, once you saw past the dirt, lack of shaving, and rough clothing.

The older man said, "No, I'm Charter, his engineer. We haven't seen Dr. Marlende for two days." He nodded to the other men. "That's Daniel, Seth, Cobbier, and Mikel."

"It's nice to meet you," Emilie said, gritting her teeth as she forced the bar down again. "Do you know where the Cirathi are?"

"We haven't seen them since we got here," Daniel said, hauling down on the bars again. He was clearly the youngest Southern Menaen, maybe only a few years older than Emilie. He had handsome features, rather unkempt curly hair, and cracked spectacles. "We think they're locked up down here somewhere, though. We keep asking about them, but the nomads won't tell us anything."

That was going to be a problem. "Have you seen Rani? She was with me, she gave me Dr. Marlende's compass, but she was captured when we got here yesterday."

There were startled exclamations from the men. "We didn't know she was alive," Charter said. "We haven't seen her since she escaped from the ship. She's here?"

Damn it, Emilie thought, and threw her weight down on the lever again. "Yes, I think so, but I don't know where." Hopefully the merpeople were keeping her with the other Cirathi.

With the next effort they managed to get the bars down far enough that the men could fit through the gap between the ceiling and the top rail. As they were climbing over the bars, Emilie checked the compass again. It pointed toward the far wall, where the door was. She hurried over to it. "The compass says Dr. Marlende is this way." Hopefully he was with Rani and the rest of the Cirathi crew. She cautiously tugged on the metal loop that functioned as a door handle. The door didn't budge, and the lock appeared to be a hole under the handle that clearly needed some sort of key. Emilie poked at the little opening. "Do you know where the key is for this?"

Charter reached her side. "Where are the others? Who else is with you?"

Emilie set her jaw, prepared for an argument. "There aren't any others. There's just me."

Charter and Daniel exchanged a baffled look. The other men looked dubious. Cobbier said, "What do you mean, 'no others'?"

"Isn't this a rescue mission?" Daniel added.

Impatiently, Emilie explained, "We came on Lord Engal's ship, me and Miss Marlende and Kenar. But we ran into the queen of the Sealands and she's forcing Lord Engal and everyone to help her attack these nomads. Miss Marlende was captured by Lord Ivers, and is aboard his airship somewhere. Rani and I were coming to free you, but she was captured this morning."

Everyone stared. "Lord Ivers is here and has Miss Marlende? We didn't even know he had a working aetheric engine," Seth said, astonished.

"Yes, he does." Emilie finished, "So you'd better stop worrying about my qualifications as a rescuer and get on with finding the others before we all get captured again."

Daniel looked mulish but Charter held up a placating hand, stepping forward to examine the door. He said, "I take your point, Emilie. We can't go out the way you got in?"

Mollified but still wary, Emilie said, "Not easily. I set a fire as a distraction, so I could get past the guards at the outside doorway, but it might be out by now."

"But is our airship still out there, moored to the top of this tower?" Daniel asked. "Can we get to it?"

"Yes." It belatedly occurred to Emilie that securing the airship might be a good idea. She had been so fixed on the goal of finding Rani and Dr. Marlende, she hadn't even thought about it. "If you're very, very quiet. The guards were maybe a few steps from the outside doorway."

"We can get past them." Charter nodded grimly. "I'll go after Marlende and the others, the rest of you get aboard that airship. Lie low for now, but don't let the ship be recaptured."

"Cobbier can get the others past the guards. I'll go with you," Daniel said, looking mulish again.

"And me," Emilie added. "I have to find Rani."

"You should go back to the ship," Daniel told her, his tone bearing an unfortunate resemblance to the way Emilie's brothers spoke to her.

Seth and Cobbier and Mikel were all protesting to Charter that they should stay together, and Emilie knew there wasn't time to argue. She said to Daniel, "You mistake me for someone you have the right to order around."

He looked taken aback, and Charter cut off all the argument with a sharp gesture, saying, "There's no time for this. Now go!"

Reluctantly, the other men went toward the doorway to the stairs, and Charter knelt to peer into the lock, ignoring the fact that Emilie and Daniel had both remained behind. Charter asked, "Have you got a pocketknife?"

"Yes, here." Emilie fished in her pocket and handed over the little knife Rani had given her.

As Charter used the blade to probe the inside of the locking mechanism, Daniel said, "It had been so long, we thought Jerom and Kenar didn't make it back to the surface."

Emilie groaned inwardly. Being the one to have to deliver the bad news was not pleasant, and this was the second time she had had to do it. "Jerom didn't make it. Kenar said the trip was much worse than they thought it was going to be. I'm sorry."

Daniel took a sharp breath. "Oh." He shook his head. "I knew I should have gone."

Still occupied with the lock, Charter said, "Jerom was a stronger sorcerer. He had to be the one to go."

"Are you a sorcerer?" Emilie asked Daniel.

He frowned at her, as if the question was too personal. "I'm studying to be one."

Though she should be feeling sorry for him, something about his attitude made Emilie say, not quite innocently, "But you couldn't do anything like get the cell door open?"

Charter snorted, and Daniel frowned even more. "It's not quite that simple—"

"Quiet," Charter muttered, still working the lock. "I'm about to open it."

They got quiet. Emilie held her breath, hoping this wasn't the end of their escape. If there were guards in the next room, there was little they could do without weapons. The other men must have gotten up to the trapdoor by this point, and she didn't hear any sounds of fighting or alarm, so that was encouraging.

The door made a dull clunk as the lock snapped open, and Charter winced. *So much for stealth,* Emilie thought. Charter eased the door open a crack and peered through, then pushed it open and got to his feet.

Daniel stepped forward into Emilie's way, but she managed to stretch to see around him. The door opened into a shadowy corridor, with a curving roof and walls of rough light-colored rock, the air dank and cool. There were no merpeople, but it couldn't be entirely deserted: a flickering lamp hung from a peg on the wall.

Charter stepped through into the corridor, Daniel managing to get in ahead of Emilie. She tugged the door closed behind them; it might slow pursuit, but only for a few moments. The merpeople had to know their captives couldn't escape through the pool's underwater passage. "What is this place?" Emilie asked as they went down the corridor. "The nomads don't live here, surely?"

"No, they use it as a stronghold," Daniel said. "It was some sort of sacred place for the old Sealands empire, built with magic. It's so old, I don't think they're sure what it was for anymore."

The corridor opened into a foyer with another pool of water. Three more shadowy corridors led away from it. The whole area under the compound must be honeycombed with tunnels, with a system of water passages below it, and one above, connecting the surface pools. Emilie quickly checked the compass again.

The arrow pointed to the corridor to the left. Emilie nodded to it, whispering, "That one."

Charter took a step toward it. Just then a merman surfaced in the pool, heaving himself half out onto the stone floor. For an instant they all froze, and he looked just as startled as they were. Then he started to push back from the edge. Charter lunged forward, punching him in the head. The merman fell backward but two more surfaced, and Charter yelled, "Run!"

Emilie ran, taking the corridor the compass had indicated before considering whether it was a good idea or not. It was a long corridor, with several guttering lamps hanging on the wall. She heard Daniel shouting behind her and slowed, looking back. Then he and Charter came pounding after her and she hurried on.

They caught up to her as she reached another open foyer, but this one had only one other way out, a narrow spiral stair up to a silvery metal trapdoor in the ceiling. The merpeople had to be right behind them and it was the only way out. Emilie started toward it, but Charter grabbed her arm and whispered, "Wait, don't move!"

Daniel stood at the open passageway, holding up a hand as if pressing against an invisible door. He was whispering quietly to himself. Emilie stared, then realized, *He's doing a spell.* She hoped he was more useful as a sorcerer than previous circumstances would seem to indicate.

Daniel took a sharp breath and stepped back from the doorway. A moment later four mermen arrived, sliding to an abrupt halt. Daniel was frozen in place, and Charter squeezed Emilie's arm, reminding her to be still.

The mermen stared through the doorway, obviously puzzled. As they looked around, their eyes seemed to slide past Daniel, Charter, and Emilie without focusing on them. *They see an empty room,* she thought, holding her breath. And it hadn't seemed to occur to them to step past the doorway and investigate further.

Tension stretched Emilie's nerves almost to the point where she felt compelled to make a sound, but finally the mermen turned away. They started back down the passage, talking agitatedly among themselves. As their voices faded, Daniel's shoulders slumped in relief, and Charter relaxed a little. Emilie let herself breathe again, feeling her pulse pounding in her ears. "It's a charm," Charter explained, keeping his voice low. "It makes people think they can't see you. But they can still hear you, and feel you."

"You couldn't use it from inside the cell?" Emilie asked. "To make them think you escaped?" Though that wouldn't do much good, unless the merpeople were incautious enough to lower the bars.

Daniel wiped sweat off his forehead. "It doesn't work if they know you're there. That's why we had to get to another room—we had to be just far enough ahead that they would be able to tell themselves that they'd mistaken the passage we took."

Emilie made a mental note that Daniel was a little more useful than he had seemed at first. And that explained why they had been so certain that Cobbier could get the other three crew members past the guards outside the tower; he must be an apprentice sorcerer too. She checked the compass again, and was momentarily puzzled when the arrow made a circle. "Oh." She looked up at the ceiling. "I think we're close."

Charter stepped past her and started up the stairs. Emilie and

Daniel waited below as he cautiously pushed the trapdoor open just enough to get a view of the next room. After a moment, he opened it all the way and motioned for them to follow him.

Emilie hurried up the stairs. The room was bigger than the foyer below, and better lit, with a larger stairwell spiraling up to the next floor, and a closed door. "I think we're on the surface," Emilie whispered. The air in this room was fresher, laced with the green scent of the forest. She checked the compass again. "It's still pointing up."

Daniel went to the door and listened at it. He shook his head. "Can't hear anything."

Charter grimaced, looking up the stairwell. He muttered, "This place is too quiet." But he added to Daniel, "You stay here, we'll go up."

Daniel nodded, and Charter and Emilie started up the stairs. She knew what Charter meant; the merpeople had seen them now and there should be more commotion outside as they searched for them. They reached the next floor, where a wide foyer held a single closed door.

Emilie hurried over to listen at it. She heard voices, and thought, *Uh-oh.* But they didn't sound like merpeople; the voices were too deep. *Wait, there is something familiar about . . .* "I think it's the Cirathi!" she whispered to Charter.

He tugged cautiously on the handle. The door didn't budge, and he crouched to peer into the opening for the lock, taking out Emilie's knife. "We don't know if they're alone in there," he said, keeping his voice low. "There might be guards inside."

"We could knock and ask," Emilie murmured. Then it occurred to her he might think she was silly enough to be serious.

But Charter just gave her an ironic smile and started to tinker with the lock. Then a bang and a muffled yell from the room below made Emilie flinch. Charter shoved to his feet, cursing, but half a dozen merpeople charged up the stairwell. Emilie ducked back against the wall with a yelp, suddenly confronted with a forest of sharp spear points.

CHAPTER TEN

One of the merpeople shouted an order and the others drew back a little. A few were female, but they all wore belts of some kind of reptile hide, they all carried knives, and they all looked angry. One held a weapon that looked like a wooden speargun. With a grim expression, Charter dropped the knife and held up his hands. Emilie held up her hands, too.

Two other merpeople dragged Daniel up the stairs, despite his resistance. He caught Charter's eye and said, guiltily, "Sorry. They just burst in through the door—" One poked him to tell him to be silent.

Charter said, "It's all right."

Emilie knew it was anything but all right.

The merpeople searched them first, taking the knife and the rest of Emilie's matches. Emilie thought they would be shoved into the room with the Cirathi, but instead the nomads prodded them up the stairs. There was a door on the next landing, with a merperson standing guard outside it. At a gesture from the leader, he pushed it open.

They were guided into a big room, lit by several lamps, bare of furniture except for a few clay water jars. But it was the occupants who captured Emilie's attention. Rani and an older Menaen man faced five merpeople. Emilie started forward, only to be dragged back by her guards. She called out, "Rani! Are you all right?"

"I'm well, Emilie." Rani looked her over, her scaled brow furrowed. "These idiots have not hurt you?"

"No, I'm fine." She hoped, for the moment. Rani didn't look hurt, and her head wasn't bleeding anymore.

The older Menaen man had to be Dr. Marlende. He had shaggy gray hair and a beard that badly needed to be trimmed, which kept Emilie from spotting any resemblance to Miss Marlende. He wore a rather shabby tweed suit coat over a somewhat-the-worse-for-wear workman's trousers and shirt. He said, "Charter, Daniel, how good to see you!"

One of the merpeople was less enthused to see them. Holding a translation shell, he turned to Rani and said, "You lied. You said you were alone." He was young, very handsome, wearing a necklace of polished shells and a reptile-skin belt set with disks of silver metal. The others with him, three young men and one older woman, wore the same kind of finery; Emilie suspected they were looking at the nomads' leaders. Or at least the leaders of this group of nomads.

Rani snorted, amused. "Of course I lied. You keep dragging me and my people off by force. We are not friends, Prince Ise." To Dr. Marlende, she explained, "That is Emilie, who came here with your daughter."

"Excellent!" Dr. Marlende said, and nodded to Emilie.

Prince Ise rounded on Charter, demanding, "Where are the others?"

They haven't caught them, they don't know they're aboard the airship, Emilie thought, relieved. His expression stony, Charter said, "I don't know. We split up, to look for Dr. Marlende and the Cirathi."

Prince Ise spoke to the merpeople guards in his own language, and three hurried off, probably to organize a search. Emilie just hoped no one thought to check the airship. Prince Ise turned back to Dr. Marlende and Rani. "You can't expect me to negotiate with you after this. You have tried to escape, to attack my people—"

Rani eyed him with contempt. "Oh, and if you were in our position, you would sit in a cell and do nothing, and wait for your captors to 'negotiate.' Is that what you would do?"

Ise set his jaw, furious. *He's young,* Emilie thought. Younger than the queen, certainly. Dr. Marlende said, "Oh, I think in our position Prince Ise would be fighting quite hard to escape. And I think we can agree that it is generous of him to speak to us at all, with everything he has to deal with at the moment."

It had given Ise time to get his self-control back. He said, more evenly, "I have been generous. I offer you an alliance. If you would help us fight the queen's forces, we would treat you as honored guests."

Dr. Marlende shook his head. "My airship is for exploration, not war. And neither we nor the Cirathi have any business interfering in your disagreements with the queen. Our involvement would cause you nothing but harm in the long run."

Ise folded his arms, his whole body communicating contempt. "I might have believed that, before the metal ship joined the queen's fleet. Our spies say they have the same magics and projectile weapons that you do. I'm only asking you to even the balance."

"They were tricked!" Emilie had to interrupt. "They think you attacked the ship, but it was the queen's people, pretending to be nomads. And now they're only helping her because they think the queen has Miss Marlende and me as hostages; they don't know I escaped with Rani and that Lord Ivers has Miss Marlende prisoner. If you let us all go, they have no reason to fight you."

"Yes, Rani informed me that Lord Ivers has my daughter prisoner," Dr. Marlende said, sounding grim. "The nerve of the man."

Ise regarded her a moment in silence, and Emilie couldn't tell if her speech had had any effect on him or not. He looked at Rani and said, "She tells the same story you told."

"Of course she does." Rani was exasperated. "It's the truth."

Prince Ise paced away from them, obviously torn. But before he could say anything, another merman pounded up the stairs, calling out. He spoke rapidly to Ise, who answered sharply in his own language. Then Ise turned to Dr. Marlende and said, "The queen's forces have found our concealed cove. We'll drive them off, but when I return—" He hesitated again, but added, "This conversation is not over."

He strode out, the other merpeople following, leaving them alone in the room. The guard outside shut the door, and Emilie heard the lock thunk into place.

Rani said, annoyed, "Well, that was not a timely interruption."

"I'm not certain it would have been any different had we talked all night," Dr. Marlende told her. "We might convince him, but the nomads have many leaders, and I don't know how much influence he has." He motioned for them to draw together in the center of the room, and said quietly, "Keep your voices low, please. Prince Ise usually leaves the translation shell with the guards."

"They've made a mistake, leaving us together like this," Rani muttered. "Surely Ise will recall it and send the guards to separate us soon."

"You can't use your magic to escape?" Emilie asked Dr. Marlende, keeping her voice low.

Daniel looked offended that she had asked the question, but Dr. Marlende smiled at her. He said, "I can create a few rather flashy illusions, but I need access to my airship's aetheric channeling devices for anything more effective." He turned to Charter and Daniel. "Any suggestions, gentlemen?"

Charter glanced thoughtfully at the door. "There's a room above this one? Is there a trapdoor in the roof?"

"Possibly, we've never been allowed up there," Dr. Marlende said.

Rani put in, "But we're three levels up, and there are guards on the ground below. This stonework is not so easy to climb." She added to Emilie, "I tried earlier. It was very embarrassing."

"We don't need to climb," Charter told her. He looked at Dr. Marlende. "Cobbier, Mikel, and Seth are in the airship."

"Ah." Dr. Marlende lifted a brow, and exchanged a look with Rani. "The guards will expect us to try to escape through the ground-level exit, so they'll concentrate their efforts there."

Rani said, "Then what are we waiting for?" and started for the door. Charter followed her.

Daniel looked from them to Dr. Marlende. "Do we need a spell, a charm? I can try—"

"They know my abilities," Dr. Marlende told him. "They wouldn't be fooled by the illusion of an empty room."

"We are doing it the old-fashioned way." Rani took up a position to one side of the door, and gave Charter a nod.

Charter pounded on it, and shouted, "Help, we need help!"

From the other side of the door, a merman's voice said, "Be quiet!"

"Please!" Charter kept pounding. Rani made a frantic gesture at Emilie. Emilie, interpreting this as best she could, shrieked as loudly and ear-piercingly as possible and flung herself on the floor.

Emilie kept shrieking, and Dr. Marlende began to caper around her tearing at his hair and giving a good impression of hysterical grief. Emilie wasn't sure how long they could keep it up; she felt she was already close to bursting a blood vessel. But a moment later, the door started to open.

The guard was cautious, entering spear-first, but Rani moved like lightning. She grabbed the end of the spear, jerked the lighter merman through the doorway, and slung him across the room. As Emilie scrambled to her feet, Daniel hit the staggering merman with a water jar. The jar cracked and the merman collapsed.

The guard still outside tried to shove the door shut but Charter wedged himself into the gap, holding it open. He cried out and Emilie gasped, knowing he must have been stabbed. But he held the door long enough for Rani to throw her considerable strength against it, slamming it open.

With the guard's captured spear, Rani slashed at the remaining merman, and he ducked away and stabbed at her. Emilie reached the door and caught Charter as he slumped, staggering under his weight. The right shoulder of his shirt was already soaked with blood. Behind her Daniel reached the doorway, just as another merman charged up the stairs. Daniel was still holding the cracked water jar and, leaning down, slung it across the floor. "Oh, clever!" Emilie said, as it rolled down the first few steps, struck the merman in the shins, and knocked him flat.

With a sudden lunge, Rani shoved the other guard's spear up, flipped her spear around and whacked him in the head with the butt hard enough to knock him back into the far wall.

Dr. Marlende reached Charter, trying to take his arm to support him. Charter said, "No, get up to the roof, signal the airship! I can make it."

Dr. Marlende snapped, "Then hurry, damn you, I'm not leaving anyone behind!" and charged up the stairs. Stumbling a little, Charter started after him.

Emilie hesitated, her first impulse to help Charter, but Rani and Daniel had plunged down the stairs, going to rescue the Cirathi. *No, better help them,* she thought, hurrying after them.

The merman Daniel had tripped with the jar had hit his chin on the stone steps and was dazed. Daniel snatched up his spear in passing and Emilie, about to step over him, remembered, *That door is locked, we need the key.* Hoping this was the guard from that landing, she stooped down to pull at his belt, looking for the key, but there was nothing there. Suddenly he grabbed her arm, and a surge of panic almost blinded her. She snatched his big knife out of the sheath and hit him across the head with the hilt. It made an unpleasant thunk as it hit his skull, and he fell backward. She pulled away, breathing hard. Hitting a person was very different from trying to hit the plant creature who had attacked Miss Marlende. She felt sick, but there was just no time for it. She hurried down the steps.

Another merman was already down, sprawled on the floor of the landing, and Rani and Daniel blocked the stairs, struggling with three others. Emilie dashed to the fallen merman, found a round metal knob attached to his belt with a cord, and jerked it free. As she stood and shoved it into the lock opening, Daniel fell backward and Rani lunged in to cover him. Gritting her teeth, Emilie forced the key to turn. The lock clicked and the door flung open, nearly slamming her against the wall. But a strong scaled hand caught her arm and steadied her as several Cirathi rushed out the door. They overwhelmed the mermen on the stairs and drove them back down the steps.

The Cirathi holding Emilie up was a young woman, only a little taller than she was. She spoke in her own language, then switched to Menaen, saying excitedly, "You are rescuing us!"

"We are!" Emilie replied.

The young Cirathi threw a worried look around. "How?"

"Oh, right! Up, we have to go up, to the airship!" Emilie said hurriedly, pointing up the stairwell. Rani shouted something in her own language that must have confirmed this, because some of the Cirathi started up the stairs, a few remaining behind to help Rani and Daniel hold off the merpeople.

Emilie followed them, past the next landing and up to the very top. They found Charter struggling up the stairs, and one of the larger Cirathi caught him, heaved him over a shoulder, and continued to climb.

They reached the landing at the top of the tower, where a doorway set at an angle opened into a large room. There was no trapdoor in the ceiling. "That's not good," Emilie said under her breath. There were windows, fortunately, big round ones with no glass panes; Dr. Marlende hung out of one, waving a lamp that burned like a white firework. As Emilie reached him, he pulled himself back in, saying with satisfaction, "They've seen it, they're coming!"

Emilie looked past him and her heart leapt. In the light from the ground lamps, the big silvery shape of the airship was lifting above the other towers, turning in their direction.

Dr. Marlende said, "Where's Charter? Ah, there he is." Charter was upright and conscious though bleary-eyed, leaning on the shoulder of the Cirathi man, holding a crumpled handkerchief to his bleeding shoulder. Five other Cirathi had come up with them. All except the man supporting Charter were fairly small, scarcely taller than Emilie. Rani must have ordered the younger ones to flee up the stairs, with the one adult to take care of Charter.

Dr. Marlende looked around the room, tapping his bearded chin. "Now if we can just hold off our captors until our transport arrives . . ." The lamp he still held was the usual sort the merpeople used, a convoluted shell hanging from a woven strap of reed or seagrass, that burned fish oil. Except this one was glowing white and spitting sparks. Emilie assumed Dr. Marlende had done something magical to brighten it so that the men in the airship could see it.

Shouting, thumps, and crashes sounded from the stairwell, and Rani, Daniel, and the rest of the Cirathi hadn't appeared yet. There was no door, nothing they could use to block off the doorway. Emilie ran to the opposite window, the one above the front of the tower. Two young Cirathi were already there, looking worriedly down at the shadowed compound. One pointed for Emilie and she saw a group of merpeople running toward the tower. "Yes, they're sending reinforcements." Emilie bit her lip. It sounded like Rani and the others could barely hold off the guards now. She turned to Dr. Marlende. "Can we do something? Outside, to keep more of them from coming into the tower?"

Dr. Marlende strode over to look out the window. He nodded grimly. "Yes, I think we'd better try a fire illusion." He glanced around the room. "If you could find me another couple of lamps . . ."

Emilie hurried to the doorway, taking down the lamp hanging near it. Even if it was an illusion, some of the merpeople might not be willing to test it too quickly. The young Cirathi didn't all seem to understand Menaen, but they saw what Emilie was doing and ran to collect the other lamps in the room. As they returned to the window, Dr. Marlende hefted the lamp he was holding, eyeing the nomads running across the compound. As they neared the base of the tower, he flung the lamp out the window.

As it plunged toward the ground, white fire burst out of it. Emilie winced away, seeing stars before her eyes. She blinked hard, trying to see what had happened. The lamp had hit the ground, still blazing, if not quite as brightly. The nomads scattered and retreated in confusion. But Emilie couldn't feel any heat from the fire, and knew in a moment or so the nomads would realize it too. Dr. Marlende said, "Now we'll try this on our antagonists in the stairwell, though I fear they'll realize it's illusory."

He started toward the doorway, but Emilie stopped, caught by the view out the opposite window.

The airship was above the tower now, the balloon huge above the smaller suspended cabin, trying to angle down to reach the window. Emilie saw Seth hanging out the open cabin door, holding a bundle of rope under his arm. Behind her, a deep voice said, "Tell them to drop a harness, this one can't climb."

Emilie glanced back. Without the lamps, the room was very dark, lit only by the dim light coming through the windows. After a moment, she realized the speaker was the Cirathi man who was helping Charter. "I can make it, Beinar," Charter said through gritted teeth.

"Of course you'll make it," Beinar said, as he helped Charter toward the window. He sounded annoyed that there was any doubt at all.

Emilie was glad Beinar was confident; it made it a little easier to ignore the tight panic in her chest. She leaned out, shouting up at the airship, "We need a harness, Charter's got a wounded arm!"

Seth waved at her and ducked back inside. A moment later, a chain ladder with wooden rungs dropped out of the airship, dangling just out of reach. It was followed by a sturdy rope with a bundle of leather straps on the end, presumably the harness. The airship angled closer, and Emilie saw the propellers at the back of the cabin starting and stopping as it maneuvered toward the tower. She stretched, reaching for the ladder. It swung toward her, she made a wild grab and caught hold of a rung.

Charter rasped, "Careful, if the ship moves up, it'll jerk you right out!"

"Right," Emilie muttered, bracing herself against the side of the window as she hauled at the heavy ladder. The airship seemed lighter than air, but it was far too heavy for her to anchor by herself.

A Cirathi girl hurried to help her, their combined strength dragging the heavy ladder up to the sill. Then Beinar propped Charter against the wall and took the ladder, pulling it into the room. Holding on to it, he stretched out a long arm and snagged the harness.

Emilie realized Beinar couldn't help Charter into the harness and hold the ladder at the same time. She motioned frantically to the Cirathi girl that she was about to let go. The girl nodded and called out to the others in her own language. Two ran back from the doorway to grab on to the ladder, and Emilie went to help Charter.

Between the two of them, with Beinar giving quick instructions, they got Charter's arms through the loops and Emilie quickly buckled the straps. In the dim light, Charter's face was pinched with pain, and he was sweating and shaking with the effort of standing.

Beinar took one hand off the ladder to tug on the straps, said, "Good," then hauled Charter around and shoved him out the window.

Emilie couldn't help a strangled noise of protest, though she knew this was what they had to do. Charter hung in midair for only a moment, before the ropes were hauled rapidly upward. *They must have a winch,* Emilie thought irrelevantly, sticking her head out the window to watch.

Mikel and Seth caught Charter as he reached the walkway and hauled him inside, then Seth reappeared, signaling wildly. He shouted, "Send the rest up!"

Emilie pulled back in, got a scrape on the cheek from the swaying ladder, and reported, "He says to come on up!"

Beinar spoke in Cirathi, and one of the girls started up the ladder, climbing quickly and agilely. As the next one started to climb, Emilie ran to the doorway. From the landing she could see bright white light glowing up the stairwell. She couldn't hear fighting anymore, though she could hear worried voices speaking in Cirathi. She called down, "Dr. Marlende, Rani, we have to go!"

She heard Rani's voice give an order, and several Cirathi charged up the stairs. Emilie pointed urgently toward the ladder, and Beinar called to them. As one of the newcomers took over helping to brace the ladder, the last young Cirathi started up.

Daniel bounded up the stairs next, breathing hard. He said, "Dr. Marlende's made a fire barrier across the stairs, making them think we've set the place alight. But he has to be there to maintain it."

"Can you do a charm—" Emilie began.

He shook his head, interrupting, "There's no way they would believe this room is empty, and they'll be able to hear us—"

"To make them think there's a door here?" Emilie finished, determined to be heard. "It's dark, and the way this doorway is angled—"

"Yes!" He grabbed her shoulders, startling her so badly she almost slapped him. "Not a door, we can't do that, but another fire barrier! It might work, just long enough."

Daniel plunged down the stairs again, calling to Dr. Marlende, and

Emilie waited tensely. After a moment, he reappeared again, with Rani and Dr. Marlende behind him.

Emilie stepped back into the room. The only Cirathi left were Beinar and one other man, anchoring the ladder. She hadn't heard any screaming or other commotion, so she hoped that meant no one had fallen.

Rani stopped, looking around the darkened room. She was breathing hard, and Emilie couldn't tell if she was wounded. She said something to Beinar in Cirathi, nodded at his answer. Then she squeezed Emilie's shoulder and started for the ladder. "We are almost there, Emilie."

"Almost," Emilie agreed, following her. She thought there was still plenty of time for everything to go hideously wrong.

At the window, Emilie leaned around Beinar to look down. Merpeople had gathered below, agitated, obviously trying to figure out what to do about the airship. Others had climbed to the top of the nearest tower, and one tossed a fishing spear at the cabin, though it fell short. "It's too high," Beinar muttered to Emilie. "So far they haven't brought out any spearguns."

"They are probably shooting at the queen's people with them," Rani said grimly. She spoke to the other Cirathi man, taking his place at the ladder. He started to climb.

Emilie watched anxiously. The merpeople on the other tower cast a few spears, calling out angrily, but the man climbed rapidly, all the weapons falling short. Emilie let out the breath she hadn't realized she was holding, and looked back at Daniel and Dr. Marlende.

Daniel stood at the doorway, his head down in concentration, Dr. Marlende standing silently behind him. "Dr. Marlende can help him do the charm?" Emilie asked.

"He hopes he can. Daniel's magic is different, apparently," Rani said, watching them worriedly. "Emilie, you climb now."

"Oh." Emilie had somehow managed to ignore the fact that she was going to have to climb the ladder too. Telling herself it wasn't as bad as climbing down the narrow tube into pitch darkness, she came around to grab the rungs and start the climb.

She found immediately that the big difference between this ladder and the one down through the island was that this one was horrifically mobile. It swayed, the chain links clicking, the wooden rungs creaking and turning under her hands. *Keep going, keep going,* Emilie chanted mentally. She looked down, saw the ground and the angry merpeople, and almost vomited. She looked up at the dark airship looming hugely above her and that was somehow worse. She forced herself to go on, ignoring the shouts from the merpeople on the other tower, refusing to look at them in case that somehow improved their aim or spurred them to throw hard enough to reach her.

When someone grabbed her arm she choked back a yelp, but it was Seth. He dragged her up and onto the airship's catwalk.

Emilie found herself clinging to the railing, the wind tearing at her hair, her legs trembling violently. She couldn't believe she had made it. And why weren't the others following her?

"Where are they?" Seth demanded. "What are they doing?"

Emilie shook her head. "They can't—They're blocking the room off with an illusion, but if the merpeople realize what it is—" She couldn't see the front of the tower from here, but the merpeople on the ground suddenly turned and ran around the curving wall. "Oh hell! Someone must have figured out the tower wasn't on fire—"

Then the ladder suddenly jerked as a figure climbed out the window. It was Dr. Marlende, followed closely by Beinar.

Emilie watched, gripping the slender railing. They were almost up to the airship when Daniel started to climb. He had his head turned, shouting back down to the window. Then suddenly the ladder came loose, swinging free.

Emilie gasped in horror, but an instant later she saw Rani hanging on to the end. She pointed wordlessly, and Seth swore. He turned, leaned into the doorway to shout, "Up, lift her up!"

Dr. Marlende reached the catwalk, pulled himself up, then turned to reach for Beinar. Below, Daniel had stopped climbing to cling to the ladder as it swung wildly. Merpeople hung out the window of the tower now, casting spears. They came within a hairsbreadth of Rani and Daniel, but the ladder's motion confused their aim.

Beinar reached the top, but hung on to the strut of the railing, waiting for Daniel. The airship was lifting up, slowly and ponderously, and Daniel had started to climb again.

Seth and Dr. Marlende looked down at Daniel and Rani, exhorting them to hurry; Emilie kept watching the merpeople, looking from the window to the roof of the nearby tower. *It took us too long,* she thought, *holding them off, getting the airship over here. They've had time to*—She saw the figures in the window make way, saw someone holding the long shape of a projectile weapon. She yelled, "Look out! Gun! There's a—"

Daniel was nearly to the catwalk, Rani just below him. Rani ducked down against the ladder, but Daniel looked wildly around. A bolt glanced off the ladder near his hand and he jerked away, lost his grip and hung by one hand. Beinar, holding on to the strut, stretched down to make a grab for him. And the next bolt struck Beinar in the neck.

Emilie froze, a sob of dismay caught in her throat, as he slumped forward. Dr. Marlende flung himself flat on the catwalk, reaching for him, but Beinar tumbled off and fell. Emilie looked down, unable to help herself, and saw his body strike the ground, far below now.

Rani scrambled up the ladder, reached Daniel and pulled him back up. Seth crouched down, and he and Dr. Marlende hauled Daniel up. Rani swung up after him. The airship was well above the towers now, turning away into the dark. Seth and the others dragged up the ladder, Dr. Marlende helped Daniel through the door. Then Rani caught Emilie's arm and pulled her inside.

The cabin was dark, lit only by the soft glow of small electric lights set under the windows. The floor under Emilie's feet was soft and oddly textured, like a cork mat. The Cirathi were silent with shock, standing numbly at the windows. They must have seen everything.

Rani drew the two nearest into a hug, and someone sobbed quietly. Emilie knew if she stood here another moment, she would burst into tears. She turned and started toward the bow of the cabin.

It was too dark to see much but she made her way past a few boxes and bags of supplies, stumbled into a padded bench, then down a short corridor lined with wooden cabinets. It was very quiet, as though they weren't in motion at all. The only indication that this was a vehicle was the faint vibration traveling through the floor from the propellers at the rear of the cabin. It was very strange.

She came out into a small round room that was mostly window, the glass curving around to form a wide port looking out into the darkness. Two small side windows were propped open, allowing in a cool breath of air. There were more lights here, set low just above the consoles of knobs and dials. They were small and tilted down, to illuminate the controls but not dazzle the eyes of the operators.

Dr. Marlende stood at the small wheel, with Seth and Mikel. Daniel was crouched on the floor, his face buried in his hands.

Emilie rubbed her forehead, trying to collect her thoughts. She asked, "Do you know where the *Sovereign* is?"

Dr. Marlende said, kindly, "No, my dear, I was going to give Rani a moment to steady herself before I asked. Do you know?"

"Yes." Emilie closed her eyes, recalling their position when they had arrived at the island yesterday. *Yesterday?* she thought in surprise. *It feels like a week.* "When we came up to the island, the Dark Wanderer was behind us. The queen's fleet was toward the end of the island, off the starboard side, and Rani thought she saw the *Sovereign* there, so that should be . . ." Eyes still closed, she pointed.

"Ah, thank you, Emilie, that is exactly what I need to know." Dr. Marlende turned the wheel, and made an adjustment to one of the knobs, and the floor tilted slightly under her feet.

Emilie nodded, pushing her hair back. It was saturated with sea salt and sweat, and felt like a dry tumbleweed perched on her head. "Is Charter going to be all right?"

"He should be," Seth told her. "Cobbier took him back to the bunk room to tend his shoulder."

That was good. Daniel was still on the floor. Emilie felt she had to do something about that. She crouched down in front of him, pulled at his wrists until he lowered his hands and looked at her. She could see his face in the instrument lights, and it was tear-streaked. She said, "It wasn't your fault." It was everyone's fault, it was no one's fault. Blaming Daniel was as bad as blaming Beinar, for being brave, for being the one who tried to help all the others, for being the one Rani sent upstairs with the younger Cirathi, knowing that he would take care of them.

Daniel shook his head mutely, and Emilie felt a flash of anger. If she could take this without breaking down, he could damn well take it too. "We don't have time to coddle you," she said roughly. "We need you. Now get up, wipe your face, and do your duty."

Daniel blinked, then glared at her in outrage. He pulled away from her and stood up. Emilie got to her feet.

Seth and Mikel stared at her, startled, while Dr. Marlende's attention was studiously on the controls. Daniel turned away, folding his arms and gazing grimly out the port.

Rani stepped through into the cabin then. "We are heading for the

Sovereign?" she asked. Her voice sounded a little raspy, as if she had been crying. She dropped a comforting arm around Emilie's shoulders, and Emilie leaned against her solid warmth.

"Yes, Emilie's given us the last position you noted for it," Dr. Marlende told her. He frowned down at a dial. "We should be passing over the outer barrier now."

Emilie heard the distant roar of falling water; they must be climbing out of the canyon. *I'm flying,* she thought suddenly. Another thing she had never expected to do. *Maybe I'll have time to enjoy it later.* "How will we contact them? If the queen didn't take any more hostages, maybe they can just run away from her."

Dr. Marlende nodded to Seth. "Try to raise them on the wireless." Seth turned, but Daniel said quietly, "I'll do it, sir." He moved to a cabinet on the far side of the cabin, opening it to reveal a small wireless set.

Seth didn't comment but exchanged a look with Mikel, and Emilie thought they were both relieved. Daniel adjusted some dials, and the wireless began to hum. He started to tap on the telegraph bar.

To Rani and Emilie, Dr. Marlende explained, "The concentration of aether in the air makes it difficult to get through over long distances, but at this range we should be able to reach them." He added, with a slight edge to his voice, "I assume Lord Ivers has returned to the surface by now, which is unfortunate. It would perhaps be more satisfying to deal with him here, out of reach of the Menaen authorities."

"Lord Engal probably thinks so too," Emilie said. "Lord Ivers kept sending men to shoot at him."

"I had no idea the philosophical community had degenerated into internecine violence, but apparently it has," Dr. Marlende muttered. He craned his neck, looking out the port. "Ah, there's the queen's fleet."

Emilie and Rani went to the side to look out. Below them in the darkness were hundreds of little flickering lights, illuminating the large oblong shapes of the big barges, and the smaller darting rafts and boats. In the faint light around the smaller craft, Emilie caught glimpses of waves and a sandy beach. "They're going ashore there."

"Yes, Ise was right," Rani said thoughtfully. "They are attacking the island."

"That must be the *Sovereign*!" Mikel said. "Here, to starboard."

Emilie went to his side and saw it immediately. The *Sovereign*'s electric lights had a steady yellow glow, completely different from the fish-oil lamps of the other ships, and they reflected off its metal hull. It was one of a group of ships lying just off the concave shore of a cove area, outlined by the lights of the smaller skiffs and rafts that had drawn up along its beach. Seth said, "That cove has a passage in through the canyon wall, to a small protected harbor where the nomads leave their boats. There's a stairway down to the valley floor."

"Yes, it must be the site of the main attack," Dr. Marlende said. "She must be using the *Sovereign* to block any attempt at escape. Hopefully Engal wasn't forced to give them any rifles."

Then Daniel said, "I've got the *Sovereign*!" The wireless was now clicking back at him. Seth stepped to the cabinet and picked up a pencil and pad.

"They're very glad to hear from us," Daniel muttered, his expression preoccupied as he hurriedly translated the code into words.

Dr. Marlende said, "Tell them we've recovered all our companions from the nomads, including the Cirathi and young Emilie here, and that my daughter is not being held hostage by the queen. Ask if they are free to break away from the fleet."

Seth scribbled down the message and showed Daniel, who tapped it out on the wireless. The answer came quickly, and after a moment Daniel translated, "They're free to break away, if you're certain the queen doesn't have Miss Marlende and Emilie. She was threatening to kill them unless the *Sovereign* cooperated."

Dr. Marlende glanced at Rani and Emilie. Rani said, "Lord Ivers has her, we are certain."

Dr. Marlende nodded to Daniel, who tapped out a brief assent. The reply was longer in coming. Seth translated it, saying, "They say if we can distract the ships around them, they should be able to break free."

"Tell them to expect a distraction in the next few minutes," Dr. Marlende said, and turned the wheel.

The deck tilted under Emilie's feet as the airship turned, angling down. She managed to catch herself on a console without turning any of the knobs. She retreated to the doorway where Rani was holding on. Emilie asked, "Are you going to use magic to distract them?" She was thinking the illusory fire could be very effective dropping out of the sky.

Dr. Marlende took the airship into a long dive. "I hope we don't have to. I'd like to conserve my resources for the moment. But I think the flares should suffice. Seth, could you . . . ?"

Phosphorus flares proved even more effective than bright illusions, as Seth, Rani, Mikel, and two other Cirathi tossed them off the catwalk. They ignited directly over the Sealands ships, lighting up the sky and causing confusion and terror. Emilie and the others watched from the windows as one long warship sideswiped another and broke off a whole bank of oars. She lost sight of the *Sovereign,* but then realized that in the midst of the chaos, it had doused its electric running lights and must be steaming for the open sea.

Emilie hurried back to the steering cabin in time to hear Daniel's report from the wireless: "The queen's naval commander forced them to abandon the *Lathi* before the battle, and they anchored it off a small island a few miles from here. They're going to retrieve it now before the queen's forces get reorganized enough to order a pursuit."

"Oh, I don't think they'll pursue us," Dr. Marlende said, bringing the airship around for a pass over the other section of the fleet. "The nomads should take this opportunity to counterattack. I know Prince Ise has forces hanging back to the south. I should think they'll all be quite occupied for a while. Tell the *Sovereign* to meet us—"

The wireless interrupted with a sudden series of clicks. Daniel frowned, startled. "That's not . . ." He scribbled hastily on his pad, then checked the code book. He looked up. "A ship called the *Philosopher's Quest?*"

Emilie shook her head, baffled, as Daniel hurriedly transcribed another message. Then his jaw set, and he said grimly, "It's a request for assistance. From Lord Ivers."

CHAPTER ELEVEN

They met up with the *Sovereign* hours later, as the eclipse was passing away across the sea. The spot they had chosen was a low-lying island some distance from the nomads' fortress. As the airship reached it, Emilie could see the Aerinterre aether current in the sky, the solid band of heavy gray cloud with the translucent column stretching up from it, vanishing high in the air.

Not having to worry about navigating shoals, the airship had arrived first. Dr. Marlende lowered it far enough to drop the ladder, so Seth, Cobbier, Daniel, and a few Cirathi could climb down to the pebbly ground and secure the anchor cables to several squat but sturdy trees. The *Sovereign* soon arrived, towing the *Lathi*. They waited impatiently on the beach as the steamer anchored and sent the launch ashore.

Kenar leapt out of it before the boat reached the beach and waded in the thigh-deep water. Rani charged at him and they flew into each other's arms, and Rani swung him around and nearly knocked him off his feet. It was the most romantic thing Emilie had ever seen in her life, and her eyes welled up with tears. All the other Cirathi gathered around, waiting excitedly for their chance to greet him. Emilie knew the happy moment would end when Rani had to tell him about poor Beinar.

Lord Engal waited more decorously until the launch had actually been drawn up on the beach, before he climbed out and strode up to shake hands. "Dr. Marlende, I presume."

"You presume correctly, sir." Dr. Marlende greeted him gravely. "Thank you for sending young Emilie to our assistance; her arrival was quite timely."

Lord Engal eyed her with exasperation and, she was startled to see, some fondness. "At this point, it hardly surprises me."

"Now if we can just extract my daughter from Lord Ivers," Dr. Marlende continued.

"Yes." Lord Engal frowned, shielding his eyes to look into the distance. "If what he said was true, which is rather a big 'if,' since the man is an inveterate liar, a criminal—"

"Yes, of course." Dr. Marlende neatly cut off the potential diatribe. "But if his aetheric engine has not been sabotaged, then he has no reason to linger here or contact us."

During the eclipse, as they fled the battle between the queen's forces and the nomads, there had been a long three-cornered wireless conversation between their airship, the *Sovereign,* and Lord Ivers' craft. He had claimed that at some point before he had left the Sealands' capital, one of the queen's courtiers who had been aboard his airship had sabotaged his aetheric engine, leaving him stranded in the Hollow World.

"You were right, Rani," Emilie had said quietly. "The queen didn't intend to let him go. She knew he wouldn't be able to get back, and he'd have to come to her for help, and she'd make him use the airship against the nomads."

"Yes, but her plan would not have worked," Rani said, lifting her brows. "The airships need fuel for the engine in the back that works the propellers. Dr. Marlende explained this, and all the limitations of this craft, when we first began to explore together."

Emilie snorted. "I bet Lord Ivers didn't explain his limitations to the queen."

"But he must have explained the aetheric engine, or the merpeople wouldn't have known how to sabotage it," Daniel said. He was taking a break from transcribing the wireless, and Seth and Mikel were manning it and the code book. Leaning against the wall near Emilie, he hadn't referred to their little altercation earlier, but he did seem to be making an effort not to act awkwardly around her. It was taking an effort on her part not to act awkwardly around him; she felt she had overstepped herself quite a bit.

Rani said, dryly, "That was stupid of Ivers."

"Yes, and naive, on his part," Dr. Marlende had agreed, standing at the airship's wheel. "He thought them too primitive to do anything with the information." He added, with grim satisfaction, "He's paying for his poor judgment now."

Lord Ivers had promised to release Miss Marlende in exchange for their help with his engine, though Emilie wasn't counting any chickens until that actually happened. She thought Lord Ivers would try until the last moment to double-cross them. But they had eventually arranged to meet here on this island, and now all they had to do was wait.

As they stood on the beach, Dr. Barshion came up to Dr. Marlende. He shook hands, saying, "It's an honor to see you again, sir. And we can certainly use your help with the *Sovereign*'s aetheric engine." He admitted, "The ship's engineers and I weren't quite up to the mark, I'm afraid."

Emilie was glad to hear him say it aloud. She didn't think it would help if Dr. Barshion got stubborn about accepting Dr. Marlende's aid the way he had when Mr. Abendle had wanted to ask Miss Marlende's opinion. But maybe it was easier for him, since Dr. Marlende was both a man and an acknowledged expert. Dr. Marlende only said, kindly, "As long as you've brought the supplies I had to send Kenar and my poor friend Jerom for. I was completely wrong about the resonance needed for the quickaether sustainers, and it contaminated the replacements I had brought along before we realized what the problem was."

Emilie missed the rest, as Kenar arrived and caught her in a hug that lifted her off her feet. His voice rough with emotion, he said, "Thank you for rescuing Rani, Emilie."

"I wish we'd been able to rescue Miss Marlende, but we were too late," Emilie said, breathless as he set her back down. "And they shot at us, a lot." She looked up at him and asked hesitantly, "Did they tell you about Beinar?"

"Yes, they told me." He squeezed her shoulders and she could see the sadness in his eyes. "He was a very good friend."

They waited through the morning. Dr. Marlende and Daniel went aboard the *Sovereign* to get the materials needed to fix the airship's aetheric engine, and to consult with Dr. Barshion and Mr. Abendle. The Cirathi spent the time checking over their ship, making minor repairs, and getting it ready for their long voyage home. "I think we have worn out our welcome in these waters," Rani said. They were in the galley cabin, and Emilie was helping her sort out which foodstuffs had gone bad and which could be saved. "We'll go back and report to our guild, and tell everyone else to think twice before they come here."

"I'm never going to see you or Kenar again," Emilie said, only realizing after the words were out how forlorn she sounded. She poked dispiritedly at a bag of meal that had something growing in it. "I mean, even if there are other expeditions, they probably won't let me come. I'm only here accidentally, after all."

"Ah, Emilie," Rani said, putting down a jar and turning to regard her. "We will never forget you. Will you forget us?"

"No, never," Emilie said, her voice thick.

"Then that will have to be enough," Rani said, and hugged her again.

Someone called out from the deck, and they ran out to see the distant shape of an airship approaching from antidarkward. "He did come," Emilie said, feeling a certain tightness in her chest ease. They would get Miss Marlende back. "He didn't lie about that, at least."

Rani nodded thoughtfully. "Now we just need to figure out what he is lying about."

* * *

Lord Ivers brought his airship in toward the far end of the island, lowered it until it was about twenty feet above the ground, then dropped a chain ladder.

Emilie waited on the beach with Lord Engal, Dr. Marlende, Rani, Kenar, and Dr. Barshion, along with Oswin and Daniel and half a dozen armed sailors. Most of the Cirathi were aboard the *Lathi,* and there were armed sailors on the deck of the *Sovereign,* just in case Lord Ivers made some sort of attempt on either ship.

Now that both craft were here for comparison, Emilie could see Lord Ivers' airship was a little larger than Dr. Marlende's, and its two-story cabin was certainly more impressive. But the wind off the sea was strong, and the airship was having to fight it, its propellers spinning rapidly as the pilot made hurried adjustments. "They aren't going to anchor," Oswin pointed out.

"No, but I wouldn't either, in his position," Dr. Marlende said. "One of the hazards of a course of betrayal and aggression is that one can never trust others. You know they have more than enough cause to betray you in turn."

Rani folded her arms, frustrated. "Which was the point I was trying to make when I suggested we simply set upon him and take your daughter."

"If we could have figured out an effective way to do it," Lord Engal muttered, "I would have embraced your suggestion wholeheartedly."

The airship steadied finally and a lone figure began to climb down the chain ladder. From his height and his clothes, Emilie could tell it was Lord Ivers himself. "He's coming alone?" she said, surprised.

Lord Engal snorted derisively. "Of course. The man's ego wouldn't permit anything else."

Lord Ivers reached the ground and made the long walk down the beach toward them. This was the first time Emilie had seen him face-to-face. He was lean, with light Northern Menaen blond hair and striking blue eyes. He was about Lord Engal's age, but he had sharper features, and was more handsome. Much more the conventional image of a noble lord philosopher. Especially compared to Lord Engal, who was big and hearty and looked like he could do a good day's manual labor without suffering unduly. Emilie expected that Lord Ivers' gentlemanly appearance probably had a lot of people fooled.

He stopped a few paces away, nodded to Dr. Marlende, and said, "Dr. Marlende, I presume."

Lord Engal said dryly, "I did that already."

Lord Ivers eyed him, his lip curled in mild derision. "I'm sure you enjoyed it. You've always been greatly pleased by your small accomplishments."

Lord Engal sputtered, "It's your petty competitiveness that turned this from a philosophical experiment into a race—"

"Oh, you calling anyone 'petty' has to be the ultimate—"

There was some restless movement among the others. Kenar gritted his teeth, Rani rubbed the bridge of her nose in tight-lipped annoyance, and Dr. Barshion sighed wearily. Emilie was pretty certain it was Daniel who had snorted incredulously. Dr. Marlende cut it off before it went on any longer, saying sharply, "Gentlemen! If this is a race, I've won it." He turned to Lord Ivers. "Now release my daughter, sir, or I'll shoot you." He rested his hand on the pistol tucked into his belt.

Now that's more like it, Emilie thought. Everyone seemed a little taken aback, except Rani, Kenar, and Daniel, who obviously knew Dr. Marlende better than the others. Lord Ivers looked affronted, and

Lord Engal startled. Lord Ivers said, "You would shoot a man in cold blood—"

Dr. Marlende was unimpressed. "My blood is hardly cold. Release my daughter. Now."

Lord Ivers watched him a moment, then evidently decided to get down to business. He said, "I will be happy to release Miss Marlende in exchange for your assistance with repairs to my aetheric engine."

Dr. Marlende countered, "Release my daughter now, and I'll forgo my desire to shoot you." He added, reluctantly, "And I'll consider not stranding you and your crew of miscreants here."

Emilie watched Lord Ivers very carefully, and she thought she saw relief and satisfaction flicker across his face, though it was too brief to be certain it wasn't her imagination. He said, stiffly, "My engine wouldn't have failed if it hadn't been sabotaged, unlike yours and Engal's. I suggest you will benefit more from my assistance."

Lord Engal laughed. "'Your engine'? I don't know who you stole it from but—"

Dr. Marlende interrupted again. "You've heard my offer. Release my daughter now, sir."

Lord Ivers' jaw tightened. "You agree to repair my engine?"

Dr. Marlende didn't budge. "As I said, I'll undertake not to strand you here. Now give me your decision. I'm just as happy to shoot you and continue this negotiation with your second-in-command."

Lord Ivers said, grimly, "I see I have no choice. I'll release Miss Marlende." He turned, and lifted his arm to wave, once, at his airship.

Emilie tensed, aware that everyone else had too. The sailors moved restlessly, shifting their grips on their weapons.

But after a moment a single figure in a battered tweed jacket and skirt stepped out of the door and onto the platform, and started to climb down the ladder. Emilie's heart leapt. It was Miss Marlende.

Emilie held her breath as Miss Marlende quickly walked all the long way down the beach, but it wasn't a trick or a trap. As she reached them, Kenar muttered something in Cirathi, sounding profoundly relieved. Lord Engal still watched Lord Ivers with skeptical suspicion. Dr. Marlende just stepped forward, and said in a thick voice, "Are you quite well, my dear? I've engaged not to shoot him, but I'm happy to retract the promise if you've been harmed."

Lord Ivers looked affronted. "I beg your pardon. I've treated the girl in a perfectly civilized—"

"I'm fine, Father. He's an arrogant and greedy cad, but he didn't hurt me," Miss Marlende assured him. She looked tired and a little mussed, but didn't seem injured at all. She reached Dr. Marlende and hugged him tightly. "And I'm so happy to see you."

Emilie managed to wait her turn behind Dr. Marlende and Kenar, but finally she could throw herself into Miss Marlende's arms. "I'm sorry we couldn't get you out too," Emilie said in a rush, aware she was babbling but unable to stop. "By the time Rani and I got back, the airship had taken off—"

"Emilie, it's all right," Miss Marlende assured her, hugging her back. "If I'd been quicker off the mark, I could have jumped into the water after Rani, but I missed my chance. There was nothing you could do."

"This is a very touching reunion, but I believe we have other more pressing concerns—" Lord Ivers began.

"Oh, shut up," Lord Engal told him, earning Emilie's approval for all time. "I want your airship anchored and your men to come out and turn over their weapons, and if they hold so much as a pocketknife back, I'll shoot you myself."

Radiating contempt, Lord Ivers agreed to everything Lord Engal asked.

Somehow, that didn't make Emilie feel the least bit reassured.

* * *

"I still feel it was too easy," Rani said, frustrated. "Ivers practically handed himself to us."

"Yes," Miss Marlende agreed. "He had to know my father wouldn't feel obligated to fulfill his end of the bargain, not after Ivers behaved like a criminal." They were aboard the *Sovereign*, in the lounge with the big windows, where Emilie and the others had spent the voyage down through the aether current. Kenar and Daniel were here too; Dr. Marlende and most of the others were working on the *Sovereign*'s aetheric engine, and Lord Engal and his sailors were busy guarding Lord Ivers' men and searching his airship. Miss Marlende added, "Lord Engal intends to press a charge against him for my kidnapping. And once the magistrates begin to investigate that, I'm more than certain we can turn up some evidence that he ordered the sabotages we suffered while planning the expedition, as well as the attack on the *Sovereign* in Me-neport."

Emilie was glad to hear that Lord Ivers would pay for what he had done, though she thought the punishment would probably be inadequate. She said, "He planned to strand us here—can't we do the same to him?"

Miss Marlende shook her head. "Abandoning Lord Ivers might be the most appealing solution, but we just can't do it. If left in the Hollow World, he would probably become a pirate or worse, and with his knowledge of aetheric and conventional engines, there's no telling what trouble he would make."

Daniel added, "Dr. Marlende is afraid the queen's people would find him, and Ivers would help them invent new devices to use against the nomads, and anyone else within range."

Kenar said, "Are we certain the airship was really sabotaged? That it wasn't a trick to allow him to contact us?"

Emilie had been wondering that herself.

But Miss Marlende said, "No, I'm certain the sabotage was real." She leaned forward on the couch. "I heard the crew talking about it. Two small but key components, including the quickaether stabilizer for the motile, were removed. Both were easily disconnected elements. I suspect the merpeople requested a tour of the airship, then removed them while Ivers and his crew were distracted or absent. They might not have known what the components did, but it wouldn't take an aetheric sorcerer or an engineer to spot them as important. I expect they thought the airship wouldn't be able to take off; when it did, they thought their plan had failed, and they pinned their hopes for overwhelming the nomads on the *Sovereign*." She added, "Lord Ivers' sorcerer is competent to maintain the spells, but that's all. He had no hope of effecting the repairs himself."

Emilie asked, "But what are we going to do with his airship? If we leave it here, the queen might find it."

Kenar jerked his chin toward the door, indicating the activity on the beach. "Engal plans to destroy it. I think it's the best course." He smiled a little. "He's looking forward to telling Lord Ivers about it."

Rani snorted. "I'm sure he will like to make Ivers watch."

It was a shame; the airship was beautiful, in its way, but they couldn't leave it here. Emilie said, "Will they set it on fire?"

Daniel nodded. "With the fuel oil from the conventional engine, after they remove the quickaether and the other valuable components."

"It will take some time." Watching the Cirathi worriedly, Miss Marlende said, "I think you should go ahead and leave, if the *Lathi* is ready to sail. You've already done so much for my father, and after what happened to your friend Beinar . . . I don't want you to sacrifice anything else for us."

Kenar lifted his brows, and exchanged a look with Rani. Rani let out her breath, and said, "We did much for your father because we owe him much, and I don't think he would leave us, if our situations were reversed. But I feel there is little we can do for you, except help you stare suspiciously at Lord Ivers." Rani shrugged. "We will stay as long as we can, and follow you to make sure your ships enter the aether current as planned."

Smiling, Kenar nudged her with his shoulder. "Good. I know the others will agree."

Miss Marlende nodded, and Emilie could tell she was relieved. "Thank you."

* * *

The conference broke up at that point, as there was nothing much they could do, and Rani and Kenar needed to get back to the *Lathi* to continue the preparations for their voyage home. As the others left, Daniel caught up with Emilie in the corridor, and said awkwardly, "I wanted to apologize for my behavior, on the airship, after Beinar . . . fell. It was, uh . . ."

Emilie thought that "natural" was perhaps the word he was looking for. He had known Beinar personally, when she hadn't, and she felt she had been high-handed, at the least. She said quickly, "No, it's all right. I apologize for being so sharp with you. I was afraid something would happen and we wouldn't escape after all. And it was a shock."

Daniel nodded, and they continued down the corridor. After a moment, he said, "You get angry when you're shocked?"

Emilie threw a suspicious look at him. Possibly he was teasing her. "Apparently so." Partly to poke back at him, and partly from real curiosity, she added, "Why aren't you helping Dr. Marlende and Dr. Barshion with the engines?"

"I'm not that kind of sorcerer." Daniel shoved his hands in his pockets, though he didn't sound too disgruntled. "I just don't have the aptitude for aether mechanics. I'm learning naturalistic magic."

Emilie frowned. "From Dr. Marlende? I thought he was an expert in aether mechanics."

Daniel smiled faintly. "He's an expert in both."

Emilie had no trouble believing that. Dr. Marlende wasn't the kind of philosopher who wrote learned articles on other people's discoveries; he was the kind who made the discoveries. "What about Dr. Barshion?"

"I don't know." Daniel sounded thoughtful. "I've seen his name in the Philosophical Society's journals, occasionally, but I don't know anything about him—"

Seth came out of the cross corridor at the end of the passage, spotted them, and waved. He said, "Come up to the wheelhouse, the doctor thinks he has it figured out!"

Daniel lengthened his stride, and Emilie hurried to keep up. Daniel called back, "What figured out? You mean—"

"How we're all getting out of here!"

*　*　*

On the chart table in the wheelhouse, Dr. Marlende spread out several maps, with Lord Engal, Captain Belden, Miss Marlende, Dr. Barshion, and Mr. Abendle looking on. Charter was here too, his arm in a sling and looking much better than the last time Emilie had seen him. He nodded to her as she and Daniel and Seth squeezed in around the table. Emilie smiled back, then looked at the maps. Except they weren't maps, but diagrams of something, covered with arrows and handwritten figures.

Dr. Marlende said, "Lord Engal has been aboard Lord Ivers' airship, and removed all the aetheric components that were salvageable. It's ready to be destroyed, and Seth and I will set that in motion as soon as we're finished here."

Lord Engal stroked his beard. "I also removed the scientific information he collected, photographic film, notes, plant and insect specimens, that sort of thing." Dr. Marlende eyed him, and Lord Engal cleared his throat. "I expect you to take charge of it, of course. I've collected my own information."

But he'd like more, since it would make for an even better presentation to the Philosophical Society, Emilie thought, managing not to roll her eyes.

Dr. Marlende said, "Of course." He turned back to the diagram. "With the array of spare parts and supplies you have generously brought along, I can quickly repair the damage to my own aetheric engine, but the *Sovereign*'s situation is far more difficult. The aether component that supports the protective shield, the 'bubble' necessary for travel within the current, is out of balance. It can be raised to enclose the ship, but it simply will not hold its shape for the entire length of the journey. I could try to recalibrate it, but it might take several days. And with the possibility that the queen's forces are searching for us, our time is severely limited. What I propose to do is finish the repairs to my airship, and calibrate the two vessels' aetheric engines to work together, and then extend the airship's protective bubble to include the *Sovereign*, so we can travel through the aether current together."

Everyone stared at him. Emilie thought she was following his line of thought, and the whole idea seemed dangerous. Not that traveling through the aether current was safe to begin with, but this seemed an even more unlikely and dubious method.

Dr. Barshion leaned over the diagrams, his brow furrowed. "So both crafts will travel through the current as one?"

Emilie realized the arrows and figures must represent the Aerinterre aether current, though she still couldn't make heads or tails of them. She said, "But what happens to the *Sovereign* once we get there?" She knew that once inside the current, it didn't matter what it passed through, but if the *Sovereign* went back through the volcano it would surely end up perched on the rocky mountain somewhere. And she couldn't be the only one who was wondering that. Captain Belden was listening with sharp interest.

Dr. Marlende told her, "This aether current has many outlets, through fissures in the ocean bottom around the island. I only used the volcano itself because it was more convenient for my airship." He tapped the diagram. "I can release the *Sovereign* from the joining here; its protective bubble should last long enough for it to be drawn with the current straight out the fissure and to the surface. There will only be a few minutes of current travel left by that point, and my airship will continue up and exit the current through the volcano's cauldron."

Lord Engal nodded slowly, his brow furrowed with concern. "I don't see that we have much of a choice, if the *Sovereign* can't make the complete journey unassisted."

Dr. Marlende said, "Very well, then." He rolled up his diagram with a satisfied air. "Now all we have to do is survive to reach the surface!"

Everyone winced.

* * *

The *Sovereign* steamed toward the Aerinterre aether current, reaching it after the end of the next eclipse. The *Lathi* trailed behind, sailing under its own power, and Dr. Marlende's airship soared overhead.

Lord Ivers' airship had been left behind on the island, a broken, charred ruin. The rigid metal framework of its balloon, exposed as the gas inside had been released and then the fabric covering burned away, had looked like a huge creature's skeleton. It depressed Emilie to see it, and somehow seemed to bode ill for their future prospects.

As Lord Engal had decided, Lord Ivers and his men were now locked up in one of the *Sovereign*'s secure holds. It made Emilie nervous to have them there, though there were four armed crewmen guarding the door at all times. Lord Ivers had thrown a fit and made angry threats when Lord Engal had given the order, but since he and his men had already given up their weapons, there wasn't much he could do.

Emilie thought Lord Engal and Dr. Marlende had taken every precaution, at least every precaution that they could think of, but she was still uneasy. Standing at the railing with Miss Marlende, watching the giant round cloud of the Aerinterre current loom overhead, she said, "I'm just worried, that's all."

"I'm worried, too," Miss Marlende admitted. She was watching the airship move closer to the *Sovereign,* angling in to get as close as possible in anticipation of joining their protective spells. This seemed to be a fairly difficult and potentially disastrous operation, and it was making Emilie edgy just to watch. Miss Marlende continued, "I won't feel easy until we're steaming into port."

"We couldn't leave Lord Ivers behind on an island and come back and get him later?" Emilie suggested, only partly joking.

"It's tempting," Miss Marlende said. "But somehow I don't think travel down here is going to become all the rage. Especially if the trip through the current tends to damage the aetheric engines. Ivers admitted that after he arrived his sorcerer had to repair the aether navigator in his motile too."

Emilie glanced up at her. "That was what you thought was wrong with the *Sovereign*'s motile, wasn't it?"

"Yes, and it turned out I was right, though there were apparently a few other adjustments that needed to be made that had confused the issue. My father repaired it fairly quickly last night. But it's the protective bubble that's the real problem, of course." Dr. Marlende had spent part of the night on the *Sovereign*, getting its protective spells ready to work in concert with his airship. Then he had called the airship on the wireless, had it lower a ladder over the *Sovereign*'s deck in the glare of the spotlights, and dramatically climbed it to finish the repairs and preparations aboard it.

"Why didn't Dr. Barshion and Mr. Abendle and Ricard know about that, then?" Emilie asked, somewhat annoyed. "At least we would have known what was wrong."

Miss Marlende grimaced. "I don't know. I don't think Barshion's in over his head, but I do think perhaps he was overworked, and overtired." She sighed. "But I suppose it doesn't matter now."

Her eyes were on the *Lathi,* which had anchored at a safe distance from the current. Emilie followed her gaze. They had already said their goodbyes before leaving the island, and the Cirathi were only waiting to watch them enter the current before they began their own voyage home. Emilie said, "I wish we could say goodbye again." She wished she didn't have to say goodbye at all, but she knew that was impractical.

"It wouldn't make us feel any better," Miss Marlende said, sounding glum, and gave Emilie a hug.

* * *

It took some time, lots of maneuvering, and various people with megaphones shouting warnings from the *Sovereign*'s decks, but they managed to lower the airship down over the water, so its cabin was level with the *Sovereign*'s second deck. Emilie watched this process from the deck above, in the enclosed promenade with Miss Marlende, both of them braced to run inside if the propellers swung their way. The rigid balloon was bigger than the *Sovereign,* blotting out their view of the sky.

Mikel stepped out onto the catwalk and tossed a line across to the waiting sailors. "Just attach it to the railing!" he called.

Lord Engal motioned for the man to go ahead, and he looped the line around the metal railing. Oswin, who had just come up from below, said worriedly, "If the wind changes and pushes the airship away, it'll take that railing with it."

"It's not meant as an anchor. It will just be slipknotted in place, as a symbolic connection between the two vessels for the spell, and will give way if needed." Engal turned to the nearest hatch and called to a waiting sailor, "Tell Barshion we're ready!"

A few moments later, a deep vibration shuddered through the deck; the *Sovereign*'s aetheric engine engaging. Emilie gripped the railing nervously, remembering how the deck had heaved last time, but Miss Marlende said, "It's considerably smoother, isn't it? My father must have made some adjustments."

There was an answering roar from the airship that made Emilie jump; before this it had been relatively quiet. Then the gold barrier rose up, cutting off their view of the water, streaming upward to enclose the airship and the *Sovereign* together in a giant bubble. The noise of the two engines rose and fell, and Emilie saw the airship's propellers had stopped spinning.

She followed Miss Marlende down the stairs and out onto the open deck. As they arrived, Dr. Marlende and Mikel were dropping a set of metal stairs down from the catwalk over the *Sovereign*'s railing to the deck. It was at a steep slant, but at least the airship was still now, steady as a rock, held in place by the protective bubble.

"We're ready when you are, my lord," Seth called from the catwalk, and stepped back into the airship.

On the deck below, Lord Engal told Oswin, "Get down to the engine room. Notify me immediately if there are any problems supplying power to the aetheric compartments." Oswin bolted off and Lord Engal turned and strode inside.

Miss Marlende pushed away from the railing. "Let's watch from the wheelhouse."

They hurried through the corridors, reaching the wheelhouse as Lord Engal was ready to give the command. The big ports around three sides of the room were filled with the golden light of the bubble, except for the one to starboard, where the bullet nose of the airship's balloon was visible. Emilie could just make out the sea past the barrier, though the glare of the sun made it difficult. Captain Belden and the other two sailors looked suitably stoic, but Emilie thought they were sweating. Lord Engal saw them and said grimly, "Better hold on."

Miss Marlende and Emilie braced themselves against the cabin wall. Lord Engal nodded to Captain Belden, who took the lever of the engine telegraph and pulled it down, sending a "full ahead" message to the engine room.

The entire ship shook, metal screeched. Then Emilie felt the deck push up at her feet. Her stomach lurched and she gripped the railing more tightly. The aether current drew both vessels up out of the water, she could see the surface dropping away below. Somehow this sensation hadn't bothered her aboard Dr. Marlende's airship; maybe because Dr. Marlende's airship was actually supposed to fly.

They went up and up, faster and faster, until the sky darkened and they could see nothing past the protective bubble. Lord Engal let out his breath and said, "That's that. All we have to do now is wait until we reach the surface, and the rift in the ocean floor."

Oh, that's all, Emilie thought, but everyone relaxed a little, breathing again.

CHAPTER TWELVE

Emilie found this return journey much more tense than the trip down, which didn't seem to make much sense. Maybe it was the fact that now she knew just how difficult and dangerous traveling in an aether current was. The first time it had just seemed like magic, the easy powerful magic of fairy stories. Now she knew that it was really the hard uncertain magic of philosophical sorcery, and that it might fail at any moment and kill them all.

It didn't help that she felt as if these short days in the Hollow World had aged her at least ten years.

She spent the time with Miss Marlende, sitting in a couple of hard chairs in the chart room. It would have been more comfortable to go down to one of the lounges, but neither of them did. It eased Emilie's nerves a little to be here, watching Lord Engal check the aether navigator and his copies of Dr. Marlende's diagrams. Sometimes he sent a sailor down to take a message with hastily scribbled figures to Dr. Marlende on the airship, or below decks to Dr. Barshion with a question.

But nothing went wrong, and tension started to segue into boredom. Emilie and Miss Marlende got up to stretch their legs, and walked around the ship a little. It was oddly quiet; everyone in the crew who wasn't manning a station had been told to stay in their quarters. It was eerie, and something of a relief to get back to the wheelhouse.

After a few hours, Mrs. Verian served a brief meal of sandwiches and tea, which Emilie helped her carry up from the galley. Having a full stomach made it harder to stay awake, at least for Emilie, and she dozed off for a bit, waking whenever she almost fell out of her chair.

She straightened up finally, blinking the sleep away, to see Lord Engal pacing back and forth in front of the wheel, rubbing his hands together briskly. He called a sailor in and sent him off with a hurried message for Dr. Marlende. "What's going on?" Emilie asked Miss Marlende.

"We're almost there." Miss Marlende stretched and rolled her shoulders. "It's getting close to the time when we'll break off from the airship and make our way out through the fissure in the ocean floor."

Emilie hugged herself, breathing out in relief. "We made it."

Miss Marlende said, preoccupied, "I'll feel better when we're out of the current." She glanced at Emilie. "What will you do when we get back, Emilie? Did you want us to drop you off at Silk Harbor?" She hesitated. "Or did you want to go home?"

Emilie frowned at the polished wooden floor, which was marred by sandy footprints and sandwich crumbs; it had been a few days since anyone had had time to think about things like sweeping the floors. Realistically, she knew her future at Silk Harbor was uncertain. Karthea would be hard-pressed to be able to provide her with any other wage than a place to sleep. *You don't even know if she'll let you work for her. But if she won't . . . I'll think of something else.* She said, "Silk Harbor. I still want to see if my cousin will let me help with her school." She added tentatively, "Perhaps I can see you and Dr. Marlende again, when you're in town?"

Miss Marlende watched her, her brow furrowed in concern. "Are you certain? I'm sure whatever difficulty you had with your family— Perhaps I could help—"

"I can't go home." Telling Kenar had been much easier, probably because he hadn't really grasped the full implication of what she had said. When she had first arrived on the boat, telling anyone else, especially Miss Marlende, had seemed impossible. But Miss Marlende knew her better now. Emilie glanced around, making sure the men in the wheelhouse were too busy to overhear, then reluctantly wrestled the words out. "Even if you and your father and Lord Engal gave me letters explaining what happened, even if you came with me and lied and swore that I'd been chaperoned the entire time, it wouldn't do any good. That's why I left."

"Chaperoned? Oh." Miss Marlende's frown deepened. "I think I see. There were accusations without basis?" She read Emilie's expression accurately. "And perhaps some threats of punishment for things you hadn't done, or didn't contemplate doing?"

"Yes." Emilie felt a tightness in her chest ease. "My mother ran off to become an actress, and although she got married . . ."

"You would think, in this day and age . . ." Miss Marlende's mouth set in a grim line. "You don't believe there is any chance of reconciliation?"

"Not now. Especially not after I ran away," Emilie admitted. "Maybe later. Years later." The situation between the Sealands queen and the nomads had given her some perspective. She thought too much had been said on both her part and her uncle's part for anyone to back down.

Miss Marlende said slowly, "Well then, perhaps, if the situation with your cousin doesn't work out, you'd be interested in a position as my personal assistant?"

"What? Yes." Emilie blinked. "Doing what?"

Miss Marlende smiled. "I do a great deal of work for my father, writing letters, monographs about his work, plus traveling and meeting with members of learned societies, that sort of thing. I could use some secretarial help. And perhaps, if I have a younger woman in tow, I'd look a bit more matronly to some of the men I have to meet with, and they would be less inclined to treat me like a frivolous debutante." She shrugged wryly. "Probably not, but it's worth a try."

Emilie nodded rapidly. "Oh, yes. Thank you." It sounded less like adventuring and more like a junior social secretary, but still . . . *Social secretary to adventurers would be far more interesting than school-teacher.* It was a fabulous opportunity.

Lord Engal interrupted then, stepping out of the wheelhouse, frowning distractedly. "Evers? Where's Evers?"

"You sent Evers with a message to my father," Miss Marlende reminded him.

Emilie thought she might as well start being useful immediately. "Do you need someone to take a message, my lord?" She had remembered to call him "my lord" that time; she hoped he had noticed.

He said, "Yes, to Dr. Barshion, if you don't mind. I asked him to send me the adjustments for the aether navigator we'll need to make for the Aerinterre surface current. It's not urgent at the moment, but I don't want to waste time once we break through to the surface."

"I'll be right back." Emilie went down the stairs, glad for a chance to work off the excitement. Her heart was pounding a little. She found herself looking forward to getting back a great deal more now.

She went all the way down to the lower deck, just above the engine room, and then turned in to the aetheric-compartment corridor. The air was hot and damp. She passed the room with the device that kept the air clean inside the bubble. It had the same mist, earthy smell, and bemused operator as the first time she had seen it.

She reached the doorway of the aetheric engine room, where a sailor stood on guard. He nodded to her, smiling, and she recognized him as one of the men who had helped search the island where they had found the *Lathi.* "Hello. I've got a message for Dr. Barshion."

Ricard poked his head out. He looked tired, and sweat was beaded on his forehead, but his expression was cheerful. It was another sign that things were going well down here. "Hello, Miss Emilie. He's not here. He went up to the wheelhouse to see Lord Engal."

"No, he's not there," Emilie told him. "That's where I've come from. Lord Engal wants the adjustments for the aether navigator for the Aerinterre surface current."

Ricard stepped back and Mr. Abendle came to the doorway. Behind him, Emilie saw the copper dome on its plinth, connected to all the pipes and tubing. It was humming loudly and hissing a little as wisps of steam escaped from its pipes. Mr. Abendle had a bandana tied around his head like an old pirate from an illustrated story. He said, "That's odd. Oh, I bet he went to Dr. Marlende first. I'll get the figures for Lord Engal and send someone up with them."

"All right, thank you." Emilie started away, feeling sweat already sticking her shirt to her back. She hoped she would have time to take a bath after they reached the surface.

She reached the cooler air of the stairwell, and stopped. The stairs that led down to the main engine room and the boilers were at the opposite end of the aetheric-room corridor. This stairwell led down to the forward hold, where Lord Ivers and his men were held prisoner.

It wasn't that she was suspicious . . . but this was an odd time for the *Sovereign's* aetheric sorcerer to go missing, even temporarily. *If, just say if, Lord Engal sends a sailor with a note, asking for the figures, Dr. Barshion pretends it's asking him to come to the wheelhouse, and no one knows where he is.* That would be one reason for Lord Ivers to put himself in Lord Engal's power, if he had a man on the inside, someone who could help him . . . *Do what? Escape after we get to the surface?*

You've read too many novels, Emilie. But now the thought was like an itch in a place you weren't allowed to scratch in public. *I'll just take a look at the guards to make sure everything is all right.*

She went down the stairs. There was a short corridor at the bottom, but only one open hatchway along it. She headed toward it, prepared to say that Lord Engal had sent her to see if everything was all right. Though that was a little unlikely. Maybe she could say—

Emilie froze in the hatchway, staring. The four crewmen left to guard the hold lay sprawled on the floor, and the door behind them was wide open. They were wearing only their shirts and drawers; their uniform jackets and trousers were missing.

It took her what felt like a full minute to believe her eyes. Especially since Dr. Barshion was also sprawled on the floor near the crewmen, a bloody gash in his forehead.

He stirred and moaned a little, and Emilie hurriedly knelt beside him and patted his cheek, demanding, "Dr. Barshion, are you all right? What happened?"

Barshion groaned, his eyelids fluttering. He said, "I told him I wouldn't do it. Sabotage, slowing Engal down, that was what he paid me for, not murder. I'm not—" His eyes opened and he focused on her. He grabbed her arm, hard enough to hurt, and gasped, "Stop him. Separating the vessels, it could kill everyone aboard . . ."

Dr. Barshion slumped back, his eyes closed, and Emilie shot to her feet. She ducked back out to the corridor and tore up the stairs. She wanted to shriek at the top of her lungs for help, but if the escaped prisoners were nearby, they could catch her, stop her from warning the others. Lord Ivers had had a crew of nine besides himself, though only four would have *Sovereign* uniforms; it was mainly those four she was worried about.

She ran down the aetheric-compartment corridor, reaching the startled sailor guarding the engine. She stepped into the doorway, where Ricard and Mr. Abendle were checking dials and writing down the readings. She said breathlessly, "Lord Ivers' men escaped! You have to lock yourselves in until they're caught."

They both looked up, incredulous. Mr. Abendle said, "What? Escaped?"

Already backing away, Emilie said, "The guards were drugged, knocked out, I have to warn everyone—No, you stay there!" she added as the sailor started to follow her. "Guard the engines!" Running for the stairwell, she hoped he listened to her.

She ran up the stairs and paused on each landing to look down the corridors, but she didn't see any other crewmen to alert. She reached the second deck and hesitated, torn between running up to the wheelhouse to give the warning and going immediately to the airship. *No, better go to the airship first.* She would alert them and then take the word up to Lord Engal. The airship was far more vulnerable than the wheelhouse.

Emilie ran lightly down the corridor, her bare feet making little noise. Losing her boots was standing her in good stead now. The ship was still quiet except for the distant engine noise, but now that seemed sinister rather than serene. As she reached the outer corridor, the one that ran parallel to the deck, she saw the nearest hatch was partly open. *Uh-oh.* She was certain Captain Belden had ordered that all hatches be kept closed. It was possible whoever had taken the last message to Dr. Marlende had left it open. *Possible, but not likely,* Emilie thought grimly. She flattened herself against the wall and peered through the opening.

The first thing she saw was Daniel, standing on the airship's catwalk above the steps that led down to the ship's deck. A sailor in the dark *Sovereign* crew uniform was just starting up toward him.

Emilie's eyes narrowed, then she swore in recognition. It was Cavin, the man who had guarded Rani's prison cell in the Sealands city.

Emilie shoved the hatch open and ran onto the deck, and shouted, "Daniel, stop him, he's one of Lord Ivers' men!"

Daniel looked toward her, startled, and Cavin charged up the stairs at him. Daniel stepped forward to block the stairs, ducked a punch from Cavin, and grappled with him.

Seth came out of the door behind him, shouted a warning to the men inside, then dove forward to help Daniel fight off Cavin. The other escaped prisoners ran out of a hatch at the stern end of the *Sovereign's* deck, Lord Ivers among them, and Emilie ducked back into the corridor. Now she had a clear path to warn the wheelhouse.

She ran back to the cross corridor and nearly slammed into the chest of a crewman. She stumbled back, saw his face and his ill-fitting jacket over a stained shirt, and yelled, "They know you've escaped, I've warned everyone—"

He grabbed her shoulders and snarled, "Shut up or I'll—"

That was as far as he got, as Oswin loomed up behind him and cracked him across the back of the head with a pistol butt. He fell away from Emilie and collapsed onto the floor. Emilie gasped in relief. She told Oswin, "There are more of them, outside, I tried to warn the airship—"

"We know, Mr. Abendle sent Ricard to the wheelhouse." Oswin brushed past her, followed by six large sailors. They ran to the outer hatch and charged out onto the deck.

Emilie started to follow them outside but jerked back as gunshots rang out. She peeked around the edge of the hatch more cautiously, saw men fighting in a confused scramble toward the end of the deck. Then the attackers retreated back through the hatch there, leaving a couple of men lying unconscious or dead on the deck. Emilie heard them pound down the corridor toward her. Alarmed, she darted out onto the deck and slammed the hatch behind her.

Oswin and his men pursued the prisoners back into the ship, obviously determined to protect the wheelhouse and the engine rooms, but Emilie saw the door to the airship hung open. *Oh, no.* She ran forward to the end of the stairs that led up to the catwalk, trying to see inside. Figures fought in the dimness inside the cabin, but she couldn't tell who they were, who was winning.

Then Daniel staggered out of the cabin onto the catwalk, struggling with another man. The other man was bigger and Emilie didn't think the outcome looked certain at all. She looked around desperately, spotted a pistol lying near the hand of a fallen attacker. She grabbed it up, finding it unexpectedly heavy.

But as she turned back to the airship, Daniel got in a hard punch to the man's chin that made him stumble back until he fell over the railing down onto the *Sovereign*'s deck. He struck the wooden surface hard, and Emilie stepped hastily away. Daniel saw her and grinned triumphantly, despite a bloody nose.

Then Lord Ivers stepped out of the cabin door behind him. Emilie yelled, "Look out!," but as Daniel swung around, Ivers pointed a pistol at him. Daniel froze.

Ivers strode down the catwalk, seized Daniel's shoulder, and turned him around, pressing the pistol to his head. He said, "Cooperate or I'll blow your head off."

Gripping her pistol tightly, Emilie bolted up the stairs. "Let him go!"

Lord Ivers turned on the narrow catwalk and dragged Daniel with him, the barrel of the pistol pressed against his temple. But as Ivers saw Emilie, his expression went from furious to amused. "Sorry, but I'm afraid I need him. Dr. Marlende has locked himself inside the steering cabin and I can't get him to open the door without a hostage."

He didn't look worried at all. *Oh, that's not a good sign,* Emilie thought. "Don't move. I'll shoot." She pointed the gun, trying to project an aura of deadly certainty. If she could have fired, she would have done it already. She had never held a pistol before and she didn't know if you had to do anything before pulling the trigger; she was afraid if she fumbled it, Lord Ivers would shoot Daniel. Also, she knew it might kick, and she was terribly afraid of firing a bullet into the airship. She wasn't sure one bullet would hurt the balloon, but they were right down near the engines and it might go through the glass. She couldn't count on any help from inside the airship; she could hear violent fighting still going on in the cabin.

"You won't," Ivers said confidently. "A well-brought-up young lady like you."

"I'm not a well-brought-up young lady," Emilie said, projecting confidence. Ivers knew nothing about her, after all. "I'm a stowaway, and a thief, and a lookout for a dock gang that steals mailbags." *And an accomplished liar,* she almost added, then decided against it.

Daniel's eyes widened. She had convinced him, at least.

Ivers stared, his brows drawing together in consternation. But he tightened his grip on Daniel. "Nevertheless, I'll kill him if you don't get out of my way."

"Why should I?" Emilie countered. "I don't like him, he's been terribly rude to me."

Daniel glared, clearly offended. At least she was distracting him from the gun at his temple.

"You don't like him?" Lord Ivers dragged Daniel forward. Emilie held her ground, though she had the feeling this wasn't going to work out for the best. From Lord Ivers' sneer, he clearly knew she was bluffing. "A handsome boy like him?"

"I'm impervious to physical attraction," Emilie tried.

"It's true," Daniel managed to gasp.

Emilie pressed her lips together. No, the stalling wasn't going to work. But she caught movement out of the corner of her eye, below the airship's catwalk on the *Sovereign*'s deck.

It was Miss Marlende. She was below and behind Lord Ivers' and Daniel's position, leaning out on the ship's railing. She aimed her pistol across at Lord Ivers, obviously trying to find an angle where she wouldn't hit the airship or Emilie.

Emilie's heart leapt but she controlled her expression and made herself focus on Lord Ivers' face. "If you let him go I'll drop the pistol," she offered.

It was the wrong thing to say. Lord Ivers' expression twisted and he muttered, "Sorry, my dear, I've no more time to waste." Gripping Daniel around the neck, he pointed his pistol at Emilie.

Emilie yelled and dropped into a crouch, covering her head, though she knew that wouldn't help. The gun went off with an ear-shattering bang, but it was Lord Ivers and Daniel who jolted forward and collapsed onto the catwalk.

Emilie scrambled forward to grab Lord Ivers' pistol out of his nerveless fingers. Ivers was half atop Daniel, and neither man was moving, and there was blood splashed on the metal beneath them. Miss Marlende must have fired at Lord Ivers and the bullet had passed through both him and Daniel. Emilie shoved both pistols down the catwalk and turned back to the men, struggling to lift Ivers off Daniel without dumping either one off the walk.

Footsteps clattered on the steps behind her and she threw a wild look around, but it was Miss Marlende. She shoved her pistol into her belt, saying, "We have to get them inside! The protection spells are about to separate."

Emilie got a grip on Lord Ivers' arms and put all her weight into dragging him off Daniel. Miss Marlende stepped around her, grabbed his belt, and heaved him off. To Emilie's relief, Daniel groaned and stirred, lifting his head. "You had to shoot them both?" Emilie asked, breathlessly, helping Lord Ivers along with a shove as Miss Marlende hauled him down the catwalk. "Not that I'm complaining—"

"It was the only angle I could get that didn't include the airship," Miss Marlende explained, her voice rough from effort. "When you ducked, I was able to take the shot. Hopefully, I just winged Daniel."

"I think so," he groaned, trying to push himself up. "Ow."

Emilie got his free arm and pulled it over her shoulders, and helped him shove to his feet. They staggered after Miss Marlende. Emilie said, "I think someone's still in the cabin. Seth was—"

The airship's door flew open and Cavin came staggering out. Seth lunged after him, delivering a punch to the head which knocked Cavin down the stairs to sprawl on the deck.

"That's the last of them," he gasped to Miss Marlende. His glasses were askew, his knuckles bloody, and he looked more like a prizefighter than a scholar. He reached for Lord Ivers and helped Miss Marlende drag him through the doorway.

A young crewman ran out of the third deck hatch, calling over to them, "Ma'am, the ship's secure, and Lord Engal says we need to go now!"

Miss Marlende told him, "Get those men and yourself inside, then shut the hatches!"

The crewman went to the rail, spotted the men lying on the deck, and waved an acknowledgment. Emilie helped Daniel toward the door into the airship, saying, "If splitting the bubbles doesn't work, will it matter if we're inside or out on the deck?"

Miss Marlende gave her an admonishing look. "Hush, Emilie."

Daniel groaned again. On the deck below, several crewmen ran out of the hatch, seized Cavin and the other fallen men by their jackets, and dragged them inside. As Emilie helped Daniel through the doorway, she saw Cobbier and Mikel sprawled unconscious on the airship's deck, with another one of Lord Ivers' men. Charter was leaning in the doorway to the steering cabin, looking gray around the mouth. The fight couldn't have been very good for a recently wounded man. Seth dumped Lord Ivers beside the other escaped prisoner, Charter tossed him a coil of rope, and he hurriedly began to tie them up. Emilie looked back out the door and saw Miss Marlende hadn't followed them inside, but had run down the steps to the deck, starting to untie the line that formed the symbolic connection between the two ships.

Emilie deposited Daniel on the first bench seat, and ducked back out again as Miss Marlende climbed back up to the airship. Together they lifted the end of the set of steps where it was hooked onto the catwalk and dropped it down to the *Sovereign*'s deck. As they stepped inside, Miss Marlende slammed the door behind them and shouted, "Tell Father we need to go now!"

Seth bolted for the steering cabin and Charter just slid to the floor. Emilie took a step toward him, then stumbled when the airship shuddered. The deck slammed up and hit Emilie in the face. At least that was what it felt like. Sprawled on the cork floor, she lifted her head. Miss Marlende had fallen too, and Daniel had been knocked flat on the bench.

Emilie shoved herself upright, using the bench as a ladder, and leaned over Daniel to look outside. The *Sovereign* was gone. She could see something past the golden glow of the bubble, and realized it was rocky walls, stretching up.

Beside her, Miss Marlende staggered to her feet, and gasped, "I think we were a bit late on the release."

"A bit?" Daniel said, still trying to struggle upright.

"What does that mean?" Emilie asked.

Miss Marlende began, "It means—" Outside, the bubble shivered, going almost translucent, before it solidified again. Emilie flinched, and Miss Marlende finished, in a smaller voice, "We might not have enough power."

"Oh." Emilie bit her lip, watching the rock stream rapidly past the fading glow of the bubble. "It was Dr. Barshion. He was in Lord Ivers' pay."

"That explains a great deal," Miss Marlende said, her voice tight with anger. "I hope he hasn't killed all of us."

The airship shuddered, metal squealed, then a powerful jolt threw them all to the floor again. Sprawled there, Emilie saw the gold glow of the bubble vanish. "Oh no," she gasped, "I think—" *we're dead,* she meant to finish, but that was daylight streaming in. Real daylight, surface daylight.

The pressure vanished and the airship jolted and shuddered again, but this time the force came from the side, like a strong wind. Emilie struggled to her feet and knelt on the bench to look out the window.

They were rising above a vast rocky cauldron, the top of the volcano. Clouds streaked the blue sky and wind whistled around the cabin. It pushed the airship over the rim, and they drifted above the outer slopes. They were rocky and bare at the top, sliding down amid boulders and old rock falls into a forest of short wind-twisted trees. Miss Marlende called out, "Father, we're losing altitude!"

"Yes, my dear," Dr. Marlende answered from the steering cabin. "I believe we've lost a number of gas cells."

"Are we going to crash-land?" Emilie craned her neck for a better view of the slope. If they were, it looked as if they were going to do it very slowly. Now that the bulk of the volcano was blocking much of the wind, the airship was spiraling slowly down. At least they were on the surface, out of the aether current.

"Yes," Miss Marlende said, "but we still have enough gas cells left so it will be more of a thump than a crash." Her brow furrowed with worry, she added, "I just hope the *Sovereign* made it."

"Can someone help me up?" Daniel asked from the floor.

"Oh, sorry!" Emilie helped Miss Marlende haul Daniel back to the bench. When they had him sitting up, Emilie turned back to the window.

"Can you see it?" Miss Marlende asked anxiously.

They were past the tree-covered slopes and over flat grassy fields, and Dr. Marlende was guiding them gently down in a wide spiral. As the airship turned, Emilie caught sight of the sea, past low rocky bluffs. She leaned close to the glass and squinted against the glare off the water. She saw light glinting off something, something coppery. "Yes, there it is!" she cried out.

It was the *Sovereign*, steaming toward the island shore.

CHAPTER THIRTEEN

"Now, you do know the way to your cousin's house?" Miss Marlende asked, looking a little worried. "It's going to be dark soon."

They stood on the dock at Silk Harbor, under a cloudy early-evening sky, near the *Sovereign's* slip. This spot had been crowded with journalists and onlookers earlier, but by the dinner hour the furor had calmed down, and now there were only the usual dockworkers, off-duty sailors, and a few passengers making their way down the wooden boardwalk above the boat slips.

Dr. Marlende's airship had attracted the attention as it was towed in this morning on a large pontoon barge by a tugboat. It had taken a few days to get the tug and the barge from the port on the far side of the island of Aerinterre, load the airship, and then travel here, so the word had flown ahead of them on the wireless. Emilie wasn't sure what had caused more sensation, the news of the successful expedition, or when Lord Engal had formally given Lord Ivers in charge to the magistrates.

He had also had to give Dr. Barshion in charge, a moment of considerably less satisfaction for everyone.

Somewhat recovered from his injury, Dr. Barshion had admitted that he had been in Lord Ivers' pay from the moment Lord Engal had hired him. He had given Lord Ivers copies of Dr. Marlende's notes and research that Miss Marlende had shared with Lord Engal, had committed some small sabotages and spied on everything Engal, Miss Marlende, and Kenar had done to prepare for the expedition. Barshion had apparently hoped to stop the *Sovereign* from ever making the attempt, leaving Lord Ivers to rescue Dr. Marlende and take all the credit and acclaim. Once they were down in the Hollow World, he had started to regret what he had done, but he had still put the sleeping spell on the guards, so Ivers and his men could escape. But he had refused to help them destroy the *Sovereign,* and Ivers had bashed him in the head and left him for dead.

Emilie felt a little sorry for him. A little. She would have felt considerably more sorry for herself and the rest of the crew if Ivers had managed to take control of the airship and destroy the *Sovereign,* and all the witnesses to and evidence of his wrongdoing. They were just lucky that no one had been killed in the escape attempt. Some of the crew, including Charter, had been left behind temporarily in the town hospital at Aerinterre, and would have to be retrieved later.

"I'm sure I know the way," Emilie told Miss Marlende now. The others would be leaving with the *Sovereign,* which was preparing to set out for Meneport tonight to arrive in the morning and meet the representatives of the Philosophical Society. The airship would also be taken there for repairs, with a shipment of the special balloon fabric from Silk Harbor's weaving factories. "It's on Caveroe Street, on Tamerin Hill. Karthea's letters said it's not a far walk from the port." She felt considerably more prepared to present herself to her cousin than she had before. For one thing, she had new clothes: a skirt, shirtwaist, and jacket, plus a cap, stockings, and a set of walking boots suitable for town or country. There was also an extra set of underthings and a nightgown, and a shoulder satchel to carry them and what was left of her old clothes. On Miss Marlende's request, Mrs. Verian had run out to a large drapery shop not far from the harbor and purchased all of it for her. Emilie could now arrive at Cousin Karthea's looking respectable. Hopefully the package with her own things had arrived in the post by now.

The Marlendes would be back here in two weeks, to collect more supplies and Emilie. She had decided to take the time to stay here and visit Karthea, so she could explain to her why she had left home, so Karthea would know the truth and be able to pass it along to the more far-flung members of the family. It would also be a good chance to write letters to her brother in the navy and her friend Porcia, to let them know she was all right. Emilie expected she would be spending much of her time at Karthea's studying up on just what it was a lady's assistant and social secretary did.

"All right, then, as long as it's not far. I'm going to give you some money—" Miss Marlende began, taking a small purse out of her jacket pocket.

"Oh no, I couldn't accept it!" Emilie said. She hadn't started her new position yet. "I'll be fine, really."

"Emilie." Miss Marlende eyed her. "Do you even have the money to buy dinner, if you had to?"

"Well, no." The last of her money had been pinned into the pocket of her bloomers, and it had been lost at some point, probably one of the times she had had to jump into the water.

"Isn't that how you got into this situation?"

"Well, yes," Emilie admitted. "Maybe I'd better take it."

"Besides," Miss Marlende said, handing her the purse. "You've already been acting as my assistant and as an auxiliary member of my father's ground crew, so we probably owe you back wages for the voyage."

"Oh, that's true." That was different than taking charity from a friend.

Miss Marlende continued, "I've also put in a note with the addresses for our town house in Meneport and my father's workshop. If you get into any difficulty in the next two weeks, please write to us or send a wire. Do contact us," she emphasized. "Don't try to stow away on anything to get there. I can send someone to get you, or I can wire you passage money for a ferry."

"I'd be a much better stowaway now than I was before," Emilie had to point out.

"Yes, I'm sure you would." Miss Marlende smiled, and hugged her again. "We'll see you soon, Emilie. Try not to get into trouble."

"I'll try," Emilie promised. She had already said goodbye to the others, and even given her direction to Lord Engal, who had said that he might need to contact her for her account of the voyage. But even knowing that she would see her again before long, it was still hard to walk away from Miss Marlende, waving goodbye.

Emilie managed it, heading down the dock toward the stairs that led up to the walkway, and the streets above it where the gas lamps were being lighted as dusk fell. The houses and shops of Silk Harbor were spread out over the low hills above the wide sweep of the port, the streets dotted with trees. She could see people on the paved walks, and house lights coming on. She took a deep breath, filled with the sea, boat tar, and the scents of grilled fish and beef from the nearest chophouse. It wasn't as busy a place as Meneport, perhaps, but much less easy to get lost in.

Footsteps pounded behind her and she glanced back, surprised to see Daniel. He was dressed in a much more respectable jacket and trousers than she had last seen him in, and had shaved recently. He carried a satchel over his good shoulder, and his other arm was still in a sling. Miss Marlende's bullet had torn his shoulder, but hadn't hit bone. It had done quite a bit more damage to Lord Ivers, though he would still recover.

"Hello," Daniel said breathlessly as he caught up to her. "Miss Marlende said you were going this way."

"Hello." Emilie lifted an inquiring brow. "What are you doing here? Aren't you going to Meneport with the others?"

He explained, "My family lives in a small village a few miles outside of town. I was going to stay over here tonight and head out to see them in the morning, then catch up with the others in Meneport." He looked a little bashful. "I thought I'd walk with you. Maybe your cousin can tell me where there's a good rooming house."

"I see." Emilie smiled, turning to head for the walkway. "Maybe she can." And they walked up into the town together.

BOOK II

EMILIE AND THE SKY WORLD

CHAPTER ONE

Emilie took a deep breath and knocked on the door.

Twilight had fallen, and the quiet street smelled strongly of dinner. Karthea's house, like all the others, had a chunky stone façade and wood-framed windows with cheerful curtains and potted flowers on the stoop. The gas lamp on the corner had already been lit, glowing bright in the failing daylight.

There was no answer immediately and Emilie began to wonder if Karthea had closed the school temporarily and gone on some journey. If so, it was less of a disaster than it would have been a fortnight ago. Emilie had money enough for a room at an inn or boardinghouse, but it would be disappointing not to see her cousin. And wandering through town looking for a suitable place to stay was considerably less daunting than it had been a fortnight ago as well, especially considering that she had company.

"Maybe she didn't get my letter, or the package I sent," Emilie told Daniel, who stood patiently beside her. "Though I'm not arriving when I said I would."

"I think I hear someone inside," Daniel said. "It's nearly time for dinner, maybe she's just busy with—"

The door flung open, and Karthea stood there, wearing an apron and holding a partially peeled beet. "Emilie, you're days late! I was so worried!" Her eyes fell on Daniel, and she frowned in confusion. "Where have you been?"

"Karthea," Emilie said, smiling. "I have had an adventure!"

Karthea's eyes widened, then narrowed. She grabbed Emilie's arm and dragged her inside. To Daniel, she said, "Excuse us, please," and shut the door.

They stood in a dim hall, lit by a gas sconce and from brighter lights in the room at the far end. Emilie could hear the voices of young girls somewhere nearby, and a clatter of dishes. It smelled homey and comfortable, of books, dust, boiling beets from the kitchen. She took a deep breath. She had meant this place to be her refuge; it felt better to be coming to it as a guest.

Karthea still held her arm, and was trying unsuccessfully to look intimidating. Karthea was mostly Southern Menaen like Emilie, with warm brown skin and dark eyes. She and Emilie looked a little alike in the face, though Karthea was taller and myopic and always wore eyeglasses. She had inherited their side of the family's somewhat unmanageable hair, and hers was just as frizzy and curling as Emilie's, in the process of escaping from the band she had tried to use to confine it. "Are you eloping?" Karthea demanded.

It was so unexpected, Emilie laughed. "Of course not!"

It was the laugh that convinced Karthea; Emilie saw the relief and chagrin in her expression. Karthea said, "Oh. But who's that young man?"

"He's Daniel, one of Dr. Marlende's students. He needs a place here in town to stay while we're waiting for the doctor and Miss Marlende to get back from Meneport. I thought you would know of a boardinghouse."

"But who are the Marlendes?"

Emilie lifted her brows. "So can Daniel come in?"

"Oh. Oh!" Flustered, Karthea pulled open the door. "I'm so sorry. Please do come in."

Daniel stepped inside, smiling diffidently, trying to look harmless. He was only a few years older than Emilie, and Southern Menaen as well, with brown skin and curly dark hair. He had replaced his cracked spectacles with a spare pair kept on Dr. Marlende's airship, and looked much more respectable than when Emilie had first met him in a cell in the sea people's fortress. Emilie said, "Daniel, this is my cousin Karthea."

"How do you do?" Karthea frowned again, but this time in concern. She nodded toward the sling Daniel wore. "Your poor arm. What happened?"

"He was shot in the shoulder," Emilie said. At Karthea's horrified expression, she explained, "It's part of the adventure. And it's a long story, so we should sit down."

* * *

The house was in the middle of dinner preparations for Karthea, the six girl boarders, and the Therisons, the older couple who helped with the cooking and housework. Emilie and Daniel ended up at the long table in the kitchen, while the others helped finish peeling the beets and cutting the other vegetables for the cold salad. A loaf of round bread from the baker sat warming on the stove, with a pot of sliced beef and gravy. Emilie had eaten lunch aboard the ship before she had left, but her stomach was grumbling at the savory odors. Karthea and Mrs. Therison were good cooks, and it had been a while since any of her meals had included fresh vegetables.

Mrs. Therison gave Emilie and Daniel tea, and the girl boarders sat in rapt silence while Emilie told the story.

She glossed over her reasons for leaving home, making it sound like she had simply been on her way to visit Karthea when things had gone wrong. Karthea knew the truth, but Emilie didn't want to talk about it to the Therisons or Daniel. Especially Daniel. She also found herself glossing over the more dangerous parts of her adventure. She didn't want to talk about how frightened she had been, and she knew she couldn't describe what had happened to the people who had died, unless she wanted to break down and cry. And talking about what she had done suddenly seemed like boasting, which was terribly inappropriate considering all the brave things everyone else had done. So she concentrated on the beautiful things they had seen, and the friends they had made, and the exciting discoveries.

To her surprise, Daniel followed her lead when he spoke. Maybe she shouldn't be surprised; these were people she knew and he didn't, so it was natural that he should take his cue from her in what to say and what to leave out. But Emilie still wasn't used to people trusting her judgment in anything, so it was somewhat diverting.

The story was so wild Karthea and the others might have thought Emilie was mad. Emilie knew she didn't look like she had been on an adventure, except for the bruises; before she had left the ship, Mrs. Verian had run out and bought her this new set of clothes, a skirt, shirtwaist, jacket, cap, and a set of walking boots, so she probably looked more like she had been out shopping. But everyone in town had seen the *Sovereign* and the airship arrive. Daniel's wound also helped. And Daniel finished with, "Some of this will be in the newspapers tomorrow. We saw journalists talking to Lord Engal on the dock."

"Journalists?" Karthea exchanged a startled look with Mrs. Therison. "Emilie, will your name be in the newspaper?"

Emilie nodded, then shrugged, then nodded again. "Maybe. Probably. They took down everyone's name, I think."

With all the talking and questions, dinner went late. After they were finished, everyone helped clean up, and then the students were sent off to the parlor with tea cakes left over from lunch for their dessert. Karthea told Emilie that the girls were supposed to study in the evening but there was also a good deal of novel-reading and playing the piano. The other students lived in their own homes in town, and only came in during the day for their classes.

Mrs. Therison was finishing up the last of the dishes and Mr. Therison had taken Daniel to their cottage, which was across the yard from the back of the larger house. The Therisons had a spare room in their attic, kept for their son on his visits home, and they were going to lend it to Daniel for the night. Karthea led Emilie to her own parlor, a small room attached to her bedroom.

It was cozy, with a couple of overstuffed armchairs that had somewhat worn upholstery, bookshelves stuffed with novels, poetry, history books, and battered old schoolbooks. It was mercifully free of tatted lace table covers and arm covers, which Emilie's aunt draped over everything and which did nothing but get caught on clothes and fingernails. Karthea's knickknacks were all old university awards and plaques, gifts from former students, and her grandmother's silver tea service, which took pride of place on the tiled fireplace mantel.

Emilie moved some books out of an armchair so she could sit down, and sank gratefully into the soft cushions. It had been a long day, and she had eaten too much of the excellent dinner.

Karthea sat down opposite her, and flopped back in her own chair. "So you're really taking this job with the Marlendes?"

"Yes, I'm going to be Miss Marlende's assistant. Like a secretary, but I'm not really sure what secretaries do, besides use typewriting machines, and I don't know how to do that." Emilie supposed she could learn. If they were going to be in Meneport for any length of time, there should be a place where she could go for instruction. It couldn't be any harder than learning how to sail a small boat, and she had learned that quickly enough.

Karthea looked a little worried. "Didn't you want to work here and go to the school?"

Emilie almost said, *But this would be a real job,* and stopped herself just in time. It wasn't that she thought teaching, or cleaning up after other people's children, wasn't a real job. As far as the actual labor went, a job mucking stables would probably be easier than teaching at a school. What she really meant was *This is a job I earned for myself, and that my cousin didn't hand me on a silver plate.* She said, "I know, and I'm sorry. I hope it won't leave you shorthanded. But . . . I think I'm better suited to a job with the Marlendes."

"Will you be at their home? Or do they keep offices? I mean . . ." Karthea fiddled with the loose threads on the chair arm, frowning. "You wouldn't be in the airship, would you? The next time they go off to explore something?"

"Probably all three," Emilie said. She thought she knew what Karthea was thinking. "I believe they travel a great deal."

"But it's dangerous travel." Karthea leaned forward, watching Emilie with concern. "You were almost killed. What if it happens again?"

Emilie was glad she had glossed over those bits. But even without every frightening detail, it had still been obvious that the trip had been fraught with peril. She said, "I'm counting on it happening again." At Karthea's aghast expression, she hastily shook her head. "I don't mean that. I didn't like almost being killed, and it was so terrible when other people were killed. I won't ever forget it and I hope it never happens again, but . . . I can't let the other part go." She wasn't certain she was explaining it well. "The part with exploring strange places, and meeting wonderful people, and learning new things. That's what I want to do."

Karthea sat back, thinking it over. "I do understand. It's an incredible opportunity, and I know you never really wanted to be a teacher. It was just a way to get out of your uncle's house. I always thought you would be so much better off if you could take university courses, instead of working in a shop or taking care of some family's children." She sighed. "But I just worry about you, flying around in an airship with people who get shot at regularly."

"I'm worried about me, too, but I think it's worth it." Emilie really wasn't keen on being shot at. It took the fun right out of exploring and meeting new people. She admitted, "And I really don't know what I'll be doing. We didn't have much time to discuss it. I may end up sitting around in a dusty library helping sort papers and books, or something."

Karthea brightened at that thought. "You can always come back here if you change your mind. Though I suppose working for the Marlendes in Meneport means that it will be harder for your uncle and aunt to cause you trouble."

Meneport might be closer to her uncle's house, but while Emilie wouldn't put it past him to send a solicitor to Karthea demanding she throw Emilie out, she didn't think he would do it to the Marlendes. Uncle Yeric was a bully at heart, and Emilie felt bullies were always afraid to bite people who might just bite them back.

Emilie also noted that Karthea hadn't made any suggestion that the Marlendes' level of respectability should be examined before Emilie accepted the position. That was one of the reasons she liked Karthea. "I suppose they'll know where I am, once they read the newspapers."

Karthea groaned. "Oh, the newspapers. The town news always gets passed along to Meneport, so any articles written about it here will show up in all the nearby towns and villages. I just hope your uncle doesn't write to me when he sees it."

"You could throw the letter in the bin," Emilie suggested. Karthea wasn't rich, but she had been independent for years. And if something ever happened to the school, she had other family to go to while she found a way to get back on her feet. If Karthea did need help, Emilie's uncle would provide nothing but censure anyway, and Emilie didn't see why Karthea should give him the satisfaction of shouting at her in a letter about something she had no control over. "Problem solved."

Karthea raised her brows in surprise, then slowly smiled. "Problem solved."

* * *

Emilie couldn't help checking the clock during breakfast, which was tea, fresh bread from the bakery down the street, butter, and sausage. Mrs. Therison apologized for the lack of eggs, explaining that the hens hadn't been laying well and she was saving what they had to make a pastry crust for dinner tonight. Emilie and Daniel assured her it was far better than anything they had had on board ship, and this was true.

Apparently everyone else had been checking the clock as well, because when it struck the hour, Mr. Therison, without being prompted, announced his intention of going to fetch the newspapers.

Karthea shooed the boarders into their parlor to get ready for their first lesson, and to wait for the girls who lived outside the school to arrive. Emilie helped Mrs. Therison clean up the dishes. Daniel tried to pitch in as well, but since he was under doctor's orders not to strain his injured shoulder by moving his arm, they didn't let him do much more than hand them towels at strategic moments.

Finally the kitchen door opened and Mr. Therison stepped in, waving the folded newspaper. "Here it is! It's on the front page." He spread the paper on the kitchen table as they all gathered around.

Emilie scanned the article, searching for her name, not sure whether she was hoping to see it or not. If it wasn't there, nothing would have changed, but if it was, her uncle would know exactly what she had been doing. She thought about her brave words to Karthea and grimaced in annoyance at herself. *You're going to have to take your own advice. Not so easy to do as to say, is it?*

The article quoted Lord Engal the most, and didn't go into much detail about the Hollow World, concentrating more on the treachery and machinations of Lord Ivers, and the rescue of Dr. Marlende.

Then she saw it and her heart started to pound. Karthea spotted it a moment later and read aloud, "'. . . Lord Engal said that essential to the survival of the ship was the quick thinking of Dr. Marlende's daughter, Miss Vale Marlende, and her assistant, Miss Emilie Esperton, both of whom bravely held off Lord Ivers. Miss Esperton joined the ship's crew in Meneport, and is an accomplished young scholar of aetheric philosophy.'" She looked up and met Emilie's gaze. "Well, there it is. Your uncle will see this as soon as the news reaches Meneport and goes out with all the village papers. If he doesn't see the article, someone is bound to point it out to him."

Baffled, Emilie said, "Why did they say I was a scholar of aetheric philosophy?"

"They had to say something about you," Daniel explained. "They always say something like that about the women, like the way they described Miss Marlende as 'a lovely lady much sought after by Meneport hostesses for musical evenings and card parties' when she hasn't gone to any silly society events for years. But if they said you were a stowaway or made it sound like you were an adventuress, Lord Engal would sue them. He sues the newspapers all the time for things like that. Sometimes on behalf of people he doesn't even know. So they just made up something that made sense and that wouldn't make him angry."

"Oh." Emilie looked over the article again, this time with a little less trepidation. "They didn't mention you. Oh wait, you're listed here on Dr. Marlende's crew. But they didn't say anything about the other things you did."

Daniel snorted. "I'm glad of that. I can live without reading 'Mr. Daniel Allwight fell down and bled on the deck while his companions fought bravely.'"

Once everyone had had their fill of the article, Karthea carried it off to read to the boarder girls, and to get ready to start the day's classes. Mr. Therison went to work in the back garden and Mrs. Therison to do the shopping. Emilie was left in the kitchen and wasn't sure what to do with herself. This was the first free time she had had in what felt like ages, but the article had unnerved her a little, and she didn't feel like just sitting and reading in the parlor or the garden.

Daniel was still lingering over his last cup of morning tea, so she asked him, "Were you going to visit your professor today?"

"Yes, I was." He hesitated. "Uh, would you like to go along?"

"To meet your professor?" Emilie hoped the desire to not sit around the house while Karthea was busy hadn't somehow been written all over her face.

Daniel explained, "She isn't really a professor, because she went to university before they gave degrees to women. But she writes a great deal and is very important in aetheric circles, and Dr. Marlende got her advice on some of his work." Suddenly a little shy, he added, "I thought you might want to meet her."

"I do want to meet her," Emilie said. She sounded like a very interesting person.

"Good." Daniel smiled. "I thought she could be an inspiration to you, since you want to work with the Marlendes. And you know, she could help you if you ever decide to go to the university."

* * *

Professor Abindon lived farther down in the town, closer to the port, and so they had to walk back down the hill and wend their way through streets with shops and town houses. There were a lot of people out now, doing early-morning shopping or heading to work in cargo and shipping offices down near the port. It wasn't as busy as Meneport, but the people were the usual mix of brown-skinned and dark-haired Southern Menaen and fair-skinned and light-haired Northern Menaen, and every variation in between. Not much different from Emilie's village. She found she preferred Meneport's excitement and bustling atmosphere, though she could see why people liked to live here.

Emilie couldn't help thinking about what Daniel had said. She had never considered the idea of going to the university before, it not being something her family would have encouraged. She wasn't sure she wanted to consider it now, though she had always liked learning new things. She wasn't sure she wanted to take on the work of a university student, particularly as it would surely mean curtailing her duties as Miss Marlende's assistant. Even if she could afford the tuition and living expenses, which she couldn't, she wasn't sure they would let her in. She didn't think her village school would compare well to a school like Karthea's, or Shipands Academy, and surely she would need more basic instruction before going on to advanced classes.

Daniel found the right street, which curved away from the shops and up a hill. There were three-story town houses along here, crowded together with no front gardens, their stones weathered with age. The carvings of ships and fanciful fish and sea serpents above the windows and pediments suggested they had originally been ship captains' or cargo merchants' homes. It was too quiet for Emilie to tell who lived there now, though some of the houses had signs indicating there were rooms to let. Professor Abindon's didn't have a sign, and while it was as old as the others and a little crumbly on the edges, its stoop was recently washed and the windows on the upper floors were open to catch the sea breeze.

"I normally send a wire or letter when I visit," Daniel was saying as they climbed the steps to the door. "But of course this time I didn't have an opportunity. I hope she's home."

Daniel knocked on the door. A housekeeper in a somewhat floury apron opened it, and the first indication that Professor Abindon didn't keep a terribly formal household was when the housekeeper exclaimed, "Why, it's Daniel!" She turned to shout down the hallway, "Professor, Daniel is here!"

"Well, tell him to come in!" a voice shouted back, but the house-keeper was already ushering them into the front hall.

It was small and a bit dark, but smelled of beeswax polish and bread-baking. Before they had a chance to move, a tall figure burst out of a door down the hallway. It exclaimed, "Daniel, why hasn't Marlende or Vale answered my wires? What the hell is wrong with them?"

"Uh," Daniel began, and the housekeeper gave him a gentle prod down the hall. Emilie followed, now certain this visit was going to be even more interesting than she had thought. Daniel said, "They've been away. Very far away. They just arrived back in Silk Harbor yesterday, but they meant to leave last night before dark."

"They were here?" Daylight fell through the open doorway, illuminating a tall woman with silver-gray hair that was as wild as Emilie's on a bad day. Some of it was confined in a band but the rest had escaped to hang in frizzy locks around her face. She was strikingly beautiful, with a mix of Southern and Northern Menaen descent in her features and her light brown coloring. "Why didn't they . . . What were they doing here?"

"Didn't you see the newspapers this morning?"

"I don't read the newspapers, it's a lot of gossip and idiocy. Why was Marlende in the newspapers?" She frowned at Emilie, though more in confusion than disapproval. "Who are you?"

"I'm Emilie Esperton, Miss Marlende's assistant," Emilie said, but Professor Abindon was already dragging Daniel into the parlor.

It was a more of a study, Emilie saw immediately, with tall windows facing the house's tiny overgrown back garden letting in morning light. The walls were lined with shelves crammed with books and papers. More books and papers and writing materials covered the desk and the library table, but a small sofa and two armchairs were free of clutter. Flustered, Daniel said, "We went to the Hollow World, Professor, we used the aetheric currents." He dropped down into a chair and Emilie took the other. "It worked just like you and Dr. Marlende thought, but we had mechanical trouble and couldn't return. Miss Marlende had to go to Lord Engal to get help—"

"Engal! Vale went to Engal? Was she out of her mind?" Professor Abindon waved her hands. "Why didn't she come to me?"

Daniel opened his mouth but no words came out. Professor Abindon shook her head sharply. "I'm sorry, I don't intend to drag you into the middle of this. Just go on."

Emilie wondered what "this" was, but she thought Daniel needed help and she dove in. "Yes, we should tell it from the beginning. Daniel, start from when you and the others took the airship to the Hollow World."

Daniel took a deep breath and launched into the story, telling it as briefly as he could given Professor Abindon's impatient expression. As he spoke, Emilie watched the professor's face. She was older than she had looked at first, though the lines around her eyes and mouth were slight. And she looked vaguely familiar, as though she resembled someone Emilie knew, though she couldn't think who it would be.

When he got to Emilie's part of the story, Professor Abindon considered her, her expression skeptical. "How do we know you aren't working for Ivers?"

"I distracted him while Miss Marlende shot him," Emilie said.

"And me," Daniel added ruefully, indicating his arm. "I was in the way."

"Hmm," the professor said, but didn't comment further.

When they were done, Professor Abindon said, "At least Marlende had a good excuse for not answering my wires, but this doesn't change the situation."

"What situation?" Daniel asked. "What was so urgent?"

Professor Abindon started to speak, then hesitated, eyeing Emilie thoughtfully. *She still doesn't trust me,* Emilie thought, which she supposed was fair. Fair, but not pleasant. Though she was burning with curiosity, Emilie said, "I can walk back to my cousin's house."

As she started to stand, the professor gestured impatiently. "Don't go. If you work for Vale . . . I trust her judgment. Come upstairs, I'll show you both."

* * *

They followed Professor Abindon up the narrow stairs to the second floor, then kept following her up a still narrower set of stairs to the third, then up again to what should have been a small attic. Emilie followed the others through the door at the top of the stairs and saw why the professor had chosen this house.

The room had once been made into an artist's studio, with one whole side of the pitched roof turned into windows, which could be unlatched and propped open with metal poles. Another set of large windows looked down into the back garden, so the room was full of light. A tiny spiral stair led up to a trapdoor in the roof, which Emilie bet opened onto a small railed platform atop the house. She had seen them on many of the houses in Silk Harbor and knew they were common for sea captains' and ship owners' homes. But Professor Abindon wasn't using this room for artistic endeavors or to watch the ships come into port.

A large gleaming brass telescope stood on a stand beneath the slanted windows, pointed toward the sky. Emilie had seen drawings of big stargazing telescopes before, but never one in person. This one had extra parts, wheels and platter-like contraptions, mounted above the eyepiece, as if for fine-tuning the view. A big table in the center of the room was spread with maps and drawing paper. Pencils and inkstands and broken pen nibs were scattered around instruments that looked like they were for navigation. Emilie thought she recognized a sextant, from the same book with the drawings of telescopes, but the rest were a mystery.

Professor Abindon went immediately to the telescope and looked through the eyepiece. She straightened up and carefully adjusted some knobs. She beckoned Daniel over. "Look here."

Emilie hadn't thought there was much point to using telescopes in the daylight. But Daniel didn't object, going immediately to peer through the eyepiece. He said, "What am I looking at, Professor?"

"Nothing, yet." Professor Abindon took one of the plates attached to the telescope and turned it upright. Emilie saw the silvery stuff running through glass insets on the metal plate and realized it was a device for viewing aether. *An aetheric telescope?* she wondered, taking an involuntary step forward. She had known there were aether currents in the air, just like there were in the sea, but she hadn't thought about what the devices for detecting them might look like. And did the aetheric streams in the air lead to another world, like the aetheric streams in the seas? Emilie's heart started to pound in excitement.

Suddenly the professor's claim of something urgent to show to Dr. Marlende began to seem far more worrisome.

The professor slid the plate into a slot in the telescope, made another adjustment, and Daniel gasped. "How long has it been there?"

The professor's voice was grim. "I first noticed it twenty-two days ago. It was much smaller then." She pushed her hair back from her face in an exasperated gesture. "I should have gone to Meneport then, instead of just sending a wire. But it's been getting steadily larger. I kept expecting it to stop."

Daniel straightened up and motioned Emilie over. She hurried forward and leaned down to the eyepiece, trying to look as if she knew what she was doing. Fortunately it was fairly straightforward, and she found the right angle to see through the glass lens without much trouble.

She saw intense blue sky, and in the center, a ring of brilliant colors— reds, greens, deeper blues than the sky—with a silver-white spiral woven through. A description of it would have sounded like something rather beautiful, rather like the description of lines of dark storm clouds against the sky sounded beautiful, until the hail and wind started. Emilie stood up and stared at the professor. "It looks like a hole."

"That's because it is a hole," the professor said. "It's an opening in an aetheric stream."

"But why would that happen?" Emilie said. She wasn't sure if that was a stupid question or not, but the hole didn't look like something that was supposed to happen. It looked wrong, strange, threatening.

"That's what we'd like to know," Daniel said, leaning down for another look through the eyepiece.

"Yes," Professor Abindon said. "There are a number of possible reasons I can think of, none of them good. But the one I'm rather afraid of is that it's opening because something is making it open. Something is out there, pushing its way through to our world."

CHAPTER TWO

Late that afternoon, Emilie, Daniel, and Professor Abindon boarded the fast steamer for Meneport. Daniel thought they would arrive some hours behind the Marlendes.

In a highly agitated conversation that morning, Daniel had convinced the professor that they could reach the Marlendes more quickly by going directly to Meneport themselves. Daniel had pointed out that the Marlendes were likely to spend all day today at the airyard with the damaged airship. And Emilie had thought, though she didn't say it aloud, that if Miss Marlende had been ignoring the professor's wires, she wasn't likely to bring them immediately to her father's attention once they reached their home again. Obviously there was some sort of disagreement or sore point between Professor Abindon and Miss Marlende.

Emilie had suggested that they could send a wire directly to Lord Engal, who was likely to have secretaries and so on who would bring it quickly to his attention.

Professor Abindon had glared at her. "You want us to send a wire to Lord Engal to tell him to tell Marlende to read his mail?"

"Yes," Emilie replied. "Why not?" Emilie was torn between the feeling that she should be showing more respect for the professor, and the feeling that she wasn't particularly in the mood to be spoken sharply to for what was a perfectly valid idea. It made her miss Rani more than she already did.

"Hmm," the professor had said, eyeing her again.

But in the end they had decided it was best to deliver the news in person, not least because then they would also be able to deliver the extensive notes and drawings that the professor had made, chronicling the aetheric disruption's first appearance and progress. "Aetheric disruption" was what the professor had told Emilie to call it after Emilie had referred to it as a sky hole. Apparently that sounded rude, though Emilie hadn't figured out why yet.

Emilie and Daniel had gone to Karthea's house to pack their belongings. Emilie hadn't explained to Karthea about the aetheric disruption, mainly because every explanation she rehearsed as they walked back to the house had sounded alarmist at best. The professor wasn't even sure it was something they needed to worry about yet, though she seemed to feel that worrying about it was the best course. So Emilie had just said that the professor needed to speak to Dr. Marlende urgently and had missed him when he was in town, and that they were going to escort her to Meneport, and that Emilie would write as soon as she had a chance.

By the time they reached the port to meet the professor, Daniel had the idea to send a wire directly to the office of the docks where the Marlendes would take the airship. It might not be delivered before they arrived, but it was worth a try, and they were sure to reach Dr. Marlende more quickly if he knew they were coming.

While Daniel was busy, Emilie took the money he had given her and purchased three passages on the steamer, something she had never done before. She considered it her first act as Miss Marlende's assistant that didn't involve being shot at.

This was a fast steamer and they should arrive at Meneport sometime late that night, so they hadn't bothered with a cabin. On the second deck of the steamer, there was a large glassed-in space with upholstered benches for seating. Daniel was ensconced on one with their bags, reading through one of the notebooks Professor Abindon had brought.

Emilie was too restless to sit down, and went out on deck to stand at the railing. They were leaving the harbor, the cliffs turned golden by the afternoon sun. The wind was cool and refreshing, the sky blue and dotted with white clouds. Emilie leaned on the railing and watched the coast go by, feeling the now-familiar chug of the engines through the deck boards. There were gray stone houses in the little pockets of green fields in between the cliffs, with narrow sandy beaches at their feet. Sailing boats and a small tug clung close to the shore, avoiding the path of the larger steamer.

Professor Abindon moved up to stand at the railing beside her. After a moment, the professor said, "Daniel looks tired."

"He hasn't had much time to recover," Emilie said, and realized neither had she. Only a few days ago they had been fighting for their lives, and now they were eating dinner with Karthea and buying steamer passages and worrying about what the newspapers printed about them. Even with the aetheric disruption to be concerned about, it didn't seem real.

"I suppose . . ." The professor's gloved hands tightened on the railing. She seemed to change her mind about what she had intended to say. "Vale was well, when you left her?"

"Yes, very well. Oh, she was tired. So was Dr. Marlende." Emilie realized then what the professor wanted to ask. *She was upset when she found out that Miss Marlende hadn't answered any of her wires.* And Miss Marlende must not have bothered to open any of them, or she would have surely taken a moment to reply. The professor and Miss Marlende must have quarreled about something fairly serious. Emilie tried to explain her position without implying that she suspected there had been an argument. "I wasn't her assistant until after we got to Silk Harbor. I mean, I wasn't there when she and Kenar were trying to find a way to get to the aetheric stream, when they went to Lord Engal for help. So . . . I really don't know anything about that." She winced, having the feeling she had just made the whole thing all that much more awkward.

From the disgruntled expression on the professor's face, she apparently agreed. Professor Abindon said, under her breath, "Well, we'll see when we get there."

*   *   *

They arrived late that night. Emilie had gone inside to doze on one of the benches, but woke in time to watch from the deck as the ship approached the port.

Mist drifted across the water, but she could see the gas and electric lights of the city sparking in the darkness like low-lying stars, hinting at the shapes of buildings and the presence of streets. She hadn't seen this before, the *Sovereign*'s departure having been far too abrupt to enjoy the view.

Closer, misty lights marked ships floating at anchor, or sitting at their docks, passenger steamships and cargo vessels, and a few big sailing ships that were probably yachts belonging to nobles or other rich families. Some of the docks were dark, but others were brightly lit, as ships were loaded with cargo or supplies or allowed passengers to board for an early-morning sailing.

The dock the steamer was headed for was brightly lit by gas lamps, with some figures standing around it waiting for the ship to arrive.

Emilie smothered a yawn. She was a little hungry, too. The steamer's steward hadn't served an actual dinner, and the sandwiches and tea provided hadn't been nearly as filling as last night's meal.

Daniel and the professor arrived then, carrying their bags. Like Daniel and Emilie, the professor hadn't brought much more than an overnight bag, though in Emilie and Daniel's case, this was because they didn't have many belongings with them. Everything Emilie hadn't posted to Karthea had been left behind at her uncle's house.

As the ship closed in on the dock, it slowed down and its engines changed in pitch. It wasn't big enough to need a tug to push it in, though the process of edging up to the dock seemed tricky. There was a stir of activity on the lowest deck, and someone called out to the shoremen.

"There's a coach," Daniel said suddenly. He pointed to the stretch of roadway between the docks and the cargo offices. A few small one-horse cabs waited there for the arriving passengers, and among them was a larger coach-and-four. "Maybe they did get my wire . . . Yes, that's Lord Engal's crest on the door, I'm sure of it!"

Professor Abindon muttered, "Oh, joy."

Emilie, caught by surprise, snorted with amusement, then turned it into a cough.

The ship came to rest against the dock, and after a little delay, the passengers began to disembark. Emilie, Daniel, and the professor followed the others down the gangway. Professor Abindon took the lead, striding through the sleepy, milling crowd to the end of the dock.

The liveried driver stood at the lead horses' heads, and Emilie expected him to step forward to greet them. But the coach door swung open and a tall figure stepped out. It was Lord Engal himself. He was Southern Menaen, with brown skin and dark eyes, contrasting against his gray hair and beard, and despite being a noble, he was burly and strong, built like one of the shoremen unloading cargo.

He said, "Miss Emilie, Daniel, I'm glad your ship arrived on . . . Good God, you didn't say she was coming."

"I'm just as pleased to see you, Engal," the professor said, her tone grim. "Now let's get on with this. Where's Marlende?"

"He's at the airship dock," Lord Engal said, and stepped warily back, holding the coach door open for the professor. Another coachman swung down from the box to take their bags and hand them up to be stowed on top.

Emilie climbed into the coach after Professor Abindon, and sat next to her on the soft leather seat. She could tell the coach was nicer than any she had ever been in before, though it was hard to see the interior with only the light from the dockside to illuminate it. The inside walls were padded with dark rich fabric and it smelled of sandalwood.

Lord Engal climbed in after Daniel, and tapped his cane on the roof to signal the coachman to go. He said, "What's this about an aetheric disruption?"

Daniel drew breath to speak but the professor said first, "I prefer to wait until we meet with Marlende. I don't want to have to go over it all twice." Then she ruined it by adding, "If you don't understand it, then he can explain it to you."

It was so rude, Emilie had to bite her tongue. Lord Engal could be annoying, but all he had done was ask a simple question, even if it didn't have a simple answer. It was a little easier to understand now why Miss Marlende hadn't answered the professor's wires.

Lord Engal sighed and said, "I see. Thank you for excusing my no doubt abysmal ignorance."

Emilie spent most of the short trip looking out the window, watching the dark warehouses and shipping offices go by. She recognized the long-necked shape of the big steam crane, like a monster rising out of the mist, that she had passed when she had been looking for the *Merry Bell*'s slip. That helped her orient herself.

The coach turned up a broad street leading away from the port. Infrequent gas streetlamps lit the signs above doorways, and most of the buildings seemed to be small manufactories or ship chandlers. Then the coach turned off to stop at a large metal gate in a wall. A moment later, a man with a lantern swung the gate open and they rolled forward into Dr. Marlende's airship yard.

From the coach window, all Emilie could see was a couple of metal-roofed sheds, lit by electric lamps mounted on tall posts. Dr. Marlende had obviously had the yard fitted with all the latest scientific devices, including electric light.

Lord Engal pushed the door open and swung out before his servant could get off the box, and held it open as they climbed out. As Emilie stepped down, she saw what the electric lights were illuminating.

In the middle of the walled yard, towering over them, the giant silver shape of an airship hung about twenty feet above the ground. Its nose was securely held in a big cone-shaped stand, and lines and heavy cables anchored it to the ground. The wooden cabin, with the narrow metal walkway around the outside, was tucked up under the gray swell of the balloon. Emilie could tell immediately that this wasn't the airship that they had returned in from the Hollow World; it showed no signs of damage, for one thing. For another, she was fairly certain it was much bigger, its cabin nearly twice as long and with at least two levels to it.

Then she spotted their airship, lying some distance past this one, its balloon partially deflated and the triangular supports that held the insides rigid showing through the fabric. Emilie knew that the airship's balloon wasn't just a big bag filled with gas, but a cover over lots of smaller bags, held in place with very light metal supports. Watching Lord Ivers' airship burn had been very instructive in teaching her airship anatomy. The battered cabin sat beside it, no longer connected to the upper structure. Men in work clothes were climbing all over it, taking it apart and carrying the pieces into a larger metal shed.

Lord Engal strode off across the yard and Emilie and Daniel hurried after him. The professor followed as well, but at her own pace.

They reached the shed and Lord Engal flung open the wooden door and shouted, "Marlende, they're here!"

Dr. Marlende, wearing a long coat dotted with oil stains and heavy protective gloves, stood beside a table spread with plans. Turning toward them, he said, "Thank you, Lord Engal, but I assure you that there is nothing wrong with my hearing and shouting is not . . ." He froze for a moment. "Abindon. I didn't realize—"

"That I was coming, yes, I know." The professor's voice was dry. "Is Vale here? I'd rather not go over this twice."

Dr. Marlende cleared his throat, regaining his composure. He was a tall, fair-skinned, weathered Northern Menaen man, with shaggy gray hair and a beard that was still somewhat out of control after his adventures in the Hollow World. "She's dismantling the steering control column in the airship."

"I'll get her," Emilie said, and bolted before anyone could argue.

She crossed the open yard to the airship and climbed the stepladder up to the cabin doorway. An electric light on a heavy cable hung from the ceiling, and the floor was covered with broken glass and more oil stains. Emilie picked her way across the floor to the open door into the cockpit.

She saw Miss Marlende's boots first, as the rest of her was tucked under the control panel working on the pillar that held up the steering mechanism. "Miss Marlende?"

"Emilie?" Miss Marlende pushed herself out from under the panel and sat up. "Father said you and Daniel were coming back tonight, that there was some emergency. Is everything all right?"

Emilie crouched on the floor so they were at eye level. "Yes, we're fine, but there was a scientific discovery, about an aetheric stream, and . . . Professor Abindon is here."

Miss Marlende didn't look as shocked as the others, but she frowned. "Abindon?" she demanded. "What is she doing here?"

"It was her discovery. She tried to send Dr. Marlende some wires about it, but it was after he left on the expedition, when you and Kenar were trying to find a way to help him and all the others, and you didn't get them."

Miss Marlende pulled her heavy gloves off and pushed her hair out of her face. She normally wore it in a tight bun behind her head, but it had come loose and, from the dark spots on the blond strands, gotten into the oil. She looked frustrated and upset more than angry. "Damn it. I did get them, but I didn't open them. I thought they were about . . . Oh, never mind. Was it terribly urgent?"

"Sort of. I don't think it was at first, but it kept getting worse. I thought . . ." Emilie hesitated, then finished, "If she really thought it was that urgent, she could have come here herself to make someone listen to her."

"Well, yes, that's what a rational person would have done," Miss Marlende said, then made a sharp gesture. "I shouldn't judge her, I suppose. It's a very complicated situation. And I've done my share of complicating it, so I can't complain." She caught the railing along the control board and pulled herself upright.

Emilie pushed to her feet. "Was she your teacher? I mean, your professor at university?"

"No. She's . . . a relation," Miss Marlende said, and stepped past Emilie out of the cockpit.

Emilie followed, thinking that one over. It certainly explained a lot, if the professor wasn't just an irascible colleague, but a relation. She knew how much trouble relations could be.

When they reached the shed, the table had been cleared of airship plans and Professor Abindon's drawings and notes were laid out in their place.

The professor looked up as they came in. Her expression was as closed and hard to read as Miss Marlende's. She said, "Vale."

Miss Marlende said, "Professor Abindon."

The professor's lips tightened, as if the greeting had been other than bland and polite. But she indicated the drawings. "I've been trying to bring this to your attention. I understand you were occupied."

It was all very uncomfortable.

It was a relief when Lord Engal, already engrossed in the notes, said, "Dear God, Marlende. Is this what I think it is?"

"An aetheric disruption, obviously," Dr. Marlende said, passing a page of notes to Miss Marlende. "But what could be causing it." He eyed the professor. "Your last observation was yesterday?"

The professor was watching Miss Marlende for her reaction. "Yes, before Daniel suggested we should come here. What do you think, Vale?"

There were lines in Miss Marlende's brow, but this time they were from concentration. "We need a better aetheric scope." She turned to Lord Engal. "Do you think you could get us into the Philosophical Society?"

"It's after midnight," Daniel said. "No one will be there to let us in. We could make an appointment in the morning . . ."

Dr. Marlende scratched his chin thoughtfully. "I'm sure I could open the lock on the front entrance. Emilie, see if someone can find my small pocket toolcase . . ."

"Father . . ." Miss Marlende began. "Breaking into the building isn't—"

"Commendable resolve but unnecessary." Lord Engal tugged his pocket watch out and checked the time. "I can send someone to get the director to meet us there and let us in. He enjoys noble patronage and late parties, so I doubt he will mind."

The professor gave him a skeptical look. "Surely you don't care if he minds? As long as the person inconvenienced isn't you—"

"We all sacrifice in the name of philosophy," Lord Engal said, and strode off, calling for his servants.

* * *

Less than an hour later, Emilie was in the Marlendes' coach, with Dr. and Miss Marlende, following Lord Engal's equipage down a wide gas-lit street. The Marlendes' coach was battered, the upholstery well-worn cloth, and the coachman was one of Dr. Marlende's airship mechanics.

Dr. Marlende had one of Professor Abindon's notebooks, holding it up to the window and trying to angle it so the intermittent gaslight fell on the pages. He said to Miss Marlende, "Even if you had opened her wires, there wasn't anything you could have done about it except to observe the situation while it developed, an activity which she was already engaged in."

Miss Marlende kept her gaze on the window. "That's not an excuse."

"It is an excuse," Dr. Marlende said mildly.

Emilie had her face almost plastered to the window on her side, trying to catch glimpses of the stone façades and pillared porticos of the buildings. She knew most of them were very fine houses, the family seats of various noble families. She had seen the houses of the wealthy gentry who lived near their village, and even gone to parties in some of them, but they were nothing compared to this. She couldn't quite believe people actually lived in these houses, or how much money they must have. *It seems such a waste,* she thought. At least Lord Engal spent some of his money on experiments and expeditions and, apparently, suing newspapers on behalf of strangers.

Ahead, Lord Engal's coach swung into the carriage circle in front of yet another imposing building, with columns two stories high fronting a wide portico with steps leading up to the entrance. Gas lamps on stands of twisted wrought iron lit the walk in front of it.

As they climbed out of the coaches, Emilie saw two men waiting by the carved wooden doors, one in Lord Engal's livery and the other in a slightly disheveled suit, as if he had donned it hastily. The doors were carved with figures of old sailing ships and views of Meneport Harbor. Not what Emilie had been expecting for the Philosophical Society, but maybe the place had been purchased or donated, and not specifically built.

"Lord Engal," the disheveled man began, "surely you realize the aetheric telescope can also be used in daylight—"

"Of course we realize that, Elathorn," Lord Engal said. "But we need to look through the damn thing now. Be a good fellow and unlock the doors."

Mr. Elathorn sighed with weary resignation, took out a large key ring, and unlocked the heavy wooden door. It opened into a dark foyer, illumined only by what little light fell through the doorway.

Mr. Elathorn stepped inside and Emilie followed with the others, bumping into Miss Marlende in the process. She could feel a tile floor under her boots and the walls were covered with more heavy carving, though she couldn't tell what the subject was. Mr. Elathorn unlocked the inner doors with a different key, and pushed them open. Emilie peered into the darkness. She had the impression the doors had opened into a large hall; something in the faintly cool air seemed to suggest a large space, but she couldn't see a thing.

She thought they might have to light lamps if the gas was turned off for the night, but Mr. Elathorn turned to the wall of the foyer and unlocked a small cabinet, fumbling in the dark. Lord Engal helpfully struck a match, holding it up so Elathorn could see.

"Thank you, my lord," Elathorn muttered. The cabinet was full of small metal levers. Elathorn pushed two down and then pushed a switch.

Clicks and a buzz echoed through the space, then electric lights flickered into blazing life all through the hall. Emilie smiled in delight. *This is more like it.*

The grand entrance hall was huge, with a massive polished stone staircase at the far end. The walls were lined with exhibits, some in glass cases and some freestanding. Light gleamed off all sorts of engines and devices, with glass bulbs, brass and silver tubes, switches, levers, and dials. There were glass cases with maps, models of steamships and airships. The electric lights on the walls were in large bronze sconces, with milky glass shielding the glowing bulbs. There were also lights set directly into the walls, between where the wooden paneling ended and the plaster facing began.

Lord Engal took the key ring and said, "That's all, Elathorn. Go home and get some sleep," and he, Dr. Marlende, and Professor Abindon headed for the stairs.

Mr. Elathorn sighed again and said, "I'll wait down here."

"Our apologies, Mr. Elathorn, and thank you for coming out here so late," Miss Marlende said, as she, Daniel, and Emilie hurried after the others.

Emilie craned her neck to see as many of the exhibits as she could as they crossed the hall. Daniel noticed and said, "We'll have to come back on a day when it's open for viewing."

"Emilie should have more than enough chances to see it all," Miss Marlende said. "We'll be planning a whole lecture series on the expedition." She nodded toward the doors in the wall past the stairs. "The main assembly hall is there, and there are smaller meeting rooms and lecture halls on the upper floors. This was a shipping magnate's mansion when it was first built. He bequeathed it to the Society more than fifty years ago, and it's been modified a great deal since then."

They started up the stairs, and continued up and up. On the third floor, they turned off through a wide hallway lined with more doors, where they had to stop along the way and look for more switches to turn on the electric lights. After several twists and turns, they went through a door into another, much smaller and more utilitarian stairwell.

The lights were less frequent here, the walls plain plaster and the wooden treads of the stairs not nearly as finely grained; this must have been a stair to the servants' quarters, back when the house had been a wealthy man's home.

They reached a door at the top of the stairs and Lord Engal selected another key off the ring to unlock it. Emilie followed the others in, staring as the electric lights popped into life. They were in a large square turret, possibly toward the back of the big house, though when they had been out on the street, Emilie had been too busy looking at the front entrance to glance up.

In the middle of the room was an aetheric scope that made the professor's look like a toy or a small-scale model. The whole was mounted on a big circular platform and the scope itself was as big as a cannon. It pointed up toward the peaked roof, which had been replaced by glass panels. Several big silver plates stood out from the base of the scope at various angles, designed to show patterns in aether.

The others immediately closed in around the telescope, Dr. Marlende and the professor in the lead. Emilie found a chair near the wall and sat down. There wasn't anything she could do to help with this part, and she was starting to realize just how tired she was. She wished she had been able to sleep more on the boat.

After a short flurry of adjustments with everyone but Emilie weighing in with a conflicting opinion, the telescope was positioned and the aetheric plates were moved in front of the lens. Dr. Marlende peered through the eyepiece. "Yes, there we are. I—" He stopped abruptly.

Emilie found herself holding her breath. Everyone waited in silence, though Daniel stirred uneasily, Lord Engal's left eyelid started to twitch, and Miss Marlende's grip on the platform's railing made her knuckles go white. Finally Professor Abindon said, "For God's sake, Marlende, what do you see?"

He straightened up, his expression deeply worried. Emilie felt a sinking sensation. She hadn't seen Dr. Marlende look this worried when they were trying to escape to the airship while being shot at by angry merpeople. He ignored Lord Engal's impatient throat-clearing noise and gestured Professor Abindon forward. He said, "I'd rather not say until I get another opinion."

Frowning, the professor stepped up and bent down to the eyepiece. "Another opinion on what? I—"

It was her turn to freeze. After a moment, she stood up and said, "It's a vessel."

Dr. Marlende let his breath out in a sharp sigh, as if he had been holding it. "I concur."

Daniel's expression was somewhere between horrified and incredulous. "What kind of vessel? An airship?"

"Something like," Dr. Marlende said. "The shape is similar."

"A vessel?" Lord Engal burst out. "But how? Even if such a craft launched into the aetheric stream from the other side of the world, we would have seen it making its way up—"

No, Emilie thought, her heart pounding, *that's not what he means.*

"That's not what they mean," Miss Marlende interrupted. "It's a vessel, but it came from the other end of the aetheric stream."

"The other end," Lord Engal repeated. "But that's . . . not impossible, I suppose."

"It's the only thing that makes sense," Miss Marlende said.

Emilie couldn't contain herself. "So it's people from another aetheric plane, coming to discover us, like Dr. Marlende discovered the Hollow World?"

"Yes," Dr. Marlende said. "They could be very much like us. Or very different indeed."

CHAPTER THREE

The next several hours passed in a whirlwind of activity. Lord Engal rushed off to find the nearest telegraph office and send a flurry of wires. Miss Marlende and Daniel followed to make sure he sent wires to everyone Dr. Marlende and Professor Abindon thought should be notified. Emilie, wide awake now, took notes for them as they made further observations with the telescope, writing down directions and rows of numbers. After a short time, more people started to arrive, men and quite a number of women, all natural philosophers, aetheric scholars, or engineers.

They entered the chamber, often disheveled and in one case still wearing a dressing gown, looked into the telescope, and then retired to join one of the many groups having low-voiced, worried conversations.

At first Emilie's head was almost spinning. She wasn't sure whether she wanted to run into the street yelling a warning, or hide under the bench. Were they actually being invaded? *Please let it be a friendly explorer.* Invasions were something that happened in books, to made-up countries. The last invasion she had read about in the history books had happened to a small country called Tuthari, far to the east. A fleet of pirates had invaded their archipelago, and had been driven off by their ships and the other traders that had been in port at the time, including two Menaen steamers.

The idea of an invasion by strange people in airships was terrifying. It certainly put the whole "Uncle Yeric seeing your name in the newspapers" episode into perspective. Emilie began to look fondly back on the time when that was all she had to worry about.

She reminded herself not to panic yet. *There's plenty of time to panic later,* she thought.

As the sky past the big windows started to lighten, a man in a very sober suit came in to speak quietly to Dr. Marlende and Professor Abindon. Emilie was close enough to hear him say, "Lord Engal has called a meeting of the Society in the main lecture hall. He wanted you to go over your findings briefly, if you could." He added, "Dr. Amalus, advisor to the Ministry and the Ruling Council, is in attendance. He expects to give a report to them based on, well, your report to him."

Dr. Marlende and Professor Abindon exchanged a dark look. She said, "Isn't this premature?"

"That rather depends, doesn't it?" Dr. Marlende answered grimly.

She took a deep breath. "Yes, of course."

They started downstairs, most of the others present following them. Emilie found her way through the crowd and trailed behind Miss Marlende. At the bottom of the stairs, Daniel fetched up beside them. There were still more people down here, milling around, though most had taken more care with their dress than the earlier arrivals.

Emilie thought Miss Marlende would follow Dr. Marlende and the professor into the lecture hall, but instead she took Emilie's sleeve and directed them both toward the open front doors. Daniel followed them.

As they stepped outside, the cool predawn air was like a welcome dash of cold water. A coach with the Ministry's crest emblazoned on the door was just drawing up in front of the building. Miss Marlende watched it thoughtfully, and said, "Let's take a break, shall we?"

* * *

They ended up in a bakery down a nearby side street, open earlier than anything else so it could supply fresh bread to the other eating establishments. It had tables in its back courtyard and also served tea. With a napkin full of breakfast rolls and a big mug of tea in her stomach, Emilie started to feel less confused and panicky. *Maybe I'm not terrified, maybe I'm just hungry,* she thought. Or maybe she had just had a little time to get used to the whole idea. Around a mouthful of roll, she asked Miss Marlende, "Why aren't you at the meeting?"

Miss Marlende stirred her tea, her brow set in a worried frown. "I know what they're going to say."

Daniel held his tea under his nose as if it were smelling salts and he was trying to revive himself. The steam made his eyeglasses cloud over. "Dr. Marlende thinks we should go up for a better look?"

Miss Marlende nodded. "It's the only thing we can do, at this point."

"Up in an airship?" Emilie asked, then realized what a stupid question it was. *No, up in a tugboat, Emilie, what do you think?* But the others were so tired all they did was nod soberly. "Have you ever done it before? I mean, in an aetheric current, not just the air."

"Yes, we've explored two of the major aether currents above Menae," Miss Marlende explained. "Father became more interested in the below-sea currents because the signs that they led to another aetheric plane were so intriguing. We didn't see any such signs in the air currents. As far as I know, no one ever has." She took a long drink of her tea. "Perhaps we just didn't look hard enough."

Daniel shook his head. "There isn't as much interest in airship travel in general. It's very dangerous. There have been at least two airship aether-current expeditions that ended in disaster. One crashed and one was never seen again."

The bad storms that plagued the seas along the best trade routes were dangerous for airships. Ships navigating via surface aether currents had always been safer and more efficient, so airships weren't popular, even for relatively safe travel between the mainland and the coastal islands. They had been mostly used as pleasure craft over land. Emilie said, "So no one really knows what's in the aetheric currents up there. I suppose because we can see the sky, we just assumed there's nothing past it." She followed that thought for a moment. "Just like everyone in the Hollow World assumed there was nothing above them."

Daniel cleared his throat. "Isn't there an old, discredited theory, that the world—the aetherverse—is a series of concentric circles?"

Emilie had seen some mention of that in a book somewhere, but hadn't paid it much attention. She had been mostly reading for the adventure stories of exploration, not the speculation on aetheric structures. But she remembered the picture that had accompanied it, all different circles, stretching out into infinity. Their world, this world, had been labeled the "surface world" and had been shown on top. "This means that theory is right, but we aren't the surface world," Emilie said. "We're not on top, we're just one of the circles."

"Yes, it's been a theory for a long time," Miss Marlende admitted.

She sipped her tea and added, "Apparently it's on its way to becoming a fact."

They started back to the Philosophical Society, and as they turned a corner to the street Emilie saw a small crowd milling in front of the building. Some clutched notebooks and pencils and were probably journalists, others just looked like confused passersby who had seen something was happening and had stopped to find out what it was. A few early peddlers had gathered on the outskirts, and a vegetable cart on its way to the open market had stopped along the curb and appeared to be trying to take advantage of the unexpected crowd.

As they approached the building, a man suddenly turned toward them out of the fringe of the crowd and rushed toward Miss Marlende.

His face was tight with fury and Emilie reacted before she quite knew what she was doing. As Daniel stepped in front of Miss Marlende, Emilie dodged sideways toward the vegetable cart and snatched up a hard-shelled melon. She braced to throw it at the man's head.

"Stop!" Miss Marlende held up her hands. "It's all right, Emilie, Daniel."

The man jerked to a halt in front of Miss Marlende and demanded, "Is it true?"

Miss Marlende gently pushed Daniel aside and said, "It is, but it isn't them. It's a strange craft."

Emilie set the melon back on the cart with an apologetic nod to the startled vendor. Her reflexes seemed to be still tuned to the Hollow World and at some point snatching up a potential weapon had become more natural to her than screaming or running.

Emilie had time to notice that the man really didn't look much like a ruffian at all. Though, of course, neither had Lord Ivers. He was young, maybe no more than twenty-five or so. His clothes were well-tailored and his tightly curled hair was carefully cut, but there was something about him which suggested that he wasn't well. His light brown skin was a little dull, his coat and jacket hanging on knobby shoulders as if he was normally slim but had also lost weight.

The man glanced at Emilie and Daniel with an impatient grimace, then faced Miss Marlende again. "Are you going up?"

Miss Marlende said, "Probably."

He nodded sharply with a brief expression of relief. "You'll look for them."

"Mr. Deverrin . . ." Miss Marlende's face was a mix of frustration and pity. "They are all dead. Surely you must know that."

He set his jaw stubbornly. "And you and I both know that means nothing. Especially after the trip you've just returned from."

Miss Marlende said, patiently, "Even if they were in a current that . . . led somewhere, there is little chance that after all this time—"

"Little chance is not no chance." He turned abruptly and strode away to shoulder through the crowd.

Miss Marlende let her breath out and rubbed her forehead. "That was unpleasant."

Emilie demanded, "Who was that?"

"Anton Deverrin. His father, Dr. Deverrin, led the second airship aether-current expedition, the one that Daniel mentioned. The one that was never seen again." Miss Marlende shook her head. "It was last year. There was a sudden storm, with a great disturbance in the aether, the day after they launched. There was no sign of the airship after that. There were twelve people aboard, including Anton's brother, sister, and two cousins, as well as his father. His mother and the other members of the family threw all their efforts and their family fortune into searching for them. It ruined them, eventually. They wanted my father to mount an expedition in search of them, but . . ."

Emilie winced. She could glimpse the scene beyond Miss Marlende's brief description: the grief and hope and desperation of a family suddenly ripped apart. No wonder the young man still looked ill. "But Dr. Marlende thought they were dead."

"Yes," Miss Marlende admitted. "We—and everyone else—thought the airship must have been torn apart over the sea. Lord Engal and some of the other explorers with steamers searched the area for survivors for days afterward, but they never even found a sign of any debris."

Emilie hesitated. "But now . . ."

Daniel's thoughts must have been moving along the same line. He said, "Maybe we were all wrong."

"Yes. In light of this new information, we could have been." Miss Marlende bit her lip. "But it's been more than a year. I don't want to get his hopes up. Even if they were trapped somewhere, it may be too late by now."

"Maybe they were lucky," Emilie said. "Maybe they found nice people like the Cirathi, who helped them."

Miss Marlende gave her a sad and somewhat ironic smile. "You usually aren't such an optimist, Emilie."

"Well, I'm trying to be better at it." Emilie agreed, though, that there was no use getting the poor man's hopes up. A year was a long time to spend trapped or adventuring in aether currents without getting killed. Their trip to the Hollow World had proved that.

Daniel didn't look hopeful either. "But if the air currents are like the sea currents, we still couldn't find them unless we knew where they left their current." He looked toward the crowd the young man had disappeared into. "I agree, we certainly can't make him any promises."

Emilie realized they had all made a rather important assumption. "So are we going up in an air aether current to look at the strange craft, then?"

"I would say there is an excellent chance of it," Miss Marlende said.

* * *

The meeting was finished by the time they entered the Society building. Coaches were starting to leave, tangling with the early-morning traffic of omnibuses and delivery carts. They found Dr. Marlende and Professor Abindon in the hall with Lord Engal, all surrounded by a small crowd of Society members and other people still discussing the strange object and its implications. Emilie thought the mood was a little less tense. Maybe confronting the problem and discussing it had helped. And if Miss Marlende was right, now they had a plan. Or at least a plan to get more information.

Miss Marlende elbowed her way through the crowd to Dr. Marlende's side, waited until the man he was speaking to took his leave, and then said, "We're going up in the airship, then?"

"Yes," he told her. "It's fortunate the larger craft is airworthy and can be made ready in a short time. If we don't get some idea of what this thing is soon, there could be a panic when the word spreads."

Miss Marlende jerked her head toward the crowd. "And with this lot, the word will definitely spread."

Dr. Marlende turned toward the door. "It was necessary to inform them." As Professor Abindon caught up with them, he continued, "Many of them have small scopes and would start to make their own observations. The professor here is an expert at aetheric interpretation, but the anomaly is growing large enough that amateurs will be able to see it soon."

Professor Abindon snorted. "If you hadn't gone haring off into the subsurface world and gotten stuck, we would have been able to start sooner."

Emilie had noted that natural philosophers seemed big on saying "I told you so." She didn't think it was very helpful in a crisis.

Dr. Marlende gave Abindon a look, but said only, "And I would know a good deal less about the practical difficulties of aether current travel." He told Miss Marlende, "Besides, we had to assemble the Society. We may need their help."

Miss Marlende's expression bordered on the bitter. "They weren't a great deal of help when Kenar and I desperately needed it."

"Did they all support Lord Ivers?" Emilie asked. The inner workings of the Philosophical Society seemed a lot more exciting than she had previously thought.

Miss Marlende said, "Many of them thought that it would have been impossible to retrace Father's route, even though Kenar himself was proof that it was possible. The ones that didn't had no real resources to offer."

Like poor Mr. Deverrin, Emilie thought. But at least in his case the storm had given everyone good reason to think that his family was dead.

Professor Abindon said, "I wish you had come to me. I'm also lacking in those sorts of resources, but at least I could have . . ." She sounded hesitant, which seemed very uncharacteristic of her. "Helped somehow."

"I didn't think you'd care," Miss Marlende said, her voice quite cool.

Emilie saw Daniel wince. Fortunately at that moment, Lord Engal caught up with them. He said, "I've sent for the coaches. I presume we're going back to the airyard immediately?"

Dr. Marlende looked both relieved and exasperated. "I assumed you would stay here and coordinate with the Society."

Lord Engal seemed to find this an astonishing assumption on Dr. Marlende's part. "Of course not. That's what Elathorn is for. If he isn't for things like that, then there's no point in having him."

"I'm sure he would disagree," Miss Marlende said.

"I don't care if he agrees." As they came out of the big double doors into the morning sun, Lord Engal jammed his hat on his head. "This is going to be an historic encounter and I'm certainly not missing it."

* * *

Once they reached the airyard, the rest of the day became a blur of activity. The larger airship that was docked there was technically airworthy, but it had to be completely checked over and prepared for aetheric travel. And the air-producing equipment, similar to what had been used on the *Sovereign,* needed to be installed and brought up to working order. Apparently the air got thinner the higher up you went, and the aether current would be taking them very high. They would need the protective-shield spell and the devices for making breathable air, just as the *Sovereign* had in its voyage through the sea bottom to the Hollow World.

Except it's not really the Hollow World, Emilie reminded herself. *It's just the next step down.* The way they were the next step down for whoever was coming in from above them.

Emilie was introduced to a dozen or so men and a few young women, some of whom worked as Dr. Marlende's mechanics and engineers, and others who were students of aetheric principles. The mechanics and engineers accepted her matter-of-factly, possibly because she was with Miss Marlende and had been on the *Sovereign.* The students stared jealously, probably for exactly the same reasons. She was very relieved to find Seth, Cobbier, and Mikel there. They had been with Dr. Marlende on the Hollow World expedition and she had helped rescue them. They greeted her like an old comrade. When she had first seen them, they had all been quite dirty and scruffy, having been held prisoner for some time. Now they all looked like what they were: advanced scholars of aetheric engineering and philosophy. She wished Charter were here too, but he had been badly wounded in their escape and had been sent home to recuperate.

Once everyone had gathered in the big work shed, Dr. Marlende climbed atop a table and said, "I believe you've all had a chance to hear what we're about to do, and why. We'll leave as soon as we prepare the airship. I've done some calculations and the optimum moment to enter the West-Median aether current is this afternoon shortly after the fourth hour." He glanced around at the group. "I know many of you have volunteered, but we will be taking only a limited crew, comprised of Miss Marlende, Professor Abindon, Daniel, Mikel, Seth, and Cobbier." Behind him, Lord Engal made a throat-clearing noise. Dr. Marlende added, "And Lord Engal."

Emilie felt her heart sink. But then, she had only been on an airship once, and she knew very little about making aetheric observations or navigating aether currents. And everyone who had been chosen had far more practical experience than she did. You would think the others would all realize this as well, but she still heard a good bit of disappointed muttering from those who hadn't been chosen. Emilie thought if she could manage not to stamp her feet and mutter, the others could as well. Dr. Marlende continued, "Now, I appreciate your efforts to work as quickly as possible so that we may launch on time!"

Emilie followed Miss Marlende and was immediately put to work checking supplies and making sure everything on Dr. Marlende's, Lord Engal's, and Professor Abindon's lists was brought aboard. This sounded easy, until they kept changing the lists, and things had to be moved around, checked for their weight, moved around again, and in some cases taken off the airship because they were too heavy and they were taking up room that was needed by something more vital. That meant a lot of writing, crossing things off, asking for clarification, and listening to debates about who got to keep what.

She did have a chance to walk around the airship's gondola, which was nearly twice as large as the one that had been taken to the Hollow World. It had two levels, a lower one with the control and steering cabin, a central living cabin whose crew facilities were mainly cabinets for storage and bench seats, and then the rooms toward the back that held the fuel tanks, the engines, and the various aetheric apparatuses needed to travel the air currents. There was also a small water closet, though from what Emilie understood, no water was involved. The second floor held three large rooms with big glass ports in the walls, all meant to hold telescopes and aetheric devices, and provide room for philosophical observations and experiments.

On one of her errands, Emilie stood and looked out over the view, which at the moment was just of the airyard and the rooftops of the buildings beyond it. *Not this time,* she thought. *But maybe the next.*

Half daydreaming about the possibilities, she went down the little spiral stairs into the main cabin. Dr. Marlende was there checking the contents of one of the cabinets, and there was muted banging and some loud voices from the engine compartments. She went out the doorway and down the gallery stairs, then ran across the gravel yard and into the open doorway of the work shed.

Miss Marlende stood at the chart table, making notes from one of Professor Abindon's drawings. Before Emilie could give her the checked-off list from upstairs, one of the students stepped into the doorway behind her to say, "Miss Emilie? There's two men here to see you."

"I don't know any men," Emilie said, startled. She amended, "That is, I don't know any men who aren't here. Not in this city."

Miss Marlende glanced up. "Is it a journalist?"

The student seemed startled. "Maybe, I didn't think—"

A figure pushed past her into the room, and the bottom dropped out of Emilie's stomach. She gasped in horror. "Uncle Yeric! What are you doing here?"

It was her uncle, not a terrible hallucination. He was a gray-haired, stocky man, his brown skin marked by deep-set lines caused by years of judgmental frowns. He was wearing a very carefully tailored town suit, and didn't look as if he had ridden all night in a coach. She wondered if he had been here in the city already, when the newspaper had pointed him to her location.

As if he had caught Emilie knee-deep in the pond looking for tadpoles, as if there were no one else in earshot, he said, "You've caused a great deal of upset and difficulty, young lady. I hope you're satisfied with it! Now come along away from here."

Emilie's pulse pounded and her face flushed from heat. She was shocked to realize it was from fury, not fear. Well, there was a little bit of fear. Maybe more than a little bit. But it was mostly fury. She said, "How did you find me?"

He seemed taken aback she hadn't followed his orders immediately, then his glare deepened. "I've been searching the town for you since you left, of course. Until I saw that disgraceful mention of you in the newspaper. Now come with me!"

"No." It felt very good to say no to Uncle Yeric. "I work here. As the newspaper said, I'm Miss Marlende's assistant."

Uncle Yeric's lip curled. "Don't spout that nonsense at me. Get your things and come with me at once. We're leaving the city immediately."

"I will not." Emilie felt her hands curl into fists. *Be an adult,* she reminded herself, *not a child.* "I told you, I work here. And you're in-terrupting the preparations for an important expedition—"

"Don't be ridiculous!" He stepped forward, but Miss Marlende stepped forward too.

Her voice hard, she said, "She is stating the facts, sir. I have hired her to be my secretary and personal assistant, and we are in the middle of some very important preparations."

"Secretary!" Uncle Yeric glared. "I don't know what your game is, young woman, but you have no right to play it with my niece. I assure you, she is not some unprotected young unfortunate whom you can do with as you will!"

"What?" Emilie was strangled speechless with outrage. "You . . . You were the one who said I was a—"

Uncle Yeric's face darkened even further and he cut her off. "Emilie, stop this nonsense at once and come away—"

Teeth gritted, Miss Marlende said, "Sir, I assure you we are perfectly respectable scholars here, and my father—"

"You will surrender my niece at—"

The door across the room slammed open and Professor Abindon stood there. She strode forward. Her face and voice were so cold, icy waves practically radiated off her. "This is private property. Leave it immediately or I shall have a constable summoned."

Uncle Yeric stepped back and Professor Abindon stepped forward. He opened his mouth, closed it, then opened it again and said, "And who may you be, madam?"

"I am Professor Abindon of the Menaen Mainland University." She kept walking toward him, and he kept backing away. "I am Miss Marlende's mother, and I deeply, deeply resent the implications you have made about her. Leave at once, and you may wait for my solicitor to bring an accusation of abuse of character against you."

Professor Abindon is Miss Marlende's mother, Emilie thought, stunned. *Estranged mother.* Then *That explains a lot.* The awkwardness between Abindon and Dr. Marlende. The reason why Miss Marlende had ignored Professor Abindon's wires. She must have thought it was some continuation of a former argument, or an attempt to interfere in her life.

Professor Abindon had backed Uncle Yeric up into the outer door-way and his choices now were either to turn and leave, or to tumble down onto the gravel yard. Or he could start physically fighting with Professor Abindon, which would probably also result in a tumble down onto the gravel yard. He sputtered and said, "This isn't . . . I'll be back with a constable!"

As he retreated, Professor Abindon called after him, "Do that. It will be convenient when I have you taken in charge for trespassing!" She turned away, dusting her hands off. "Is that loud, tiresome person really your uncle?"

"Yes." Emilie took a deep breath.

Lord Engal came out of the back room, clutching a rolled-up sheath of papers. "What in the blazes was all that noise? Was it a journalist? Get his name and I'll summon my solicitor."

"No, it wasn't a journalist." Miss Marlende cut him off impatiently. "Emilie, are you all right?"

"Yes." She wasn't, but she didn't have time to be upset now. "I didn't think he'd come to Meneport after me. I thought they would assume I was hiding in the neighborhood. I thought at worst they would write to Silk Harbor, to bother my cousin." Someone must have seen her making her way along the road, and told Uncle Yeric. She remembered the student had said there were two men and she stepped to the doorway to look out. The sight made her set her jaw. Uncle Yeric stood in the yard with her younger brother Efrain. *Traitor*, she thought. Coming here to help Uncle Yeric carry her away like a prisoner. *I don't like him anymore either, but I wouldn't turn on him like this.* Emilie had always gotten on with her brothers, up until Erin, the oldest, had left to join the merchant navy. After that the two youngest had seemed to blame Emilie for the fact that he had taken her into his confidence before he left. They had sided with Uncle Yeric in every argument, and seemed to completely take on his opinion of Emilie, even though they had to know better. "One of my brothers is with him."

Miss Marlende stepped to her side to look too. Emilie saw Uncle Yeric stomp away, leaving Efrain standing in the yard. Emilie said, "He must be going for a constable." The professor's bluff hadn't worked. She turned to Miss Marlende. "I'll have to leave before you all do. Sneak away and hide until you get back. Otherwise, when the airship takes off, they'll drag me home. They'll tell the constable I'm a vagrant, or morally compromised, or something." Emilie bit her lip and made herself take a deep breath. After all, she wasn't friendless and moneyless anymore. She hadn't spent any of the pay Miss Marlende had given her in Silk Harbor, and she had more than enough for several days of food and lodging. Though she would need a good suggestion of where she could hide. Uncle Yeric might search for her in hotels or boarding-houses, but there must be a lot of them in the city.

"Morally compromised?" the professor said, startled. "By us? I may have to bring an action against that man."

Lord Engal told her, "You may use one of my solicitors."

Ignoring them, Miss Marlende asked Emilie, "Is he your legal guardian?"

"He was, but when my oldest brother turned nineteen, it switched to him." Emilie had known that Erin had been designated to be their guardian at his majority, since the time she had been old enough to ask about her parents' death and see the papers they had left behind. She had even daydreamed that Erin would get a position somewhere in another town, and she and her other two brothers would live with him in a little cottage. Her aunt and uncle hadn't been nearly so bad back then, but Emilie had still known things would be better if it had just been the four of them. And surely Erin would want to go some-where to make his own life. Well, Erin had, but he had done it more than a year before his majority, when he had run away to be a mer-chant sailor. But it didn't matter where he was, he had turned nineteen several months ago and was still Emilie's legal guardian now. "Uncle Yeric still acts as if he is, but he has no legal right. However, my older brother's in the merchant navy, I don't know where, and there's no one to defend me."

"Is this recorded somewhere?" Miss Marlende asked.

"In the village hall at home." Emilie thought that perhaps Lord Engal's natural inclination was right, maybe there was a legal solution. "I need a solicitor, I think. How much do they cost?"

Miss Marlende started to speak, stopped, frowned, and turned to Lord Engal. "Where's your wife?"

Lord Engal was taken aback, but replied, "She's at our country home with the children. She took them out of town when Ivers started shooting at me. She should be back by tomorrow morning." He fol-lowed Miss Marlende's reasoning and added, "You want someone to take charge of the girl so her family can't remove her without the older brother's consent? Your instincts were quite correct, my wife is obstinate and determined and would have made an excellent ally. But since she is unavailable, perhaps Professor Abindon—"

"No, you're not getting rid of me that easily," Professor Abindon interrupted. She grimaced in frustration and said, "Why not simply bring the girl with us? There's room, and if she doesn't lose her head—"

"Emilie doesn't lose her head," Miss Marlende cut in, her voice so acid even Professor Abindon stopped talking. Miss Marlende turned to Emilie. "Would you do that, Emilie? Come with us?"

Combined relief and excitement made Emilie's knees weak and she lost what little control she had over her mouth. "Yes, of course! I wanted to come all along, but I didn't want to make trouble by insisting—I mean, asking."

"That would be a first," Lord Engal put in.

Professor Abindon glared at him, apparently just on principle, then said, "Well, that's settled."

Lord Engal turned away. "Good. Now if we can get back to work without any more interference from overbearing relatives . . ."

Emilie looked out the doorway again. It struck her suddenly how embarrassing it was for Uncle Yeric to show up like this, throwing accusations around and disrupting everything. Efrain still stood there, looking around a little nervously. Uncle Yeric hadn't returned yet. Emilie had the sudden urge to tell Efrain off. She said, "I'm going to tell him there's no point in standing around out there."

"Careful," Miss Marlende said, watching her worriedly.

Emilie stepped out and strode across the yard toward Efrain. He was younger than her by only a year and a month, and they had the same brown skin and brown eyes, though she didn't think they had ever looked much alike in any other way. She had always looked more like their younger brother, Emery. Efrain was a few finger widths taller than her, and his dark hair was cropped close to the scalp. He was dressed very correctly in his best town suit. He saw her and came forward to meet her. "Emilie—"

She said abruptly, "I'll be on the airship when it leaves, so when Uncle Yeric returns tell him he can't kidnap me."

Efrain stared at her. "Going on the airship . . . What do you mean?"

"What does it sound like I mean? This is part of my job as Miss Marlende's personal assistant. Don't play ignorant, I know you saw the newspaper story."

"I didn't believe it was true!" Efrain still stared at her as if she was mad. "Why would they want you?"

Emilie felt her lips form a sneer. She said, sweetly, "Perhaps they've taken leave of their senses. After all, I'm obviously completely worthless to anyone."

Efrain winced and shook his head slightly. "That isn't what I . . . How long will you be gone?"

"I don't know. As long as it takes. Probably a week or more." Dr. Marlende had said he thought it would only take a few days at most, but Emilie hoped Uncle Yeric would be too cheap to pay for a hotel if he thought it would be several days, and would give up and leave the city.

"But what for?" Efrain glared suspiciously toward the crew who were still loading supplies. "What will they make you do?"

"Make me do?" Emilie had been angry before, stomach-churning and hand-tremblingly angry. Now she felt as if the top of her head had opened up to let the steam out. "You mean sexually?"

"Emilie!" Efrain actually took a step back in horror.

Emilie took a step forward, pushing him to retreat farther, a tactic she had picked up from watching Miss Marlende and Rani and now Professor Abindon, a tactic that she hadn't realized she knew until now. "That is what you mean, isn't it? That there's no possible reason in the world that anyone would want my assistance. That as a useless, pathetic little girl I couldn't take notes or carry things or learn to sail a boat or use a wireless or pilot an airship or be anything except a prostitute, that's it, correct?"

Efrain's mouth hung open but he couldn't seem to get any words out.

Emilie laughed at him. The phrase about some people being able to ladle it out but not take it came to mind. "You're just like Uncle Yeric. Go home and tell each other how right you were about me."

She turned away and started toward the airship's stairs. Daniel stood on the gallery, and had obviously heard the argument. He was facing the other way, shoulders stiff with embarrassment. She heard footsteps crunch on the gravel right before Efrain grabbed her arm. Prepared, she spun and twisted out of his grip so fast he almost fell. Breathing hard, she didn't run. If he wanted a fight, he was going to get one. He was stronger now than he had been when they were children, but

Emilie didn't intend to restrain herself in the matter of eye-gouging, nose-breaking, and throat-punching.

Efrain's expression was too complicated to read. He said, "What do you mean, 'You're just like Uncle Yeric'?"

"Go ask him." Emilie turned away again and reached the stairs, and started up.

She paused on the gallery, taking a deep breath, trying to regain her composure before she went inside. This journey was important and she couldn't let her idiotic family disrupt the preparations any more than they already had. Uncle Yeric had already made her look like a helpless fool in front of everyone. She would have to make that up by being as competent as possible on the trip.

Daniel glanced warily at her, then frowned toward Efrain. "Are you all right?"

"Yes." She saw he was cradling his bad arm, and asked, "Are *you* all right?"

"Huh?" Still staring toward Efrain, he blinked in confusion, then realized she was asking about his injury. He slipped his arm out of the sling and stretched it cautiously. "Oh, yes, I'm fine. Just a little sore from sitting up on the boat all that time."

They stood there a moment. Emilie gritted her teeth. "Is he still there?"

Watching Efrain, Daniel narrowed his eyes. "Yes, he's just standing there."

Emilie swore, too in need of venting to worry about shocking Daniel. She stepped over the seal and through the doorway, and hurried down the narrow passage past the engine compartments toward the hold. As she passed the small chamber where the air-producing apparatus had been installed, the heavy odor of wet plants and earth filled her lungs.

In the hold, one of the students was there checking off the supplies on a sheaf of notepaper. Emilie took it away from her and sent her out rather precipitously, starting on it herself. She finished the list, found three items that were missing, and sent another student to collect them, and to get her bag of belongings from the workroom. Then Cobbier came in to ask her how much she weighed so they could adjust the airship's ballast. This necessitated some changes in the list, and she rechecked the final version again just to be sure. As she was marking off the last item, Seth poked his head in and said, "Are we all finished back here?"

Then he looked at her more closely. "Are you all right?" He was the youngest of the Marlendes' three crew members, tall and slim, with very dark skin and short curly hair. He was a year behind Daniel at the university, though he was studying engineering and not magic or aetheric sorcery.

"Yes, I'm fine, I'm just making certain we've got everything." Emilie didn't know what disaster might fall if they had missed some key item, but she really didn't think they had. She followed Seth forward toward the main cabin. The air compartment smelled even more fragrant and the big turbines that powered the airship's engine hummed quietly.

Miss Marlende was in the main cabin and the door was open into the control area. It was almost as big as the main cabin, with the tri-angular glass port in front, and an array of controls with leather seats placed in front of them. Dr. Marlende was at the controls, with Lord Engal and Professor Abindon standing beside him. Daniel was seated at the wireless station. Or at least, it looked much like the wireless station from the other, smaller airship.

Excitement washed away the lingering sour anger the confronta-tions had left behind, and Emilie tried not to bounce. They were really going! At some more quiet moment, Emilie was going to have to ask Miss Marlende what all the control stations did. If someone shouted at her to do something in an emergency, she wanted to have some idea of what to do and where to do it.

Emilie remembered Professor Abindon and Miss Marlende's rela-tionship, and wondered how awkward things might be between them on the trip. She had been so occupied with her own problems she hadn't even thought about their situation. She couldn't tell if the atmo-sphere was tense and strained, but it seemed like it should be.

Seth told Miss Marlende, "We're ready to lift off."

"Very good." She checked the watch pinned to her vest. "Right on time. Everyone get to their station and we'll go." She stepped through the doorway into the control cabin.

Emilie went to the nearest port. The students and some of the ground crewmen had formed a human barrier in front of the ship, holding back several people who might be journalists and a number of others who seemed as if they had just come to watch the airship take

off. Then she spotted Uncle Yeric, standing with a uniformed constable. Uncle Yeric was gesturing angrily, and the constable just looked
confused. She didn't see Efrain, but there were enough people milling
around that he might just be hidden in the crowd.

She felt the deck shudder and one of the anchor ropes swung loose.
The other ground crew must be releasing the anchors. Mikel and Cobbier
appeared on the gallery, hastily reeling in the loose lines, and the airship shivered again. The deck pushed on Emilie's feet and she felt that
wavery sensation in the pit of her stomach that meant they were moving upward. She took hold of the railing but the airship's movement
was so smooth she didn't really need to steady herself.

The airship lifted high enough that she could see over the city to the
port, the ships at dock, the ones steaming out to sea, sunlight sparkling
on the water. The view had been her favorite part of riding on the other
airship, and this was the first time she had been in one flying over
a city. Looking down on the streets and the slate and wood rooftops
from above was fascinating. She could see people looking up as the
airship rose, pointing it out to others. *I wonder if they know why we're
going yet,* she thought. Probably not. It wouldn't be in the papers until
tomorrow. She hoped there wouldn't be a panic before they got back
with more information about exactly what the strange craft was. She
also hoped there wouldn't be a panic after they got back.

The buildings grew smaller and the airship moved out over the sea.
Watching the ships cut through the water, spotting tiny islands and
rocks, kept her so occupied Emilie almost didn't hear the sudden commotion from the control cabin.

Cobbier and Mikel came inside, letting in a rush of cool air tainted
with woodsmoke. As they shot the bolts in the cabin door, Seth hurried past and scrambled up the spiral stair to the second level. Miss
Marlende stepped into the main cabin and her expression was highly
irritated. "What's wrong?" Emilie asked.

"We heard footsteps up on the second level." Miss Marlende's voice
was grim. "It must be one of those damned journalists."

Daniel stepped in from the control cabin. He was pointing up and
started to speak, then stopped as he saw everyone already staring at
the ceiling.

Emilie realized she could hear creaking metal as feet crossed the
level above. She just hadn't noticed it, assuming any noise was natural

to the airship. With all the confusion, and the students and ground crew going back and forth, it must have been just possible to slip aboard the airship. She asked, "Will he write about us? I know the newspapers were probably going to anyway, but—" Her voice strangled in her throat when a young man clattered down the steps, prodded by Seth.

It was Efrain.

CHAPTER FOUR

Emilie stared. "You . . ." she began, and couldn't seem to get any further.

Miss Marlende clapped a hand over her eyes. "Oh, for the . . ."

Seth stepped off the stairs, watching Efrain warily. "Emilie, you know this kid?"

Apparently seeing that Emilie's jaw was locked with rage, Daniel answered, "He's her brother." He added grimly, "He came to the airyard with another relative who was trying to force her to leave."

Cobbier eyed Efrain without favor. He was an older man, short and stocky, with sparse hair and dark brown skin and a normally good-humored expression. He had been with Dr. Marlende the longest. "This isn't a joke, son. This is an important job we're doing, and we don't have time for shenanigans."

Efrain lifted his chin stubbornly. "You have my sister on board. I couldn't leave her here unchaperoned."

The rage obstruction in Emilie's throat finally gave way at that. She said, in a particularly acid tone she hadn't known she possessed, "*Unchaperoned?* Miss Marlende is right here, with her mother, Professor Abindon. I am better chaperoned than I ever was at home."

From Efrain's expression, she might have punched him in the stomach. He said, "Oh. Uncle Yeric didn't mention that."

"Of course he didn't, because he's a horse's ass. And these are all respectable men, not the sort of people you and Uncle Yeric evidently keep company with."

Efrain glared. "That's ridiculous! And it's not what I—"

Miss Marlende began, "Emilie! And young man, you . . ."

"How is the fuel mix working?" Lord Engal strode in. "Are you taking notes? Who is checking the gauges?" He looked around at them all. "Well? What's the . . ." He noticed Efrain and frowned. "He's new. Are you new? Who are you? Is Dr. Marlende raiding the primary schools for students now?"

Efrain opened his mouth but couldn't seem to answer. Seth said, "He's Emilie's brother, my lord. He stowed away without her knowledge."

Lord Engal stared, then shook his head in exasperation. He turned to Emilie. "So it runs in the family, does it?"

"Apparently," she admitted grudgingly. "I won't do it again now that I know what it's like from the other end."

Lord Engal didn't appear to know how to respond to that. He finally said, "Well, see that you don't." He turned and walked back out of the cabin.

Efrain watched him go, bewildered. "So . . . he's not going to do anything about me?"

"He's not in charge of this expedition. My father, Dr. Marlende, is," Miss Marlende explained. She sighed. "And it's not as if there's anything we can do with you."

"We could toss him off the ship," Emilie said darkly. "That's what Lord Engal wanted to do to me aboard the *Sovereign*."

Lord Engal strode back in. "I never said that, you ungrateful child. We are a civilized society, we do not throw people out of moving vehicles of any sort." He eyed Efrain without favor. "You'll just have to find something useful to do while you're here." He turned and went out again.

Efrain lifted his chin, apparently emboldened by the fact that no one was shouting at him. "You could take me and Emilie back to the ground."

That was the last straw on an already badly strained donkey's back, as far as Emilie was concerned. She took what she was fairly certain was a menacing step forward. "I wasn't joking about throwing him off the ship. He's endangering the whole expedition."

Efrain glared at her. "You wouldn't."

Miss Marlende caught the collar of Emilie's jacket and pulled her back. "She might if suitably provoked, but I'm afraid I'll have to forbid it. And we can't take you back. We have to enter the aether current at the correct time or we won't end up anywhere near where we want to go. We have no leisure to wait another day for the right moment again." She added, "I'd better go inform my father about our new passenger.

Considering that he thought a journalist had managed to sneak aboard, he'll probably be relieved, but the weight ratio will still have to be adjusted. Please endeavor to be civil to each other," she added, with a stern look at Emilie.

Miss Marlende went into the control cabin and closed the door. Emilie swore, not entirely under her breath. On her first real day on the job, she was not making a good impression, and it was all her stupid family's fault.

Daniel cleared his throat, sounding uncomfortable. "Well, we'd better get back to work."

The others all seemed to remember that this wasn't a spectator event at the same moment. They headed toward different parts of the ship, Cobbier and Mikel going up to the second level while Seth and Daniel went through the passage to the engine compartments.

Since they were giving her the opportunity for a private conversation, Emilie took advantage of it. "You're getting me into trouble with my employers," she hissed. "Why couldn't you stay at home and feel self-satisfied there? Why did you have to come here and try to ruin my new life?"

"We didn't know you had a new life!" Efrain glared back at her. "We thought you were in trouble . . ." He waved his hands hastily. "And I don't mean that kind of trouble! We thought you'd be lost in the city, with no money."

"You thought I was a fool." Emilie had no intention of mentioning it was her money problem that had led to her meeting Miss Marlende and Lord Engal. "I was going to Cousin Karthea's, I was going to help her with her school. Then I decided to do this, instead." She folded her arms. "And don't pretend Uncle Yeric was concerned for me. He thinks I ran off to the big city to become a prostitute."

"He does not! Stop saying that!" Efrain looked around to make sure no one had heard, but the rest of the crew was staying as far away as possible from them without actually leaving the airship. "You're crazy. Why would he think that . . . ?"

"Because our mother was an actress, and he thinks all actresses are secretly prostitutes, no matter how many plays they're in." It struck her as horribly unfair, that while her uncle had never gotten along perfectly with their older brother Erin, he had clearly not had the same problems with her younger brothers, and had certainly never seemed to see them as just marking time until they could embark on careers in some criminal enterprise. Deliberately provoking, she added, "They do have boy prostitutes, you know, so I'm surprised he didn't accuse you of wanting to be one too."

Efrain hesitated, mutinous and obviously confused as to what he wanted to argue about first. She expected him to attempt to deny the existence of boy prostitutes but instead he said flatly, "That's crazy. Uncle Yeric didn't accuse you of that."

Being called a liar didn't improve Emilie's temper any. "He did. At tea, in front of Aunt Helena, Porcia, Mr. Herinbogel, Mrs. Rymple, and Mrs. Fennan. It was humiliating." It had been more than humiliating, it had been a terrible shock. Emilie had thought she had lived with people who knew her, even if they didn't always seem to like her much. To be so completely misunderstood had been like suddenly discovering that she had been living with strangers.

And the more time she had to think about her feelings, the more Uncle Yeric's opinion of her seemed to put her off men entirely. Human men, at least. She wouldn't mind meeting a nice Cirathi man, like a younger version of Kenar, but that wasn't likely to happen.

Maybe the detail, or her tone, was convincing. Efrain's expression was less disbelieving. "But . . ."

"All I wanted was to go off to Karthea's school, to help her with it and maybe take lessons. She had written to me about it before. It wouldn't even have cost him anything, just the passage on a steamer and it's not very expensive." She folded her arms. "If you don't believe me, you can write to Karthea and ask her yourself. I had my things sent to her from home, and I stayed in Silk Harbor at her house the night before last. Daniel was with me. He stayed in the housekeepers' cottage. I was going to visit her there for a few days, then we found out about this—" She waved an arm around, taking in the airship and the aetheric disturbance they were heading toward. "—and we had to come back to Meneport with Professor Abindon."

"Oh." Efrain seemed taken aback, possibly at all the witnesses to her actions and behavior that Emilie could bring to bear if necessary. "I thought . . . I thought you were trying to find Erin, that you thought he was in Meneport."

Emilie felt her lip curl. Anyone with any sense knew that naval ships spent months at sea, transporting cargos of their own and protecting other merchant and passenger ships and ports from pirates and raiders. The only address Emilie had for Erin was the general one for the naval shipyard, but it took ages for letters to the ships to be forwarded from there. "You thought I'd just come to the docks and perhaps run up and down crying, shocked that his ship wasn't here? Besides, he doesn't care about us. He left us all behind and if we all died tomorrow he wouldn't shed a tear." She stopped, a little shocked. She hadn't meant to say the last part; it had come out all on its own, a fear that had been buried in the back of her mind since Erin left.

Efrain stepped back, and pressed his lips together. "You left just like he did. You don't care about us, either." He turned away, going back toward the rear compartments.

"You stopped caring about me first," Emilie retorted to his retreating back. It was a cruel parting shot, and she knew she had gone too far.

* * *

Emilie went into the control cabin and shut the door behind her. She was still angry, in that unsettled way when you knew the argument was more your fault than anyone else's. Miss Marlende was at the controls, and Dr. Marlende and Lord Engal were occupied with the aether navigator. It was mounted on a pedestal between the two control stations, and looked very like the one Emilie had seen used on the *Sovereign*. It had a flat silver plate, etched around with the symbols and degrees of the compass directions. Two silver rings could be rotated around it, to help determine longitude and latitude. On a shallow dish on the plate itself, there was a liquid silvery substance that looked like mercury but was actually drops of clarified, stable aether. It rolled around when the plate was turned and rotated, and pointed the way toward aether currents in the air and water.

Lord Engal and Dr. Marlende made minute adjustments to it, probably trying to pinpoint the best location to enter this aether current. Dr. Marlende was saying, "I wish young Deverrin had spoken directly to me. I feel I owe him an apology. If I had known then what I know now, I would have gone up after them."

Lord Engal said, "But any aetheric traces of the Deverrin airship's passage would have been scattered by the lightning of the storm." He adjusted the plate again. "Even if they did enter another aetheric plane, we wouldn't have been able to track them. And if they haven't managed to make their own way back by now, they must be dead."

Dr. Marlende adjusted the plate back where it had been before, and made a "hmph" noise.

The professor was seated at the other control station, taking notes or writing down her own observations. She said, dryly, "Even you can't work miracles, Marlende."

Emilie let her breath out, not sure whether she felt relieved or even more awkward that no one wanted to shout at her about Efrain. *They're busy with things that are far more important than your stupid family,* she reminded herself. She just hoped Efrain didn't cause any more trouble.

Finally Dr. Marlende checked another instrument on the control board and said, "Yes, that's it! Just there."

Lord Engal stepped back, rubbing his hands together briskly. "Good. Interesting that the current hasn't been disturbed by the object . . . or craft, or whatever it is."

"It hasn't disrupted it yet." Dr. Marlende picked up a speaking tube. "Seth, please confirm that our recycling apparatus is producing air."

Seth's voice came over the tube, tinny and small. "Yes, Doctor, it's working well."

"Very good. Prepare for entry into the aetheric current."

Emilie's first inkling that taking an airship into an aetheric current might be somewhat different from taking a steamship into one was when Miss Marlende turned to her and said, "Strap into a seat, Emilie. It can get a little rough."

Emilie took a padded chair at the back of the compartment that wasn't near any of the equipment the others might need. The worn leather seat had been designed for a bigger person and she fumbled to get the straps adjusted. As she did, Miss Marlende spoke over the speaking tube, asking the others in the back to confirm that they were all strapped in. Daniel answered for himself and Efrain. Emilie, who had just been recovering from the whole argument, felt her face heat with embarrassment again. It was good of Daniel to take charge of her brother, but she just hoped Efrain wasn't saying anything horrible about her. All these people knew her—had known her—as Emilie the Adventurous Stowaway; she wasn't happy that Efrain might paint a different, considerably more pathetic picture of her. *You shouldn't have told him what Uncle Yeric said to you,* she thought. *Idiot.* She already knew she had talked far too much and said things she regretted. She was beginning to think opening her mouth at all had been a bad mistake.

Once everyone had strapped in, Dr. Marlende put his hands flat on the control board and closed his eyes. Emilie knew he must be invoking the protective spell, and looked out the port in time to see it shimmer into existence, rising up like a crystalline curtain being gently draped over the airship. It was necessary to protect the craft from the pressures of the aether current, and to keep the air inside once they had gone up so far that there was hardly any to breathe outside.

Dr. Marlende took hold of the wheel. Miss Marlende, her eyes on one of the dials on the panel, said, "On my mark . . . Mark."

Dr. Marlende turned the wheel and the airship twisted. Or at least Emilie's stomach twisted.

The deck underfoot trembled, then the ship started to move upward, faster than it had before.

Emilie sat back in her seat and felt her heart thump nervously. Miss Marlende and Lord Engal checked their straps, and Emilie tightened hers. Dr. Marlende's expression was rapt with concentration. Miss Marlende adjusted the controls carefully. The light outside dimmed and shimmered, and the push of the deck against Emilie's feet grew harder until her whole body squished down with the force of it.

The ship jerked, wrenched sideways as if a giant hand had snatched it out of the air. The straps bit into Emilie's chest and waist as she jerked forward. Everything rumbled and shook. Emilie's ears popped and she gasped in a breath, and wriggled back to ease the pressure of the straps against her waist. From across the cabin, Lord Engal grunted in pain and muttered, "I've always hated that part."

Emilie was rather glad she hadn't known about it; tensing up in anticipation would have made it far worse. The deck still pressed up against her feet and she knew the ship was being carried along in the powerful aetheric current. Cautiously, she stretched up and looked out the port.

Through the misty surface of the spell bubble, she could see blue sky stream past, streaked with white that might be clouds. She blinked and squinted. No, it wasn't sky, or not exactly. Or not the right sky. In the distance there was purple-tinted indigo darkness, like a thunderstorm rising on the horizon. Except it wasn't the horizon because she couldn't see land below them anywhere. "Is it always like this?" She hadn't realized she had spoken aloud until she heard the words.

"Like what?" Miss Marlende asked, starting to unbuckle her straps. "Oh, you mean the colors? Yes, this is perfectly normal. And you can get up now. We should be stable for the next three hours."

Emilie unbuckled herself and carefully eased to her feet. The feel of the deck pushing upward was disconcerting, and not at all like the way it had felt aboard the *Sovereign,* when the steamship had been traveling through the sea-bottom aether current. "What should I do? Is there any work you need help with?"

"Not right now." Miss Marlende stretched and yawned. She looked at the professor, who was still writing in her notebook as if nothing had happened, and shook her head wryly. "Just get some rest."

Emilie's first impulse was to go see if Efrain was all right, and she grimaced at herself. After a moment of struggling with her conscience, she went to look for him.

She found him in the back compartments with Seth and Cobbier, listening to a detailed explanation of how the engines worked, and apparently, infuriatingly, no worse the wear for the startling experience of entering an aether current for the first time. Emilie would have liked to listen to the explanation too, but didn't want to look as if she was waiting on Efrain's convenience, so she left the compartment.

Emilie walked around a little, and found Daniel and Mikel on the second level making sure their various telescopes and aetheric observers had made it through the bumpy transition all right. Mikel was another student, but an older one, and like Seth he was also an engineer. He was lean and rawboned, with brown skin and lighter Northern Menaen hair. He had a weathered face from spending a great deal of time at sea when he was younger, and it made him look older than his actual years. He told her, "Take a look at the view, it's best from up here."

She paused to look out at the aether current through the big observation windows. There were mists and eddies of other colors in the darkness, violet with a hint of red, swirls of silver trickling over them like whitecaps on waves. It was like watching clouds, you could make fanciful shapes out of them if you . . . Emilie stared, blinked hard, and stared again. That wasn't just a shape. She pointed. "Uh, Daniel, Mikel . . ."

Lifting over a bank of violet-streaked darkness was a wing, a giant wing, curving and pointed at the end, made of the same darkness as everything else but Emilie could see the etched lines of scales. Daniel stepped up beside her, leaned forward so his nose almost touched the glass. From behind them, Mikel said, "It's an aether ghost. You see them occasionally in the air currents. We saw some on Dr. Marlende's last trip up here."

"How do you know . . ." Emilie began, meaning to ask how one knew this was a ghost and not an actual enormous flying creature. But the wing dissolved into mist, fading away into the darkness. "Oh."

"I suppose they're in the sea aether currents too," Daniel said, staring intently after the wing. "We just can't see them."

"But what are they? Where do they come from? Are they really ghosts?" Emilie scanned the moving colors, hoping for another glimpse.

"We don't know, really," Mikel said. "The theory is that the current passes things and carries their images along with it for a while."

The world was an even stranger place than Emilie had realized. After a while Daniel and Mikel went back down to the main cabin to get some sleep, but she stared for a long time, looking for more ghosts. Then her eyes started to hurt and she realized she was drifting off. She managed to use the waterless WC without incident, and took the opportunity to find her bag and change out of her skirt and into the clean but somewhat battered pair of bloomers that had survived her trip to the Hollow World. Both Miss Marlende and Professor Abindon were also wearing bloomers, much more practical for climbing around the airship. Then she went back to the control cabin again so she could sit and look out the big port. She fell asleep still watching for more aether ghosts.

*   *   *

They had to strap in again to exit the aether current. Miss Marlende said it wasn't usually as rough as entering it, but they had never come this far up before so they had better be cautious. Emilie completely agreed with that sentiment. With the others, she took her seat and got her straps tightened. Lord Engal was the last to get situated, muttering to himself as he buckled in.

"Are you ready?" Dr. Marlende asked irritably. "The aether current won't wait for us."

"Yes, yes, go ahead, I'm ready." Lord Engal yanked on the last strap.

Emilie thought it was nervousness on both their parts. Everyone was on edge, watching the controls with worried concentration. Miss Marlende made some careful adjustments to the dials, then nodded to Dr. Marlende. He flicked a switch, then turned the wheel slightly.

For a moment there was nothing, except the sky outside the port began to darken. The sensation of rushing movement and constant pressure began to ease and then stopped altogether; Emilie had gotten used enough to it that it felt odd to be without. The cessation of it was so gentle, it came as a complete shock when the airship shuddered violently and jerked sideways.

Emilie clutched the arms of her chair, glad she hadn't been expecting that one, either. The airship shook once, hard, and then went still.

"There we are," Dr. Marlende said, sounding satisfied. "A successful journey." Emilie was glad he was so much better at traveling through aether currents than Dr. Barshion and Lord Engal.

The others began to unbuckle their straps and stand. Daniel poked his head in through the doorway and Emilie heard movement and Cobbier's voice from the main cabin. She looked out the side port and saw the colors had changed to a very deep blue that shaded to black as she craned her neck to look up. She couldn't see clouds, or stars, or anything below them. That was disconcerting. The spell bubble was just a faint shimmer now, nearly transparent, and it felt like little protection between the airship and all that immensity of sky and empty space.

Lord Engal stared through the front port, and said, "And there it is."

Emilie hastily unstrapped and climbed out of her seat. She stepped up beside Miss Marlende and the professor to see the shape of the strange craft just becoming visible in the upper portion of the forward port. At first it looked small, then she realized those little round dots along the hull must be windows. She blinked and suddenly saw it in the right perspective: the strange craft was huge.

It had three long cylindrical hulls, all of dull but silvery metal, like pewter. One hull was in the center, with the two others attached on either side. Above them were three enormous sails, square but curved on top, like shovels slanted backward, which gave the whole craft a sense of forward motion, even though Emilie thought it must be standing still. It was like a very odd sailing ship. There were no open decks or promenades, and the little windows seemed to be the only way to see in or out.

Beside her, Daniel gasped in amazement. Professor Abindon lifted a small telescope to study it more closely.

Lord Engal whistled in appreciation. "That is a fine sight."

"The sails are fascinating," the professor said softly. "Can it possibly use them to sail the aether current?"

"It must," Dr. Marlende murmured, his expression rapt. "Surely they aren't decorative."

"How does it land?" Emilie asked. She didn't see any sort of landing apparatus, though she supposed the rounded hulls could float in water. "Or is it meant to stay in the air?"

"Or something far stranger." Miss Marlende's expression was simultaneously intrigued and fascinated and worried. "We don't know anything about the place where it comes from. It could be . . . completely different."

"How different?" Emilie asked, then realized it was a question without any sensible answer. If the ship had never been meant to land, and the sails looked so delicate . . . "Like a world that might be made all out of aether? But what would the people be like?"

"A good question," Dr. Marlende said, his voice turning grim.

Emilie felt a chill settle in her stomach. Looking at the beautifully strange vessel, she had forgotten for a moment that it would be piloted by somebody. Hopefully they would be like the Cirathi, friendly explorers not so different from themselves. Hopefully.

"I don't see any lights," Miss Marlende said. "Can any of you?"

"Lights in the portholes, you mean? No." Professor Abindon adjusted her telescope. "Its position hasn't changed since we launched, either."

"Really?" Dr. Marlende turned to her. "But your record of its earlier progress showed that it was moving at a steady rate."

"It was, but it's stopped. It hasn't moved at all since our last observation, late last night." She lowered her telescope. "Perhaps it somehow detected when we entered the current and paused to wait?"

Dr. Marlende's brow furrowed. "Hmm."

Lord Engal absently scratched his beard. "How odd. If they had stopped to wait for our arrival, you would think they would have spotted us by now, and tried to signal."

Emilie glanced at Daniel. Keeping her voice low, because she wasn't certain if it was a silly observation or not, she said, "Maybe they're so different, they don't have signals."

"If they're that different, I don't know how we're going to talk to them," he murmured back.

"Yes, communicating may be a significant problem," Lord Engal agreed, though Emilie had thought he was too distracted to listen to them. "It's too bad the sea kingdom people were too involved in their own hostile interactions for any meaningful exchanges of ideas. The translation spells they used might have come in quite handy now."

Miss Marlende eyed Lord Engal. "I thought our goal as decided by the Society was only to observe the object up close and ascertain whether it was really a foreign craft."

"We've done that," Lord Engal pointed out. "Our next goal as decided by the Society would obviously be to attempt to contact it and ask it what it wants. There's no point in returning to report when we'll only have to turn around and come back."

"Yes." Miss Marlende looked toward the silent craft again. "I'd rather hoped to see some sort of friendly crew waving at us, which would have rendered the whole point moot."

"As did I." Dr. Marlende turned to Daniel. "We'll try signaling them. Daniel, tell Cobbier to ready the signal lamp."

Professor Abindon snorted. "I don't suppose they'll know International Lamp Code."

Dr. Marlende said, rather tightly, "No, Professor, but I hope they'll see it blinking at them and interpret it as an attempt to greet them."

Professor Abindon sighed. "I wasn't criticizing you. It's the only course open to us at the moment."

Emilie followed Daniel back through the main cabin. She wondered if signaling was a good idea. What if the strange vessel thought they were attacking it? She pushed the thought away, recognizing it as another symptom of panic. The others were right, all they could do was try to contact the strangers the way they would anyone else, and hope for the best.

They were in a situation where anything they might do, any choice they made, could turn out to be horribly wrong. She should be used to that from the trip to the Hollow World, but apparently it was a sensation that one couldn't get accustomed to.

They found Cobbier with Seth and Mikel and Efrain in the room adjacent to the engine and air-processing room. It was lined with cabinets and had two more padded chairs with safety straps. They were all glued to the large port, Efrain as well. As they stepped in, Efrain turned to stare at her, his eyes huge. "It's really a ship from another world!"

"We know," Emilie snapped, conveniently forgetting her own awe of a few moments ago. "We're going to try to signal it."

"With the lamp?" Cobbier asked. Then added, "That's our only choice, I guess. It's not as if we can use the flags up here." He crossed the room to a storage cabinet and started to rummage in it.

"But . . ." Efrain stared at the ship again. "What if it does something?"

"It has to know we're here," Daniel said, before Emilie could snap again. "The way these aether currents work, it would have seen us coming from a long distance. Just like we could see it. If it was going to . . . do something, it would have done it by now."

Efrain didn't look much reassured. Cobbier lifted out the lamp, a big metal cylinder with glass slats on both ends and a hand crank. As he carried it to the port, Seth unrolled a cable from the engine-room doorway. Emilie knew that the lamp ran on electricity, and that to make it blink you used the crank to open and close the slats. They attached the lamp to a half-circle metal brace that was set up in front of the port, fastened it down, and connected it to the generator with the cable. The cylinder hummed and crackled as the bulbs inside it warmed. Daniel used the speaking tube in the wall to call the control room. "We're ready, Dr. Marlende."

The tinny reply came over the tube. "Very good. Signal at will."

Cobbier looked at Daniel. "What should we say?"

"Uh . . ." Daniel bit his lip. Emilie thought it was rather a big responsibility to have, to be the one to decide what their first message would be to this potential new friend that they all hoped very much did not become an enemy. She was rather glad she wasn't the one deciding it. Finally he said, "Just the standard greeting to an unknown ship." He glanced worriedly at Seth and Mikel. "Does that sound right to you?"

Mikel shrugged. Seth admitted, "I don't know what else we'd say."

Cobbier moved the crank, and the cylinder clacked as he sent the coded signal. With the others, Emilie watched the strange ship, her heart thumping in anticipation.

But the ship just floated there silently.

"Keep trying," Daniel said softly.

There was a quiet step behind them. Emilie looked back as Miss Marlende stepped into the compartment. Emilie said, "It doesn't seem to be working."

"Maybe they aren't looking at us," Efrain said.

Emilie gave him a withering look. "There's a strange airship in the same aether current. What else would they be looking at?"

Efrain glared back at her, but didn't argue. As the light clacked and hissed with heat, Miss Marlende folded her arms, regarding the ship. She said, "I'm beginning to wonder if something's happened to them."

Emilie had to admit that the ship's lack of activity did make you consider that possibility. Several different scenarios came to mind, mostly from the Lord Rohiro novels and from histories of exploration she had read. "There could have been illness aboard, or food that went bad, or pirates . . . No, I suppose not pirates."

"We hope not pirates," Daniel said. "I don't want to see what sort of pirates would be traveling aether currents from another world." Cobbier nodded fervently.

Emilie found the idea intriguing, but she would much rather read it in a book or watch it in a play, and not experience it in real life.

"But some sort of disaster befalling the crew doesn't explain why the ship is still here." Miss Marlende shook her head. "Without anyone to guide it, it should have started to drift by now. It would eventually fall out of the current and be destroyed. Something must be holding it in place."

Mikel seemed intrigued by the thought. "Maybe it has mechanisms aboard that we just haven't thought of yet, that keep it on course even though the crew isn't there to tend them."

Emilie was watching Miss Marlende's expression now. "We're going aboard it, aren't we? If they won't answer us . . . there's no choice, really, is there?"

The others all looked grim, except Efrain, whose expression was incredulous. He said, "'We'?" When the others just looked at him, he cleared his throat and said, "Shouldn't we let someone official do that?"

Miss Marlende lifted a brow at him. "Just who do you think we are, young man? Tourists?"

Efrain fumbled for an answer, and Emilie set her jaw. She said, "Anyway. Dr. Marlende will want to board it, won't he? And Lord Engal." She would be rather surprised if Lord Engal didn't demand to be part of the boarding party.

"Yes." Miss Marlende let out her breath. She looked weary and worried. "I don't like the idea, but . . . We have to find out who sent this ship, and it would be helpful to know why it seems to be uninhabited."

"If it is uninhabited," Daniel said quietly.

Miss Marlende acknowledged that with a nod. "Well, I'm fairly certain it wasn't uninhabited when it started out."

CHAPTER FIVE

Just to be certain they had tried every option, Dr. Marlende also had Daniel use the wireless to try to signal the strange ship they had dubbed the aether sailer. As Daniel tapped the code onto the machine's plate, it sounded hollow and echoing, as if the signals were going out into the vast empty air with no one to receive them. At least, that was how Emilie's imagination saw it. After many repetitions of the message, there was still no answer. After that, Dr. Marlende decided to keep signaling the ship with the lamp, at least for the next hour, to give the aether sailer plenty of time to respond. But in the meantime he began to work on the spell that would be needed to board the aether sailer from the airship.

"We'll have to get as near as possible," he said, leaning on the railing in the main cabin to look thoughtfully toward their goal. Seth was at the wheel in the control cabin, listening to the wireless just in case, with Cobbier still manning the signal light. "I'll construct a variation on the protective spell that encloses the airship. It will have much the same function, but on a smaller scale. Once it's active, we'll be able to pass through the protective barrier and, hopefully, into the other ship."

"If we can find an entrance somewhere," the professor said.

Dr. Marlende said, "Yes, we'll have to locate one first before we attempt the crossing, since we have no portable version of the air-producing apparatus, and our time will be limited."

Miss Marlende lifted her brows. "You mean it will be like walking inside a giant soap bubble. When the air runs out, you could asphyxiate."

"Well, in a word, yes," Dr. Marlende admitted.

"What if the aether sailer has no air aboard it?"

Dr. Marlende shrugged. "Then we'll have to turn around and come back, and think of something else?"

Miss Marlende did not appear to think this a very good plan. Emilie was doubtful of it as well, but had no idea what to suggest in its place.

"Not an ideal solution," Lord Engal agreed. He rubbed his hands together briskly, obviously more than ready to begin. "But I don't see that we have a choice."

Daniel and Professor Abindon and Mikel all nodded, though the professor looked grim. Efrain just watched incredulously, as if he couldn't believe what he was hearing. Emilie just hoped he didn't say anything stupid and embarrass her again.

The hour went by slowly while Dr. Marlende made his preparations. Emilie spent the time ignoring Efrain and getting a quick tutorial in how to signal for help in lamp and wireless code from Daniel. Or at least she tried to ignore Efrain. He came into the compartment where the signal lamp was mounted, where Emilie and Daniel sat at a little table that folded down from the wall. Daniel had marked the codes on paper and Emilie was tapping them out by knocking on the table. Cobbier was still working the signal lamp, though Daniel was due to take over for him in a few minutes.

Efrain stood there a moment at Emilie's elbow, looming in annoying younger brother fashion, then said, "Can I talk to you?"

Emilie didn't look up. "No, I'm busy. I need to learn this."

Efrain hovered for a time, then finally left.

Emilie saw Daniel's expression and heard him draw breath to speak. She said, "No, I have no intention of making up with him so I'm a terrible mean person."

"I think you're a very upset person," Daniel said. He glanced up at her. "Has he really been awful to you?"

Emilie started to say yes, then thought it over. Daniel deserved a better answer. A more honest answer. "He probably doesn't think he has."

"I'm not giving you advice." Daniel held up his hands, as if to ward off any accusation of giving advice. "But what we're doing is not safe, and . . . It's just a good idea not to leave things in a way you might regret later."

"I know," Emilie grumbled. She really did know. But it felt like the hardest thing in the world.

* * *

The first thing they had to figure out was how they were going to get aboard. From this angle, the only openings in the aether sailer were the window portals, and those appeared to be covered with glass or some other transparent material. They needed to find some sort of door.

By stopping and starting the engine, and turning the aether rudder at the stern of the airship, Dr. Marlende maneuvered around and brought the airship closer to the aether sailer. Watching from the port in the control cabin, Emilie held her breath, but the other ship still didn't seem to notice they were there. The airship dropped slowly, the curved wall of the far larger aether sailer looming over it. This close Emilie could see scratches and pits in the dull silver metal, as if the ship had been struck by windblown debris, or had spent years traveling in heavy weather. "It's old, isn't it?" Emilie said aloud. For some reason that seemed strange, as if part of her had assumed the aether sailer had sprung into being just before the professor had detected it. "Do you think it's been traveling for a very long time?"

It was the professor who answered, watching the view out the port with her arms folded. "It's a possibility. We've assumed that the concentric-worlds theory is correct, and this ship is a visitor from the world just above ours. But if it's designed for long aether current voyages, it could have traveled through many such levels to get here."

That was rather encouraging, Emilie thought, as the airship followed the curve of the lowest hull. Pirates or other people who wanted to cause trouble would surely stick to targets close to home. The only people who would have reason to travel through many different worlds were explorers and philosophers. *You hope,* she told herself. It didn't explain why the aether sailer seemed to be ignoring them.

"There doesn't seem to be anything at all down here," Lord Engal said from the other port. He sounded disappointed. "Perhaps . . . Wait. There toward the middle. There's a round shadow."

Miss Marlende, manning her side of the control board, stood up from her seat to look. "Move forward, Father. About ten degrees."

Emilie leaned against the port and craned her neck. All she could see was more curving pitted metal; the strange light filtering through the aether current reflected off it in shafts of blue. The airship nudged forward and she saw what Lord Engal meant. Toward the center of the hull was a round depression, gently curving up.

As they drew closer, she saw it must be some sort of docking plat-form. It was a bell shape hollowed out of the bottom of the hull, with a platform half circling it. Emilie couldn't imagine what sort of craft it was meant for, except that whatever it was must be round. The airship angled around and she spotted the circular shape of a door, just above the platform. It was closed, but it was there, and it was the only door-like thing they had seen so far.

Miss Marlende said, "Hmm. I don't suppose we're far enough up in the current to roll the airship sideways."

"No, unfortunately, we must stay on this plane of reference." Dr. Marlende picked up the speaking tube. "Seth, find the grappling gear and bring it up to the main cabin, if you would be so kind."

* * *

The protective spell around the airship extended out over the gallery that ran along the main cabin, so though it was more exposed it was just as safe as the cabin interior. It was purely Emilie's nerves that made it seem like a bad idea to open the door and step out on it.

But that was what Dr. Marlende did when Seth brought in a rolled-up bundle of ropes. Seth deposited the bundle on the deck and went back for more, and Dr. Marlende moved to the railing and peered upward. Lord Engal and the professor joined him. Miss Marlende was still in the control cabin, keeping the airship in place. Taking a deep breath, Emilie stepped out after them.

It shouldn't be that different from looking out the ports, but it was. The view was vast and forever, the shadings of blue more vivid and alive. It was as if there was no world below them, nothing existing in all this emptiness but the fragile construction of metal and cloth that their lives depended on. Emilie was suddenly aware that she couldn't let go of the doorframe.

Dr. Marlende, Lord Engal, and Professor Abindon were all look-ing up as if they were on a balcony in Meneport, contemplating the stars. Lord Engal said, "It's rather a bad angle, with the balloon in the way. But it can't be helped. You don't think the aether current's natural buoyancy will interfere with the grappling launcher?"

"Natural buoyancy?" Emilie wondered.

"The current makes things float," Professor Abindon explained.

Dr. Marlende said, "There will be some interference. But the grappling launcher should be powerful enough to get the hook to the platform."

"You're both mad," Professor Abindon said, but added thoughtfully, "It should work, however."

Emilie made herself look up, and almost ducked in involuntary reaction. The aether sailer filled the sky above them, the great long curved shapes of the triple hull as big as mountains from this angle. The bell-shaped depression with its half circle of platform and tantalizing door looked terribly far away.

Daniel stuck his head out the cabin door and she jumped a little. He said, "All the way up there? Huh," and stepped back in.

Emilie ducked in after him and saw him crouching on the floor with a spring-loaded device used to shoot a grappling hook attached to a line. It was useful for attaching ropes to objects at a distance, so an airship could be tied off to them if they were solid enough, or to attach lines and draw up a rope ladder.

Daniel, Cobbier, Mikel, Seth, Dr. Marlende, and Lord Engal all began to lay out the various ropes and hooks they would need, something that took up most of the main cabin and the balcony. Emilie retreated up the stairs to the upper cabin to watch from there, where she was out of the way.

She had only been there a few moments when Efrain came up the stairs. Emilie grimaced, aware she had allowed herself to be trapped into a private conversation. She said, hoping against hope, "The water closet is back there."

Efrain ignored that. He said, "Seth told me what you did."

Emilie was instantly suspicious. "What did I do?"

"How you rescued them, from the cell when they were held prisoner by the sea people." He paused for a moment and seemed somewhat bemused, as if he couldn't believe he was saying those words to his despised and useless older sister. Emilie had to admit it did sound rather unlikely, though it was true. He continued, "It was . . . I just . . . Weren't you afraid?"

That wasn't what Emilie had expected him to ask. She hesitated, tempted to say she had never been afraid, that she had sailed through the whole experience without a qualm, even when people were trying to kill her. Efrain would never have believed her if she had told him about it, but he had believed Seth, even though he was a total stranger.

A strange man who is a crew member on an airship Efrain stowed away on has more credibility than me. But she thought of poor Beinar, and suddenly couldn't lie about it. "I was very afraid. But there was no one else. Rani had just been captured, Miss Marlende was being held prisoner by Lord Ivers, I wasn't sure where Lord Engal and the others were." Even remembering it was making her insides curl up. She had been afraid, but it was the feeling of being completely alone that she remembered the most. "But I was more afraid to just stay where I was, so I had to keep going forward."

Efrain bit his lip, obviously conflicted. "It's like I don't know you," he said finally.

"You don't," Emilie said, and it startled her to realize just how much she resented it. It almost put what Uncle Yeric had said to her in the shade. "You stopped knowing me when Erin left. I went away and you pretended there was a useless, stupid girl in my place, who said stupid things and was easy to ignore. Don't think I didn't notice."

Efrain shook his head, confused and mulish. "That's not what . . . You were . . . You changed!"

If that was all he had to answer her with, Emilie didn't care to continue the conversation. She retorted, "I didn't change. I was always the same. But it's not nice, having someone who knows you suddenly unknow you."

Emilie turned away, took three long strides toward the stairs and almost ran into Professor Abindon. The professor's expression might have been mistaken for her not-uncommon angry frown, but this close up Emilie could see it was really consternation, as if she had just heard something that had startled or upset her. Before Emilie could speak, the professor said, "Forgive me. I didn't mean to overhear."

"It's all right," Emilie said hastily, and waved her hands, trying to indicate that the interconnected compartments of the airship made privacy almost impossible. "Can't be helped, here, I mean." Then she fled before it got any worse.

* * *

It was Cobbier who fired the hook launcher up toward the platform. The hook skittered across the metal and caught on the far edge. Everyone ducked a little, waiting tensely. Emilie saw she wasn't the only one who had thought that appearing to shoot something at a strange ship could possibly be problematic. But there was no reaction, and after a few moments, everyone breathed again.

Cobbier detached the line from the launcher and leaned on it, testing the hold. The hook didn't move. "It's holding."

"Good." Dr. Marlende shed his coat and absently held it out. Emilie hastily stepped forward and took it, glad to feel a little useful. He continued, "I'll go up first and secure the ladder, then come back and extend the spell to cover the rest of you."

Miss Marlende said, "Have you tested the smaller protective spell?"

Dr. Marlende smiled at her, pulling on a pair of leather gloves. "This will be the test."

Miss Marlende drew a sharp breath, and didn't look especially happy with that answer. Professor Abindon sighed wearily and rubbed her forehead. Emilie could see that being married to Dr. Marlende might prove to be a little too much on a daily basis. Perhaps it wasn't surprising that the professor had decided to give it up.

Dr. Marlende wrapped his legs around the line and shinnied up it like a long pole. Cobbier reached for the end but Lord Engal got it first, and leaned on it to hold it taut so the doctor could climb more easily.

It was a long way, and he had to climb past the bulk of the balloon, near enough that he could have stretched out and touched it. As he reached the top of the shimmering curtain of the protective spell, Emilie held her breath. But as he climbed past the faint wavering light, a globe of it detached like a droplet from a dipper of water and clung to him as he continued up.

"Ah, it worked just as expected," Lord Engal said, sounding pleased. Cobbier wiped sweat off his brow and exchanged a relieved look with Mikel.

The professor muttered, "I wonder at the man's sanity, but he is competent."

Emilie realized she was holding her breath only when it abruptly ran out, and she choked a bit and coughed. Miss Marlende put an arm around her and squeezed her shoulder.

Everyone sighed with relief when Dr. Marlende reached the platform and scrambled up onto it. Lord Engal and Cobbier hurried to attach the rope ladder to the line, and Dr. Marlende drew it up until he could hook the end to the platform. Then he turned toward the door.

"What the . . ." Lord Engal was outraged. "He's supposed to wait for us!"

"Quiet," Miss Marlende and the professor both snapped. Miss Marlende added, "He has to check the air supply. Otherwise there's no use in the rest of you going up there."

It was too far away to see what Dr. Marlende was doing in any kind of detail, but Emilie could make out that he was searching all around the doorframe. Finally he turned and crouched down, swinging onto the ladder with practiced ease and starting down. Emilie found herself wiping sweat off her forehead. *And we haven't even gotten to the really scary part yet,* she told herself.

Miss Marlende turned to her and said, "Start bringing out the packs, please, Emilie. I want to have this over with as soon as possible."

Emilie nodded, and hurried back into the main cabin.

From the control cabin, Daniel called, "Is everything all right? We can't see a thing from here!"

She looked to see both Daniel and Seth staring worriedly from their seats at the control console. Efrain peered around the door at her. She called back, "It's fine! So far. I'm getting the packs."

She slung two over her shoulders and picked up the other two, then stepped out onto the gallery just as Dr. Marlende climbed down the last rung of the ladder onto the deck.

"What did you discover?" Lord Engal demanded.

Dr. Marlende rubbed his hands together briskly. "I found the catch to the door, and was able to open it slightly. No one seemed to be immediately visible. I was also able to determine that the air inside is breathable."

"Good," Lord Engal said, somewhat mollified. He slung the pack Emilie handed him across his back. "That will make this much easier. If the crew is merely incapacitated inside somewhere, we can more easily come to their aid. If the crew has had some misadventure and is dead, it will probably take some time to try to determine how to land the ship."

"Land it?" The professor raised her brows. "You're planning to keep it?"

"If we can find no sign of the crew, what else are we to do?" Lord Engal waved upward at the bulk of the aether sailer. "We can't leave it up here! Some brute like Ivers could come and steal it."

"We could leave it up here," Miss Marlende countered. She looked up again at the bulk of the craft looming over them. Her brows drew together in concern. "But perhaps it wouldn't be ideal. If it really has stopped moving, it could disrupt the aether current even further."

"When I finish my calculations, we'll know," the professor said, somewhat darkly.

They watched while Dr. Marlende, Lord Engal, Cobbier, and Mikel got their packs on and readied themselves for the climb. Miss Marlende said, "Just be careful."

Dr. Marlende kissed her cheek. "If all goes well, we'll report on the hour."

"If all goes well?" Miss Marlende repeated.

"Well, the crew may in fact be alive and aboard and studiously ignoring our attempts to contact them, and may order us—or chase us—off the vessel as soon as they lay eyes on us," Dr. Marlende said. "But somehow I doubt it."

Emilie did, too. There was something ominous about the giant aether sailer's silence.

Dr. Marlende started up the ladder first, followed by Lord Engal, Mikel, and then Cobbier. Emilie and the others watched until they reached the platform, and one by one disappeared through the door.

"Are any of them armed?" Professor Abindon asked.

"My father and Lord Engal are, as am I," Miss Marlende said. "Though it's more because of the trouble with Lord Ivers than anything we expected to encounter out here."

"Hmm," Professor Abindon said, and stepped back into the airship. It was not a very reassuring "hmm," Emilie thought.

* * *

They waited.

At first Emilie was tense and jittery with excitement, and she knew she wasn't the only one. They took turns as lookout on the gallery, keeping watch in case the exploring party returned or tried to signal them earlier than the one-hour mark. Emilie took her turn, though she hated standing out there alone. There was just something daunting about that much empty space, with only the thin barrier of the spell between her and it. It helped to keep the door open, and listen to the others talking and moving around inside.

After about an hour, Efrain, who was taking a turn at watch, called out excitedly. Emilie, Miss Marlende, and the professor hurried outside. Emilie looked up to see that Cobbier stood on the aether sailer's platform. He waved to them, and attached something to a line that ran parallel to the rope ladder, then pulled on the line to send it down to them.

As it drew closer Emilie saw it was a metal tube, meant to hold a written message. She tried not to bounce with impatience. *We're about to get answers to all our questions!* Miss Marlende snatched the tube off the line as soon as it dropped within reach, wrenched off the cap, and pulled out a rolled-up square of notepaper. Emilie thought, *Uh, that looks a little small to have all the answers on it.*

Miss Marlende read aloud, "'No sign of any crew aboard. Continuing the search.'" She crumpled the paper, staring incredulously up at the aether sailer. "That's all? After an hour? You have to be joking."

Up on the platform, Cobbier waved again and went back through the open door, vanishing into the ship.

Everyone stared up in frustration and disappointment. Professor Abindon swore. "That man."

Miss Marlende's glance at her was annoyed and a little defensive. "It's Lord Engal's handwriting."

"If your father had meant him to add more he would have dictated it in exactly . . ." She registered Miss Marlende's expression and shook her head. "I'm sorry."

Miss Marlende pressed her lips together, smoothed the note and tucked it into a pocket. "Never mind. At least we know they're all right."

Emilie let her breath out, controlling her own dissatisfaction at the lack of information in the note. Maybe all the answers was a little bit much to expect, she thought. She stepped back inside to go to the control cabin and tell Daniel what the note had said. He also stared incredulously and said, "That's it?"

Emilie nodded. "If you had been able to go with them, would you have written more?"

Irritated at the implied accusation, Daniel said, "Of course!" As she continued to regard him, he added, "Well, probably I would have. Maybe they haven't discovered anything else."

Emilie grudgingly admitted that was possibly true and went back to the main cabin to start waiting again.

* * *

The wait continued for the next hourly report. Emilie had spent the time looking over the wireless manual and memorizing some of the basic codes. It was very dry reading, though, and after a time she drifted off. She woke abruptly when the bench seat shook violently and the book slid off her lap. She sat up, suddenly wide awake.

Seth, out in the gallery on watch, was now braced in the open doorway. Efrain stared at her from the opposite bench seat. "Was that normal?" he asked her.

"No. At least, I don't think so." Emilie pushed to her feet, keeping hold of a support post, but the deck had stopped shivering.

"It wasn't normal," Seth confirmed. Still holding on to the doorframe, he stepped cautiously out to look up at the aether sailer. "Can't see anything out here that might have caused it."

Professor Abindon clattered hurriedly down the stairs from the upper cabin. "Did something hit us?" she demanded.

"We don't know, we can't see anything," Emilie told her. She had rather been hoping the professor knew.

She followed the professor into the control cabin, Efrain trailing behind them. Miss Marlende had taken over for Daniel at the controls, and he stood looking over her shoulder as she checked various dials and adjusted levers. She glanced up, frowning. "Before you ask, I don't know. It must have been a fluctuation in the current. If something had hit the balloon, we would have heard the impact."

Daniel was nodding. "It felt like something just grabbed the whole ship and shook us. That had to be the current."

The professor checked the aether navigator, then compared it to a long list of figures in her notebook. "The current has shifted three degrees."

"It can't have." Startled, Miss Marlende glanced over her shoulder. "Are you certain?"

"Yes." The professor's face was grim. "I've been checking our position frequently. Something is disrupting the current."

Miss Marlende turned back to the controls, and said, "They must have felt that aboard the aether sailer. Hopefully Father will make a more complete report this time."

When the time came, Emilie and Daniel went out onto the gallery to wait with Seth. The professor followed them, and Efrain came to stand in the doorway. They waited expectantly, staring up at the aether sailer.

After a time, Professor Abindon checked her pocket watch, and snorted with exasperation. "Of course he's late."

But Seth was frowning. He said, "He wouldn't miss a report."

Daniel looked concerned too. The professor conceded, "Well, the craft is large, and they may be at some distance from the door by this point."

Daniel bit his lip. "They may not want to split up, either."

Emilie felt a sinking sensation. *No one is coming,* she thought. She didn't know how she knew. There was just a sense of emptiness and silence and . . . *It's like how you're expecting the post to come, but it doesn't, and you just know there was a problem with the wagon and even if they fix it they won't send it out this late.*

They waited, but no one opened the door.

CHAPTER SIX

After three hours had passed, Miss Marlende said, "We'll have to go after them."

Daniel nodded. "I'll go, with Seth. I can do the protective spell. Dr. Marlende showed me how he constructed it. We'll need—"

"Daniel, you can't climb that ladder, not with your shoulder," Miss Marlende interrupted impatiently. "If you tear that wound open, you could lose control of the spell and you and whoever was with you would die, in a very unpleasant fashion." Daniel drew breath to argue, and she added, "Do not attempt to cross words with me."

Daniel hesitated for a long moment, then let the breath out, words unspoken. His expression was torn between frustration and grim anger. *He knows she's right*, Emilie thought. At least he was sensible enough to acknowledge it. He said, "But who will go?"

"I will," Miss Marlende said.

"But the spell—"

"The professor can do it." Miss Marlende's gaze met the professor's.

Professor Abindon lifted her brows, then said, "I can. I will."

"But can you climb the ladder, Professor?" Daniel asked. "It's such a long way—"

She gave him a withering look. "Please. I'm not decrepit. I've climbed the lighthouse at Silk Harbor every week for the past two years, to adjust their aether weather-scope. And the current's buoyance means we won't weigh as much while we're climbing."

Miss Marlende nodded firmly, though Emilie read the relief in the set of her shoulders. She hadn't been entirely certain the professor would agree to go. She said, "Very well. Seth, you'll remain here also."

Seth stared in astonishment. He had clearly been counting himself as a member of the party. "But Miss Marlende, you can't go alone, just you and the professor . . ."

Miss Marlende fixed him with a steely gaze. "Neither Efrain nor Emilie can pilot the airship, and Daniel will need a relief pilot. We may be gone for some time, and we can't risk the airship changing position and breaking the lines to the aether sailer." He started to speak and she interrupted, "Are you going to present a relevant argument or are you going to make an emotional appeal?"

"But . . ." Seth deflated. "Just the two of you . . . It's not . . ."

"Safe?" Professor Abindon's mouth twisted in ironic comment.

Emilie took a deep breath. She felt a flood of fear, and was surprised to note that it didn't seem to be any easier to get used to, having felt it so much in the Hollow World. But it subsided and she said, "I'll go with you."

"Emilie." Miss Marlende rubbed her eyes, betraying just how tired she was. "There is no reason for you to risk yourself . . ."

Emilie said, "Are you making a relevant argument or an emotional appeal?"

Miss Marlende froze, and stared at her. Emilie figured this would either work, or she would be fired on the spot.

The professor gave Emilie an appraising look. "I like this girl."

Miss Marlende glared at her mother, then at Emilie again. Daniel's expression was hard to read; possibly he wanted to object, possibly he felt that adding more members to the party was only sensible. Miss Marlende appeared to wrestle with similar thoughts, then finally said, "Very well. You may come along."

Emilie's heart thumped, mostly in relief that Miss Marlende wasn't going to dismiss her from her assistant position. "Thank you. You won't regret it, I promise."

Then Efrain said, "I'm going too."

Miss Marlende said, "Oh, please."

Efrain lifted his chin. "You can't stop me."

Miss Marlende regarded him. Her eyes narrowed.

Seth told him, with emphasis, "She could stop you."

Daniel seconded, "Oh yes, yes, she could."

Efrain looked from one to the other, then at Miss Marlende. His eyes widened a bit as he saw they were serious. He quite obviously decided to take a different tack. He said, "Please. I can't let my sister go without me. And there's nothing useful I can do here. I'd be a waste of . . . of air. With you, I can carry things, and guard your back. I know how to shoot a pistol."

"You know how to shoot a duck-hunting gun," Emilie interposed. "It's not the same thing at all."

Before Efrain could retort, Professor Abindon said, "A little brute strength might come in handy, depending on what we find."

She meant come in handy if they had to help injured men back to the airship. Emilie bit her lip and decided to stop talking. Miss Marlende met the professor's gaze again and seemed to draw the same conclusion as Emilie. She said to Efrain, "You must obey my and Professor Abindon's orders exactly. And if I ask Emilie to tell you to do something, you must do it at once, with no argument. Can you swear to me that you will do that?"

Efrain's expression was serious. "I swear it. On my mother's grave."

Emilie felt her jaw tighten. She wasn't sure what she wanted to object to. Having become an ally of Uncle Yeric, Efrain hadn't actually given up any right to their mother's memory. But she felt like he had.

Miss Marlende nodded. "Very well. Let's get ready."

*   *   *

They hastily assembled supplies. Emilie had a pack that contained, among other things, a hand-cranked battery lamp, a coil of very strong line, matches, a water bottle, packages of lifeboat rations, a notebook and pencils, and a first aid kit. She put on her jacket in case it was cold aboard the aether sailer, shouldered the pack, and was ready to go.

Miss Marlende finished with her own pack and asked the professor, "Do you have everything you need?"

Professor Abindon said, rather grimly, "We'll find out, won't we?"

The professor went first so she could do the protection-bubble spell, then Miss Marlende, then Emilie and lastly Efrain. Efrain had a pack too, and had exchanged his good town shoes for an extra pair of Seth's work boots, which had been left in a supply locker aboard the airship from some earlier trip. Efrain was lucky he had big feet for his age.

Emilie had climbed a very long ladder down into a very dark hole, but this was worse. At least in the dark hole she had suspected that the fall would be enough to kill her painfully but she hadn't known it for certain. Here she knew it for certain.

As she started up the rope ladder, she thought suddenly of climbing the ladder up to the other airship, with the angry sea people shooting at them, and what had happened to poor Beinar. It made her stomach lurch and she had to take a deep breath, and force her hand to reach for the next rung. Once she got past that moment, it wasn't so bad. She concentrated on the movements of Miss Marlende's boots and trousers above her, and tried not to think about anything else.

Emilie wasn't aware of the protective spell until she realized the balloon was no longer in the peripheral vision of her right eye, and the shimmer of the barrier was suddenly within arm's reach. It had formed around her as she had climbed out of the range of the airship's spell, without her noticing. And oddly, she did feel lighter, as if she didn't weigh as much. That must be the aether current's buoyancy. She still didn't succumb to the temptation to look down.

Finally Miss Marlende stopped, then moved forward again, and Emilie heard her say, "Emilie, do you need a hand?" Her voice sounded hollow and distant, an effect of the separate spells.

Emilie made herself lift her head and her neck bones creaked. She had been staring so fixedly at one spot that her shoulders had gone stiff. "I'm all right."

But it was still a relief when Miss Marlende's firm hand grabbed her pack strap and guided her as she scrambled up onto the platform. Emilie couldn't really feel it through the protective spell; she knew there was hard metal under her hands, but it felt curiously neutral, neither hot nor cold. She pushed to her feet and moved over a few steps to give Efrain room. She was breathing hard and the back of her head hurt, probably from tensing her muscles so much.

As Efrain scrambled up onto the platform, she heard a muted thunk behind her. She turned and saw Professor Abindon had already opened the door of the ship. Emilie stepped to her side to peer in.

It was dim but not completely dark. The walls were a bronze color, and the golden diffuse light seemed to come from chased metal strands embedded in the curved ceiling. Like a container of molten metal had fallen and splashed, then hardened into strings of rivulets. Emilie found herself exchanging a look with the professor.

Miss Marlende stepped past and into the aether sailer. The professor moved after her, and Emilie followed.

The corridor was a good ten feet wide, at least, and the ceiling was well above their heads. It made sense for a ship this big to have room to spare. Efrain hesitated in the doorway, then stepped through.

The floor had little ridges in it, possibly meant for traction in rough weather. The walls were textured too, with raised ridges that formed abstract patterns. Emilie looked up and down the corridor. It curved away behind them, following the shape of the hull; ahead it went some distance and then dead-ended into a little circular chamber. "I guess they didn't go that way," she said. Her voice came out as a whisper, and she cleared her throat.

"But they did." Miss Marlende moved to the wall, pointing to an arrow hastily drawn with light-colored chalk. "This is Father's mark."

"Well, I certainly hope it's not anyone else's mark," Professor Abindon said. "One party of explorers lost in this ship is enough."

Miss Marlende's jaw clenched and Emilie could see the tendons in her neck. She thought the professor was just being sarcastic out of nerves, and not meaning to aim it at anyone in particular. But it was always easier to see that sort of thing when you were standing outside looking on, than when you were one of the people involved.

Miss Marlende said, "It looks safe at the moment, but take care where you step. Don't touch anything." She pulled the outer door closed, then moved down the corridor, and they all followed her.

The arrows continued, and there were no other doors or cross corridors. Emilie thought the little circular chamber ahead must be some sort of optical illusion, like when straight lines looked wavy, or when you frightened yourself by mistaking the shadows at the bottom of curtain folds for feet.

But as they reached it, it was still a round chamber, the ceiling open to a shaft that stretched up into the ship. The second-to-last arrow pointed toward it, and the last pointed up into the shaft.

Miss Marlende stepped into the chamber, her brow furrowed in thought. Emilie leaned in and looked up. The walls of the shaft were also bronze, lit with alternating bands of golden light, the wavy texture making the light bend as it reflected. She could see another chalk arrow about fifteen feet up. *The arrows are a trick?* she thought, and felt a cold chill settle in her stomach. Maybe someone . . . something . . . had captured the others and taken their chalk to trap—

Then Miss Marlende reached out to touch the wall. She snatched her hand back, startled. The professor asked, "What is it?"

"I think . . ." Miss Marlende lifted her leg and placed her foot on the wall. And then she was walking up it.

Emilie blinked, floored. *Or maybe they actually did go this way.* She hadn't quite seen how the transition was accomplished. Still walking, Miss Marlende said, "Come on, this way!"

Emilie stepped forward and put her boot on the wall. It was suddenly like walking down a steep slope, as her momentum pulled her forward and the next thing she knew the wall was the floor, and she put one foot in front of the other and kept going. Behind her, she heard Professor Abindon say, "How odd." And Efrain laughed with delight.

Emilie kept her eyes on Miss Marlende's back, a little worried that if she looked around too much it would break the spell and she would fall down the shaft. They passed two more chalk arrows, then Miss Marlende stopped, confronted by an arrow that curved into a loop. Emilie carefully turned her head, craning her neck to follow the direction it seemed to be indicating. There was an open circular doorway in the wall directly behind them. "That way?"

"It must be. Let's see if this works . . ." Miss Marlende slid one foot to the side, moving cautiously, then took a full step. She turned and walked around the circular shaft toward the doorway. Watching her made Emilie dizzy. She managed to make herself turn and follow.

Miss Marlende reached the doorway and stepped down into it, and suddenly stood at a right angle to Emilie. Emilie lunged forward and stepped before she could change her mind, felt the pull of that strange momentum, then suddenly she bumped into Miss Marlende. Miss Marlende steadied her and drew her back a few steps to allow the professor and Efrain to follow.

They walked into a large open chamber that appeared to encompass two levels of the ship. A bronze metal gallery ran around the second level, with no railings. There was a large rounded door directly across the room in the far wall, and other doors opening off the second level. Emilie noticed that the door in the left-hand-side gallery midway along looked as if it led to a much brighter room. *Maybe they're in there, maybe those are their lamps,* she thought.

More arrows were marked on the lower level, leading them along to a half-circle shaft in the wall. Miss Marlende stepped into it and was immediately propelled upward onto the gallery. Emilie saw her stumble a bit as she exited, then Miss Marlende called, "Yes, it's this way!"

They followed, all managing to reach the gallery without falling off. The next arrow was chalked on the wall, pointing to the lit doorway.

The light in the chamber was brighter because it had several of the curved windows in the far wall. There were tables on one side of the room, set with a lot of disks that looked somewhat like the instrument dials in the airship, only there were no glass covers and they didn't show words and numbers, but tiny little folds of what might be paper. Looking into them was fascinating; they only got more elaborate the longer Emilie stared. She had to tear her gaze away.

Beside them were switches and levers and knobs, though they too were made of something that looked like paper, all twisted into elaborate folds. Emilie was afraid to touch any of them to make sure, for fear of breaking them or accidentally turning something on. There were chairs, or at least round contoured benches, and the dark material upholstering them was very soft. There was a doorway in the far wall, leading into another, similar room.

Emilie moved toward one of the windows and looked out, but they were high in the hull here and she could only see the far curve of the airship's balloon. She turned back to look around again.

Professor Abindon picked up a piece of thin metal that was covered with more of the tiny elaborate paper folds, twisting around each other into patterns. Stepping up beside her to look, Emilie thought it must be art. But the professor said, "This could be writing." The professor held it flat on one hand, and touched it very gently. "Hmm. It's tougher than it looks."

Emilie touched it too, gently brushing her pinkie finger across it. It did feel more like metal than paper, deceptively strong, so it could be touched and maybe even crushed, and still hold its shape. She said, "That's why there's more of this on the panels. Maybe it's instructions for the switches and levers?"

"And this could be a control room," Miss Marlende said, "but it's odd that it's not more toward the prow of the ship. Do not touch that, Efrain," she added, and Efrain jerked his hand back from one of the levers. "We don't know how it operates. If it's like that lifting wall, it may only require a touch to do something quite dramatic."

Efrain looked suitably sobered and took a step backward from the table for good measure.

Emilie swallowed her irritation and started to look for the next arrow. She found it by the door, pointing to the next chamber. "Here, Miss Marlende."

Miss Marlende shook her head slightly, as if more than a little dazed at all these strange sights, and strode forward again. The next chamber was nearly identical to the first, except that it had big cabinets textured the same way the walls were. These seemed promising, but after a brief search they proved to contain nothing but sheets of the metal-paper writing. The next room, however, had something astonishing in it.

It was a big sphere, nearly three feet tall and about as wide. It looked to be made out of one long twist of the metal-paper. The folds extended deep into the sphere so it was almost like peering into the insides of a plant or a strange sea creature. It could have been a sculpture or a decoration, but after the professor had speculated that the metal-paper folds were writing, Emilie wondered if this had some other purpose. *Though if it is writing, I don't see how they read the bottom without lying on the floor.*

Then Miss Marlende said, "I wonder if they can't see." She stretched her hands out toward the globe, but didn't touch it. "If they don't read this by looking at it but by touching it."

"What about the windows?" the professor said. Her tone was deeply thoughtful, not argumentative. "If they are blind, they wouldn't need them."

Miss Marlende nodded. "True. Perhaps they need light, or can see light, but they need their hands to interpret things that are this detailed."

Emilie thought of the textured handles and the metal-paper patches on the control boards. Were they instructions? Or were they dials like the ones on the airship, that showed what fuel was left and the air temperature and the compass directions? "Maybe this moves," she said. "Like compass needles or gauges."

"A possibility," the professor acknowledged. "If true, then this object is . . ."

"A map," Miss Marlende finished. "But a map of what?"

Efrain had gone to prowl around the other doorway, and now he said, "Miss? I can't find any more arrows."

"What?" Miss Marlende turned, frowning.

Emilie went to the doorway. "They probably just didn't bother to leave any because this just leads to the next room—"

"It doesn't." Efrain stepped forward, making a gesture. Emilie reached him and saw he was right, this junction had a doorway into the next chamber and an opening into another corridor. "They could have gone either way, so there should be an arrow."

Miss Marlende moved toward them. "Look carefully." The professor came to search too. The next chamber and the one after it were mostly empty, with the round bench-chairs arranged for seating and some low tables but no control panels or giant globes. They went some way down the corridor, far enough to find another walking shaft that must give access to the rest of the ship. But no arrows.

They came back to the room with the globe and stood and looked worriedly at each other. "They were here and then they weren't," Professor Abindon said.

"It doesn't look as if there was a fight. There's no blood," Emilie pointed out, trying to be encouraging. "And if someone had knocked into the globe, surely the ends of the metal-paper would be bent." Efrain winced and the professor gave her an odd look, and Emilie realized that perhaps that hadn't exactly been tactful. Emilie felt her cheeks flush and she looked at Miss Marlende. "Sorry."

Miss Marlende just said, "No, Emilie, don't apologize. I appreciate your candor. And you're right, there's simply no sign of a struggle here. Not that we've seen any sign so far of anyone that they might have struggled with."

"Yes, though it's a large vessel, and we've seen little of it so far." Professor Abindon tapped her chin thoughtfully. "If we're being blunt, one or more crew members could have killed the others, and still be hiding on board."

Emilie nodded. "Yes, that's happened before, on the *Thalandia*, out of Isenland, twenty years ago." There had been a chapter based on the incident in one of the Lord Rohiro novels, and Emilie had looked it up in a natural history book to see what had actually happened. She misread Efrain's expression as baffled and explained, "They were caught in a surface aether current and couldn't get out, and they think it did some odd things to the crew."

Efrain said, "Why do you know these things?"

Emilie felt her cheeks heat again, this time from rage, but Miss Marlende said, "Young man, disparaging others' perfectly reasonable contributions to the discussion is a waste of everyone's time." It sounded

mild, but knowing Miss Marlende better, Emilie thought she was trying very hard to control her anger. *She's upset,* she thought. She really
expected to find them all wrapped up in searching or trying to figure
out some strange device, so that they just forgot to check in.

"I wasn't . . ." Efrain started to object, caught Miss Marlende's expression, and subsided. "Sorry."

The professor frowned at him and continued, "But the point that
there is no sign of a struggle is still valid. There may be something in
this room that they touched, which drew them into another part of the
ship. Like the walking shaft, but perhaps more abrupt. They may be lost
or trapped somewhere aboard or otherwise unable to get back here. I
suggest we search this room thoroughly, with a great deal of care."

Miss Marlende directed them to each take a section, and Emilie
ended up with the wall that held the windows. She thought it was an
unlikely place for a device of any kind, but searched thoroughly anyway. She didn't touch it, but stood as close as she could and made her
eyes trace the textures of the wall, looking for hidden switches.

At the point where the patterns in the textures were making her
dizzy, Emilie stepped away to let her eyes adjust. Miss Marlende and the
professor were carefully searching the control boards on the far side of
the room, and Efrain was doing the opposite wall, studying it with the
frowning concentration of someone who had no idea what they were
looking for. Emilie repressed the urge to sneer, knowing that none of
them really knew what they were looking for. Not that Efrain would
have resisted the urge to sneer at her—

The deck shivered underfoot. Just a brief, violent quiver, hard
enough to make Emilie's teeth rattle. She stepped away from the wall,
though she hadn't been near anything. The others turned, staring in
alarm. "Did anyone touch anything?" Miss Marlende said.

Efrain shook his head and Professor Abindon held up empty hands.
She said, "That wasn't the ship, it was the aether current again. There's
been some disturbance—"

And then the globe moved. The whole surface of the metal-paper
twitched, then shifted seamlessly into motion. The twists and folds
flowed like fluid, then settled into new patterns.

After it was still, they slowly stepped toward it. Emilie leaned down
to look closely. Some of the individual folds of metal-paper were still

waving gently, as if moved by a soft breeze. In the next moment, they had all stopped. Miss Marlende said, "I think you're right, Mother. It is a map."

The professor nodded slowly. "But not of a surface world. I believe . . . It's a map of aether currents. It moved when the current shifted." She lifted her brows. "I just wish we could read it."

Emilie didn't think either one had noticed that Miss Marlende had called the professor "Mother"; both were too intent on solving the mystery. Emilie certainly didn't intend to point it out.

"I wish we knew why the current shifted," Miss Marlende said, a little frustrated. "It happened before Father and the others went missing, and we think they were in this room."

"Could it have done something to them?" Emilie eyed the globe warily. "It didn't do anything to us."

"We weren't close to it, though," Efrain pointed out. "We were all back around the walls. And we didn't touch it."

Miss Marlende's mouth twisted ruefully. "True. I find it hard to believe Lord Engal or my father resisted the urge to touch this device."

Emilie hated to admit that made sense. The professor's thoughtful frown was hard to read. She started to speak, then a loud bang sounded from down the corridor. Everyone flinched and Emilie's heart thumped. "Maybe we just didn't search enough," she blurted.

"Maybe." Miss Marlende strode to the doorway and the junction with the corridor. Emilie followed with Efrain and Professor Abindon, feeling her nerves jump. The soft gold light in the corridor seemed dimmer than it had before, with more shadows and less illumination. She wanted to speculate but just managed to keep her mouth shut; they needed to hear anything that might be moving in this corridor. Maybe the first, more violent shift in the aether current had trapped Dr. Marlende and the others somewhere in the ship, and the second had released them. Or maybe the ship's crew was aboard, and just . . . *Sleeping?* she asked herself. *In the water closet? Otherwise indisposed? The airship has been here for hours.*

They came to the shaft without seeing anything that could have caused the noise. The shaft only led down, and Miss Marlende hesitated for just a moment before stepping into it. Emilie followed her, too occupied this time to notice the odd sensation of suddenly walking down a wall.

Miss Marlende headed toward the open doorway into what should be the next deck. As she neared it, she circled around the shaft so she could see out. Emilie followed her example, edging cautiously forward when Miss Marlende stopped at the opening to peer out.

Emilie leaned around her to look past her shoulder. She thought the person breathing right behind her ear was Professor Abindon.

Ahead was an open two-level chamber much like the one near the control-room compartments. The shaft led into the second-level gallery, again with nothing like a handrail or balustrade, that looked down on a lower deck about twenty feet below. A few doorways and what must be another walking shaft were set into the walls. Emilie couldn't see what was on the deck below. This was more proof that while the crew might read the metal-paper with their hands, they could certainly see to some extent. The galleries with no railings would be terribly dangerous for a person who was completely blind.

"Hmm," Miss Marlende muttered under her breath. She started to step down to where the shaft would place her upright on the platform floor. Emilie leaned forward to follow when Miss Marlende froze.

A moment later Emilie saw it too. Something, a dark shape, moved across the lower deck, just visible below the platform. The movement was halting, uncertain, as if they were watching the head and shoulders of someone who was feeling their way in the dark. Except Emilie rather thought the shape had too many shoulders.

Miss Marlende leaned forward to see better, and Emilie shifted for a better angle. The next instant Emilie's feet jerked out from under her and she suddenly slammed into Miss Marlende. They fell out of the shaft, landed with a thump, and stumbled on the platform.

The shape below vanished. Miss Marlende caught her balance and lunged forward to the edge of the platform. Emilie landed on her hands and knees and scrambled to look. The space below was empty, and Emilie could see a doorway in each wall. She hung out over the edge, trying to see under the platform, where the lower level stretched out a long distance back through the ship. She caught a glimpse of a moving shape, a strange outline against a gold-lit wall, and then heard the loud clang again. This time she could tell it was a metal door swinging shut.

The professor and Efrain landed behind them and Efrain flung himself down next to Emilie. He demanded, "What did you see?"

"It was something, someone." Emilie looked at Miss Marlende and saw her own bafflement and consternation reflected in her expression. A member of the crew? But why only one? *And why did they run?* "What do we do?"

Miss Marlende's expression hardened and she shoved to her feet. "Follow it."

CHAPTER SEVEN

Emilie looked wildly around. There was no stairwell, no ladder, no immediate way down. "Oh, there!" The corner of the platform was supported by a pillar twisted into a spiral.

Miss Marlende ran for it, swung off the platform, and climbed down the pillar. Emilie hurried after her. She made the scramble onto the pillar far less gracefully than Miss Marlende had, but once she had managed to grab it the texture and the twists of the spiral provided hand- and footholds like a ladder. She dropped the last few feet and looked up to see a wide-eyed Efrain climbing down after her. The professor, still standing on the platform, waved her on. "Go, don't wait for me!"

Emilie obeyed, darting after Miss Marlende, who was already pelting down the corridor.

Racing to catch up, Emilie knew this was probably the exact opposite of what they should be doing. Miss Marlende was obviously so worried for her father and the others that she had disregarded all caution. So Emilie would have to be cautious for her.

She caught up with Miss Marlende just as she ran under an archway and into a large high-ceilinged chamber. They both slid to a halt, staring up.

The walls weren't walls, but huge bronze ball-and-socket joints, like giant metal knees, towering over them. Each was several feet wide, the beams they were attached to stretching high up to disappear into shafts on each side of the room. They were all still at the moment, though they clearly looked as if they were meant to move something heavy. Emilie kept her voice low. "What's this?"

"It must be part of the mechanism that moves the sails," Miss

Marlende whispered back. She looked around again. "I'm sure I heard a door. There!"

She darted off toward a triangular door set in between two of the joint-gears in the far wall. Emilie hurried after her.

As they reached the door, Efrain and the professor caught up to them. The door was just a triangle of bronze, no handle, but with a medallion in the center carved in the shape of what looked like a bundle of snakes. Miss Marlende hesitated, then pushed against the medallion, and the door slid open.

They stepped into a room that must have been in the lower part of the aether sailer. It was long and the far wall was dotted with the round windows.

And at the far end, a creature whirled around to confront them.

It was like a flower. Or maybe a whole bunch of flowers, attached to each other with fireflies and gossamer. There was a big round globe of them where the head should be, and delicate fronds like lace lined with blossoms that gently waved in the still air. It lifted them like arms, except there were four instead of two.

Emilie supposed it might attack them, but it looked so delicate, that was hard to imagine. The legs, all four of them, were covered with blossoms too, and didn't look any sturdier than the rest of it. It must have run on those delicate limbs, but it was so light, it couldn't need much effort to hold itself up. It was like confronting a large hyacinth.

"What is it?" Efrain whispered.

"No one knows," Emilie said, more to get him to be quiet than anything else.

Miss Marlende held up her hands and said, "Hello. Is this your vessel?"

The head part seemed to study her, and it lifted its four arms to mimic her gesture. Miss Marlende pressed her lips together in frustration. "It doesn't understand."

Professor Abindon gestured toward the strange being, and it turned to her and mimicked her motion. "Its language, its way of speaking, must be completely different to ours."

"But what happened to the rest of the crew? And my father?" Miss Marlende said. The stranger waved its four arm blossoms in a swirling way, and she duplicated the motion.

"I suppose it could have attacked and killed them," the professor said dubiously.

"It doesn't seem likely, does it?" Emilie said. "And it's not attacking us."

The stranger waved its blossoms again, and Emilie thought she read frustration in the gesture, as if it was just as annoyed at the language barrier as they were. Though maybe that was wistful thinking.

"We have to think of a way to communicate." Miss Marlende pulled her pack around and dug through it.

The stranger watched her, the blossoms on its head area pointing toward her inquiringly. Emilie thought, *It doesn't seem afraid of us.*

Miss Marlende pulled a notebook and pencil out of her pack, braced it against her forearm, and began to sketch rapidly. Emilie stepped closer and watched her draw the rough outline of the aether sailer, and the airship below it, with the ladder connecting the two. She turned the notebook to show the stranger, then pointed at all of them and herself, and then to the airship. "We came from here." She pointed at the stranger. "Where did you come from?"

The stranger leaned toward the notebook, its lighted blossoms waving at the page as if studying it. Then a blossom reached out to the pencil and took it out of Miss Marlende's hand. Emilie had to lean closer to see. Dozens of little feelers lining the stem of the blossom gripped the pencil just like fingers. The stranger moved the pencil over the paper, clearly trying to draw something.

Emilie shifted from foot to foot anxiously, then realized her balance felt so unsteady because the deck was trembling. "Do you feel that?" she said, just as Miss Marlende said, "The aether current is shifting again."

The stranger dropped the pencil and waved its blossoms in agitation. Then it whirled like a bundle of flowers caught in a windstorm and bolted away up the corridor. Miss Marlende called out, "Wait!" Efrain started forward, meaning to run after it, and Emilie also started forward, meaning to run after him to make certain he didn't do anything stupid like grab the stranger. But the trembling turned to shaking. Emilie staggered sideways and bounced off the wall.

Miss Marlende and the professor both swayed, and Efrain grabbed the doorframe to stay upright. He turned toward them, then gasped and pointed.

Emilie twisted around to look. The end of the corridor was blocked off by something, a white wall. No, it wasn't a white wall, it was a storm, a roiling tempest, slamming down toward them. She yelled in alarm, and the next instant it hit.

Emilie tumbled, fell, slammed into something hard. Her body stretched almost to breaking point. It happened so fast the flash of burning pain was over before she knew what had happened. She fell into something soft and collapsed.

Emilie groaned. Her face was smashed into something fragrant, like grass. *Grass? On the aether sailer?* She felt limp and numb, as if her brain was awake but not the rest of her body. After a long moment she realized the heavy thing on her head was her pack, one loop still wrapped around her arm. She shoved it away. That got her moving, but it took a huge effort to drag her arms underneath her and push herself up.

She lay on a bank of tall grass, dark green with violet-tinged tips. *This is . . . not the aether sailer.* She lifted her head, focused her blurry eyes. She was in a clearing, surrounded by trees with dark purple trunks and bushy green canopies. The knee-high grass brushed against her trousers.

The air was damp and warm, sweat already sticking her shirt to her back and chest. A breeze made the leaves rustle and she could smell green plants, wet earth.

She staggered to her feet, staring around. She had been on the aether sailer with the others, and now she was somewhere else. *Others . . . Where are the others?*

Emilie's heart pounded in alarm, as if it had awoken to the strangeness and the danger before her brain had. She took a deep breath and heard a hitch in her throat. She told herself, *Don't panic. You've been alone in strange places before.*

Yes, but at least I knew where the Sovereign *was, even if I couldn't get to it. And I knew where I was, and what had happened.*

Except she thought she knew what had happened this time, too. The aether current had been shifting, just like it had before. *The aether current did this. It grabbed me—us?—and brought us . . . here.* The others had to be here too.

She moved through the grass, searching for more fallen bodies, but she didn't see anyone. They had to be here. It was odd enough for an aether current to slam through the aether sailer and grab people and transport them without crushing them to death or asphyxiating them; it was too odd to contemplate the thought that it might have just grabbed her and left the others alone. Making herself think about whys and hows at least made the frightened hitch in her breathing smooth out.

There was no sign of anyone in the clearing. Emilie thrashed through the grass in case it was hiding an unconscious body, stopped when she realized it was no use, they just weren't here. She looked around, made herself think. Past the trees she could see the ground rose up into a hill. *I need to get higher so I can see if they're nearby.*

She started through the trees, instinctively wary for snakes or biting insects. It was warm enough that you expected gnats or other little flying bugs, or grasshoppers fleeing from her boots swishing through the grass, but there was nothing. It was odd: even in Meneport, in the center of the city, there had been bugs.

She came out of the trees and concentrated on plowing her way up the hill, which was a little steeper than she had thought. At the top, she looked around.

And she thought, *Uh-oh.*

This was the strangest country, unlike anything in the Hollow World, unlike anything she had ever seen pictured or described in books.

She was surrounded by steep-sloped forested hills, with the purple-green trees and grass. But beyond them were higher mountains, their shapes like nothing she had imagined a mountain might be before. Some were tall pillars, others were spirals. Some were pillars with plateaus balanced atop them, and some were like huge mushrooms. They were wreathed with clouds, and she could see the craggy shapes of rock, and different-colored swaths of trees or other vegetation, some green, some a dark blue, some red. But there were strange gaps between them. She could see the broken rock where sections had been torn from the ground. *Did the aether do that?*

Looking up, she realized she couldn't see the sun. The light seemed to come from everywhere and nowhere, evenly across the sky.

She looked around again, slowly, at the strange shapes of mountains, none of which looked as if they came from the same continent as these hills. Were the mountains even real? Maybe she was just seeing solid aether ghosts. *So does that mean I'm an aether ghost too?* There didn't seem any point in assuming that. If she had died and become an aether ghost, there wasn't anything she could do about it.

Except maybe have a good panic. She was probably overdue for a panic.

"Emilie!"

She spun around at the shout. It was Efrain, emerging from the trees at the bottom of the hill. He was disheveled and his pack was half off, but he was here. Her heart thumped with relief and she waved and started down toward him. If she was a ghost, and she was beginning to doubt it, at least she wasn't alone.

Efrain charged up toward her, so she stopped to wait for him. He reached the top of the hill, breathing hard, and started to speak. Then he looked around.

Emilie gave him time to absorb it. Finally he looked at her, wide-eyed, and bit his lip. She said, "If you start to cry, I will slap you."

Efrain blinked, then glared at her, offended. "I wasn't going to cry!"

"See that you don't." Emilie looked around again. "You didn't see the others?"

"No. I thought I was alone." His voice cracked a little and she gave him a warning glare. He glared back, snatched out his handkerchief, and noisily blew his nose.

She said, "Well, we're here. They have to be here too. Where were you?"

"What? Oh, down there, just past those trees." He felt his hair, and pulled a few twigs out. "I think I got dragged through one of them."

"I was down there. I didn't get dragged through a tree." They had both ended up in different copses, but you could draw a straight line between them. Or a triangle, with the hill as the third point. That gave Emilie an idea.

Efrain was saying, "I'm sure only inferior people like me get dragged through trees . . ."

"Quiet! The current seemed to come toward us from the end of the corridor. You were standing beside me, just a couple of feet away." Emilie frowned, trying to remember. "Miss Marlende and the professor were in front of me, next to each other. The stranger, Hyacinth, was—"

Efrain lifted his brows. "You're calling him Hyacinth?"

"What would you rather I call him? And we don't even know if it's a him! He might be a her, or a neither, or a both."

"All right, fine, Hyacinth. He—or she or neither or both—was in front of the professor and Miss Marlende, but over to the side of the corridor." His brow furrowed. "Only when we saw the current-thing coming, I think he moved closer to me. He was waving his arms, like . . . maybe he was trying to tell us to move?" Efrain looked around again, glumly. "I guess we should have listened."

"I think it was too late by then." Emilie took a deep breath. "But I think, based on where you ended up and where I ended up, we should look for the others that way." She pointed to where another clump of tree-covered hills rose. "I think we should walk that way, sort of at an angle."

Efrain nodded. "All right."

Emilie was a little startled by his ready agreement, but he had already started down the hill. She caught up with him in a couple of steps and they walked together, the grass swishing at their pants legs. Efrain said, "So . . . This is where Dr. Marlende and Lord Engal and the other men went too? And the crew of the aether sailer?"

"They must have," Emilie said, but she was aware that was a big assumption. Maybe even bigger than the assumption that said that Miss Marlende and the professor and Hyacinth had been deposited in the trees in this direction and not just flung into empty space.

"And they haven't come back." Efrain's expression was deeply worried. "Is there a way back?"

"I don't know." Emilie had been wondering about that herself. She was fairly certain if there was a way, it would require far more knowledge of aether currents than she had gleaned from the Lord Rohiro novels and from listening to the Marlendes' and Lord Engal's conversations. Neither she nor Efrain was a sorcerer or a natural philosopher, and she thought it would take both to get back to where they had started.

"But you know everything . . ." Efrain began, then looked at her. "I didn't mean it like that! I just meant . . . You've done this before."

Emilie swallowed her first knee-jerk acerbic comment. Maybe he really hadn't meant it that way. "Yes, but I had help."

Efrain pressed his lips together and didn't say anything.

They reached the copse of trees and found the going far more difficult. The trees were tall and the light beneath them was gloomy and tinged with violet. The ground was spongy with dark-colored moss which was soft enough, but it was growing over rocks and lumpy clumps of dirt. This hill was much steeper too, but at least the trees gave them something to steady themselves on. They struggled to the top of the hill and then had to be extra careful on the way down, their boots sliding through the moss and losing purchase on the rounded stone. Emilie managed it by half sliding from tree to tree, and Efrain copied her. This would be a very bad time for a broken ankle for either of them.

They couldn't see much of anything ahead except more trees, and Emilie started to call out for Miss Marlende and the professor. Efrain tugged on her sleeve. "Are you sure you should do that? What if there's . . ."

"What?" Emilie asked. She dug her heels in on the next slope, half sliding down and stopping herself on a tree at the bottom.

"I don't know." Efrain gestured in frustration and almost lost his grip on the tree he was using to keep from falling. "Aether monsters."

Normally, Emilie would have scoffed. But after everything else she had seen she supposed it wasn't beyond the realm of possibility. "I just don't know how we're going to find them otherwise. Even if we're right about where they landed, they probably started running around searching, just like we did." Through the trees ahead she could see more light, and thought they might be coming to the edge of a bluff.

"That's true, but . . ."

"Wait. Be careful here, the ground's all torn up." The dirt and moss and rock were disturbed and the trees leaned forward, their roots half ripped out of the ground. Emilie stepped carefully, trying not to put her weight on the unstable trunks. The ground did drop away ahead, and as she reached the edge, she saw "drop away" was exactly how to describe it.

There was a bowl-shaped section missing from the hilly forest, at least a hundred yards wide. Emilie looked down the rough side of the cliff to see clouds, and miles below a misty dark-blue mottled area that might be distant land. *Or it might be the colors of the aether current.* It was like whatever had been here had just fallen away. It had left a few fragments behind, irregularly shaped chunks of rock and dirt, floating on thin air—or thin aether—in the empty space.

Emilie's whole body prickled with unease, and the ground underfoot suddenly felt delicate and apt to dissolve at any moment. Efrain whistled in awe. "What happened?"

"The aether current. It took the land somewhere else, just like it did us." It had to be.

"But it wasn't our current. It happened a while ago. You can see how the tree roots are all dry. They've been out of the ground awhile." Efrain pointed along the side of the bluff.

"Oh. Well, that's good." It was good. It meant it might be a fluke that wouldn't happen every time an aether current fluctuated. And maybe Efrain was good for something after all. "We'll have to go back and around—"

Movement on a small fragment-island stopped the words in her throat. What she had thought was a bundle of dead vegetation rippled and stood and turned to face them. It was Hyacinth, trapped on a chunk of rock and dirt barely ten feet wide. It was floating somewhere around ten or twelve yards from the bluff.

"Uh-oh," Efrain said, low-voiced.

Emilie felt a little sick. "The aether current must have dropped it there." It meant they had veered a little off as they had made their way through the forest. Miss Marlende and the professor must be farther to the left. She lifted her hand and waved.

Hyacinth lifted its four arms and waved back, then drooped again. After a moment, it sat back down.

Emilie clearly read dejection in the way those blossoms hung loose. "It's stuck."

"What do we do?" Efrain hesitated. "Do we have to leave it?"

"No." The word was out before Emilie completely formed the thought. The idea of leaving it, or anyone, stuck out there to die was horrible. It could have easily been one of them.

She stepped back from the edge, looking up and down the bluff. They needed something to reach the floating fragment. "Didn't you have rope in your pack?"

Efrain leaned on one of the trees to steady himself and pulled his pack around. He rooted through it and dug out a coil of climbing line. "We could tie a rock to the end and try to throw it, but Hyacinth would have to jump and we'll have to pull it up, and it'll hit the side of the cliff."

That was true. Even if they tied their end of the rope to a tree, there was nothing to secure it to on the fragment. And that was if they could manage to throw the rope out far enough so Hyacinth could grab it.

Efrain could throw farther than Emilie, but she had never noticed him being particularly accurate.

The tree Efrain leaned against creaked alarmingly, a small avalanche of dirt and pebbles sliding down from around its roots. Emilie grabbed for his arm and they hastily scrambled back. A little unsteadily, he said, "These trees aren't as stable as they look."

"No. No, they aren't." It gave Emilie an idea. It was probably a bad idea but it was still worth trying. "Come on, this way."

She led the way along the bluff's edge, scrambling in the clumps of dirt and rock. She could see scooped-out scars in the edge where other trees must have finally pulled loose and fallen. After a short search and some wandering back and forth, she found a slender tree that seemed to be tall enough and that was leaning at the right angle. Efrain followed her, his expression reflecting increasing consternation as he realized what she was doing. He said, "It could crush him! Though I guess that's better than starving to death."

"Maybe it lives off sunlight, like a flower. It might be out there forever." Emilie climbed carefully around the selected tree, examining the roots' grip on the edge of the bluff. She pushed hard on the trunk and heard an encouraging crack underfoot. Efrain yelped and scrambled away, dragging on her pack strap.

"This one is perfect." Emilie told Efrain, "Take the rope and tie the end to one of those trees up there. Make sure it's a good solid one."

Efrain nodded sharply and started up the slope. Emilie felt a start of surprise that he was listening to her. It felt very odd to be doing something constructive with Efrain again. The last thing they had actually cooperated on was the aborted construction of a tree fort.

It had been a death trap of a tree fort due to rotted lumber. She only hoped they were better at this.

Hyacinth had stood up again and appeared to be watching them. At least, when Emilie looked at it, it waved its blossoms. She waved back, and pointed significantly at the tree, then toward the rock island. Hyacinth waved its blossoms again.

Efrain slid back down, leaning his weight on the rope to test it. Emilie shrugged off her pack and hooked it over some tree roots upslope, and they tied two loops in the rope, one for each of them. The first set of loops didn't allow for enough slack between them, but once they got that sorted, they were able to pull the loops over their heads and up under their arms. "Are you sure the rope is tied off securely?" Emilie asked.

"Of course I am!" Efrain bristled.

"We're both going to die if it isn't, so I won't be around to say I told you so," Emilie pointed out. Her heart was thumping a little at what they were about to do. It wasn't so much that she was afraid of heights as she was terrified of falling from heights, having come very close to it a time or two.

Once they had the rope loops secured around them, they slid down to the base of the tree that clung insecurely to the edge of the cliff. It was a very tall tree, but slender, and they sat in the tumbled dirt clods at its base and pushed with all their strength. The tree creaked and Emilie heard dirt and pebbles rattling below it, but it didn't fall. "Use your legs," Efrain advised, and they twisted around to push with their feet. Roots popped and tore, and Hyacinth must have figured out what they were doing, because it was now huddled on one side of the fragment, making itself as small as possible.

"It's working," Emilie said, breathing hard from the effort. "Just not as fast as I imagined."

"Get closer, here, like this." Efrain dug his way farther into the roots. "And push up!"

"I think . . ." Emilie lost that thought when the tree jerked forward and started to fall, the roots tearing free in a shower of dirt, and the edge of the bluff dissolving under them.

Emilie clawed frantically at the sliding dirt before the rope caught her. She banged into Efrain and they both dangled down the edge of the cliff. The rope was so tight under her arms it squeezed the air out of her lungs. Struggling to find a hand- or foothold in the bluff, she was barely aware that the tree was still held in place by its lower roots, that it hadn't toppled all the way down, so the top must have hit the rock fragment as planned. But as Efrain tried to use the roots to drag them up, they tore out of his hands and the tree slipped down.

Then something wrapped around her upper arm and yanked her up, flinging her forward. She landed face-first in loose dirt, Efrain landing heavily on top of her. She scrambled up, half dragging Efrain, until she felt rock and sparse grass.

She spit dirt out and pushed herself up enough to look around.

Crouched next to them was Hyacinth, its blossoms shaking with agitation, or maybe reaction to their extremely close call. Efrain, still face down in the dirt next to her, groaned. "That hurt."

Emilie twisted to look and saw the very top of the tree had struck the fragment, and lay delicately poised there. That was close, she thought, her throat dry. It was lucky Hyacinth must be as light as a feather; a person of any weight whatsoever would never have been able to cross that tenuous bridge. And she and Efrain might not have been able to climb back up the cliff, might have strangled themselves in the too-tight rope, if Hyacinth hadn't been strong enough to lift them. Then the last of the tree roots gave way with a crack and another chunk of the cliff went with it as the tree dropped away.

Hyacinth tugged at her arm again, urging her farther up the slope. Emilie grabbed the back of Efrain's jacket and dragged him up. Once they were farther up on more solid ground, she and Efrain managed to struggle out of their rope loops. Efrain tried to brush the dirt off his shirt and pants without much success. He said, "I'd better go up and try to get the rope loose. We might need it again."

"Cut the knot if you have to," Emilie told him. She retrieved her pack and sat for a moment, contemplating Hyacinth. "Thank you," she told it. Her upper arms and chest still hurt, she was fairly sure the bruises were going to be terrible, and breathing still felt like a luxury. But she was very glad they had taken the chance. Walking away with Hyacinth trapped on that fragment would have been impossible.

Hyacinth fluttered its blossoms inquiringly. The next step was obviously to figure out how to talk to it, so they could make plans. It must know more about the situation here—wherever here was—than they did. And she couldn't keep calling it Hyacinth. It needed a real name. "I've been calling you Hyacinth," Emilie said. "I hope you don't mind."

Hyacinth fluttered its blossoms again. If it could understand her, it didn't appear to mind.

Efrain came back down the slope, moving slowly, coiling the rope up. "Let's get out of here," he said, "before something else happens."

Finding Hyacinth had told them that Emilie was right about where Miss Marlende and the professor must have ended up. She pushed to her feet. "We need to go back this way." She turned to motion to

Hyacinth to follow but it was already beside her, flowing easily over the rough ground.

* * *

Emilie and Efrain moved much more slowly, though the next set of hills wasn't nearly so steep. It wasn't so much from caution, but from aches and pains and a growing tiredness. Emilie just didn't think they were going to make it much farther without a rest. Hyacinth didn't seem tired, but its body seemed so light and it had four legs to walk on. They both had water bottles in their packs, but Emilie was relieved to encounter a stream flowing down one of the rocky slopes. It flowed down through the forest, narrow but fast-moving in a wide gravelly bed that ran to the edge of a bluff and dropped away. At least if they were stuck here for any length of time, they wouldn't die of thirst.

They stopped to rest by the stream by common consent. Once they drank and refilled their bottles, and Hyacinth had drooped some blossoms in the water, they sat on the smooth rocks on one side and looked out over the valley. Efrain said, "It's funny that there's no insects. That doesn't make sense."

Emilie had noticed that too. "Why doesn't it make sense?"

"Because there are flowering plants. You can't have flowers without insects, and bees. Or, most of the time, anyway. The bees carry the pollen around from flower to flower, and if they didn't, there wouldn't be any flowers."

Emilie frowned at him. It was more erudition than she had ever heard Efrain show on any subject that didn't involve throwing balls and being contemptuous of sisters. "How do you know that?"

Efrain glared at the water and nudged pebbles around with his boot. "I read."

"I've never seen you read."

Efrain's chin grew even more stubborn. "I don't show you and Emery everything. I have secrets too." He rolled his shoulders uncomfortably. "Erin knew I read."

Emilie eyed him. Regardless of that, he was right about the lack of insects. They were both sweating and even Hyacinth smelled more flowery; surely they should be attracting midges. There weren't even any beetles or stinging bugs around the water.

Then she looked at the stream, at the wide channel and the narrow trickle of water. The stone she was sitting on was still damp. No insects, no birds, no sign of animals. She looked around at the hill, and thought of the gap and the fragments where Hyacinth had been trapped, the strange mountains, so oddly shaped and so different from each other. "Uh-oh."

Efrain, still frowning, stared. "What?"

Emilie hesitated. She was a little worried Efrain would panic, but . . . She had to say this to somebody and Hyacinth wouldn't understand the words and couldn't answer in any way she understood. "I think . . . What if we weren't brought here, to this place, by the aether current? What if the aether current brought all of this here? These hills, the ground, the mountains. That's why it's in clumps, like this, and why there was a section missing."

Efrain's eyes widened. Then he shook his head. "But there's water here. This stream. Water has to come from somewhere. And the trees . . ."

Emilie grimaced. "The water is running out. This stream should be three times as wide. But the lake or spring or whatever that was brought here with it isn't connected anymore, and it's slowing down to a trickle."

Efrain pushed to his feet and looked up and down the stream. Emilie looked at Hyacinth. She thought she had figured out where its eyes were, buried among the blossoms roughly in the center of the area that was probably its head. There were several small round bumps there that she caught occasional glimpses of, and they were dark and shiny like eyes. Now they appeared to be regarding her soberly, or at least she thought so. *I bet it came to the same conclusion,* she thought. *I bet that it knows what this place is, and what happened. It just can't do anything about it.*

Efrain said, unsteadily, "But . . . What . . . What do we do?"

Emilie pulled her pack strap over her shoulder again. She said, "We walk faster so we can find the others."

Efrain rubbed his eyes but didn't sniff. Hyacinth flowed to its feet. It looked from Emilie to Efrain and back. Then its blossoms rustled and it held something out. Emilie stepped close to look.

It was a little ball of the metallic folded paper, just like they had seen on the ship. Emilie leaned closer. The tiny folds were moving, just a little. It looked like a miniature version of the globe they had seen in the control area . . . Emilie lifted her brows. "It's your version of an aether navigator, isn't it? It moves when the currents move?"

Hyacinth waved its blossoms gently and tucked the little device away again.

"Can he get us back to the airship with it?" Efrain asked, suddenly hopeful again. "After we find all the others?"

"Not if it works like an aether navigator. But it should be able to tell when the current changes again, and what direction it shifted to, and that sort of thing." Emilie wondered if Hyacinth could understand something of what they said. Or maybe it was just much better at interpreting their expressions and actions and gleaning information from them than they were from it. She said, "We're looking for our other two friends." She gestured, and held up four fingers and then two, and tried to pantomime the absence of Miss Marlende and the professor. "We think they must be over that way. That's why we're going in this direction." As she pointed, they all turned to look.

Three hills away, over the tops of the trees, a thin column of smoke was rising. Just enough for a small campfire. "A signal!" Efrain bounced happily, pointing. "They're signaling us!"

"Of course they are," Emilie said in relief.

CHAPTER EIGHT

It made sense, Emilie thought, as they hurried through the forest. Miss Marlende and the professor must have decided to wait where they were and build a signal fire. On reflection, Emilie could see that it was the most sensible course of action and that she and Efrain should have done it as well. But Miss Marlende must have looked for a signal from them, not seen it, and decided to do one of her own so they didn't miss each other while running around through the woods and up and down hills. Maybe Dr. Marlende and Lord Engal and Mikel and Cobbier had found them as well. With everyone putting their heads together, and Hyacinth's device for showing the aether currents, surely they could find a way out of here.

That was what she was telling herself, anyway.

The slopes and bluffs allowed them views where they could spot the signal again and keep to the right direction. "It's getting thinner," Efrain pointed out after they had walked about an hour and were only one hill or so away.

Emilie shaded her eyes to look. The smoke column did look more wispy. "Maybe it's just the angle we're at, or the wind."

"Or they need to get more wood," Efrain added practically, and they moved on again.

As they came down through the thick trees on the last part of the hill, Emilie tried hard to hear voices ahead. She supposed Miss Marlende and the professor could just be sitting around quietly resting, but it must mean the others hadn't found them. She couldn't imagine Lord Engal being in this situation and not talking about it.

She could think of a dozen reasons for it to be quiet, but it still filled her with dread. *Something's wrong.*

They emerged from the trees above a clearing that was studded with a few white boulders. Emilie saw the camp immediately. A spot among the rocks had been cleared roughly of grass, and a fire had been built. A heap of sticks had been piled nearby, ready to feed it, but the fire had almost burned out. There was no sign of anyone.

Emilie's throat went tight. She hurried down the last slope, Efrain and Hyacinth following. The area around the dying fire showed no signs of a struggle or fight. The grass that hadn't been pulled up to keep the fire from spreading was flattened a bit, as if two people had walked or sat on it. Then she saw a pack leaning against the base of a boulder, its white canvas blending into the gray-white stone. She ran over and snatched it up.

Efrain said, "Where are they?" He flung his arms out. "They aren't here! It's not fair, we thought they were here!"

Emilie, sitting on her heels to look through the pack, paused to stare at him incredulously. Efrain sniffed and rubbed his nose, and admitted miserably, "That didn't sound so whiney inside my head."

"I don't know where they are," Emilie said under her breath. In the top of the pack she found the professor's notebook. Everything else seemed as it should be. Her water bottle was still there, the packets of food, and a collection of items that were probably for magic, such as little bottles of minerals. There were also some instruments that might be for navigation or drawing that Emilie couldn't identify. One she recognized from descriptions in the Lord Rohiro books and from glimpsing one on Dr. Marlende's workroom bench. It was a combination clock and aether compass, with a pocket-watch face on one side and on the other a little miniature aether navigator with a tiny bit of aether in a glass bubble, floating a tiny compass needle atop it.

She stood up and looked around again, then walked around the perimeter of the camp. Miss Marlende's pack wasn't here. "If they left on their own, they wouldn't have left the professor's pack here."

Efrain watched her uneasily. "If they left on their own. You mean, someone made them leave?"

Emilie couldn't think of any other reason they would build a signal fire to draw them here and then go away, especially without the professor's things. If Dr. Marlende or any of the other men had found them and required help urgently, they could have torn a page out of the notebook and left a message to that effect. She realized she was pacing in a tight circle and made herself stop. "Someone else found them before we did. Someone made them run away, or took them away."

"What someone?" Efrain rubbed his eyes again, clearly fighting back tears. Hyacinth waved its arm blossoms in agitation. There was no telling if it understood what had happened, but it clearly knew something was wrong. Efrain continued, "What do we do? How do we find them now?"

Emilie drew breath to snap at him, then let it out. Efrain might pretend to be a mature young man around Uncle Yeric, but he was a year younger than she was and he had never been through anything like this before. Standing there, she became aware of how much her feet ached from walking on sliding rocks, how dry her throat was. She should be hungry, but she just felt queasy. It had been a long time since either of them had slept, and the unchanging light of the aether had kept them from noticing. They would have dropped from exhaustion if they hadn't been so afraid. None of that was going to help her find the others.

She said, "We need to rest first. Sit down and have some water and some food."

"But . . ." Efrain hesitated. He scrubbed his fingers through his hair. "All right."

Efrain sat down and opened his pack. Hyacinth settled next to him. Emilie sat across from them, and thought about building up the fire again. *No, if anyone we actually want to find could see it, they would be here by now.* And more smoke might draw the attention of whoever had come after Miss Marlende and Professor Abindon.

Efrain took a drink from his water bottle, and pulled out a wax-paper-wrapped sandwich packet. He handed a second one to Hyacinth. As Efrain ate, Hyacinth picked the sandwich apart with the delicate tips of its blossoms, examined it carefully, then handed it back. Efrain wrapped it up again and put it away. "I guess it does eat sun, like a plant."

Emilie got her own bottle and food out and made herself drink and eat. It settled her stomach, and after a while each bite seemed to make it a little easier to think. She wished Rani were here. Rani had always known what to do, and would surely know how to track people through this grass and dirt.

Emilie frowned as she finished off the last crust of her sandwich. Hunters in books were always looking for faint traces invisible to the naked eye. Maybe it wasn't that complicated. Maybe she should just look and see if she could find anything, and not write it off as a lost cause just because she wasn't an expert hunter like Tagaff, the midshipman from Atalera in the Lord Rohiro books.

She tucked the wax paper back into her pack and got to her feet. "Stay here and rest. I'm going to look around."

Efrain, drooping over his pack, started to struggle upright. "I'll go with you!"

"No, I'm just going to be right around here. I'm looking for tracks and evidence. I don't want you to step on it." Emilie wasn't sure what it was but she was pretty certain Efrain would step on it if given the opportunity, especially as tired as he was now.

Efrain sank back down and yawned. Emilie started to circle around the various boulders that surrounded the camp, carefully examining the grass and dirt between them. Hyacinth followed her, watching what she was doing with interest. The first time around she didn't see anything, then she turned back and did it again, circling out a little wider. Coming at the camp from the opposite direction, this time she saw a gouge in a patch of dirt between two clumps of grass. Emilie sat on her heels and considered it. Hyacinth crouched beside her. The mark looked too sharp and defined to have been made by an animal. Not that they had seen or heard any hint of animals, birds, or insects here. "I think this was made by someone's heel," she told Hyacinth.

It touched the gouge with a tentative blossom.

Emilie started to search the ground in a straight line out from the heel mark, heading toward the forest. Hyacinth had realized what she was looking for now, and lowered itself to within a foot or so of the ground, flowing gently back and forth over the grass, hardly disturbing it. It had gotten a bit ahead of Emilie, and she saw when it stopped abruptly and stood up again, waving its arms at her. She hurried forward.

They were about halfway to the trees on the far side of the clearing from where they had entered it. In an area of patchy grass and dirt, there was a blurred outline of a boot print. Emilie put her own foot beside it for comparison. It was three or four times the size of hers, too big to be Miss Marlende's or Professor Abindon's.

Emilie's heart started to pound. Up until this moment, she hadn't really believed in the mysterious strangers who had made Miss Marlende and the professor leave their camp. She had theorized their existence, but there had been a lot of theorizing by her and everyone else since they had first seen the aether sailer and they didn't know the truth of any of it. But here was proof.

It cut straight through the fog of exhaustion. "We have to get out of here," she told Hyacinth. She shoved to her feet and strode back toward the camp to shake Efrain awake. Whoever had done this might come back.

*　*　*

Emilie made them walk several hundred yards into the forest, until she found a sheltered spot where they could rest. It was a little hollow shielded by another boulder, and Efrain folded up in it and went to sleep immediately. Emilie sat down beside him. She meant to stay awake and just rest her feet, but she woke abruptly, still half sitting up, her face propped on the professor's pack. She sat up, groggy, rubbing her eyes. Efrain was still curled against the rock, snoring a little. A small pile of white vines was heaped nearby; after a moment she realized it was how Hyacinth looked when it was asleep.

She squinted up at the tree canopy overhead. The light hadn't changed at all. Or she had slept through a whole day . . . She dragged the pack open and got the portable aether compass out. The clock on it showed that only a few hours had passed. She let her breath out in relief and shook Efrain's foot.

He groaned. Hyacinth flinched, then popped upright, waving its arms wildly. "It's all right," Emilie told it. "You fell asleep."

The blossoms' wild motion slowed, and it sank down again and drooped. Emilie wondered what had happened to it, if the other flower people crew members were trapped here somewhere too. *If they were, surely it would be looking for them, not following us around.* It acted as if it was stuck, and that staying with them was its only option.

She wondered how long it had been trapped alone on the aether sailer.

Efrain sat up and scrubbed his hands through his hair. Emilie told him, "Come on, we need to go."

"Go where?" Efrain said, still groggy. "We don't know how to find them."

"We know they went in this direction." Emilie stood and shouldered the professor's pack along with her own. She had marked the direction on the aether compass before they had left the clearing. Without a smoke beacon to follow, keeping to a straight course through the forest would have been difficult. At least this way they knew they were heading in the same direction that Miss Marlende and the professor had been taken away in, and not just going in circles.

After a few minutes of trudging after her, Efrain said, "Who could have taken them? If this place has been just put together from chunks of other places that got picked up in the aether currents like we think, there wouldn't be any people still alive here. They would have run out of food and water pretty quickly. Unless a whole lake got taken with them."

It showed the sleep had made Efrain's brain start working again. That was a relief. "Unless they were taken recently, like we were."

Efrain frowned down at his boots. "But you don't think they're friendly, because they didn't let Miss Marlende leave us a note, and the professor left her pack behind."

To give them both something else to think about, Emilie said, "Maybe they're pirates." Pirate adventure stories had been Efrain's favorite when he was younger. Emilie had thought that if there were really that many pirates, there wouldn't be any shipping at all, since the stories implied hundreds more ships than the Menaen merchant navy had ever needed. But then she remembered how much Efrain had changed in the past year. She didn't even know if he still read those stories.

But Efrain said, with relish, "Or ghosts."

"Ghost pirates," Emilie suggested. Impulsively she smiled at Efrain and he smiled back. Hyacinth waved its blossoms at them, as if it felt it should participate but had no idea how.

Then Emilie blinked and focused her attention on the compass instead. It had been a long time since she and Efrain had smiled at each other.

Efrain seemed to realize it too. He shifted his pack uncomfortably and didn't say anything else.

They had only walked about half an hour according to the compass clock, when Emilie started to glimpse something gray between the trees ahead. At first she thought it was mist or a haze; as they drew closer she realized she was looking at a cliff. She groaned under her breath. The ground had been relatively even through this part of the forest so far. She had climbed and slid down all the steep stony slopes she ever wanted to in this place.

. But when they emerged from the trees it was clear this wasn't just another rock formation. The cliff was only about twenty feet tall, but it was dark gray streaked with a glittering blue, with broken shards of blue crystal sticking out of it. The mossy ground of the forest floor came right up to it with no rocks or stones or anything, and some of the trees were uprooted and leaning against it. It looked like two different places.

"Oh," Emilie said aloud. "Because it is two different places."

Efrain nodded. "This part came from somewhere else, and it just got mushed together with the forest." He looked up and down the cliff, though the trees crowding it made it hard to see very far. "They must have climbed it. We need to find where they went up."

He was probably right. With the trees crowding so close there just wasn't much room along here, and the base of a cliff seemed an odd place to pick for a camp anyway. And along the top they might be able to find more tracks. She went to one of the uprooted trees that leaned against the cliff. "Let's try to get up this way. It'll be easier to see where they went from up top."

She stepped on the trunk and awkwardly crab-crawled up the steep angle. It was rough going; the wood slipped under her feet, and the branches were all at the top. Then Hyacinth flowed past her, using all its limbs to rapidly scale the side of the trunk. Then it paused and extended an arm toward Emilie.

They could have it carry the rope up for them, but this was faster. Emilie stretched and grabbed the blossom-covered arm, and it hauled her easily up the trunk as if she weighed nothing. She let go when she reached the branches and could pull herself up and scramble onto the cliff top. Hyacinth made sure she didn't fall and then went back for Efrain.

Emilie picked twigs and leaves out of her hair, looking around. The top of the cliff was rocky and flat, with blue crystal slabs sticking up from the mottled gray stone, and little veins of crystal between them, glittering like streams of water. It stretched out for a few hundred yards to a forest of light green ferny foliage, clearly completely different from the forest they had just crossed through. Rising up from the forest, perhaps no more than a mile or so away, was a great lumpy hill all of gray rock, hundreds of feet tall, almost big enough to be a small mountain. It was studded with pockets of foliage that must mark various clearings and folds that might lead into little valleys. It seemed to have been here for some time, because she could see streaky white grooves that might have been waterfalls at some point, but were now dry.

Then a glint of metal caught her eye and Emilie stared. *That can't be right.* She dropped the professor's pack and hastily dug through it.

Efrain and Hyacinth stepped up beside her as she pulled the little telescope out. She straightened and peered through it at the gleam of metal on the side of the stone slope, adjusting the lenses to bring it into focus. *No, that's what it is.* Sticking out from the side of the hill, as if it had landed on a ledge concealed by a fold of rock, was the metal frame of an airship's balloon.

Emilie wouldn't have recognized it if she hadn't seen the ruined skeleton of Lord Ivers' airship, after Dr. Marlende had burned it. It might be something else that just happened to look like an airship frame, but whatever it was, that was clearly the place they needed to go.

"What is it?" Efrain demanded.

"I think it's a wrecked airship," Emilie told him. A blossom arm snaked the telescope out of her hand before Efrain could grab it. Hyacinth jammed the end of the telescope somewhere into the region of what Emilie thought its lower chest was. It had it pointed at the airship frame, so Emilie assumed that was actually where its eyes were. Or at least some of its eyes.

"But how . . ." Efrain began. "It's not our airship, is it?"

"No. No, it isn't." If it was a Menaen airship, there was only one that it could be. "Come on." Emilie shouldered the professor's pack again, tucking the telescope back under the flap as Hyacinth handed it back to her. "They might see us. We need to hurry."

* * *

Emilie didn't breathe easy until they reached the trees. They weren't very tall, but she and Efrain were both short enough to walk under the ferny foliage without crouching down. It also provided some welcome shade, since she was sweating from the run across the crystal-shard fields.

She wasn't certain how they were going to get up the hill until they got to the base of it. From there they could see the folds in the rock had formed natural ramps and pathways, much easier to climb than the steep smooth slopes of stone. The hard part was trying to find a way that would allow them to spy on the spot with the airship frame without walking directly up on it. After some fumbling on Emilie's part and some bad advice on Efrain's, Hyacinth took the lead, climbing rapidly ahead of them, then returning to show them the way it had found.

After a long scrambling climb, with skinned knees and bruised knuckles, Hyacinth returned from one of its scouting forays and crouched in front of Emilie. It waved its blossoms and then gently touched her face.

"You want us to be quiet," she whispered. She glanced back to make certain Efrain had heard, too.

It waved its blossoms again, but seemed satisfied and turned away, moving slowly so they could keep up with it.

It led them up a winding narrow channel that might have been part of a watercourse at one time, now choked with dark green-gray weeds. They came to a spot where the side of the channel opened into a little cliff. Hyacinth stopped and pointed down. Emilie leaned past it to look, and saw another dry water channel below this one, running parallel to it for a short stretch. But this one had been carved into wide steps, the weeds cleared away.

Efrain squeezed in to look over her shoulder. They exchanged a grim look. *We're almost there,* Emilie thought.

Hyacinth led them around a bulgy curve of rock, and then up the side and out of the channel onto a ridge. The top of the airship frame loomed above it. Moving slowly and carefully, they flattened their bodies against the rock and climbed to the top of the ridge to look over.

Below was a steep-sided well in the side of the hill, which might have been formed by water. It now held the cabin of an airship, still partially attached to the giant skeletal balloon frame and leaning at an angle. It was a large two-story cabin like the one on their airship, but it was battered and crushed along the bottom and had clearly been in a crash landing, perhaps even dragged over the stone of the hill. Shelters had been built into the side of the cliff with walls of piled rock and roofs made of slender wooden poles, and there was also a rock firepit and a square box made of slabs of stone that might be an oven.

And there were people. Menaen people, at least ten of them, dressed in ragged clothing, two carrying rifles . . . Efrain gripped Emilie's wrist and drew in a sharp breath. She stretched to look and spotted them: sitting in a small group near the airship cabin were not only Miss Marlende and Professor Abindon, but Dr. Marlende, Lord Engal, Cobbier, and Mikel.

They were sitting on the dusty ground, facing two strange people, a man and a woman, who were speaking earnestly to them. Emilie could see Lord Engal's stiff posture, and the professor's frown, and knew these weren't friends.

She edged back, drawing Efrain with her as Hyacinth followed them. Back in the shelter of the channel, keeping her voice to a bare whisper, she said, "We have to rescue them."

"How do we know they're captured?" Efrain asked. "Those are Menaens. They must be explorers who were trapped here too."

She shook her head. "Then why did Miss Marlende and the professor not leave us a note? Or say, 'No, we can't go yet, we have to wait for our friends Emilie and Efrain, who are here somewhere too'? Why didn't the professor take her pack? The ones who came for them didn't see it where it was lying against the rock, and she left without it, so we could find it and know something was wrong."

Efrain frowned. "But . . ."

"Lord Ivers and his men were explorers and Menaens and they almost killed us. The other Menaen explorers were the most dangerous people we met in the Hollow World. Without them, it wouldn't have been nearly so bad." She sat back. "Those people have to be the Deverrin expedition. They were lost last year sometime. Miss Marlende knew them. But why are they holding our people prisoner?" Could they think Dr. Marlende was trying to steal their work? That didn't make any sense, but it was the sort of nonsensical idea that explorers seemed to tend to.

Efrain didn't look convinced. "Are you sure?"

"They have rifles."

Efrain's stubborn expression turned troubled. "Miss Marlende and some of the others had pistols . . ."

It didn't change the point. "We had pistols because people like Lord Ivers keep coming after us. But the Deverrins are supposed to be friends of the Marlendes. Their brother, Mr. Anton Deverrin, asked Miss Marlende to look for them."

Efrain said, "Maybe someone was after them, like Lord Ivers was after Lord Engal, and they're suspicious of everyone now."

Emilie still rather resented it when Efrain said something smart, but there was no denying he had a point. "Maybe. But why would they think it was the Marlendes?"

Efrain lifted his brows. "Because it was?"

Emilie felt her cheeks flush, mostly with rage. Her first impulse was to punch Efrain in the face, or to tell him to take it back, or preferably both. But that was childish and she didn't have time for it. "I need a plan. And I need to know more before I can make one."

Ignoring Efrain's "But what . . ." she climbed back up the rock to the vantage point for another look at the camp.

The young woman and the man had moved away from the Marlendes and were talking with the others now. The Marlende group sat where they had been before, still watched by the two men with rifles, talking quietly together.

She realized the Deverrin party wasn't guarding their camp like people who expected intruders. There were no lookouts posted, no one watched the approaches to the hill. The elementary sort of thing one learned from playing pirate-fort as a child, or at least that was where Emilie had learned it. All their attention was on their prisoners, as if they were the only source of danger.

Maybe they were. Maybe the Deverrins had never seen any other people here, and thought the Marlende party was the only threat. If the situation was as tense as it looked, the Marlendes certainly wouldn't have mentioned the fact that there were a couple of their party still missing.

Emilie needed to get closer to where the Marlendes were being held, and maybe try to signal them if she could.

She climbed back down to where Hyacinth and Efrain waited. "I'm going around to the other side. There's a fold of rock there I can use to get down near the airship. From there I should be able to hear what they're saying."

Efrain glared at her. "You'll get caught!"

"Quiet!" Emilie glared back. "I won't get caught. I've done this sort of thing before."

Hyacinth stirred uneasily, its blossoms pointed toward them like it was disturbed by their behavior and trying to understand what was wrong.

"Emilie . . ."

"Just be quiet and stay here!"

Efrain started to get up. "If you're going to do this stupid thing, I'll come with you."

Emilie's jaw hurt from gritting her teeth. "Stupid? All right, Efrain, you're in charge. What do we do next? How are we going to free my friends? How are we going to get back to the airship? Hurry, before the aether current destroys it or snatches up Daniel and Seth and we're stuck here until we die."

Efrain stared at her, frustrated. "I don't know."

"Then sit here and be quiet." Emilie hurried away, moving quickly and quietly on the stone. She didn't look back.

* * *

It took Emilie a little time to get around to the airship and climb down that fold of rock. It was a good deal narrower than the one on the other side that Hyacinth had led them to, and it wasn't nearly as good cover. She had to wriggle on her belly through the last section, until she could finally hear voices.

Lord Engal was saying, "Believe me, my dear, we all understand your concern. We've just come back from an expedition where we were harassed unmercifully and nearly killed by Lord Ivers of the Philosophical Society. But I fail to see why you believe that we are a danger to you."

At least she had been right about that. The Deverrin expedition was suspicious and frightened. *But surely we can work that out,* Emilie thought. Suspicion was one thing but everyone would want to work together to get out of here before the aether current ripped this place apart or decided to drop a mountain on top of them.

The young woman's voice said, "My father will explain. I have no intention of being fooled by your false concern—"

"False concern?" Miss Marlende burst out. "I wish I'd never heard of any of you! You're all as mad as mercury-sniffers."

Dr. Marlende broke in, "Miss Deverrin, you've been gone a year.

If we had anything to do with it, why would we wait so long to come after you?"

"And why in the world would I participate in it?" Professor Abindon asked. "You, or at least your father, must know our history."

Emilie hoped she would elaborate, but Miss Deverrin said, "Perhaps you were duped."

Her voice acid, the professor said, "Young lady, no one 'dupes' me."

Someone called out and Emilie flinched, but Miss Deverrin said, "My father has returned." It should have sounded overblown and self-important, but there was a faint quaver in her voice.

It gave Emilie pause. Maybe it did the others too, as no one said anything as Dr. Deverrin's footsteps sounded lightly on the packed dirt. The silence was so tense that when a mild voice tinged with a Menaen country accent spoke, Emilie flinched. He said, "Well, this is quite a surprise. But I suppose you meant to come after us eventually."

Lord Engal said, "Deverrin, are you seriously suggesting that you believe we somehow sabotaged your expedition? Everyone believed your ship had broken up over the sea. No one had any notion that you were alive and trapped."

"This is exactly what I expected you to say, of course."

Professor Abindon said, "How exactly was this accomplished, by the way? I assure you, if Engal or Marlende could force an aether current to do their bidding, they would find better things to do with it than to attack the expedition of an inferior scholar."

Lord Engal sighed. Miss Marlende said, "Perhaps not the best point to raise, at the moment, Mother."

Dr. Deverrin said, "And what say you, Dr. Marlende? You're being uncharacteristically quiet on this subject."

Dr. Marlende said, thoughtfully, "I say that you're not Dr. Deverrin."

There was a moment of stunned silence. Or at least it was stunned on Emilie's part. She frowned, baffled by what Dr. Marlende might mean. That Dr. Deverrin wasn't behaving like himself? He couldn't mean that this person actually wasn't Dr. Deverrin. Some of these other people were members of the Deverrin family, and they were all known to the Marlende party. It didn't make sense.

Dr. Marlende continued, "I don't know what you are. I find this a very curious circumstance, and not something I have ever encountered before. You have Deverrin's face, and his body. But you do not have more than the most rudimentary elements of his mind."

Someone made a choking noise, almost a sob. Emilie was certain it was Miss Deverrin. After that the silence stretched again. Emilie's skin prickled all over and her throat went dry. *If someone accused me of not being me, I'd throw a fit. Or something. I wouldn't just stand there.* But Deverrin was just standing there.

Dr. Marlende said, "And now you're trying to exercise some sort of influence over my mind. Very odd. It might have worked, if I hadn't already seen through your deception."

Finally Dr. Deverrin said, "I see you've gone mad. Perhaps that's why you attacked us."

As if he hadn't spoken, Dr. Marlende said, "You see, Dr. Deverrin and I were very close, intimate friends when we were young men. We went to university together. We learned philosophy and magic together. We performed spells in tandem. I can't describe to you, whatever you are, how a deep aetheric bond can form between individuals. Particularly individuals who already share a great deal of sympathetic connections. We were not as close after university, as he was called on to marry and continue the Deverrin line, which we both knew would eventually happen. So the bonds of that time may no longer be as immediate, but they still exist. I would know if Alaine Deverrin was standing in front of me. And he is not."

"I see," Dr. Deverrin said, his tone unchanged. "It's a rather ridiculous accusation, and there isn't much I can say to it, is there? I assume you hope the rest of your party still on your airship will be able to carry out your plot against us?"

There was a moment's pause. Dr. Marlende said, "How did you know there is still crew on our airship? None of us mentioned it."

Dr. Deverrin just said, "Come away, this is pointless."

Miss Deverrin said, "Yes, Father."

Their footsteps crunched away across the dirt and gravel.

Lord Engal spoke first. "That wasn't some sort of ruse? You really believe that isn't Deverrin?"

"I wish it was a ruse." Dr. Marlende's voice was grim. "I have no idea how this could have happened. It must be something that . . . attached itself to him after his airship entered the aether current."

"There's never been any hint of the possibility of something like this in all the years of study of the sea aether currents," the professor objected.

"But there has," Miss Marlende countered. "There have been instances of crewmen acting in wild uncharacteristic ways, behaving violently, attributed to overexposure to the sea aether currents."

Lord Engal said, "Yes, but some of those men were recovered alive, and examined carefully by physicians and aetheric sorcerers. Surely some evidence of this, whatever this is, would have been found."

"I believe this is something native to the air currents," Dr. Marlende said. "And I think this creature knew about the crew left behind on our airship because it has some contact or connection with the aether sailer. From the way Miss Deverrin spoke, he leaves the camp frequently, but she seems to have no idea why."

A ghost pirate. Emilie would have to tell Efrain that they had been right.

Miss Marlende sounded worried. "That's frightening. If he . . . it . . . does something to Daniel and Seth or damages the airship—"

The professor said, "Perhaps it, or something like it, is why the aether sailer was abandoned. If we could speak to that member of the crew we encountered, so many questions might be answered."

Yes, if we could speak to it, Emilie thought in frustration. She wondered how she was going to get all this information across to Hyacinth. It clearly understood their broad attempts to communicate things like "we're going this way," "we're searching for others," and "those people might hurt us." But she didn't think she had much chance of explaining this and even if she somehow managed to, she had no chance of understanding its replies.

And if she couldn't get close enough to speak to Miss Marlende and the others, she had to at least let them know she was here so they could form a plan. She was going to have to try to let them see her, without letting anyone else see her.

She crawled farther along the ridge, heading for the airship frame. It took her what felt like forever to reach it, moving slowly and carefully, the rock scraping her knees and elbows. She squirmed around folds of stone, wiggled between narrow boulders. At the point where the rusted frame loomed over her, she began to wonder if she hadn't made a terrible decision. Or another terrible decision. The folds of rock were covered with gravel and stone chips and it was like climbing over broken glass. And she had to creep along very slowly to keep from making noise. She knew she should just turn around and go back, but she had come too far and wasted too much time to stop now.

Finally she got to a spot where she could crane her neck and see through a gap between two girders in the frame. She could see the little group of prisoners sitting in front of the airship's wrecked cabin. Some of the Deverrin crew sat nearby, gathered around the small campfire, their weapons in evidence, but the others were over by the stone shelters. Their attention was still on guarding their prisoners, not on anything or anyone who might come at them over the rocky ridge surrounding their camp.

Miss Marlende was seated with her legs folded and facing this way, though she wasn't looking up toward Emilie's position high in the ridge above the cabin. Emilie chewed on her lower lip, then decided to take a chance.

She pushed herself up slowly and cautiously, keeping an eye on the nearest Deverrins, the group sitting around the fire. Miss Marlende still wasn't looking up. As Emilie drew her feet under her, she felt something shift below her heel. Gravel rattled, slid through a gap in the rocks, and clattered down on the metal frame.

Emilie ducked and froze, cursing herself. The sinking sensation of having made a terrible mistake made her stomach want to turn. She wished she had listened to that feeling earlier. Someone yelled, "Up there!," and she heard footsteps crunch on the rock and gravel below.

Cursing herself again, Emilie scrambled farther along the fold, moving as fast and as quietly as she could. She came to a dead end, where she couldn't go any farther without climbing up the side of the rock and letting the whole camp see her. But it wasn't as if they didn't already know she was here. She gritted her teeth and started to stand, just hoping they didn't shoot her.

Then someone called out, "There he is!"

Emilie stopped. *He?* The footsteps all sounded as if they were running away from her now. *Oh, he didn't!* A shot went off and Emilie flinched. It echoed against the stone and her skin went cold.

But a few moments later she heard Efrain's voice, though she couldn't distinguish the words. She scrambled quietly back down the fold to where she could get a view of the camp again. Efrain was alive, being conducted down the stairs cut into the wall by one of the men. It must have been a warning shot. She leaned against the rock, dizzy with relief. The idiot must have deliberately showed himself, to distract from Emilie's blunder. What did he think he was doing? Maybe he hadn't thought anything, maybe he just hadn't wanted her to be caught. At least Hyacinth hadn't followed suit. If the Deverrins were this suspicious of the Marlendes, there was no telling how they would react to a flower person.

The man had Efrain by the arm, and pulled him off the steps and into the center of the camp. Several of the Deverrins still stood guard over the Marlendes, their guns at ready, but most gathered around Efrain.

Efrain stared at them with the wide-eyed innocence that had been so infuriating when he had used it on Uncle Yeric while tattling on Emilie. He sniffed and rubbed at his nose, making himself look even younger than he already did.

Dr. Deverrin strode forward. Emilie watched him nervously. This would have been anxious enough if it was just a somewhat paranoid Dr. Deverrin in there, but if it was really some sort of aether being . . .

Deverrin stared down at Efrain, who sniffed again, blissfully oblivious to the fact that he was facing something strange. Deverrin said, "There was another one, another young person. Where is she?"

Emilie froze. *How did he know that?* One of the others could have said something, but it was hard to imagine them being so foolish.

Efrain hesitated, taken aback, then blurted, "She's dead. We . . . I think the aether current dropped her too close to a cliff, and she fell, and she's dead!" He choked and sobbed, scrubbing at his eyes to cover up the fact that he wasn't tearing up. It was a tactic of his that she remembered well from the times when Efrain had claimed she had done something terrible to him. At last it was coming in handy.

Miss Deverrin put a hand to her mouth and the others shifted uncomfortably, looked to Dr. Deverrin or at each other. "There was nothing that could be done," Dr. Deverrin said. Which there wasn't, if it had really happened. But one usually expressed sympathy first before one got around to the "oh well, it was bound to happen" stage. At least in Emilie's experience.

Lord Engal swore and turned to the others, and Emilie saw Mikel and Cobbier exchange a worried look. Dr. Marlende squeezed Miss Marlende's arm, both of them watching Efrain carefully. The professor turned her face away, shielding it from the guards, and said something quietly. *They don't believe it,* Emilie thought. She just hoped Dr. Deverrin did.

CHAPTER NINE

Emilie made her way back around to where she had originally left Efrain and Hyacinth. She was tired, covered with sweat and dust, scratched and scraped and bruised, and angry with herself. *You really messed this one up,* she thought grimly. In hindsight, her overconfidence seemed obvious; it was frustrating that she had been too stubborn to see it at the time. And what Dr. Marlende had said made her wonder if he and Professor Abindon had fallen out because he had still been in love with Dr. Deverrin, who had now been taken over and possibly killed by an aetheric monster, and that seemed so sad. She would rather they had broken up over a difference in opinion on philosophical theories, or because their personalities were so irritating to each other. Thinking about it, she couldn't imagine the latter hadn't been a factor.

When she reached the fold in the rock where she had left the others, at first Hyacinth seemed to be gone as well. That wasn't encouraging. It might have had to withdraw, to keep any possible searchers from finding it. Or maybe it had just gotten fed up with her stupid decisions and had set off on its own.

She found their packs stuffed hastily under a clump of weeds. If the Deverrins had searched up here, they would have found them too, but at least Efrain had tried. She couldn't carry all three, so she took the water flask, rations, and anything else that looked useful out of Efrain's pack and put it into hers, then hid it more carefully. She started to stand, to shoulder her pack and the professor's, when Hyacinth swarmed over the nearest rock and plopped itself in front of her.

Keeping her voice carefully hushed, she told it, "Efrain got caught, and it was my fault. He did it to save me. And Dr. Deverrin isn't Dr.

Deverrin, he's something else, probably an aether monster pretending to be Dr. Deverrin."

It waved its arm blossoms in a beckoning motion, and turned away, heading back the way it had come. Emilie stared after it. It turned back, waved at her again, then returned, still waving. It seemed to be trying to point over the rocks, away from the camp.

"You want us to leave?" Emilie said. That seemed a little harsh, for it to want her to abandon Efrain. But maybe it was trying to show her something. "Do you want me to follow you?"

An arm wrapped around her wrist and tugged, trying to pull her away. "No, wait, I have to stay here and—" It stopped and waved at her urgently. It occurred to Emilie that the only other times Hyacinth had touched her was when it was trying to stop her from falling off a cliff or tree trunk. She took a deep breath. She had made a terrible mistake and gotten Efrain captured. It was time to at least listen to someone else. And maybe Hyacinth had found something important while she was off spying and being an idiot. "All right, I'll follow you."

Hyacinth led her up and around the side of the hill, away from the camp. Emilie kept her grumble of frustration to herself.

They followed another fold of rock for a time, then Hyacinth motioned for her to duck down and did its "quiet, danger ahead" blossom wave. Emilie crouched down and watched her steps, avoiding the loose rock. She could see the top of the airship frame jutting over the rock now, and had some idea where they were going, just not why. Then they came out to a ledge where they could see roughly cut steps leading to a gap in the rock: the main entrance to the camp.

Hyacinth settled in, sinking down into a sprawl on the ledge that made it hard to distinguish from a clump of foliage. Emilie hunkered down and tried to follow suit.

They waited for a while, the stone grating on Emilie's knees, until she began to get very thirsty. She was about to climb back down into cover so she could get her water flask out of her pack when she saw shadows move in the gap that led into the camp. She froze and huddled down as far as she could.

It was Dr. Deverrin who stepped out of the gap, followed by Miss Deverrin. Emilie could tell they were talking but couldn't make out the words. Miss Deverrin seemed to be worried and Dr. Deverrin was reassuring her. Then Dr. Deverrin turned away and started down the steps.

Emilie watched with narrowed eyes. He did move awfully easily for an older man. She had been thinking of him as being under the control of some creature or being, something that was mentally affecting him. But maybe that wasn't him at all, just something that had made itself look like him. She really wasn't certain what was worse.

He made his way down the steps and into a ravine in the side of the hill, then climbed down it until he disappeared from view. Hyacinth flowed into motion, slipping back down the fold in the rock to follow. Emilie scrambled after it.

What followed was an exceedingly difficult exercise in climbing, crouching, and crab walking up slopes, at least for Emilie. Hyacinth, with its light weight and extra limbs, was able to make it all look easy. Sweating and struggling to keep up, Emilie knew it was anything but.

Hyacinth kept darting ahead to watch the route Dr. Deverrin took, then returning to lead Emilie. They went down and around the side of the hill, through several jumbles of boulders, across a dry riverbed, and then into a shallow canyon whose floor was studded with giant shards of the blue crystal. The ground was flatter and easier to walk on but Emilie didn't like the idea of what would happen if they stumbled and fell against a crystal; all those edges looked sharp.

Then Emilie spotted something ahead, a metal spire, towering over the tall shards. She brushed Hyacinth's blossoms to get its attention and pointed up at the spire. It froze for an instant, then began to move rapidly sideways, making its way toward the wall of the canyon. They climbed the smooth sloping stone wall and took cover behind some tumbled rock.

Ahead, at the far end of the canyon, they could see what the spire was attached to. It was a ship of some kind, an aether ship. Hyacinth quivered all over with excitement.

The little ship was made of bright pewter-colored metal, with a rounded flat-roofed cabin studded by little windows. Standing above it was a metal sail, at least three times as large as the rest of the ship. The resemblance to the aether sailer was hard to miss. "It's your ship," Emilie said to Hyacinth in a voiceless whisper. "A small version of the bigger one?" Then the obvious explanation struck her. "Oh . . . It's a lifeboat. Or a launch?"

Dr. Deverrin was just coming out from between the blue shards, making his way toward the little ship. He came up to a round opening at the back, and climbed inside. Hyacinth made a noise she hadn't heard it make before, a sort of long hissing sound. She realized she hadn't heard it make any sort of noise before and thought it must be in the grip of some extremely strong emotion. Emilie dug in her pack and pulled out the professor's telescope, hoping to get a close look at Dr. Deverrin's expression when he left the ship.

After an interminable time, Deverrin finally emerged. Emilie focused the telescope on him, but his expression was completely blank. It was so blank, it was like looking at the face of a dead person, laid out by the undertaker for the relatives to take their last look. It gave her a cold sensation all up and down her back. It was just one more sign that Dr. Marlende was right. And she wondered if the other members of Dr. Deverrin's party had any idea this ship was here.

She would bet they didn't.

They watched Dr. Deverrin walk back into the forest of blue shards, then sat quietly, giving him time to cross it. He appeared briefly at the far end, just before he disappeared around a fold of rock. They waited some more, for safety's sake, then climbed down to the canyon floor.

This wasn't something she and Hyacinth had to discuss; it was clear they were going to the little ship.

Hyacinth bolted for it. Emilie had to keep stopping and looking toward the top of the canyon, in case this was a trick by Dr. Deverrin and he meant to double back and catch them. But there was no movement among the crystal shards.

The aether ship sat at an angle against the wall of the canyon, but it didn't look as if it had crashed. It looked as if it had simply been deposited there. Maybe it had, by the aether current, just like everything else here. Hyacinth went to the stern under the sail, where the round hatch was. The door stood partway open and it flowed inside without hesitation. Emilie stepped in after it.

There was no mistaking that this ship had been built by the same people as the big aether sailer. The walls of the long cabin were the same bronze color, with the same sort of chased metal strands embedded in the curved ceiling, except these didn't glow with light. Hyacinth went forward to the little round windows at the front, where there was a smaller version of the folded metal-paper globe, only about a foot across. In front of it was a panel with the same metal-paper controls as on the aether sailer.

Hyacinth moved its blossoms over the panel, and light flickered in the metal strands in the ceiling. "It still works!" Emilie pointed upward. She had thought the little ship was a derelict. They might be able to use this to get everyone out of this place and back to the airship. A terrible thought hit her. Did Hyacinth mean to leave now? "Uh, it still works, and everything, but are you actually planning to leave, because I can't go with you but if you would care to wait . . ."

She trailed off, as Hyacinth wasn't listening. It had opened a panel in the wall and drew out a handful of the metal-paper. It turned to hand it to Emilie. After a moment of hesitation she held out her cupped hands and took it.

Hyacinth turned to the panel and took out another clump of metal-paper. This one it kept, balancing it in several of its front blossoms. Emilie felt her metal-paper warm slightly against her skin. She hoped Hyacinth wasn't planning to leave and expecting her to help it pilot the ship. "What is this?"

The clump it held moved by itself as if in response, the metal-paper shifting into different patterns. It moved its blossoms over it again, then turned to face her expectantly. She stared back at it. It poked at the metal-paper clump in her hands and Emilie looked down at it.

The center of the clump had formed words, words in Menaen. They said, *It is a translator.*

Emilie sat down heavily, her knees weak with reaction. Hyacinth hadn't spoken aloud, or at least not in any way that she could hear. But this device would let them talk, and if they could talk, they could plan. She said, "That is a huge relief."

It sat down too, dropping down onto the deck, most of its blossoms limp with weariness. *For me also.*

* * *

So they talked. It was much easier than waving at each other. Its name and the name of the place it had come from didn't translate into Menaen, but when she told it she had been calling it "Hyacinth" it said it didn't mind. She supposed the word didn't translate, any more than its name for her did.

It had come with its people on the aether sailer, to explore this new current they had discovered. From what it said about the aether currents, the whole system was far more complex than the concentric circles of worlds that the Philosophical Society had envisioned, but Emilie didn't need to understand it to follow the story.

All had been going well aboard the aether sailer when one of the crew members began to act oddly, injuring others, and then had sabotaged the ship. The ship had gradually started to slow down, then finally became stuck in place in the aether current. They had quickly realized that some creature had actually taken over their friend's mind, and caused him—or her, the translator wasn't clear on gender, but that wasn't important either—to behave this way.

"That's what happened to Dr. Deverrin, the man we followed here," Emilie told it.

Yes, it told her, *I suspected this when we viewed the camp. I knew this lifeboat was missing, and the* something something *had disappeared. The creature must have destroyed it, and then stolen the lifeboat and come here.*

"Wait, that one didn't translate. Destroyed the what?"

Hyacinth turned back to her. *It was a mechanism, a device, for driving the creature out of a host. The* something *aboard our ship assembled it, to force the creature out of our friend. I had it with me, but when I woke after being incapacitated by the aether current, it was not there.*

The flower people had used the device to force the aether creature out of their friend, but they hadn't been able to repair their ship. The other crew members had taken the additional lifeboats and left, but Hyacinth had felt it was its duty to remain behind with this lifeboat, to make one more attempt to free the aether sailer. But the aether current had started to behave erratically, and had snatched the lifeboat away while Hyacinth was working on the aether sailer. It had seen the airship arrive, and it had been afraid to answer their hails, thinking they had been the ones who sent the creature. It had spied on Dr. Marlende's party, and had just decided to try to contact them when the aether current had swept over the ship again. Hyacinth had not been caught by the current but had been incapacitated by it, and had lain dormant for some time. It had just woken and heard movement on the ship again before it had run into her party. After a short time it had become clear, even without being able to understand their speech, that they had not sent the creature and were just as much at the mercy of these erratic aether currents as it was.

Emilie nodded. "Do you think the creature is making the currents do all this? That it made them grab your ship, and all of us?"

Yes. But how, or why, is unknown to me. Do you know what this place is?

"I was going to ask you that." It wasn't reassuring that Hyacinth didn't know. "It looked to us as if the aether current picked up chunks of land and brought them here. Is there any reason why someone would make an aether current do that?"

It seems dangerous and unwieldy. But there must be some compelling reason to create this construction. It might be a natural phenomenon, but it is not one my civilization has ever encountered before.

"We've never seen anything like it either." She told it about the disappearance of the Deverrin party in their airship last year, and how they had been presumed dead, and how Professor Abindon had detected the aether sailer and they had come up through the current to see what it was. "So the creature must have come here on the lifeboat after it sabotaged your ship, and it took control of Dr. Deverrin the way it did your crew member." But why was it doing this? Was it just collecting aether ships and people or did it have some sort of goal? "But why would it attack your ship and sabotage it so it would be trapped in place?"

We talked much on this, before the others left. We thought it must want something from our ship, or perhaps to use it to try to travel somewhere within the current. But this makes little sense in light of its later activities. It has succeeded in this; why is it still here?

"Yes, exactly. And does this little ship still work? I mean, if the creature wanted to use it to go somewhere, could it do it?" *Could we do it?* she wondered. Perhaps they could pick the others up and flee back to the airship or the aether sailer.

Hyacinth's blossoms shivered in agitation. *The power is low, and the* something *is a little damaged, but flight is still possible. But I also wonder . . . Why did the creature come here at this moment?*

Emilie felt another cold chill travel down her spine. "Oh. Maybe it was setting a trap for us. Maybe it realized we were watching it."

They both turned to peer out the little windows. Nothing moved in the canyon, though there could be a dozen people hiding among the blue shards. Emilie forced down the fear and made herself think. She looked up at Hyacinth, though she didn't know if it could really see her face, or if it did if it could read her expression. "If you help me free my people from this creature, we'll help you fix your aether sailer so you can get it out of the current and take it home."

Hyacinth waved its blossoms. *This was what I hoped we could do.*

Emilie nodded tightly. It was going to help her, they were going to help each other. That made her breathe a little easier. "I think . . . If we can get back to our airship, Daniel and Seth are there, and they can help us."

Hyacinth considered briefly, its blossoms opening and closing, and Emilie realized she was asking it to extend them a great deal of trust, just on her word. But it said, *We will do this. If we leave immediately, the creature will not be able to trap us, if that was its intention.*

Hyacinth turned to the panel at the very front of the ship and ran its petals over the metal-paper control. Emilie felt a hum travel through the deck, and the bronze lights blinked and began to glow softly. There were no chairs to sit in, so she crouched down on the deck where she could peer out one of the lower windows and hold on to a rail built into the wall.

The deck pushed against her feet as the ship lifted off the ground. The blue shards dropped away below, and Emilie was glad to see they were moving away from the camp, so there was no chance of the Deverrins seeing the launch. If Dr. Deverrin wasn't lurking out there waiting to trap them, then the longer it took him to realize the ship was gone, the better.

The ship moved away from the canyon, out over a dried empty lake bed. Then it shuddered and Emilie fell back, sitting down hard. "What happened?" It occurred to her belatedly that Dr. Deverrin's trap might have involved a weapon that could shoot them out of the air.

Hyacinth didn't answer, too occupied to look at the translator. The ship shuddered again, and the metal-paper controls and the globe flowed and changed like water. Another shudder, and Hyacinth waved its petals in agitation. Then the ship started to sink gently down toward the ground.

Once they had landed on the lumpy surface of the lake bed, Hyacinth turned to her and the translator said, *Something is wrong. The ship will not enter the aether current. We cannot travel away from this place without making repairs to the aether-navigation equipment.* It drooped a little. *It may take some time.*

Emilie eased back into a sitting position, and let go of her death grip on the railing. "Well, now we know why the creature didn't use the ship to escape." She let her breath out in frustration. "But we still don't know why it left the camp and came to the ship. If it knew we were following it and it meant to trap us, it should have done that right away, and not given us a chance to move the ship. It must have come here for another reason."

Hyacinth pivoted, as if looking over the interior of the ship for anything that was different. *Perhaps it has hidden something here.* It got up and started to search, finding little cabinets in the walls to look through that Emilie hadn't even seen were there. She followed it around, watching as it pulled various incomprehensible—at least to her—objects out and examined them. If this was a lifeboat, she supposed most must be supplies and survival gear for flower people. The paper started to move in her hands again and spelled out *There is nothing here that does not belong.*

Emilie turned around again, looking over the ship. It didn't seem disturbed, except by the search Hyacinth had just made. "So why did the creature come here in the first place and take over Dr. Deverrin? I mean, here to all these jumbled-up pieces of land, this construction. If it wanted to fly away, it had the aether sailer. I mean, yes, you said it sabotaged it, but then it should know how to fix it again, right?"

Hyacinth's blossoms suddenly all opened. The metal-paper formed the words *You said the people in the camp had been here for some time?*

"Around a year. That's a long time," she added, in case it didn't translate. "Before your aether sailer arrived." She realized the problem. "But this construction must have been here for at least a year, because what was left of the Deverrin airship crashed on it. So if the aether creature created this place, it could have taken over Dr. Deverrin first. It could even have sabotaged the Deverrin airship, just like it did your aether sailer."

And it did not have access to this lifeboat until recently, so it could not have been traveling back and forth between here and the aether sailer.

"It makes more sense if there's two of them." Emilie's throat was suddenly dry. "If the creature that attacked your crew is still on the aether sailer. If the creature who took over Dr. Deverrin has been here with the Deverrins the whole time."

If so . . . Perhaps the creature came to this ship to communicate with its companion. Hyacinth flowed toward the front, to crouch in front of the control panels again. Its petals moved over the metal-paper surfaces. After a moment, it swung back to face her. *We are correct. The communications device has been used. It has contacted the aether sailer.* Hyacinth's blossoms shivered. *It must have been talking to someone.*

Emilie nodded to herself, the cold feeling settling in the pit of her stomach. The creature had been there while they had searched the aether sailer, it had seen them all, and told its friend about it via the flower wireless in the lifeboat. "These two creatures are planning something. They don't just want to escape. If they did, Dr. Deverrin would be trying to repair this ship, so he could get back to his friend on the aether sailer and the two of them could leave."

Hyacinth turned back to her. *This ship has not been here until recently. Perhaps they have not been able to communicate until recently.*

Emilie sat down on the deck and thought hard. "I'm not sure we can count on that. The one that's back in the aether sailer isn't inside a person anymore, right? They're aether creatures, so they must be able to travel in the aether. Maybe it can still travel between here and the ship." She shook her head in frustration. There was still so much they didn't know. "I don't think it matters what they're planning so much, at least not at the moment. We just need to get my people and you and your ship, and this ship too, away from them." She looked up. "The other Deverrins don't seem to know that the creature is there at all. They think he's just Dr. Deverrin. But Dr. Marlende—he's the leader of our expedition—he knew right away it wasn't Dr. Deverrin." It had to be very difficult to believe that a strange ghost-aether-creature had taken over your father or mentor. But still, with all this time to witness his odd behavior . . . "Do the creatures confuse people, make them believe things? I'm trying to figure out why the other Deverrins haven't noticed anything odd."

Hyacinth thought that over, its blossoms opening and closing. *I did not witness that. But perhaps it has a different effect on your people. I have noticed that we must perceive sound and light waves in very different ways.*

"Yes, I noticed that too. I think you can see with your hands, and we can't do that at all, for example. Perhaps the ghost pirates can fool Menaens in a way they couldn't fool you and your crew."

Ghost pirates?

Emilie felt her cheeks flush. "Sorry, that was just a joke, between me and my brother Efrain—the one who just got caught, so the Deverrins wouldn't catch me. We thought something strange might be in the aether current, then we realized there were strange people here, and we called them ghost pirates."

If the translation is correct, that seems to be an accurate name.

Emilie had to agree. Calling it the ghost pirate seemed terribly irreverent, but Emilie doubted she could explain that to Hyacinth without sounding foolish. "Well, yes, I suppose it is."

Hyacinth's leaves and blossoms quivered. *We must try to force this ghost pirate from its new host. That will convince the rest of the host's family/clan of the danger, and perhaps they will assist us as well.*

First they had to rescue the Marlendes. Once they were free, it would be much easier to rescue the Deverrins and deal with the ghost pirates. And then hopefully get out of here and back to the airship and the aether sailer.

As Emilie thought about it, the rudiments of a plan started to come together. She said, "We have to lure the ghost pirate Dr. Deverrin away from the camp again. You can fly this ship anywhere you want around here, just not back out to the aether current where we came from, not until it's repaired?"

This land construction is a mass of aether currents, knotted together. It is only surprising that it has not come apart yet. Its blossoms were all pointed at her now, which she assumed meant it was very interested in what she was saying. *But yes, I can fly it within this construction, as long as the power lasts.*

She held up the metal-paper translator. "Is this like a wireless telegraph? Can it work from a distance?"

Yes. Hyacinth's blossoms waved in excitement. *I think I see what you are thinking. We will need to move the ship back to the canyon.*

CHAPTER TEN

This was going to be the scary part. Or at least, Emilie amended, one of the scary parts.

She felt very alone, walking back along the trail from the blue-shard canyon to the Deverrin camp. She kept trying not to think too hard about exactly what she wanted to say, for fear of sounding as if she was repeating a school lesson by rote. She stopped once along the way to smear even more dust on her face and her clothes, trying to make herself look pathetic and helpless. She had left both the packs with Hyacinth in the little lifeboat; she didn't want it to look as if she might be carrying something, since it would be a disaster if they searched her.

As she started up the crude steps to the camp's entrance, she heard a shout from inside. She froze, fighting the urge to dive off the steps and run. *You're a little girl,* she told herself, helpless. *Just like you were before you realized that you weren't.* She rubbed a little dust in the corner of her eyes to make them water, and kept climbing.

Two men appeared at the top, both young, around Daniel's age, both with the darker skin and hair that meant their families had Southern Menaen roots, like the Deverrins. Their clothes were ragged from hard use and their faces a little gaunt from rationing food, but other than that they both looked like university students or young-men-about-town. Except that one carried a rifle. They also seemed considerably startled to see Emilie.

"It's a young girl," one called out to someone behind them. The other asked her, "Who are you?"

Emilie sniffed and rubbed at her eyes again, trying to project an image of youth and harmlessness. "I'm Emilie. I was with the Marlendes. I don't know how I got here."

The one without the rifle reached down to help her up the last few steps, and she walked through the stone gap into the camp with them.

The airship's cabin and the skeletal remains of its balloon were on the left, looming over the stone hollow. The shelters and makeshift kitchen were built into the wall directly across from her. From here she could see that the Deverrins had taken the big fuel tanks out of the airship and moved them into shelter on the far side of the camp. She wondered if they still held fuel, then realized they must have been cleaned out and used to store water, taken from the lakes and streams that were transported here.

The Marlendes, Lord Engal, Professor Abindon, and Mikel and Cobbier were still seated near the airship's cabin, guarded by an older man with a rifle, and she was glad to see Efrain was still with them. Hopefully Efrain had had a chance to tell them that Hyacinth was helping them, which would make the rest of the plan go a bit more smoothly. When they saw Emilie, they all surged to their feet, staring.

Dr. Deverrin came toward her, followed by Miss Deverrin. They were both tall and slender, though Dr. Deverrin was several inches the taller. Miss Deverrin was lovely, even under all the dust and a year of what must be very difficult circumstances. Her brown eyes were clear and warm, her dark skin still unlined, and her curling dark hair tied back with a scarf. There was a definite resemblance in Dr. Deverrin's strong features. His hairline had receded and there was gray in his beard, but he was still a very handsome man. Except for something about his eyes.

Miss Marlende called out, "Emilie, are you all right?"

"Yes, miss," Emilie called back, and sniffled loudly.

Miss Marlende stared, as if startled by Emilie's demeanor. Emilie just hoped she wouldn't say anything that might make the Deverrins or the ghost pirate suspicious.

Miss Deverrin came forward. She knelt beside Emilie and clasped her hands. "Brendan, who is this?"

The young man who must be Brendan replied, "She said her name is Emilie, and that she was with them."

Dr. Deverrin glanced toward the Marlendes. "I see. Is that your brother? He said you were dead."

Emilie sniffled again. "I suppose he thought I was. We were on the aether sailer together and then we were here, and we got separated and I fell . . ." She looked up at Dr. Deverrin, earnest and trembling. The trembling was from nerves and some fear, but she thought it just made her story seem more believable. All the bruises and scrapes, and the little tears in her clothing from climbing rocks and tripping down slopes must help as well. "There was something there. A creature, on the aether sailer. It followed us here and tried to kidnap me."

At the words "creature on the aether sailer" an expression flicked through Dr. Deverrin's eyes that would have told Emilie that something was badly wrong, if she hadn't known it already. *He's wondering if I mean the other ghost pirate.*

The expression was gone a heartbeat later when Miss Deverrin looked up at her father. "This is the ship the Marlendes spoke of? They said it was empty."

"We thought it was." Emilie drew a shuddering breath, as if she was trying to be brave. "But there was this creature on it. When we came here, I got separated from Efrain, and it was nearby, and I didn't know what to do. I couldn't talk to it." She saw the professor and Miss Marlende exchange a look. "I didn't know what it wanted." She found herself almost enjoying the worry she must be causing Dr. Deverrin, making him wonder how much she knew. She reminded herself not to get overconfident again.

Dr. Deverrin said, "And what did this creature look like?"

"As if it was covered with flowers." Dr. Deverrin didn't betray any open relief, but she thought the set of his shoulders relaxed just a bit. Emilie could see the Marlende party past him and they looked more suspicious than the Deverrins. Cobbier kept glancing up at the rim of the canyon, as if he expected something to come at them over the top at any moment. Efrain just looked confused. He started to speak and Miss Marlende squeezed his shoulder and whispered something to him. Emilie wiped her eyes to hide her reaction. She hoped Efrain was sensible enough to just keep quiet.

"Flowers?" Miss Deverrin said. "Surely you imagined—"

Dr. Deverrin cut her off. "Where is it now?"

Trying to be as vague as possible yet still seem to be answering the question, Emilie said, "I'm not sure. The creature made me walk a long way. I saw the top of the airship." She pointed toward the airship's frame. She remembered she wasn't supposed to know anything about the Deverrins. She had meant to work more questions in earlier. "I guess you crashed here too?"

Miss Deverrin started to answer, but Dr. Deverrin cut her off. "What happened then?"

"We went past this place, into this canyon where all the rock was blue. And there was another little ship there."

That flicker went through Deverrin's gaze again. The other Deverrins were startled. The young man Brendan said, "What sort of ship? An airship?"

"No, there was no balloon. It was like a little sailboat." Emilie shrugged in what she hoped was convincing bewilderment. "It just let me go then. It went into the ship, and ignored me. So I ran as fast as I could. I came back here, because of the airship wreck. I thought there might be people here."

Brendan and Miss Deverrin seemed baffled, as if they didn't know whether to believe her or not. Dr. Deverrin lifted his head, as if listening to something no one else could hear. Then he focused on Emilie. "Are you telling the truth?"

Emilie nodded earnestly. "Yes." She seized on the point Miss Deverrin had clearly doubted, as if that was what Dr. Deverrin was questioning. "There really was a flower creature, I swear. I know it sounds mad."

There was a moment that seemed to stretch forever, as his regard bored into her. Then he said, "Put her with the others. I need to leave."

Emilie sniffled and wiped at her eyes again, to make certain she didn't betray any relief.

Miss Deverrin said, "But Father, we have to find out what . . ." She stared at him a moment, then blinked and looked away. "Yes, Father."

Some of the men standing nearby shifted uneasily, but didn't object. Dr. Deverrin strode away toward the camp's entrance without another word. Miss Deverrin watched after him, her lips pressed together in frustration.

Brendan took Emilie's arm and led her over to the Marlendes. She looked up at him; his expression was distracted, as if he couldn't remember something he had meant to say. That made a shiver run up her spine.

The ghost pirate must have an influence over all the Deverrin party. It didn't seem to have an influence over her yet, and hopefully not the other Marlendes. Maybe there hadn't been enough time for it to influence them.

Maybe it felt it needn't bother.

Brendan pushed her gently toward the Marlendes. Emilie flung herself into Miss Marlende's arms and sobbed into her shirtwaist. She snuck a glance back to make sure Brendan had retreated and the other guard was out of earshot, then whispered, "It's all right, I have a plan."

"You said she was quite capable, and I should have believed you," the professor said dryly.

"It wasn't fun growing up with her," Efrain said, sounding sulky. "She's a very good liar."

"In case you haven't noticed, you haven't finished growing up, and there's no point in pretending you have," Emilie told him.

"It was a masterful performance," Lord Engal said, his head turned away from any Deverrins still watching. "I thought you were actually weeping at one point."

Emilie was flattered. "My mother was an actress," she explained.

Dr. Marlende said, "I don't believe such talents are carried in the blood, my dear. You must take credit for it yourself. Tell us about your plan."

"Yes." Miss Marlende added, "I hope the bit about the ship was true."

"It was. Efrain told you about Hyacinth?"

Miss Marlende nodded. "He did. It's an ally?"

"Yes. I call it Hyacinth, because I can't say its name." She stepped away from Miss Marlende, drying her pretend tears on the handkerchief Lord Engal handed her. "An aether creature came aboard the aether sailer somehow, and took over a member of their crew, and then sabotaged the ship. The other flower people all got away, but Hyacinth stayed to try to get the aether sailer working again. We think Dr. Deverrin is possessed by a similar aether creature, working with the one still on the aether sailer. When Dr. Deverrin left earlier, Hyacinth and I followed him to a little wrecked lifeboat that came from the aether sailer."

"How did it tell you this?" Efrain said. "I thought it couldn't talk."

"Of course it can talk," Emilie hissed. "There's a translator on the lifeboat."

Miss Marlende and Dr. Marlende exchanged a startled look, and

Lord Engal said, "We'd barely got the hang of the idea that there was one aether being, and now you say there's two?"

"Yes. It's the only thing that makes sense. We think they're talking to each other, that maybe the one on the aether sailer was going back and forth between here and there on the aether current, but now they have the lifeboat and they're using its wireless."

"This lifeboat has a wireless?" Cobbier asked. "Can we—"

"It's not at all like our wireless. Hyacinth didn't know how to call our airship on it." Emilie thought she had given Dr. Deverrin enough time. "Are they still watching?"

Lord Engal glanced around, as if taking stock of their situation. "Not closely. It depends on what you need to do."

Emilie considered trying a faint, but she thought Miss Deverrin or some of the others might come running over. They all seemed awfully normal except for the control Dr. Deverrin had over them. It was probably better to just try to be unobtrusive. She wiped her face with Lord Engal's handkerchief, then leaned over and unlaced her boot. She whispered, "Warn me if they come this way."

The metal-paper was wrapped around her ankle, beneath her sock. It had already given her a bit of a rash, rubbing against her skin, but as she carefully worked it loose it moved in her hands. She curled the handkerchief around to hide it, lifted it and said, "It worked. He's coming your way."

The answer was almost immediate. *Success. I will be there.*

Dr. Marlende tried to lean in to see the device without it being apparent that that was what he was doing. "Ingenious."

Mikel and Cobbier both edged closer, trying to get a better look at the translator without making it obvious. Mikel said, "That's the metallic paper from the aether sailer. We wondered what it did."

"So it's like a wireless, but it can only call a similar device?" Cobbier asked.

"This one is a translator, really," Emilie said. "But Hyacinth thought it would work over this distance. It's powered by the aether current."

"They're coming back over here," Efrain whispered.

Emilie looked up, holding the handkerchief against her chest. Miss Deverrin and Brendan came toward them. They stopped to speak to the guard with the gun, then moved forward.

Miss Deverrin's expression was harder and more decisive. She said to Emilie, "Was this story rehearsed?"

Emilie shook her head, wide-eyed, too startled to formulate a reply. Miss Marlende came to her rescue with a cold "What story?"

"First you accuse my father of being some sort of . . . Of not being himself. Then this young woman says that there is some sort of creature running around here that looks as if it's covered with flowers—"

"Not a creature," Lord Engal interrupted. "A member of the crew of the aether sailer, left behind after the ship was abandoned. The aether sailer that did not appear in this area of the current until less than forty days ago, that your father seemed to know all about—"

Brendan interrupted, "That would be impossible. He didn't know about it."

"What have you done since you've been here?" Miss Marlende gestured to the airship. "You must have had fuel left, and your wireless and other equipment. Did you try to send a message in the current? Construct some sort of signal buoy? Or even to repair your ship?"

"We could do nothing," Miss Deverrin said, but she stared at the cabin of the wrecked airship as if she had forgotten it was there. As if she was shocked to see it.

Emilie followed her gaze, and saw there were dusty weeds around the doorway. She burst out, "Don't any of you even go in it anymore? What if someone tried to call your wireless?"

Miss Deverrin swallowed hard and didn't answer. Brendan looked away.

"Where did your father go?" Dr. Marlende added, watching her carefully. "He leaves often, doesn't he? Expeditions that have nothing to do with gathering food, or water, or wood. Does anyone ever go with him? Do you ask him where he goes?"

Miss Deverrin shook her head. Brendan said uncertainly, "He's scouting."

Lord Engal said, "I also have a large family, many associates, and more servants, and I can't go near the front door of our house without at least dozen people demanding to know what I'm about. Your father traipses off in the middle of this place, a howling wilderness of clapped-together bits of land from who knows where, and none of you thinks to object, or even question him?"

Professor Abindon said, "You're an intelligent woman. You know something is wrong."

Miss Deverrin's jaw set stubbornly. "There is nothing . . ." But she couldn't seem to finish.

The professor frowned. "Nothing wrong? You can't bring yourself to say it, can you?"

Emilie felt the metal-paper move in the handkerchief and snuck a glance down at it. It formed the words *I am near, be ready.* "It's almost here," she said aloud.

Miss Deverrin stepped forward, her expression turning angry. "What is that? What are you hiding?"

Emilie skipped back, snatching it out of reach. "Don't touch it. If you want it, you'll have to have me shot in the head."

Miss Deverrin stared, aghast, and Miss Marlende said, dryly, "Miss Deverrin, this is the real Emilie. I don't believe you met earlier."

Then Mikel, who had been watching the top of the canyon, said, "Is this our ride?"

The little aether ship floated up over the canyon wall, as light as a milkweed blossom, gleaming in the light. The Deverrins stared in shock, pointed, called out to each other. Miss Deverrin and Brendan and the other guard stared up at it too, but both guards still held their rifles. Emilie bit her lip, seeing the flaw in her plan. If the Deverrins shot at the ship, or shot at them while they were trying to get aboard, they could be in a lot of trouble.

But Miss Marlende flicked a look at Dr. Marlende, and then stepped toward Brendan. "That's the little ship Emilie saw, proof that she was telling the truth about everything. And proof that we're telling you the truth about your father."

Brendan shook his head, started to turn toward her. And Miss Marlende grabbed the barrel of his rifle. Surprised, he tried to wrench it away, but Dr. Marlende surged forward and punched him across the jaw. Brendan lost his grip on the gun and staggered back. Lord Engal grabbed Miss Deverrin by the arm. Cobbier and Mikel hurried toward the one remaining guard but he spun and leveled his rifle at them. Miss Marlende pointed Brendan's rifle at Miss Deverrin and said, "Drop it. You've threatened us and held us prisoner. I won't hesitate to shoot."

Miss Deverrin gasped, "No, don't believe her. She wouldn't—" But the man dropped his rifle. Cobbier hurried forward to grab it.

Miss Marlende ordered, "Get our things." Mikel and Efrain hurried to get the packs that had been stacked against the rocks nearby.

As the little ship hovered lower over the camp, Emilie ran toward it. Dust swirling around her, she waved and motioned for it to land. It sank gently toward the ground.

"We seem to have a hostage," Lord Engal said, pulling Miss Deverrin forward. In a lower voice, to Dr. Marlende, he added, "I've never had a hostage before and I'm not certain what we do next."

Brendan shoved to his feet and shouted, "Let her go! We won't try to stop you."

Miss Deverrin said stiffly, "If you mean us no harm as you claim, you should let me go."

Dr. Marlende hesitated, Brendan's heartfelt appeal clearly having an effect on him. Emilie didn't like it either, but now that they had Miss Deverrin, she was extremely reluctant to let her go. Miss Marlende said, "We should take her with us. Perhaps if she's away from the creature's influence long enough, she'll come to her senses."

"Odd, I was thinking the same thing about you!" Miss Deverrin snapped.

Professor Abindon said, "Vale, I believe you're right. The girl is already a good deal more spirited. We should take her with us."

The lifeboat touched the ground and bounced as if it didn't weigh anything. Emilie ran around to the hatch at the stern and pulled it open. "Hurry, everyone!"

Efrain climbed in first, then the professor and Lord Engal, pulling Miss Deverrin along with him. Cobbier and Dr. Marlende hung back, pointing the rifles at the other Deverrins, as Miss Marlende and Mikel stepped in. Emilie followed them, backing in to give the others room to get aboard. Inside, everyone was crowded along the walls, staring at Hyacinth, who crouched over the controls, its rear blossoms pointed toward them. Efrain had taken a position up next to it, looking out the front window.

Emilie said into the translator, "Everyone, this is Hyacinth. Its real name doesn't translate to Menaen, and I don't think our names translate to its language, so . . . it may be a bit confusing now there's more than two of us."

The translator formed the words *I will point at who I mean to speak to. Or perhaps we could assign you numbers.*

"Now you're teasing me," she told it.

Stepping into the hatchway, Dr. Marlende called out to the Deverrins, "We will return for you all, as soon as we're able!"

He backed inside. Cobbier scrambled aboard, then handed the rifle off to Mikel so he could pull the hatch shut. Emilie told the translator, "That's it! Please take off now."

The ship's deck swayed as the ship lifted up. Emilie glimpsed the top of the ridge, and felt the tightness in her chest unknot. *We did it.* Miss Deverrin folded her arms stubbornly, glaring at all of them. She said, "You're common criminals."

"Young lady, you were holding us prisoner," Lord Engal said, exasperated. "You don't get to call foul when we escape."

Professor Abindon added, "And if you still believe our story is a lie, why is there an intelligent plant flying this craft?"

Miss Deverrin's jaw set and she didn't answer. Emilie could tell she was going to be a tough nut to crack. She could understand why: if Miss Deverrin admitted they were right about her father, she had to admit that she had been a fool, who had been tricked or mentally controlled by an alien creature. And she would also have to admit that her father might be dead. Or that he couldn't be saved.

Then Efrain shouted, "He's coming back! I see him!"

Emilie turned and squeezed in between Miss Marlende and the professor to see out the window. Dr. Deverrin stood on the path up toward the camp entrance, just staring at the ship. His lack of reaction was chilling.

Everyone found a window, watching him. Sounding more curious than afraid, Cobbier said, "That's just not normal. You think Deverrin is still in there at all?"

Dr. Marlende shook his head. "I don't know." He looked toward Hyacinth. "Perhaps our new ally can help us find out."

As the ship pulled away, Dr. Deverrin disappeared behind the trees. Emilie felt the translator move in her hand. She looked down to see it read, *Where should we go?*

"Hyacinth wants to know where to land," Emilie said. "We can't take the ship out into the aether current yet. It needs to be repaired."

Dr. Marlende said, "Go back toward where we were first deposited in this world. It will be far enough away that Deverrin won't easily find us, and perhaps the current will be easier to access from that point."

Emilie consulted the translator, and said, "It wants you to point out the direction, please."

Dr. Marlende did so, and they all swayed as the ship turned.

* * *

Hyacinth landed the lifeboat on a large flat spot on a hill near where they had first been deposited in the construction.

After a long talk with Hyacinth via the translation device, Dr. Marlende, Professor Abindon, Lord Engal, Cobbier, and Mikel began to consult on a way to get the little ship able to enter the aether current again.

Before they started to work, Lord Engal told Miss Marlende, "We'll need to keep watch. Deverrin—or the creature, whatever it is—may try to come after us."

Miss Marlende held one of the rifles, looking out over the hills and the purple-tinged forest. "He shouldn't be able to tell what direction we fled in, but we don't know what his abilities to track us are."

"Do you think he could tell when the aether current fluctuated and brought us here?" Emilie said. "Either that, or the creature aboard the aether sailer called on the lifeboat's wireless and told him."

"Hmm." Lord Engal said, "I suppose we won't know until we can ask him," and went back to join the others.

Once they helped Hyacinth repair the lifeboat, they would need to figure out what to do about the Deverrins, and the other ghost pirate still on the aether sailer. Emilie was feeling a little overwhelmed.

She was so overwhelmed she thought she was having a conversation with Miss Marlende, until she woke abruptly, lying in the grass, with her head pillowed on a pack. She sat up, looking around blearily.

Efrain lay nearby, curled around a pack and sound asleep. Miss Marlende sat next to him, keeping watch with the rifle across her lap. Miss Deverrin sat a short distance away, her arms folded, grimly staring down the hill. Miss Marlende said, "You were exhausted, so I just let you sleep."

The others still gathered around the lifeboat. The hatch was open and Emilie could see Lord Engal sitting with Hyacinth and talking on the translator, while Mikel and Cobbier had their packs open and strewn around and were working on something that looked like a small portable wireless. Dr. Marlende and the professor had their heads together, both writing in notebooks. They must be working out a spell. Emilie said, "Did he leave her because he was still in love with Dr. Deverrin?" Then she realized she had said it out loud, and felt her cheeks flush.

Before the embarrassment set in too heavily, Miss Marlende sighed and said, "No, I think that was all over with long before they separated. I blamed my mother for it, for a long time. But watching them now . . . I think both of them just realized they didn't want to be married. They were always very good colleagues, it had been so long since I'd seen them together, I'd forgotten about that. I suppose they thought that because they worked so well together, they should marry. But they fought so much."

"Oh." It must be odd, to watch that happen to your parents. Emilie's parents had died so young; they were preserved as a perfect couple in her memory. She decided on the whole it was better to have imperfect but living parents, even if they were living in different towns.

She looked at Miss Deverrin's stiff, angry back. What must it be like to see someone—something—else in your father's body. "Hyacinth said the ghost pirate took over the body of his crewmate, but they made it leave. But Hyacinth also said it must be different, for his people and us. Maybe we can still get it out of Dr. Deverrin."

Miss Deverrin didn't react at all.

Miss Marlende said, "I hope so. I just wish we knew why the creature, or creatures, if your theory about the second one aboard the aether sailer is correct, did this in the first place."

Emilie agreed. So far, the ghost pirates had had the Deverrin airship, an aether sailer, and an aether sailer's lifeboat, and done nothing with any of them. They had to be planning something. Emilie sighed in frustration, and looked toward Miss Deverrin. It might be helpful if Miss Deverrin could tell them about what Dr. Deverrin had done since they had arrived here, when his behavior had changed, and if he had ever spoken of creatures living in the aether. "Do you think she's listening to us?"

"Yes." Miss Marlende frowned. "It's a great deal to take in, in such a short time. But if she doesn't listen to us, the rest of her party is doomed."

Miss Deverrin flinched.

Dr. Marlende called to them from over by the lifeboat. "My dears, we think we have it!"

Miss Marlende stood. "Emilie, wake Efrain, please. Miss Deverrin—"

The ground underfoot rippled. Emilie, caught as she was about to stand, thumped back to the ground. Efrain sat bolt upright. Miss Deverrin shoved to her feet and looked around wildly. "There!"

Emilie stepped back, wary that it might be a trick, then looked.

In the distance, a big dark shape dropped toward one of the rounded, oddly formed mountains. It was like watching an airship land, but it was so far away, it had to be huge. It plummeted down toward the mountain and hit the slope. The ground shook, hard enough to rattle Emilie's teeth.

Chunks of rock tumbled down the mountain, and an avalanche started as all the slopes below started to slide. The whole mountain shuddered and settled into a different shape.

Emilie's throat was suddenly dry. "That's right. They aren't mountains. They're piles of . . . pieces." It was one thing to theorize about it, another to see it happen. She turned to look at Miss Marlende.

Dr. Marlende stood next to her and Miss Deverrin. Efrain had run to the doorway of the lifeboat. He called out, "I think we should go inside!"

"Yes. Yes, we should," Dr. Marlende agreed. He stepped back to let Miss Deverrin and Miss Marlende go first, and motioned for Emilie to hurry.

CHAPTER ELEVEN

Emilie stepped into the lifeboat. The panels at the front had been lifted off, and Hyacinth was crouched over the strange objects inside. Lord Engal, Cobbier, and Mikel had already carried all the packs and tools inside. Professor Abindon sat on the deck with her notebook in her lap. They all stared worriedly, including Hyacinth, who had all its blossoms extended. "What was that?" Lord Engal asked.

Dr. Marlende said, "The current fluctuated and brought in another section of ground from somewhere. I suggest we make our departure as soon as possible."

Miss Marlende asked, "You've repaired the ship?"

Dr. Marlende explained, "Hyacinth has been able to ascertain that the only function that is damaged is the mechanism that allows the lifeboat to enter the aether current. We can't repair it with the tools and material available, but we can construct a spell to replace it. Fortunately, the aether-navigation device the ship uses is still functional. Once the lifeboat is in the current, we should be able to use its own navigation equipment to guide it back to the aether sailer and our airship."

Her voice cold, Miss Deverrin said, "And what will you do then?"

Professor Abindon turned to regard her. "Then we will find and confront the creature we believe is still aboard. Hopefully at some point you will break free of its influence and help us try to rescue your father and the others in your expedition."

Miss Deverrin grimaced and looked away. She said finally, "Then . . . you don't plan to kill my father?"

"Of course not." Dr. Marlende sighed, wearily frustrated. "My dear young lady, we are trying to help you."

"How?"

Lord Engal gestured to Hyacinth. "Our friend here has described in detail the device its crew constructed to force the aether creature from its first host. That device has undoubtedly been destroyed by the creature still aboard the ship, but we may have the materials aboard the airship to construct something similar."

"Or at least," the professor added, "use an aether navigator to demonstrate that there is something very odd about your father."

Miss Deverrin's brow furrowed, and her expression was conflicted. Emilie seized on that. "Didn't you have an aether navigator on your airship? Did it do anything odd?" She remembered the disused condition of the airship's cabin. It had been strange that the Deverrins hadn't used the airship cabin as a shelter. Emilie had put it down to Dr. Deverrin's influence, but hadn't thought further than that. "You must have had an aether navigator. And other equipment. What happened to it?"

Miss Deverrin shook her head. "It was broken in the crash."

Miss Marlende's voice was highly skeptical. "If the plate for your aether navigator 'broke' I don't see how the rest of the cabin survived intact."

Emilie knew what she meant. The plates for aether navigators were solid silver. And she knew from the Lord Rohiro books that they were relatively easy to assemble, if you had a sorcerer who could manipulate aether. If something had happened to the one aboard the airship, Dr. Deverrin should have been able to repair it or build another.

"He didn't want any of you near it, did he?" Professor Abindon watched Miss Deverrin speculatively. "Tell me: Your father was known as a sorcerer of great skill. Has he done any magic since you've been here?"

"No, but . . ." Miss Deverrin shook her head. "This place affected him!" she burst out. "It affected us all. You can't understand."

Professor Abindon grimaced in irritation. "Talking to this woman is pointless. Are we ready to go?"

Cobbier picked up the translator and relayed the question. Hyacinth waved its blossoms in assent, and Cobbier said, "It says to close the door and hold on."

Mikel pulled the hatch shut and they all found a place to brace themselves.

Emilie managed to get a spot close enough to see the translator, which Cobbier still held. The lifeboat's deck pushed up against her feet as the ship left the ground, and Emilie breathed a sigh of relief. Then Mikel said, "Look. We had about another hour, if that."

Emilie turned toward the nearest window, sharing it with Miss Marlende. "I don't . . . There!"

Two hills away, in an area where the trees were sparse, several human figures were visible. They stopped as they saw the lifeboat, and Emilie was certain the one in the lead was Dr. Deverrin. A cold feeling crept down her spine. *Too close,* she thought.

She turned away from the window to see Hyacinth's blossoms lifted inquiringly.

"It was the Deverrins," Emilie told the translator. Cobbier held it up so she could speak into it more easily. "They were coming toward us. Somehow they knew where we were."

That is disturbing, Hyacinth replied. *The ghost pirate must be very sensitive to the aether currents caught in this construct to detect our movements in that way.*

Emilie read the answer aloud for the others, forgetting to change "ghost pirate" to something more dignified. "Ghost pirate?" Efrain said, grinning at her.

"If the name fits, use it," Emilie said, embarrassed.

"Names aside." Professor Abindon said into the translator, "Guide us to the current, please."

The ship lifted up and up, but there was no gradual darkening of the sky. The light was the same. "Is the light coming from the aether current itself?" Emilie asked softly. "We wondered when we got here."

"Yes, it seems to be a side effect of whatever is attracting and holding these pieces of world in place." The professor stared intently out the window, then looked back at the translator. "I'm not sure this is a mystery that we will ever solve."

Unless we can get the ghost pirates to talk, Emilie thought. She had the feeling they knew everything about this place.

With the others, Emilie had been keeping an eye on the ball of metal-paper that functioned as the ship's aether navigator. Her gaze on the translator, the professor said, "We're nearly there, and the current is starting to fluctuate."

Dr. Marlende crouched near the little device he and the others had assembled earlier. It was made mostly from silver wire, along with the disassembled parts of an aether compass and a jar from their rations that had originally held pickled vegetables. "It's to contain and amplify the spell," Lord Engal told Emilie.

The professor read off the translator: "It says, 'Be ready, be ready.'"

"Everyone hold on," Cobbier warned. "It's going to be rough."

Emilie wrapped her arm more firmly around the rail and looked to make sure Efrain had done the same. Miss Deverrin grudgingly gripped a rail.

The professor said, "Now!"

Dr. Marlende touched the jar and Emilie saw a faint shower of sparks. The lifeboat shuddered and jerked, and she bumped against the wall despite her efforts to hold steady. Then it was as if a giant grabbed the lifeboat and shook it.

Emilie's feet slipped out from under her but she held on, even when she slammed against the wall again. Someone fell into her and she grabbed hold of an arm with her free hand.

The shaking stopped abruptly. Emilie blinked, dazed. It was dark outside the lifeboat, the interior lit only by the bronze lights in the curved ceiling. The person who had fallen onto her was Efrain, and Miss Marlende had grabbed his other arm to steady him. Hyacinth had turned some of its blossoms into suction cups to grip the front panel.

Lord Engal muttered, "I hope we've done it."

"I would think the ship would have fallen apart by now if we hadn't," Dr. Marlende said, pushing to his feet. The pickling jar lay broken on the deck.

Everyone managed to stand, turning to look out the windows. Emilie's heart leapt as she saw the darkness was the familiar rich purple cloudscape of the aether. She pressed her face to the window and could just see the tip of the aether sailer's sail. "We did it! It's down there, below us!"

The lifeboat swept around, turning back toward the aether sailer and giving them a better view. The airship was still connected by the lines and ladder. Daniel and Seth must be very worried by now. She wondered if Seth might have tried to go aboard the aether sailer when they had failed to return. He could have, with Daniel to cast the protective spell over him.

"I hope Daniel and Seth are all right," Miss Marlende said, her voice low.

Emilie turned to stare at her. She hadn't thought of something using the connection to climb down to the airship. "The aether creature . . ."

"Yes." Miss Marlende's expression was troubled. "We don't know how it—or they—choose victims to attack. And it may have wanted to secure the airship."

Emilie turned to look again. The lifeboat circled to the stern of the aether sailer, and only the topside of the airship's balloon was visible. She turned away in time to catch an expression of doubt and fear cross Miss Deverrin's face. *She can't believe all this is acting for her benefit, just to fool her,* Emilie thought. No one was that self-centered. They must be getting through to her, no matter how much the aether creature had clouded her thinking.

As the lifeboat came about, the aether sailer loomed over them, huge and shadowy in the half-light of the current. Its rounded stern had a dozen or more small doorways in it, each big enough for the lifeboat to pass through. One had been left open, and Hyacinth guided them toward it. "Marvelous," Lord Engal said under his breath.

Emilie agreed. It was almost exciting enough to make you forget the huge ship was infested with a body-stealing aether creature.

The ship wobbled a bit as it approached the doorway. A slithering thud just above her head made Emilie jump, but she realized it was the lifeboat's sail folding down. The lifeboat slipped through the doorway and bumped gently to a halt inside.

The professor looked down at the translator and reported, "Hyacinth says to wait for the *something* to take effect, so it will be safe to leave the ship." She glanced up, craning her neck to see out the window. "I assume it means some sort of protective spell."

Emilie pressed her face to the window again. The interior seemed dark, but after a moment her eyes adjusted and she saw the bronze lights glowing down from a high ceiling. The ship rested against a dock in a long rounded room, with a door at the end. A large section of one wall was covered with the metal-paper, moving gently and reshaping itself.

"The outer door just closed," Mikel reported from the stern window.

Hyacinth moved away from the panel. The professor translated: "It says, 'All is well, open the hatch.'"

Mikel moved to unlatch the hatch, and climbed out first. The dock was wide, and there was a window in the outer door looking out into the aether current. Emilie followed with the others, Cobbier and Lord Engal pausing to hand out the packs and rifles. Professor Abindon handed off the translator to Emilie.

Hyacinth emerged from the hatch, its part of the translator clutched in its blossoms. *We must hurry to the work area.*

Hyacinth went to the inner door and pressed a blossom against the wall next to it. The door popped open.

The bronze corridor beyond was empty, leading a short distance into the ship before one side opened up to the giant metal levers they had seen before. It helped Emilie connect their current position to the part of the ship they had briefly explored. They were on the other side of the left-hand wall of the large room they had chased Hyacinth through. Hyacinth extended its blossoms into the corridor for a moment, then cautiously moved out into it.

From behind her, Mikel said, "This thing can't jump us if it's not in a body. Can it?"

"Relay the question, please, Emilie," Dr. Marlende said.

Emilie did. Hyacinth replied, *I thought it could not. But I fear it will have thought of some method. It has found ways to affect things inside the ship, the way it destroyed the device we used to drive it out of our companion.*

That's not good, Emilie thought, and read its answer aloud. Miss Marlende muttered, "Lovely."

They followed Hyacinth down the corridor, past the giant levers, and then through a junction and up a walking wall shaft to the upper levels. Hyacinth swarmed up the shaft effortlessly, and watching it do so made the design seem quite sensible.

Emilie glanced back at one point to see Miss Deverrin's expression of wonder and consternation. She realized it had been some time since Miss Deverrin had accused them of lying and plotting against her father. Hopefully all this was helping to knock her back to her senses. If they had her help, it would be easier to rescue the rest of her party, and do something about the creature inside Dr. Deverrin.

Hyacinth led them to the starboard side of the aether sailer, to a set of rooms they hadn't seen before. It was a windowless interior space where the walls were lined with twisted spills of the metal-paper. There were bronze metal canisters stacked around, and weird little instruments that must be tools. Hyacinth said through the translator, *This is our workroom, where the device was originally constructed.*

Everyone set their packs down on the floor and began to unload tools and notebooks and other things, and Emilie brought Professor Abindon's pack.

"Oh good, you found it," the professor said, coming over to sort through the contents. She looked around thoughtfully. "We'll need more materials and tools if we're to re-create this device."

"Yes." Dr. Marlende pulled his pack off his shoulder and began to empty it. "Cobbier and Mikel, I want you to take Emilie and Efrain back to the airship—No arguments," he said, as Emilie drew breath to argue. "I'll be sending you with a list of supplies that we need, as soon as I draw one up."

Emilie folded her arms. It was annoying to be sent away, but she wasn't going to follow Miss Deverrin's example and cause trouble by resisting simple precautions. Efrain said, somewhat reluctantly, "We could stay and help guard you."

"A kind offer, but not necessary." Dr. Marlende smiled, and unrolled a leather flat of tools. "We don't know how this creature chooses its victims, and if there is one still aboard this ship, we want to give it as few options as possible."

"And Daniel and Seth need to be warned," Cobbier pointed out. "They must be going out of their heads with worry by now."

"What is the principle of this device?" Miss Marlende asked. "I missed that discussion."

Through the translator, Hyacinth said, *It is similar to your aether navigator that was described to me, but its only purpose is to identify aether within living beings.*

The reason Dr. Deverrin had avoided the aether navigator in the wrecked airship. Emilie asked, "So people don't normally have any aether inside them?"

"We don't, as such," Lord Engal told her, taking tools and some instruments she recognized as being for aether manipulation out of his pack. "Though there are substances that seem to be similar that have yet to be truly understood. The presence of aether in a human—or apparently, in any living being—would be an indication that something odd was going on."

Once the aether is identified, it can be forced out, Hyacinth explained. *I will read off the plan to you. Hopefully the translation device will be able to keep up.*

Hyacinth went to one of the metal-paper spills in the wall and removed it, unfurling it out into a large ball. It managed this while still holding the translator device in another set of blossoms. Miss Deverrin walked around the room, staring at all the strange things. Emilie noticed Miss Marlende was keeping an eye on her, and was glad. They still had no real idea how cooperative Miss Deverrin meant to be. Or if she was still under the control of the aether creature.

Professor Abindon turned suddenly, one hand lifted to her temple. "Did you feel that?"

Miss Marlende frowned. "What?"

"A pressure, as if the air was drawn out of the room for a moment." The professor stared around in consternation. "None of you felt that?"

"No." Lord Engal pushed to his feet, his brow furrowed. "Anyone else?"

Worried, Emilie shook her head. "Nothing. You think it's a problem with the ship? Its protective spell?"

Mikel stepped to the doorway to look into the corridor. "It can't be. We'd have felt it. And, you know, we'd be having trouble breathing."

The others looked around the room warily. Hyacinth had gone still, blossoms lifted as if testing the air. Then Emilie saw that Miss Deverrin had pressed her hands over her mouth, as if she had had a bad shock. Emilie pointed at her. "She knows something!"

Miss Marlende stepped toward Miss Deverrin, caught her by the shoulders, and held her firmly. She said, "Tell us. You must tell us."

Miss Deverrin lowered her hands and her expression was horrified. She said, "Just before our airship was torn out of the current, my father said he felt the same thing, that the pressure had dropped, but none of us felt anything . . ."

Miss Marlende stepped away from her and looked at Professor Abindon. "Are you all right? You don't . . . feel anything else?"

Everyone stared at the professor, and Hyacinth pointed all its blossoms at her. She planted her hands on her hips and frowned thoughtfully. "I don't think I've been possessed by an aether creature. Surely there would be some indication."

That was when Emilie realized that Dr. Marlende hadn't said

anything. He was still in the same position, kneeling on the floor over his roll of tools. *Oh. Oh, no.* A sick fear creeping over her, Emilie said, "Miss Marlende . . ." and pointed.

Miss Marlende turned to look. Her face went still. "Father? Father, look at me."

Dr. Marlende didn't respond. Then he suddenly jumped up and bolted for the door. Emilie yelped and flinched away, then realized she should be trying to trip or tackle him. That wasn't Dr. Marlende, it was a monster who was kidnapping Dr. Marlende. Lord Engal was the first to lunge forward. But before Dr. Marlende could reach the doorway, Hyacinth pushed its blossoms against the wall and the door slammed shut. Dr. Marlende turned at bay, and the professor yelled, "Grab him, now!"

Dr. Marlende darted toward the pile of packs where one of the rifles lay. Emilie was closest and flung herself on top of the weapon. She knew she couldn't stop Dr. Marlende herself and had no intention of trying to shoot him; she just meant to keep him from getting the gun until the others could tackle him.

He grabbed her shoulders to shove her away and Emilie hung on to the rifle, jamming her hand in behind the trigger so it couldn't go off accidentally. Lord Engal went flying past over her head and an instant later Dr. Marlende lost his grip on her. She rolled away, still holding on to the gun. Lord Engal had landed on Dr. Marlende and flattened him to the floor. Cobbier hurried to help and Mikel grabbed the other rifle.

Miss Marlende pulled Emilie to her feet and carefully pried the rifle out of her hands. She said, breathlessly, "Thank you, Emilie."

Emilie looked up into her face and swallowed hard. Miss Marlende's face was drawn and hollow, as if she was about to faint or be very ill. Emilie knew she wouldn't do either, but it was terrible to see her in this state and know what she must be feeling. "It's going to be all right," Emilie blurted.

Miss Marlende said, "Yes, of course," and then unloaded the rifle, putting the bullets away in her pocket.

Miss Deverrin had put her back against the wall, a hand pressed against her chest. Her expression made Emilie think the woman was reliving some nightmare moment. Maybe it was a nightmare moment she had just remembered. Maybe whatever influence the creature had confused her mind with was finally broken.

Efrain edged forward, trying to get a better look at Dr. Marlende. "Is he all right?"

His voice tight from effort, Lord Engal said, "I believe so . . . He certainly isn't making any effort to pretend to be Marlende."

Professor Abindon said, "The creature must realize we were suspicious. And it must have known we were about to build the device." She pulled a white canvas medical kit out of a pack and opened it. "Just hold on to him for a moment."

"I'll certainly try," Lord Engal said grimly.

Miss Marlende shook her head helplessly. "Why him? Did it try to pick the leader of our party?"

The professor checked the vials of different drugs in the kit. "Where's the translator?"

"I've got it!" Efrain hurried to pick it up where it had fallen on the deck. The metal-paper had unraveled when it hit the floor but as Efrain gathered it up it coiled back into shape.

"Ask Hyacinth if the member of its crew who was taken over was a sorcerer," Professor Abindon said, her voice harsh with worry. To Miss Marlende she added, "Dr. Deverrin was the only sorcerer aboard the Deverrin airship."

Efrain reported, "It says yes, the crew member who was taken over was an aether manipulator." He frowned. "I think that means the same thing as sorcerer."

The professor nodded, her expression determined. "That would explain it. It tried both of us, and it must have gotten Marlende first. He was distracted, thinking about the device we were about to construct, that may have helped it. Ah, here it is." She pulled a vial out of the padded pocket in the kit, then a hypodermic needle. "This creature must be attracted to those who have the most magical ability, or perhaps those who are the most experienced. Perhaps it's incapable of taking over a person with little or no magical ability."

As Professor Abindon began to prepare the hypodermic, Emilie felt her eyes get wide. She asked, "Are you going to drug him?"

"Yes, I am."

Miss Marlende said, "Mother, is that wise? If he can resist the creature—"

"Deverrin wasn't able to resist it, and neither was the sorcerer aboard this ship. I doubt your father will be able to." The needle ready, she walked over to the struggling men. "I just don't want this thing interfering with him while we build the device. And with your father incapacitated, I need Engal's help. Someone's going to have to do the menial labor."

"That's very good of you to say, Professor," Lord Engal managed, struggling to pin Dr. Marlende down. "It's always nice to be needed."

"Wait." Miss Marlende stopped Professor Abindon with a hand on her arm. She took the vial and the hypodermic out of the professor's hands and checked both, then handed them back.

The professor lifted her eyebrows. "Really, Vale. This is too much. Your father and I had our difficulties, but I never wanted to murder him. And if I had, I certainly wouldn't do it in front of my only child."

Miss Marlende gave her a level look. "I wanted to make certain that the creature hadn't possessed you, and was somehow forcing him to behave this way."

Professor Abindon's expression cleared. "Oh, of course. Good thinking."

Cobbier helped Lord Engal hold Dr. Marlende's arm down and pushed up his sleeve so the professor could give him the injection. Emilie found she really didn't want to watch, and went over to where Efrain sat beside Hyacinth.

Efrain held the translator while Hyacinth crouched nearby, working with several different constructions of the metal-paper. Efrain was clearly frightened and upset. He kept glancing toward Dr. Marlende and the others and then looking away. Emilie took the translator away from him. She needed something to do besides sit around and be worried.

Hyacinth said, *This is disturbing. I am readying our materials so we can begin work as quickly as possible.*

Dr. Marlende's struggles were starting to get weaker and the professor said, "We'd better tie him up."

Emilie winced. She asked Hyacinth, "Do you think the thing you're building will work on us? The others didn't seem to think so."

I do not think it will work on beings so different, but it will be easier for me to explain how it works once it is assembled, so your matriarch will be able to construct her own device.

"Matriarch" was a good way to describe the professor, Emilie considered.

It seemed to take an inordinately long time, but finally Dr. Marlende lay still.

"Let's get started," Lord Engal said, taking something out of his pack that looked like a disassembled aether navigator. "Emilie, if you would translate, please. Ask our friend to explain the principles of its device."

CHAPTER TWELVE

After a consultation with Hyacinth, Professor Abindon wrote up a list of items for Emilie and Mikel to get from the airship. Emilie felt bad that they hadn't managed to send someone to Daniel and Seth before then, but helping Dr. Marlende took priority.

As they prepared to leave, Mikel asked Miss Marlende, "Should we take Miss Deverrin with us and leave her aboard the airship?" He glanced toward where Miss Deverrin sat back against the wall, watching all the proceedings with an expression that was hard to read.

Miss Marlende shook her head. "They would still have to guard her, and I doubt either would have the . . . poor manners to do it effectively. They haven't seen how far under that creature's spell she was." She added, "Here, I can keep an eye on her."

The track back through the empty aether sailer was more nerveracking than Emilie would have expected. The silence was absolute, and shadows gathered in every corner. The place would be very different if it was still filled with flower people, going about their daily tasks. But now it felt haunted. It would have been much worse if they didn't know that the aether creature was in Dr. Marlende.

As they walked down the long bronze-lit corridor to the nearest wall shaft, Emilie said, "Does it feel like someone is watching us?"

Mikel shrugged, though he didn't look terribly happy with the situation either. "We're in a ship from another world. And an aether current might come along at any moment and sweep us off it. It would be odd if we didn't feel that way."

"Yes, but . . . We've been here a while now. We should be used to it."

"I think you get used to things faster than other people," Mikel told her wryly. "It's interfering with your perspective."

That might be true. But Emilie thought it mainly meant that Mikel felt uneasy as well, though he seemed reluctant to admit it.

They reached the outer door and opened it carefully. Professor Abindon had renewed their protective spells, but it still took Emilie a bit of effort to step out onto the little gallery. The view of the aether current seemed even more vast than it had before.

Mikel checked the ladder, making certain it was firmly attached, and then started down. Emilie took a deep breath and climbed down after him. She kept her gaze locked on the ladder rungs, tracking her progress by the swell of the airship's balloon in the corner of her eye.

She twitched in alarm when she heard a voice, but realized an instant later that it was Daniel, below them on the airship's gallery. The wave of relief made something inside her chest unclench; she had been far more worried than she had realized.

She risked a look below and saw Mikel step off the ladder. Daniel stood on the platform demanding, "What in the name of everything holy happened? Where are the others?"

As Emilie reached the deck, Mikel said, "It's a long story, and we have to tell it quickly. Emilie, have you got the list?"

Her arms quivering a little from her death grip on the ladder, Emilie pulled the folded paper out of her jacket pocket. "Right here." She told Daniel, "We have to hurry. Dr. Marlende's in trouble."

Daniel was clearly baffled and impatient and a little angry, but his expression cleared and he turned to lead them into the ship.

Seth called plaintively from the control cabin, "What happened? We thought you were all dead!"

"I'll tell you as soon as they tell me," Daniel called back, as they hurried through to the hold. He grabbed a bag with a long shoulder strap and Emilie started down the list of supplies. It was all things like certain types of wire, a disassembled plate for an aether navigator, several different kinds of lens, and some metallic powders. She felt very glad she had been the one to help stow the supplies; knowing where everything was would make this a much quicker process. It was probably why Miss Marlende had sent her with Mikel.

As they found the materials stowed away in various boxes and containers, she and Mikel took turns telling Daniel the story. Daniel finally said, "But did these creatures cause the aetheric disruption that constructed that place you were trapped on?"

"Maybe," Mikel said, hastily tucking away the jars of metallic powder into the satchel. "If they did, we've got no idea why, and the one that got Dr. Marlende didn't seem inclined for conversation."

With everything collected, they went back out to the main cabin. Emilie was glad there was no question of her remaining behind; for one thing, the two satchels of supplies would have been difficult for Mikel to manage alone on the ladder.

Daniel stepped out onto the platform with them. "Be careful," he said. He rolled his shoulder and grimaced. "I wish I could help more."

"We've got the professor," Mikel told him, making sure his satchel was fastened. He gave Daniel a quick grin. "With her in charge, there's not much call for more help."

Emilie tied off the satchel's extra strap around her waist, wishing the long climb was already over. "We'll come back if we need anything else," she said, and looked up in time to see Daniel staring pensively at the deck. As one of Dr. Marlende's favorite apprentices, he must be very upset. "It'll be all right."

Daniel looked up, startled, and gave her a distracted smile. "I know."

Mikel thought Emilie should go first so if she slipped he could catch her. Emilie severely doubted Mikel's ability to catch a falling body in these circumstances, even though they didn't weigh as much when they were on the ladder, but she appreciated the thought and went ahead anyway.

They managed the long climb, and the trek through the ship. The empty corridors felt much less spooky. Emilie thought it must be because they knew the others were waiting, and there wasn't time to feel uneasy.

They arrived back to universal relief. "Is everything all right on the airship?" Miss Marlende asked, taking Emilie's satchel.

"They were fine, just very worried about us," Emilie reported. She saw Dr. Marlende still lay unconscious and suppressed the urge to ask if he was all right. It wasn't as if any of them knew.

While Mikel watched over Dr. Marlende, and Miss Marlende kept an eye on Miss Deverrin, Lord Engal and Cobbier set to work building the workings for the device, which would be placed inside a metal tube like a telescope. Professor Abindon sat on the floor a little distance away, concentrating on a metal plate with a small quantity of liquid aether on it. She seemed to be trying to urge it to cover a glass lens.

The aether glowed a little and it hurt Emilie's eyes to look at it too long. Hyacinth had subsided into what looked like a heap of disconnected blossoms, and hadn't spoken for a while. Emilie thought it was probably asleep.

Finally, Lord Engal said, "Any time you're ready, madam."

"Quiet." The professor didn't look up.

Miss Deverrin moved closer to Miss Marlende, causing Emilie to tense warily. But Miss Deverrin said, "If this works . . . can you use it on my father?"

Miss Marlende shifted her position a little, and eyed Miss Deverrin thoughtfully. "That was our intention, even before this creature attacked my father. You believe that we're telling the truth, now?"

"Yes." Miss Deverrin stared at the floor, her face etched with exhaustion. "I'm not certain why I didn't, before. It seems . . . obvious. I feel my memory of the past months since our accident is confused, and . . . I should have known something was wrong with my father immediately, as you did with yours."

Emilie said, "Perhaps you did, and the creature kept you from remembering it."

Miss Deverrin stared at her, startled. Emilie added, "There's no real way to know, is there?"

Then Professor Abindon said, "Ready. Bring the casing here, Engal."

Lord Engal hurriedly stood and carried over the telescope casing, while Cobbier brought the wire frame. Lord Engal carefully slid the wire and other small devices into the casing.

Emilie waved her hand over Hyacinth. It puffed out again and its blossoms fumbled for the translator. Emilie told it, "The device is ready."

Hyacinth waved in acknowledgment and pointed all its blossoms at the professor.

Professor Abindon carefully set the aether-coated lens in among the wire, and slid the whole into the case. She said, "This should cause the creature's aetheric aura to become visible. Then the spell should detach it from Marlende's aura and expel it."

Everyone watched, tense and expectant. The professor lifted the case and pointed it toward Dr. Marlende.

After a long, fraught moment, Efrain said, "I don't see anything. Is it working?"

Emilie glanced at him, annoyed. "We can't see it because we're not sorcerers."

"No, we should all be able to see it." Lord Engal glared at the device, then turned to Hyacinth's translator. "Isn't that how it is meant to work?"

Hyacinth waved its blossoms anxiously. *Yes, that is how our device operated.*

Professor Abindon swore, using a very bad word Emilie hadn't heard anywhere but the docks in Meneport. The professor turned, pointed the device at each of them, including Hyacinth, and then swore again.

Lord Engal huffed in frustration. "Are you certain it's working?"

The professor grimaced. "Yes, I can feel the spell, ready to initiate. Cobbier, is the mechanism attached properly?"

Cobbier stepped forward and took the device, examining it carefully. "Yes, everything's still in the right position." Then he stepped back and pointed it at the professor. Emilie's breath caught in her throat. But then nothing happened. She breathed again as Cobbier handed the device back and said, "Sorry, ma'am. Just checking."

In bitter realization, Miss Marlende said, "It was a trick! It's had us here, watching Father, while it's . . . moved somewhere else."

"But where?" Lord Engal made a sweeping gesture. "If we're correct in our assumptions and it can only infect someone who has a certain amount of magical ability—"

Emilie was having a horrible thought. "Daniel's a sorcerer." She blurted out the words. She couldn't remember his expression, as they had left the airship with the supplies. She had been in such a hurry, she hadn't looked at him properly. "On the way to the airship, I felt like something was watching us. But not on the way back."

Mikel clapped a hand to his forehead, appalled. "I did too. I thought we were both just imagining things—"

"Oh, if it's taken the airship—" Miss Marlende bolted out the doorway.

Hyacinth shoved the translator back into Emilie's hands. She read the words there and shouted, "Go forward down that corridor! You'll be able to see the airship from there."

The others ran after her, Lord Engal ordering, "Mikel, stay with Dr. Marlende!"

Emilie ran with Hyacinth and Efrain at her side and caught up with the others at the end of the corridor. It ended in a domed room that must be the prow of the aether sailer. The round windows were studded all over the front wall, giving a much wider field of view. Emilie ducked under Miss Marlende's arm for a look, just as Professor Abindon said, "The airship hasn't moved."

"I don't understand." Miss Marlende bit her lip, deeply worried. "If the creature did take over Daniel, it's had plenty of time to act. What is it doing?"

Lord Engal stepped back, shaking his head. "We may have just panicked over nothing, but I don't like it. I'm going down there. Cobbier, you come with me."

Professor Abindon drew back from the window, her expression still troubled. "I'll bring the device. We can't take the chance and it would be too dangerous to bring Daniel all the way up here."

Miss Marlende said, "Yes, it's been hours since the aether current fluctuated. At least if we split up it can't get us all." She turned back down the corridor. "I'm going to try to revive Father."

The translator moved in Emilie's hands and she looked down to read, *I will secure the controls. It was not necessary when we thought the creature had taken your elder, but now I am concerned.*

"Yes, good idea. I'll go with you." It would be useful at least. She wasn't sure how well Hyacinth could fight, and if Daniel tried to get to the controls they would need to subdue him. She went to the doorway of the compartment. Miss Marlende had the medical kit open and had taken out the bottle of smelling salts. "Miss Marlende, I'm going to help Hyacinth guard the control room."

"And me," Efrain said.

"I'll go as well," Miss Deverrin said.

Miss Marlende had glanced up, but hesitated at that. "Miss Deverrin, I know you must realize why we can't exactly trust you."

"I have to do something," Miss Deverrin protested. "I give you my word. Besides, I haven't the slightest idea how these controls work. There's little I could do to this ship even if I wanted to."

Miss Marlende started to speak, but Dr. Marlende stirred a little. Mikel said, "His eyelids moved, miss. He might be coming around."

Distracted, Miss Marlende turned back to her father. "All right, go on."

Emilie started after Hyacinth, who waited impatiently for them at the end of the corridor. As Efrain and Miss Deverrin followed, Emilie said, "She's very worried about her father."

"I understand completely," Miss Deverrin said, her voice grim. Emilie winced. She had forgotten Miss Deverrin's situation for a moment; she wished she had just kept her mouth shut.

Efrain filled the uncomfortable silence. "If we can just get your father and that device they made in the same place, we could save him."

The tense set of Miss Deverrin's shoulders relaxed minutely. "I hope so," she whispered.

Hyacinth led them to a wall shaft and they went down a level, then along a corridor that led toward starboard. As they turned off into a series of rooms, Emilie recognized the route. "We're going back to those rooms we found with the globe and all the panels. We thought it might be the place where they steered the ship."

"That was where the aether current grabbed Dr. Marlende and the others," Efrain pointed out. "We should be careful."

Efrain was just full of good advice. "What exactly do you suggest we do—" Emilie began, as they stepped into the first of the three control rooms they had explored. At the far end, she could see through the doorway to the center room with the giant globe. And standing in front of the globe was Daniel.

For a heartbeat, Emilie froze. Even though she had been the one to suggest it, until this moment she hadn't really believed that Daniel had been taken over by the creature. It was a possibility that had to be eliminated, that was all.

But there he stood in the control room of the aether sailer, running his hands over the metal-paper globe as if he knew exactly what he was doing.

Hyacinth surged forward. Daniel spun around. He wasn't wearing his glasses and the shoulder of his shirt was stained with blood from where he must have torn the healing gunshot wound open when he climbed the ladder. He flung himself sideways toward a control panel. A door suddenly slammed down into place, blocking off the room.

Emilie belatedly lunged to the door and felt around the edge, looking for some sort of catch or switch. "How do you open it?" she demanded. Hyacinth frantically ran its blossoms over the metal-paper, clearly trying to make the door open again. But nothing happened.

"That was him?" Miss Deverrin asked, startled.

"We can get in through the other way!" Efrain yelled and bolted toward the corridor.

"Efrain!" Emilie caught him by the collar and yanked him to a halt. Of course if there was a way to seal this door there must be a way to seal all of them.

While Efrain pulled at his collar and glared, acting as if she had strangled him, Emilie asked Hyacinth, "What do we do?"

Hyacinth shoved away from the unresponsive panel and flowed toward the door. *This way,* it said, managing to convey a world of anger in the words.

It charged down the corridor and Emilie and Efrain raced after it. She had never seen it go this fast before; it flowed halfway up the wall as it rounded the corner and disappeared through a doorway. They ran onto the gallery of the big open space next to the series of control rooms.

The door there was sealed as well, and the door in the room on the far side of the globe room. Hyacinth hurried to a panel and started to manipulate the metal-paper on it. Emilie started to follow, then swayed as the deck rolled underfoot. She staggered back and stepped on Efrain's foot. He caught her but fell against the wall. Miss Deverrin gripped the edge of the doorway and managed to stay on her feet. She called out, "We're moving!"

Emilie struggled upright and braced her back against the wall. She could feel the aether sailer turning, the motion more like a steamship than an airship. "What happened?" she asked Hyacinth. "I thought we couldn't move, because of the sabotage!"

She realized what the answer must be even before Hyacinth replied. *The creature must have repaired it. That was what it was doing while we were distracted, thinking it had taken your elder.*

Reading over her shoulder, Efrain said, "Uh-oh."

"But where is it taking us?" Emilie shoved away from the wall and fought her way up the slope of the deck to the nearest window.

Her breath caught in her throat. She had forgotten about the airship.

When the aether sailer pulled away, the ladder had ripped from both ships' platforms and come loose. Now it floated some distance below the airship. The airship itself had been yanked around sideways by the force of it. Horrified, Emilie pressed her face to the cold glass. She could see the propeller and it wasn't moving, wasn't making any attempt to adjust its course. *What did that creature do to Seth?* Emilie thought. It would have had to do something to him, for Daniel to be able to leave the airship.

But Professor Abindon, Lord Engal, and Cobbier had been on their way there. Maybe they had already reached the airship to find Daniel gone and Seth unconscious, maybe they hadn't reached the outer door of the aether sailer before . . . Emilie's eyes widened.

As the airship lifted up she had a better view of the ladder. Both ends had come loose, and it was floating away from the airship's platform, caught in the aether current. And three figures clung to it. "Hyacinth!" she cried out into the translator. "Hyacinth, help!"

Almost before the words were out, Hyacinth reached the window. It brushed against her side, smelling strongly of lilac. It stuck all its front blossoms against the glass.

Efrain ran to the next window to look out, Miss Deverrin with him. He said, "The airship . . . Oh no!"

Hyacinth pulled back from the window and said, *They live?*

Emilie's throat felt thick. "They have protective spells. But the air is limited. Dr. Marlende said not to be trapped in the current, not to fall off the ladder, it wouldn't last . . . We have to do something!"

Hyacinth surged for the door. *We will go to the lifeboat. It has a mechanism we can use to retrieve them.*

Emilie ran after it, Efrain and Miss Deverrin following her. "What about Daniel?" Efrain said.

As they reached the wall shaft down to the first floor of the gallery, Emilie managed to look at the translator. It said, *He has taken control of this ship. We must reach the lifeboat before he thinks to jettison it.*

She read the words aloud and added, "It's right. We have to get to the professor and the others now, they don't have time." She stepped into the shaft, slipped, and had to steady herself against the wall. "But Miss Deverrin, will you go to Miss Marlende and Mikel and tell them what's happened? Maybe they can sabotage the ship again and keep Daniel and the creature from taking it away."

Hyacinth had already started down the shaft, but the translator replied, *Yes, a good idea.*

Miss Deverrin hesitated an instant then nodded sharply. "Yes, I'll go."

She stepped off the shaft at the next level and Emilie and Efrain followed Hyacinth down. They took the route Emilie had followed with Miss Marlende and the professor what seemed like days ago now, down the corridor to the compartment with the engine shafts. Then Hyacinth took a doorway which led into the individual lifeboat docks.

They ran to the single sealed door and Hyacinth stopped, turning toward them. The translator said, *We must be quick. If the being is watching the controls, it may see that this door has opened and realize we are in the dock. It may choose to open the outer door.*

Emilie glanced at Efrain to make certain he had seen the warning. He nodded, his expression serious. She told Hyacinth, "We'll be right behind you."

Hyacinth turned back to the door and touched the panel. The door slid open and they all ran for the lifeboat. Hyacinth moved swiftly, circled around to the rear hatch and ran its blossoms over the control there. Emilie heard the outer doors make a clicking noise. She stifled her first impulse to yell at Hyacinth to hurry; she didn't want to distract it.

The hatch swung open and Hyacinth flung itself inside. Emilie and Efrain piled in after it and Hyacinth shoved the hatch shut. Efrain pushed forward to the nearest window and looked out. "The door's opening!"

Emilie clutched the translator to her chest and steadied herself on the wall. Hyacinth was already at the controls of the lifeboat. She felt the deck shift under her feet as the little boat pulled away from the dock. The translator said, *That is for the best.*

The boat surged backward suddenly and they were outside in the current, the wall of the aether sailer towering over them. Emilie staggered, and said, "Good, in another minute it would have thought of stopping us."

Efrain picked himself up off the deck and stumbled back to the window. "Won't it let all the air out from inside? Or is there a spell?"

There are automated protections that will force the inner door to shut. The lifeboat wheeled away from the aether sailer.

Emilie pulled her way along the wall so she could look out a front window. The airship grew larger as they approached, then the lifeboat dipped down toward the floating ladder.

Emilie saw with relief that the three figures still clung to it. They had managed to climb closer to the end, but the gap between the end of the ladder and the drifting airship was just growing wider. "What are we going to do?" Emilie asked.

The lifeboat has a towing mechanism, for recovering damaged craft from the aether current, Hyacinth explained. *I have no means to bring them aboard, but I will try to get them back to your craft.*

Emilie nodded, watching anxiously. "That would do nicely."

The lifeboat slowed as it approached the airship. The deck moved underfoot again as the lifeboat angled downward, drawing near the ladder. Emilie gripped the rim of the window. She could see the professor clinging to the ladder, Lord Engal a few feet lower, and Cobbier below him. They stared toward the lifeboat; they must see that it was trying to get closer. *They're probably wondering if we know what we're doing,* Emilie thought. She hoped they did.

Hyacinth lifted up, stretched its hand-blossom out, and splayed it over a patch of metal-paper to one side of the window. The paper began to move, shifting and changing, and Emilie felt something thunk against the deck underfoot. Hyacinth said, *I am releasing the tow device.*

Efrain ran to look out the stern windows. "I see it! It's like a long chain with hooks on the end."

Emilie stepped back so she could see out the nearest window. The tow chain curved out from beneath the lifeboat, stretching toward the drifting ladder. "Do you want me to direct you?" she asked.

That would be helpful, Hyacinth said. It hunched over the panel, and she saw with alarm that a few of its petals had wilted and fallen down onto the deck.

That wasn't good when it happened to a normal plant and it must be that much worse when it happened to a plant person who used its petals for hands and eyes. *I hope it's not sick,* Emilie thought, but didn't allow any of her concern to enter her voice. "Just keep going like you are, it's curving toward the end of the ladder . . . No, stop, back toward the lifeboat. Yes, that's right."

The hooks had almost reached the end of the ladder, but the ladder was caught in the buoyance of the current, slowly twisting away, starting to double back on itself. The professor climbed toward the end and stretched to reach the hooks. Emilie bounced on her feet, jittering with anxiety. "Can you reel it out a little more? It's almost there."

It is fully extended. Hyacinth moved its blossoms over the metal-paper. *I will try to move closer.*

The lifeboat dipped down, but the movement was jerky.

The current is moving again, Hyacinth said. *I fear—*

It cut off there, concentrating on finely adjusting the controls.

Emilie gripped the windowsill, willing Professor Abindon to reach the hooks. The professor got to the end of the ladder and stretched, but it was just a little too far. Emilie watched her pull back and loop a rung of the ladder over one foot, then the other. Emilie winced in horror, knowing what would come next. It was what she would have done if she had been in the professor's position, but watching someone else have to do it was nerve-racking.

Her feet secured to the ladder, the professor lunged out and grabbed the hook. She contracted her body and pulled the slack of the ladder toward the tow line.

The professor managed to loop the end of the ladder over the hooks. Emilie gasped in relief. "She's got it!"

Efrain cheered. Emilie added, "Wait . . ." as the professor freed her feet and climbed down a little away from the attached hooks. "There, you can pull on it now."

Hyacinth's blossoms shivered and the lifeboat moved slowly back toward the drifting airship. Emilie saw the metal-paper on the panel seemed to be moving independently of what Hyacinth was doing. It had to be the growing disruption in the aether current. She clenched her teeth, and didn't say "Hurry!" Hyacinth had enough to deal with at the moment, it didn't need its elbows jogged.

The ladder gradually straightened as the lifeboat drew it back toward the airship. The lifeboat couldn't get too close, but as it approached it started to turn, angling so the ladder began to swing toward the airship's gallery. Realizing what the lifeboat meant to do, Cobbier climbed down toward the end. As the ladder neared the airship, he stretched out his hand.

Blue light sparked when the individual protective spell around Cobbier passed through the greater barrier around the airship. That end of the ladder went limp and bumped the top of the cabin, the rest still drifting out into the aether current. Cobbier climbed down and scrabbled for a handhold, then caught the bracket above the door. Emilie sagged in relief as he wrapped a rung of the ladder around it. Lord

Engal climbed rapidly down toward him, passed into the protective spell and jumped down onto the gallery. Cobbier swung down beside him and they both began to reel the professor in.

As Professor Abindon reached the gallery, she fell into Lord Engal's arms in a way that was probably highly embarrassing to both of them. Emilie said, "That's it! You've done it! Now—"

Emilie wasn't sure what they were going to do now, so it was just as well she didn't have to finish that sentence. The lifeboat shuddered and Hyacinth said, *The aether current! It is shifting! Hurry, we must—*

It didn't get a chance to finish that sentence either. On the airship's gallery, the others felt the same shudder. They abandoned the ladder and Cobbier wrenched open the door. Lord Engal shoved him and Professor Abindon inside and stepped in after them.

As the lifeboat wheeled away from the airship, Emilie turned back to the front window. Ahead was the stern of the aether sailer. Emilie wondered for an instant if the lifeboat should try to get back aboard, if they could help Miss Marlende take control of the ship from the creature/Daniel. Then everything in front of her seemed to ripple.

Emilie grabbed a handhold and shouted "Hold on!" just as the aether current seized them and flung them away.

CHAPTER THIRTEEN

Terrified that they would be plucked off the lifeboat by the aether current, Emilie gripped the handhold for all she was worth.

The whole ship jerked and rolled. She slammed against the wall and heard Efrain yell in pain and alarm. Light and dark flashed across the windows, then light again, then the lifeboat tipped forward and they were falling like a rock.

Emilie screamed but couldn't hear herself. Possibly because of the roaring in her ears, possibly because of the screaming Efrain was doing. Hyacinth moved frantically over the controls, all its limbs flailing, rolling its whole body over the panels and metal-paper. There was definitely an advantage to having more than two hands and Emilie hoped fervently that it might save their lives.

She got a confused glimpse of blue rock flashing past outside, far too close to their windows, then the lifeboat's nose lifted. Its headlong fall slowed, but the little ship waffled like a toy boat caught in a storm. Then it dipped sideways and rammed into a stand of trees.

Emilie fell forward, slammed into Hyacinth's back. It made a soft cushion to bounce off and she landed on her side on the floor. She lay there, stunned. They weren't moving anymore.

She managed to push herself up on one elbow, her head pounding. Efrain was huddled in the back, braced against the wall. "Are you all right?" she croaked.

He nodded, staring at her wide-eyed. "Are you? You fell . . ."

"I'm fine." Emilie struggled to disentangle herself. She knew she was lucky not to have bashed her head in. "Efrain . . ." It hit her suddenly, what Daniel had said about how dangerous this all was, and how her last words to Daniel were something inconsequential, and now she might never get a chance to say anything else to him in his right mind.

"Efrain, I suppose we'll always argue but you're my brother and I'm very fond of you."

"Oh." Efrain, trying to stand, hesitated. "Are we going to die?"

"I don't really know. I just thought I'd take the chance to say it." Emilie sat up, wincing at all the new bruises.

"I see." He nodded in relief. "I'm fond of you, too. And I don't think anybody else has a sister who can do things like you do."

"They do," Emilie assured him. "You just never hear about it." She stumbled to her feet and looked for Hyacinth.

Hyacinth slumped over its panel, its blossoms trembling. Emilie wasn't certain if she should touch it or not. She couldn't have done it any good by slamming into it. She looked for the translator.

It lay in a scrambled pile under her left foot. She collected it in both hands, and it formed the words *Hold on*. That must have been the last thing Hyacinth had managed to say.

Emilie struggled to her feet, her legs trembling. Out the window she saw the shattered trunks of a stand of small saplings, with blue-tinted trunks and leaves. Hyacinth must have used them to slow the lifeboat down enough to stop the impact from killing them. She brushed her hand lightly over its blossoms and said into the translator, "Are you all right?"

The blossoms stirred. After a long worried moment, the translator said, *I do not feel well. But I am functional.*

That didn't sound very good.

Clambering around in the back, Efrain said, "Where are we? Are we in that same place, with the gaps and the funny mountains? We're not somewhere different?"

Emilie leaned forward to peer out the window. The trees looked a lot like smaller versions of those in the forest they had trekked through to get to the Deverrin camp. "I think it's the same place."

Hyacinth lifted up a little and pressed its blossoms against the window. *Yes, it is the same. The current has brought us back here.*

"But then why did the aether creature take the aether ship this time?" Efrain peered uncertainly out the window. "Before, it just took people."

"It took the Deverrin airship." Emilie lifted the translator and said to Hyacinth, "The aether creatures are controlling the current, aren't they? This is proof."

Hyacinth shook itself and pushed upright. The translated words formed more quickly. *Yes. Perhaps they did not bring the aether sailer earlier because they had no use for it. Or perhaps something in the current has changed.*

That didn't sound good either.

"The airship's here!" Efrain stared out the back window. "Look!"

Emilie hurried to his side and craned her neck to see where Efrain was urgently pointing. The Marlende airship hung overhead, just visible past the jumbled branches of the broken saplings. She twisted the handle of the hatch to unlock it. It swung open just enough to jam against a broken tree trunk.

Efrain planted his shoulder against it and pushed. Emilie wedged herself in beside him and together they managed to force the hatch open. Emilie shoved her way out first, gripping the hatch to keep from tumbling into the saplings. Her ears still rang a little from the crash but the strange birdless, insectless quiet of the aether construction was almost too familiar.

The lifeboat sat at the end of a trail of shattered trees, cutting straight through the forest. The airship was several hundred yards away and high above the tallest treetops. The cabin had been battered around. The ladder still dangled from the bent railing of the gallery. She couldn't see the aether sailer, if it had been brought here as well. With the path the lifeboat had cut through the forest, there was no way it could fail to see them.

As she struggled through the debris, she saw the lifeboat's outside looked worse than the inside, the silver metal gashed and scratched and the sail crumpled. As Efrain climbed out, Emilie leaned back in to ask, "Do you think you can take off again?"

Hyacinth climbed toward her, clutching its translator device. *I do not think so. Much of the power is gone. Is the aether sailer here?*

"I can't see it, but I think it must be here." Emilie moved to give Hyacinth room to get out the hatchway. Efrain had already made his way down the pile of broken trunks to the floor of the forest. With Hyacinth, Emilie followed, the wood cracking and shifting under her feet.

The patch of forest wasn't large and they came to open ground after only a short walk. As soon as they were clear of the trees, Efrain jumped up and down, waving at the Marlende airship. They were at the edge of a field set below the big circular ridge of the Deverrin camp. Emilie could just see the top of the Deverrin airship from here. The creatures had made the aether current deliver them here like a wrapped parcel.

She looked up then and spotted the aether sailer. It was much higher in the air, but was dropping down toward the ground. As if it meant to land, perhaps down into the bowl of rock where the camp was. "Can it do that?" she said, startled.

With difficulty, Hyacinth said. All its blossoms were pointed toward the aether sailer in what Emilie interpreted as consternation.

Emilie bit her lip, trying to form a plan. The creature/Daniel must not mean to stay locked up in the control room, not if he was trying to land the ship. If he came out, Miss Marlende could get him with the aether device. But if he managed to land and the Deverrins' party and Dr. Deverrin got aboard . . . "We have to get aboard before he lands."

Hyacinth said, *You are right. It will be our only chance.*

"Daniel—that thing in Daniel—isn't going to let us aboard again," Efrain said. "We'll have to fight, somehow."

Well, obviously, Emilie thought, but there was no point in saying it. The Marlende airship angled down toward them. Emilie waved at it and shouted, "Lower a ladder!"

Fortunately there wasn't much wind in the constructed place and the airship was easily able to maneuver. It dropped down until it was about fifty feet off the ground, then the door opened onto the gallery and Lord Engal stepped out. He released the boarding ladder that was stowed in a roll along the edge of the gallery. As it plummeted toward them, Emilie yanked Efrain back so it didn't hit him in the head. Once it was down they both grabbed and used their combined weight to steady it. Emilie told him, "Climb, hurry!"

Efrain started up. Emilie fumbled for a place to put the translator while she climbed; it was too big for any of her pockets. But Hyacinth took it, tucking it away among its petals.

Emilie followed Efrain up the ladder, so preoccupied with what they needed to do next she forgot to be nervous at the height and the swaying. Hyacinth swarmed easily up behind her. As she reached the gallery, Lord Engal leaned down to catch her arm and pull her the rest of the way up. Hyacinth scrambled up after her and Lord Engal said, "That was a timely rescue; thank you very much indeed. We were all quite relieved." He looked battered, his hat missing and his tie askew.

"Daniel was taken over by the creature, and he seized control of the aether sailer," Emilie reported breathlessly. "We need to board it before it lands."

"Like pirates," Efrain added helpfully.

"Yes, we thought as much. The professor has also ordered us to board the aether sailer." Lord Engal started to crank the ladder up. Emilie grabbed the railing as the airship swayed toward the ridge. Lord Engal added, "Better get inside, the woman flies like a maniac."

Emilie headed for the door and stumbled into the main cabin with some relief. Efrain flung himself immediately onto a bench. Hyacinth's petals extended to study the room. "Where's Seth?" Efrain demanded.

Emilie was afraid to hear the answer. She went forward into the steering cabin, where Professor Abindon was the only one at the controls. "Is Seth all right? Daniel didn't . . . Did he?" If Daniel had killed or injured Seth, he would feel terrible. If they could get the aether creature out of Daniel.

Most of her attention on the steering yoke and the port, the professor said, "He was hit on the head, and Engal and Cobbier carried him back to recuperate in the rear cabin. He was regaining consciousness, but very woozy."

"Good. Good that he's not dead, I mean." Emilie leaned on the back of the copilot's seat. The professor's clothes were torn and in disarray, and there was a bad bruise developing on her cheek, but her expression held nothing but grim determination. It was very reassuring. Emilie told her, "Miss Deverrin went to warn Miss Marlende about Daniel. He had locked himself in the control room and we couldn't get to him. We decided to rescue you all first."

"A wise decision," Professor Abindon said. The airship had lifted up above the aether sailer, looking down on the ridge and the camp on the other side. She turned the control yoke to swing in toward it.

Hyacinth handed Emilie back the translator and began to move around the steering cabin, closely examining everything. It said, *There is an emergency door in the top of the aether sailer. We should make for it. It is not much used, and even if the ghost pirate knows of its existence, there is no way to lock it from the control room.*

Emilie read this to Professor Abindon, who said, "Excellent," and guided the airship down.

Cobbier came to the doorway. "Good to see you all. Seth's awake and talking, but he can't get up without falling down. What are we doing?"

"We're attacking the aether sailer," Efrain told him.

The professor said, "Yes, and if you would, Cobbier, tell Lord Engal to leave the ladder partway down. About twenty feet should do it."

The professor guided the airship toward the silver curved top of the aether sailer. Emilie tried to hold the question back, but it came out in spite of her. "Do you think we'll be able to save Daniel?" She was realizing how Miss Deverrin must feel. It was awful. Was Daniel himself even still there? Was he trapped in his body and painfully aware of what the creature was doing with it? Hyacinth's crew member had come through the experience alive, but would it be horribly different for a human?

The professor shook her head slightly. "I don't know, my dear. Theoretically, it should work. But we won't know until we try."

Emilie nodded, and took a deep breath. She couldn't worry about Daniel right now. She had to focus on getting aboard the aether sailer and preventing the Deverrins from making everything worse.

The aether sailer was having difficulty landing, probably because neither Daniel nor the aether creature had ever landed anything like it before. As the airship drew closer, Emilie saw the aether sailer was still a good distance above the ridge.

The airship came in low over the top of the larger craft. The dangling boarding ladder dragged over the side of the hull, between two of the sails. The professor flipped switches to adjust the propellers and said, "Cobbier, take over. If Marlende is still unconscious, we're going to need a sorcerer in there."

Emilie stepped back as Cobbier came forward and took the wheel. Professor Abindon slipped out of the seat. Emilie followed her out to the main cabin with Efrain and Hyacinth. Lord Engal stood there, loading a revolver. He explained, "If the Deverrins manage to get aboard and have more weapons—"

Professor Abindon said, "I'm not objecting. But if we have to shoot Daniel, best to let Vale do it. She's an excellent shot and will be able to stop him without killing him."

Efrain made an involuntary noise of protest but Emilie nodded; it only made sense. Though she hoped they didn't have to shoot Daniel again while he was still recovering from being shot while escaping the Hollow World.

"Practical as always." Lord Engal held the door for them as they went out onto the gallery. Needing something to carry the translator, Emilie stopped to grab a shoulder bag lying on the bench and found it already contained a medical kit. She slung it over her head.

The air out on the gallery was oddly still. The rocky ridge off to the side seemed awfully close, but any sight of the camp was blocked by the pewter-colored bulk of the aether sailer. Cobbier kept the airship as still as possible, about twenty or so feet above the hull of the other ship, between two of the huge sails. Hyacinth moved forward. *I will go first and open the door.*

Emilie translated for the others as Hyacinth flowed down the ladder. Lord Engal gave it time to get a little way down and then followed. Emilie turned to Efrain. "You should stay up here and help Cobbier."

Efrain snorted. "Help him with what? I can't fly an airship. I don't know what all those buttons and switches do. I'd just crash into something."

He was right about that. "You don't have to help him fly, you could . . . hand him things."

Efrain snorted incredulously. "Like what?"

Emilie glared at him. "You should stay up here, out of danger."

"It's just as dangerous up here, if those two ghost pirates get their way." He glared back. "And I want to help Daniel. He was nice to me when you were being horrible."

Emilie found that hard to argue with. Still, she had to make the effort. "If you do something stupid and get yourself killed, I'll be more horrible to you than you can imagine."

"Children, I'd prefer to leave you both behind," Professor Abindon said, leaning over the gallery railing to watch the progress below, "and it's only the facts that you saved our lives and that we'll surely need all the help we can get that make me hesitate. So if you're going, start climbing."

Emilie hurriedly tucked the translator into her bag and went first, rather glad the professor gripped her arm to help her through the difficult moment of climbing from the gallery onto the ladder. She went down quickly. The ladder swayed with the airship's slight movements, but her view was mercifully blocked by the metal curves of the aether sails. She reached the bottom and stepped cautiously onto the aether sailer's hull. Lord Engal steadied her and she managed not to grab on to his coat sleeve. The surface wasn't as slippery as she feared. The texture was rough underfoot, more like stucco than a slick metal. Lord Engal said, "Try not to stamp or move around much. I'm not certain how well sound would carry through this hull."

Emilie tried to stand quietly. The door was round and large, almost ten feet across. Hyacinth crouched to one side, using its blossoms on a circular metal-paper control set into a niche in the hull. Efrain reached the bottom of the ladder and shakily stepped down, the professor not far behind him. Then the door popped and began to swing open.

Hyacinth slipped inside and Lord Engal crouched down to look. Emilie pulled the translator out of her bag. After a moment, it said, *This corridor is empty, at the moment. Follow quickly, please.*

"It says to come on in," Emilie whispered.

Lord Engal sat on the edge and swung his feet down, then disappeared almost immediately. Emilie realized it must be a walking shaft. She sat down and put her feet on the wall, and it jerked her forward into the ship.

The shadowy dark was broken by the now-familiar bronze lights, except they were blinking and trembling, like candles or gas flames caught in a breeze. Emilie walked down the wall shaft and let it spit her out onto the floor of a short corridor with only one door in the left-hand wall. Hyacinth and Lord Engal were down there, carefully peering through it. She hurried to join them, stretching up on her toes to look over Hyacinth's head.

The doorway led to a junction with several different doors, all thick with shadows that jumped with the fluctuating lights. Emilie stepped back and whispered to the translator, "Can you see anyone?"

I feared the pirate might set a trap for us, but there is nothing ahead. I hope it does not realize we are on board.

"Why are the lights blinking?"

It is a warning, that the ship may be damaged if it continues to fly in this manner.

Lord Engal read the translation over her shoulder. Efrain and the professor reached them, and Engal said, keeping his voice low, "We need to find Dr. and Miss Marlende and Mikel before we proceed. Ask him—"

A loud bang echoed up through the ship. Emilie flinched in alarm. Lord Engal finished, "Never mind, I think I know where they are. To the control room!"

Hyacinth led them hurriedly down the darkened corridor to the nearest wall shaft. The deck of the aether sailer trembled under their feet, its engines protesting the effort of being awkwardly guided lower to the ground. "Was that a shot?" Efrain asked. "Are they shooting at Daniel?"

"Of course not," Emilie snapped. She hoped they weren't. "They must be trying to get the door into the control room open by shooting at it."

"I don't think that was a shot," Professor Abindon said repressively.

After another wall shaft and a corridor, Emilie heard Miss Marlende's voice somewhere ahead and her heart thumped in relief. They reached a door that led into the cabin next to the locked control room, and Lord Engal motioned them to wait. Emilie bounced in impatience as he stepped forward and cautiously looked through the door.

Then he exclaimed with relief. "There, I see you've recovered, Marlende. Any success?"

With the others, Emilie crowded into the doorway. Miss Marlende and Miss Deverrin stood beside the still-blocked entrance into the control room. Dr. Marlende crouched beside it, near a large scorched spot on the wall. There were various dents and pry marks along the edge of the door, but so far it must have resisted all their efforts. Miss Marlende swore in relief. "We were afraid you were dead!" She and Miss Deverrin both looked disheveled and weary, but not hurt.

"It tried to kill us," Emilie admitted. "We crashed the lifeboat, too, but the airship is all right."

"We've tried using gunpowder from the pistol's ammunition to construct a small explosive to get the door open, but it hasn't worked," Dr. Marlende explained. "Mikel is guarding the door on the far side of the room, in case the creature attempts to escape that way, but escape doesn't seem to be its plan." Dr. Marlende looked drawn and exhausted. He might have recovered, but the attack by the aether creature had obviously been difficult on him. "I see you're all well." He peered at them anxiously. "Are Seth and Cobbier accounted for also?"

"Seth was hurt when the creature seized control of Daniel, and

Cobbier is flying the airship." The professor stepped into the room. "We have to get in there, now. Daniel is attempting to land this ship so Dr. Deverrin and the others can join him."

"Yes, Mother, we know that." Miss Marlende gestured pointedly toward the observation window. "If you have any suggestions . . ."

Emilie had been thinking frantically. "I have one. I can go around to the other door and try to convince it to let me in." Everyone turned to look at her. Even Hyacinth extended some blossoms to see her better. "I mean, we never figured out how much it knows about the person it takes control of, did we? And we don't know if it's been listening to our conversation. Maybe I can convince it I'm silly enough to think it's Daniel in there, and not something who has taken Daniel prisoner."

Professor Abindon frowned. "I don't think it's much of a chance, but we might as well try it."

Miss Marlende seemed even less convinced. "But what would you do if it let you in?"

"Try to hit the lever to let you all in." Emilie turned to Hyacinth. "You'll have to describe where it is."

I can do that. It added, *This creature must know little about your people, not like the other one who has inhabited the elder of the camp here for so long. I hope your plan may work.*

Lord Engal had already taken off his pack and was unloading various tools. "Yes, go ahead and try. Even if it only distracts the creature for a moment, it could be of use."

Emilie turned back down the corridor, with Hyacinth, Miss Marlende, and even Miss Deverrin all moving to go with her. She stopped Efrain and told him, "Stay here. They might need your help." That was a more diplomatic way of saying that they might need someone to hand them things while they worked on the door controls, but she didn't want Efrain to distract her while she was doing this. And mostly, she knew she would have to act very silly, and if they survived this she didn't want to be teased about it later.

Efrain nodded. "Be careful," he told her, and went back to Lord Engal.

Hyacinth led the way down the corridor to the gallery and around to the cabin on the far side.

Mikel stood by the sealed door into the control room, and turned in surprise as they came in. "You're back!" he said, relieved. "We didn't know what had happened."

"It was bad for a bit," Emilie told him.

Miss Marlende said, "Emilie is going to try to trick the creature into opening the door."

Mikel lifted his brows. "It's worth a try, I suppose."

Emilie wished they would all be just a little more confident. She handed the translator over to Miss Marlende, wanting both hands free.

Hyacinth pressed its blossoms against a metal-paper control near the door. Miss Marlende reported, "It says it will open a speaking device that will let the creature hear you inside the control cabin. And the rest of us ought to conceal ourselves in the corridor."

As they left, Miss Deverrin stopped in front of Emile and said, "Take care. Great care. These creatures . . . Remember they can affect your mind." She took a sharp breath. "I know it seems an obvious piece of advice, and probably ridiculous, coming from me. But if someone had told me last year that my father could be possessed by some aetheric monster and I would not notice the difference . . ."

"I understand," Emilie said quickly. And she had needed to be reminded of the creature's strange ability to affect belief. She would like to think she was too strong and knowledgeable to fall for it, but she knew where overconfidence had landed her before.

Hyacinth signaled that it was ready, and Emilie stepped over to the wall. Hyacinth tapped a blossom on a small hole that had opened in the square of metal-paper there. She leaned close and whispered, "Daniel. Daniel, can you hear me?"

She heard something rustle, though the room behind her was empty and neither she nor Hyacinth had moved. *This lets me hear inside the room, too,* she realized. *That's handy.* "It's Emilie. I can help you. Please let me in." She tried to make her voice low and conspiratorial, though she didn't know how sensitive the creature listening would be to nuance. If this was really the first time it had taken over a human, it might not have any idea how they would really talk to each other.

There was a long pause. Then she heard a quiet footstep. She thought the creature must have stepped closer to the talking device on its side of the wall. She said, "It's safe. The others are all in the room on the other side. I don't know why they're doing this to you, and poor Dr.

Deverrin. They say you've been taken over by some sort of monster, but I told them I don't see any monsters around you." Emilie hesitated, wondering if that had crossed the boundary into too stupid to be credible. She thought Miss Marlende must be listening from the corridor and whispering a translation to Hyacinth, because it was staring at her with all its blossoms. The deck shuddered underfoot again, a reminder there wasn't much time, and she added, "I have a weapon that can help you, if the others get in." She needed to make it more urgent. "They have a bomb, to blow up the door! They'll use it at any moment."

There was silence except for a hollow thud and a muted bang that must be coming from the effort to get the other door open. Then Daniel—or at least Daniel's voice—said, "What . . . What weapon?"

"A gun," Emilie answered. "They don't know I have it." She made herself sob, though to her ears it sounded unconvincing. More like a muffled squawk. "I don't want you hurt." She winced in anticipation, and made herself say, "You know I love you." She hoped the real Daniel couldn't actually hear her. She felt a great deal of friendship and affection for Daniel, but certainly not romantic love. "I'll help you any way I can."

She tried to think of something else to say, but knew piling on more reasons the creature should open the door would just make it all sound like the lie it was.

Then Daniel's voice said, "I'll open the door, Emilie. You know I trust you and love you. Pass me the weapon through the opening."

The hair stood up on the back of Emilie's neck and every nerve tingled. The words themselves were strange to hear in Daniel's voice, but there was a tone underneath that made her skin crawl. She said, "I will."

Hyacinth eased away from her, flattening itself against the wall.

Emilie stepped close to the door, not sure what she meant to do. She hoped Hyacinth was telling Miss Marlende what was happening through the translator.

The door creaked and started to slide and Emilie tensed. It opened just enough to reveal Daniel.

Emilie meant to lunge through the door as soon as it was open wide enough, but instead she found herself just standing there.

Daniel still looked like himself, though his clothes were mussed and he had lost his sling. His shirt was torn enough to reveal the bandages on his shoulder. They were bloodstained and the skin around them was purple-black with bruises. "You're hurt," she said stupidly. And it was very stupid, because of course she had been there when Miss Marlende had shot him in the Hollow World. It must have made the healing wound much worse when he had climbed the ladder.

She couldn't remember why he had climbed the ladder.

He said, "Give me the weapon."

She actually reached into the bag still hanging from her shoulder and grasped the medical kit inside before she realized what she had done. She froze, staring at him. *Oh. Oh, my.* This was the effect that had clouded the minds of Miss Deverrin and the rest of her party. It chilled her straight to the bone. What would have happened back at the camp if Dr. Marlende hadn't been able to resist it and warn them about Dr. Deverrin? Would they all still be sitting beside the corpse of the wrecked airship, listening to Deverrin and nodding along with everything he said?

Emilie forced herself to smile. "Of course." She drew out the medical kit and held it out. "I hid it in here." When he reached for it, she jammed it into his face and shoved through the door.

He wrenched backward and hit something on the wall beside him. The door rammed into Emilie's shoulder, squeezing her painfully as it tried to close. The breath shot out of her lungs and she couldn't even cry out. Then Hyacinth was beside her, then above her head, forcing its body into the shrinking gap. The door slid open abruptly. Emilie staggered forward, gasping for air. Daniel swung away from her, lunging for the controls on the central table.

Her voice a strangled croak, Emilie shouted to Hyacinth, "Get the other door!" She flung herself forward and tackled Daniel around the knees. They both hit the ground with a painful thump.

She remembered at that point that Hyacinth wouldn't have understood her request to open the other door. But it must have realized that was the best course of action because it leapt across the room and hit the control. Daniel struggled under her, twisting and sitting up to hit at her. Dr. Marlende and Lord Engal charged in. Then Miss Marlende grabbed the back of her jacket and hauled her off Daniel.

They surrounded him. Efrain and Miss Marlende stood by Emilie, and Miss Marlende had her pistol drawn. Dr. Marlende held the aether device. Daniel scrambled backward, his expression confused and terri-fied. "Help me, Emilie!" he said, desperate.

Emilie said, "If you were really Daniel, you'd know that thing won't hurt you." She was flushed and dizzy, and her shoulder hurt where it had taken the brunt of the door's weight.

Dr. Marlende lifted the aether device and triggered it.

CHAPTER FOURTEEN

Daniel went still, then slowly lifted his hands to his face.

Emilie bit her lip so hard she tasted blood. *Come on, come on, work,* she pleaded with the device. Then Mikel said, "What's that?"

Emilie thought he was talking about Daniel, then realized she could hear someone shouting. It wasn't someone in this room. Professor Abindon swore and said, "The Deverrins! They've managed to get aboard."

Lord Engal stepped quickly to the doorway. "Dr. Deverrin won't know we have the device. This is our chance."

"You're right." Miss Marlende turned to Mikel. "Get back up to the airship and have them break off. We can't risk the Deverrins reaching it. Efrain, show him the way to the topside hatch."

Efrain hesitated, threw a worried look at Emilie. She jerked her chin, telling him to go. He nodded and ran out the door with Mikel.

Dr. Marlende was already striding out with Lord Engal, Miss Deverrin right behind them. Dr. Marlende said, "Vale, keep an eye on Daniel. We have to set a trap for Dr. Deverrin."

Emilie looked at Daniel again. He had fallen over sideways, curled into a ball. She started to step forward, then made herself stop. If the device hadn't worked, he might grab her and hold her hostage. Miss Marlende said, "Emilie, take the translator, please."

One hand occupied by her pistol, Miss Marlende held the translator awkwardly tucked under her other arm. Emilie took it, wondering if Miss Marlende just wanted to distract her from Daniel. But Hyacinth stood at her elbow and she realized it must not have understood what had just happened. She said into the translator, "The Deverrins got aboard and we're setting a trap for the creature in Dr. Deverrin."

Hyacinth flowed toward the door immediately to follow Dr.

Marlende and the others. Emilie realized as the one with the translator, she had to go too, and hurried after it. Professor Abindon said sharply, "Emilie, be careful!"

Emilie waved an acknowledging hand as she ran out the door.

She and Hyacinth went through the outer rooms and found the others in the corridor overlooking the gallery. Dr. Marlende, Lord Engal, and Miss Deverrin had taken a position to one side of a supporting arch. Lord Engal had a pistol, one of the spares from the airship, and was saying, "They must have climbed up along the ridge and reached the lower hatch of the aether sailer. Part of the ladder was still attached to it when it broke away from our airship."

Dr. Marlende was armed only with the aether device. His expression severe, he said to Miss Deverrin, "Young woman, I am asking you to withdraw. Surely you realize what effect seeing this creature again may have on you—"

"This creature is holding my father prisoner inside his own body." Miss Deverrin's voice was quite sharp. "I assure you I am very aware of that now. I will be here when that device frees him."

Dr. Marlende was not impressed. "And I'll remind you we don't know if it worked on Daniel yet or not."

Lord Engal hissed, "Quiet, they're coming."

Emilie drew Hyacinth back and crouched down behind another arch. She glanced back and saw Professor Abindon had taken up a position in the doorway to the control room, where she could hear what happened but also keep an eye on Miss Marlende and Daniel.

If Lord Engal was right and the Deverrins had gotten in through the underside hatchway, they would be coming down the main corridor from the first wall shaft. They would enter the open area below the gallery through the large doorway in the far wall. Emilie heard movement from that direction now, booted footsteps on the metal floors.

Dr. Marlende eased forward, carefully cradling the aether device. Lord Engal lifted his pistol and said in an almost voiceless whisper, "Careful. Miss Deverrin, do they have other firearms?"

"Besides the ones you took, there is another rifle and three pistols," Miss Deverrin whispered back.

"I'd rather avoid a gunfight inside this ship," Dr. Marlende murmured.

Emilie would, too. She spotted movement past the large doorway, a flash of metal, the gray of someone's coat sleeve, and heard low voices. She tensed. If Dr. Deverrin would just step out into view . . . That would leave the other Deverrins to deal with, but with Miss Deverrin here to talk to them, they might be able to avoid a fight.

Then Dr. Deverrin's voice rang out across the large space. "I know you're there. I assume you have weapons pointed at us."

Dr. Marlende didn't move, but Lord Engal shifted uneasily. Dr. Deverrin shouldn't know about the new aether device, Emilie told herself. He was only worried about the guns. The other ghost pirate would have told him that it had destroyed the original device. Unless they had some silent way to communicate with each other once they were both in the same place.

"We have no desire to injure you." Dr. Marlende pitched his voice to carry. "But you have held us captive before and we have no intention of allowing you to do so again. Perhaps if we can discuss the situation?"

"You wish to bargain with me?"

Emilie thought Dr. Deverrin's voice was oddly unemotional, as if the ghost pirate wasn't bothering to play the part anymore. She snuck a look up at Miss Deverrin and then wished she hadn't. Miss Deverrin's face was taut with dread, her expression sickened.

"You obviously want this ship. You and your companion went to a great deal of trouble to seize it and keep it in the aether current, and now you've brought it here. I assume your need for it is now urgent," Dr. Marlende said. "If you admit what you are, we can bargain."

"Admit what I am?"

Dr. Marlende smiled. "Oh, come on now. Surely there is no point in attempting to conceal yourself further."

"Very well," Dr. Deverrin said. "Perhaps there is no more point in hiding. We are exiles. Our own people sent us out here to die, and closed the aether current stream to our world, so we could not return."

Emilie whispered the words into the translator for Hyacinth.

Lord Engal muttered, "He must have the rest of the party under very strict control, to be able to speak so openly. That doesn't bode well."

Miss Deverrin took a sharp breath, as if suppressing the urge to speak. Lord Engal glanced back at her, and she shook her head. She whispered, "Perhaps. I don't know what he's done to them."

"He obviously suspects a trap." In a crouch, Dr. Marlende backed up to the wall, then motioned for Emilie to come toward him. Staying low, she reached him and he whispered, "Take this and the translator and give it to Abindon. Ask Hyacinth to guide her around to the other side of the gallery. She may be able to get a shot from there." He dumped the aether device into Emilie's arms.

She quietly scrambled back to the doorway, saying softly to Hyacinth, "Did you get that?"

I did. I will guide the matriarch.

To Dr. Deverrin, Dr. Marlende raised his voice and replied, "That's very unfortunate, and you have my sympathy. But that doesn't give you the right to torment and drive away the crew of this ship, or to attack the Deverrin party and use them to assault us."

In the cabin, the professor stepped forward, taking the aether device and the translator. "I heard. Come along, my friend."

Hyacinth led her back through the control room where Miss Marlende waited with Daniel. Emilie hesitated in the doorway. He still lay curled in a huddle on the floor, and Miss Marlende looked deeply worried. Emilie was torn between following Professor Abindon and Hyacinth, or joining Miss Marlende. She decided two people moving through the ship was less likely to alert the Deverrins than three, and she didn't think she could stand to sit and watch Daniel and not know whether it was all him in there or not. She slipped back to her former vantage point in time to hear Dr. Deverrin say, "We needed to return home, and used what was available to us."

Dr. Marlende frowned, trying to understand. "And did you cause the disturbance in the current that created this place, this amalgam of other worlds?"

"This is our way home. We have stirred the currents to bring us fragments of all the worlds along their path. These fragments join the whole, which will soon have such weight and power to break the seal and force open the aether current to our world. We will ride this vessel down it and our people will not be able to prevent our return."

Dr. Marlende and Lord Engal exchanged dubious expressions. Emilie whispered to them, "Will that work?"

Lord Engal replied softly, "I have no idea. It sounds possible though unlikely. But these beings obviously understand much more of the aether than we do."

"I see," Dr. Marlende said to Dr. Deverrin. "If that's your goal, then I want to bargain with you. Have your companion release my assistant

Daniel, and you release Dr. Deverrin, and we will leave you in peace to carry on with your endeavors."

Emilie held her breath. This depended on whether the two pirates could communicate with each other over distances through the aether, or if she and Hyacinth were right and they had needed the communication device aboard the lifeboat to speak.

"If that is truly all you want," Dr. Deverrin said, "prove you have no ill intent. Come down where I can see you."

Dr. Marlende glanced across the room. Emilie followed his gaze and saw Professor Abindon standing just inside a doorway on the opposite gallery, Hyacinth beside her. They were directly above the Deverrins' position. If Dr. Deverrin would just walk out into the room . . . Dr. Marlende said, "Will you agree to release Dr. Deverrin, and my assistant Daniel?"

"Of course. But first come out, so we can speak like gentlemen."

Emilie shifted uncomfortably. The ghost pirate hadn't been speaking as Dr. Deverrin since it had started the conversation; despite the reference to "gentlemen" it still didn't sound like him. Emilie suddenly didn't think Dr. Deverrin was in there at all anymore.

She didn't want to think about what that might mean for Daniel. He hadn't sounded at all like himself, either.

Lord Engal muttered, "I'm afraid we have to. He won't come out unless we do."

"Yes." Dr. Marlende threw another look across at Professor Abindon, who waited in tense impatience, the aether device held ready. "Emilie, Miss Deverrin, stay up here."

"I'm coming with you," Miss Deverrin said. "Don't argue. It will be to your advantage—he'll think he can manipulate me." At Lord Engal's glance, she added, "He can't. Not anymore."

"Very well." Dr. Marlende stepped toward the wall shaft. "But Emilie, stay up here with Vale. She may need you."

"I will," Emilie promised, trying to sound firm and not like someone who was sweating anxiously.

Lord Engal and Miss Deverrin walked with Dr. Marlende down to the wall shaft. Emilie edged back farther into the doorway, pressing herself against the side. It was harder to see the floor of the room below from here, but it would be harder for the Deverrins to spot her, too. She didn't know what she could do to help. She didn't want to just huddle here. But she didn't want to do anything foolish and make things worse, either.

She watched Dr. Marlende, Lord Engal, and Miss Deverrin go into the wall shaft and emerge below, Miss Deverrin stumbling a little as she reached the floor. Lord Engal slipped his pistol into his jacket pocket, but kept his hand on it.

Dr. Marlende moved a few steps farther into the space, then stopped.

Emilie held her breath, watching the doorway. After a long moment, two young men stepped into the room. One was Brendan, and the other she recognized as one of the men who had been guarding the Marlendes; both held pistols. Brendan said, "Alea, are you all right?"

"I'm fine," Miss Deverrin replied, sounding calm and certain. "There is no need for firearms. These people want to help us."

Emilie didn't move, didn't turn her head for fear of attracting attention, but out of the corner of her eye she saw the professor ease silently forward to the edge of the gallery and lift the aether device.

Dr. Deverrin stepped through the doorway. He said, "Come here, Alea."

Professor Abindon took aim and fired.

Dr. Deverrin staggered two steps forward. Emilie was ready to cheer in relief. It was working on him, just as it had on Daniel.

Then Dr. Deverrin straightened up, apparently unaffected. His face shaped a smile. "My companion told me he destroyed that device. I thought you might try to rebuild it."

Emilie looked across at Professor Abindon and Hyacinth. The professor looked annoyed and angry and Hyacinth had all its blossoms extended in alarm. She heard a quiet "Damn" from Lord Engal.

Dr. Deverrin said, "But it is far too late to use it on me. I have been in this body too long."

Emilie looked at Brendan and the other man, the other Deverrins she could see through the doorway. Their expressions hadn't changed, they still looked worried, a little confused. *They can't hear what he's saying,* she thought, just like in the camp when Dr. Marlende had accused him of being an imposter. Dr. Deverrin still had them under tight control.

Miss Deverrin shouted, "You bastard, let my father go!" and surged forward.

Lord Engal caught her around the waist, holding her back. "Don't get near him!"

Dr. Deverrin held out a hand to her. "But I am your father, my dear. We are one."

"It's horrible," Emilie whispered aloud. Poor Dr. Deverrin . . . And Daniel, if the device hadn't worked on him either.

"But why?" The words burst out of Dr. Marlende in a tone of anguish. "Why steal the bodies of other beings?"

Dr. Deverrin said, "We cannot cross the bridge we have constructed in our true forms. We took these bodies because we needed them. There was no other suitable shell for my companion among the ones we already had, and if you had not come we would have had to delay our crossing until—"

Then behind her Miss Marlende shouted a warning. Emilie twitched around to see Daniel staggering toward her. She hesitated for a heartbeat, not sure if this was Daniel or the ghost pirate. Whichever, he shouldn't be out here. She lunged forward to tackle him back into the room.

Prepared this time, he grabbed her shoulders and twisted away from her. She stumbled back and sat down hard. Miss Marlende tried to seize him from behind and he flung her off. He made it the last few steps out onto the gallery.

He stopped right at the edge. As Emilie struggled to her feet, he started to shudder. The motion was jerky and awkward, as if something inhuman was trying to move his body and no longer knew how. Emilie took a step toward him but Miss Marlende grabbed her shoulder. She could see everyone on the floor below staring up at him. For once Dr. Deverrin had a real expression on his face. It was horror.

Daniel's body convulsed and then light shimmered out of his skin. It was the deep red Emilie had seen reflected in the aether current clouds, shot through with black shadows. It stretched away from Daniel's body, dragged itself free. It formed a shape with multiple limbs, nothing that looked like a head. This was the aether creature leaving Daniel's body. It should have been a relief, but it was awful to watch.

The translucent shape writhed away and Daniel stumbled back. Emilie and Miss Marlende darted forward as one and caught him before he could fall. He breathed heavily, blearily half conscious. He gasped, "What happened?"

"You were taken over by an aether ghost pirate, but it's gone now," Emilie told him.

As they eased him to the floor, Miss Marlende muttered, "I didn't expect it to happen like that."

Emilie didn't think anyone had. The aether creature had disappeared over the side of the gallery. She stepped to the edge to see it lying in a gently glowing pool on the floor below. *I hope it doesn't go after Dr. Marlende,* she had time to think. Then abruptly its light winked out.

And Dr. Deverrin screamed in rage. "You murdering filth!" Brendan and the other man lifted their pistols. The rest of the Deverrins surged into the room.

Dr. Marlende pushed Miss Deverrin toward the nearest corridor opening and yelled, "Run!"

Miss Marlende snapped, "Emilie, take Daniel!" As Brendan lifted his pistol she fired a warning shot down into the room. It scattered the startled Deverrins, gave Dr. Marlende and the others time to get through the doorway.

Emilie grabbed Daniel's good arm and helped him shove to his feet. She pulled his arm across her shoulder and they staggered down the gallery as fast as they could. He gasped, "People are shooting at us?"

"Yes, again." Shots rang out and Emilie stumbled, just short of the opening at the end of the gallery. Miss Marlende caught up with them and grabbed Daniel around the waist, pulling them both on through the door.

"This way." Emilie dragged Daniel down the corridor. "We need to get up to the topside hatch."

They ran, awkwardly supporting Daniel. Hyacinth and Professor Abindon appeared at the end of the corridor. The professor shouted, "Marlende and Engal don't know the way up to the wall shaft!"

Emilie remembered there was a short wall shaft in the next corridor over, that connected to the level where Dr. Marlende and the others were. "I'll go get them," she said, and shifted Daniel's weight over onto Miss Marlende.

"Emilie, what—Where—" Daniel was still confused.

"Hurry," Miss Marlende called after her.

Professor Abindon added, "We'll meet you at the wall shaft up to the topside hatch!"

"Don't wait for us, we'll be right behind you!" Emilie called back.

She ran down the cross corridor, hoping she recalled this area from their earlier explorations as well as she thought she did. She took the two turns she remembered, then reached the junction area with the wall shaft to the level below. A shout echoed up from it and the clang of a bullet hitting a metal wall told her she was in the right spot. She shouted down the shaft, "Dr. Marlende! Lord Engal! This way!"

She flung herself down on the floor and gripped the edge of the opening, resisting the pull of it, and hung her head down. At first she couldn't see anyone; the corridors leading away from the junction below were empty. Then she heard running feet and Miss Deverrin appeared at the end of a corridor. "Here, this way!" she called out again.

Dr. Marlende and Lord Engal came into view behind Miss Deverrin, Lord Engal turning to fire a shot at their pursuers. They ran toward the wall shaft and Emilie scrambled back out of the way.

As they came up the shaft, Miss Deverrin was saying, "Are you absolutely sure?"

As the shaft deposited him on the floor, Dr. Marlende replied, "Unless that was some sort of play put on for our entertainment, I don't see—Emilie, was Daniel all right?"

"Yes, it's him. He's back," she reported hurriedly. "He doesn't seem to remember what happened."

Lord Engal stumbled out of the shaft. "The creature must have been telling the truth, Miss Deverrin. I fear your father is in effect dead. I am very sorry."

Miss Deverrin dashed a hand across her face and didn't reply.

"It's this way." Emilie led the way down the corridor. There might be a quicker way to that main wall shaft but she felt it was better to stick to the one she knew. If the Deverrins cornered them in a room, there would be no escape. "I guess it's no good telling Dr. Deverrin that we didn't mean to kill the other ghost pirate?"

"No, and I don't think our intentions mattered." Dr. Marlende caught up with her as they rounded the corner. "There was clearly a difference between extracting an aether being from a human and from a member of Hyacinth's species, something we failed to understand." He sounded calm again, the way he usually did, but Emilie remembered his voice when he had asked Dr. Deverrin why it did this to people. She thought Dr. Marlende was very good at making himself be calm, even when he was in great emotional turmoil; it must be a necessary skill for an adventurer.

"The other one knew it was killing my father," Miss Deverrin said from behind them, her voice harsh with grief.

"Yes, there is that," Dr. Marlende admitted.

They made a turn into another long corridor and with relief Emilie saw the professor, Miss Marlende, Daniel, and Hyacinth waiting at the far end. They were in the junction with the wall shaft that went up to the top level of the ship. Emilie waved at them and yelled, "Go on!"

As they hurried down the corridor, Miss Marlende and Professor Abindon had an abrupt discussion, then Miss Marlende hauled a protesting Daniel into the shaft. The professor and Hyacinth waited, the professor waving impatiently at them.

They had just reached the junction when the deck rolled. Emilie staggered sideways with the others and bounced off the far wall. The professor grabbed the edge of the wall shaft to steady herself, and Hyacinth rolled a little before it caught itself on the floor with its four lower limbs. The aether sailer shuddered and righted itself, and metal groaned from somewhere far down in the ship. "What was that?" Emilie gasped. "The aether current again?"

Lord Engal staggered upright. "We may be too close to the ground. Surely this ship wasn't designed—" Another shudder cut him off, and the deck tilted again. This time it didn't right itself, but stayed at an angle. Emilie braced herself against the wall. This was clearly very, very bad.

"Hurry." Dr. Marlende pushed away from the wall, pulling Emilie with him.

Professor Abindon steadied a stumbling Miss Deverrin. "Is it the block in the aether current breaking up? Perhaps it took both of them to maintain—"

A shot shattered the air and Emilie clapped her hands over her ears. A heartbeat later she realized she should have thrown herself on the floor, but it was too late now. She twisted around, sliding on the steep incline.

At the far end of the corridor, the Deverrins rushed toward them, Dr. Deverrin in the lead. They moved fast despite the slant in the deck. Lord Engal had slipped and fallen back against the wall . . . No, he had been shot. A red stain showed on his white shirt, under his open jacket.

Emilie lunged toward him. Professor Abindon lifted the aether device and fired it. The effect hit Dr. Deverrin like a bullet. He staggered, clutching his head. Dr. Marlende drew a pistol out of his jacket pocket and fired twice down the corridor. Deverrins halted in confusion and fear, though he must have fired over their heads because no one fell down.

Emilie reached Lord Engal and grabbed his arm to drag him back. He was too heavy for her, especially on the sloping deck, but terror seemed to lend her extra strength. Hyacinth was suddenly beside her, gripping Lord Engal's jacket and other arm with its blossoms. With its greater strength, they dragged him rapidly toward the wall shaft.

Lord Engal struggled to use his feet to help them, his face set in a grimace of pain. Then Dr. Deverrin straightened up and charged toward them again. Someone else fired another shot and Hyacinth fell heavily against Emilie. She caught it and found her hand wet with a white fluid. *It's been shot,* she thought, panic racing through her. She held its light body against her side and kept her grip on Lord Engal's arm, braced to feel the next bullet herself. *At least Efrain and Miss Marlende and Daniel got away,* she thought.

Dr. Deverrin stopped barely ten steps away. His face was a mask of rage; he was barely recognizable as the man Emilie had seen in the camp. He said, "Put the weapons down or I'll have them kill all of you." The other Deverrins pointed their guns, waiting for his order.

Dr. Marlende braced himself on the wall near Emilie. "You mean to do that anyway."

Dr. Deverrin lifted his lips in a terrible imitation of a smile. "Then shoot them. But you won't, will you? They've done nothing to you, except allow themselves to become extensions of me."

Dr. Marlende's jaw hardened. "Let the others here go. I'll stay, and you can take your vengeance on me."

"Put down the weapon," Dr. Deverrin said again. "Without my companion our aether bridge is breaking up, and will destroy this ship. I have no time to argue."

Lord Engal's breathing was harsh in the quiet and Emilie could feel Hyacinth sagging in her arms. Part of her brain worked furiously, trying to see a way out, but the rest of her was paralyzed with growing despair.

Miss Deverrin said, "I'll take it." Emilie flinched. She had almost forgotten Miss Deverrin was with them, the woman had been so quiet.

Miss Deverrin stepped forward as best she could on the slanted deck, and held out her hand for the gun.

He's taken her over again, Emilie thought, angry, then, *hasn't he?* Miss Deverrin's face was rigid, hard with grim determination.

Dr. Marlende met Miss Deverrin's gaze, and put the gun into her hand.

Dr. Deverrin said, "Now, my dear, shoot—"

Miss Deverrin turned and fired at Dr. Deverrin.

Emilie squeezed her eyes shut, just an instant too late. The thump as the body hit the floor made her flinch.

Emilie opened her eyes to see the other members of the Deverrin party staring in shock. Light shimmered out of Dr. Deverrin's body, just as it had Daniel's. Dark red translucent limbs stretched, and for a moment she thought the aether pirate would flee. Then it collapsed into a puddle on the deck, and all its light went out.

With barely a tremor in her voice, Miss Deverrin said, "That was the obvious solution." She took a deep shuddering breath. "I understand why you were reluctant, but as Lord Engal said, my father was already dead."

Dr. Marlende took the gun out of her hand. He just said, "Can you make your companions follow us? If they remain behind here they will surely die as well."

CHAPTER FIFTEEN

Miss Deverrin went to Brendan's side and put her hand on his arm. He shook his head in confusion. The other Deverrins seemed too shocked to move. Down the hall, one of them slid to the floor.

Dr. Marlende and Professor Abindon moved to haul Lord Engal up and toward the wall shaft. His breath wheezing, his voice tight with pain, Lord Engal said, "You may have to leave me, I'm afraid."

"Don't be ridiculous." Dr. Marlende shouldered Lord Engal's arm.

"Yes," the professor added, supporting his other side. "Don't make a bigger spectacle of yourself than you already have."

Lord Engal rallied and said, "Madam, if I'm to die, I have some rather frank things I would like to say to you about your personality—"

Dr. Marlende interrupted, "Emilie, is Hyacinth all right?"

"No, it was shot." Emilie swallowed back a sob and tried to lift Hyacinth. For a moment it was like holding a limp bag of laundry. Then it suddenly shoved itself up and shivered its blossoms. It weaved back and forth, then wrapped an arm around her forearm. She kept her arm around it, telling it, "There, you can walk. It's not so bad." She hoped it wasn't so bad.

The professor fished into her bag and pulled out the translator. Without letting go of Lord Engal, she handed it back to Emilie. "See if our friend is well enough to move."

Emilie held the translator up and read the words *I can move. Is the pirate truly dead?*

"It's a puddle, like the other one," Emilie told it.

A relief. And perhaps a sadness. I do not know what else we could have done. It shivered. *Ouch. That was an extremely painful weapon.*

"Just try to keep moving," Dr. Marlende said, with a glance back at the Deverrins.

He and the professor hauled Lord Engal into the wall shaft and Emilie followed with Hyacinth. It was easier to support Hyacinth with the force in the shaft pushing them slightly upward. Emilie looked back over her shoulder but the Deverrins still weren't following. She admitted to mixed feelings; the Deverrins had tried hard to kill them and might very well have permanently injured Lord Engal and Hyacinth. But they had been in the power of the aether pirates, just like Daniel had been. And she didn't want Miss Deverrin to be left behind. Or maybe she didn't want any of them left behind. *I think I'm having a fit,* she thought. *If I was inclined to it, I might faint.* Maybe later she could have a good faint, once they got out of this place.

"Is the creature really dead?" Lord Engal asked, his voice raspy with the effort of staying upright in the wall shaft. "It's not going to be sneaking about after us, is it?"

"I believed it lingered too long in Dr. Deverrin," Dr. Marlende told him. "Perhaps the being inside Daniel died for the same reason; after inhabiting a human, it was unable to switch to a different host, or to exist in its normal state."

They reached the top of the shaft and stepped out into the corridor, which seemed a lot longer than it had when they came through here the first time. As they reached the turn that led to the topside hatch, Emilie heard something and looked back to see Miss Deverrin and Brendan stumble out of the wall shaft. She said, "Dr. Marlende."

He turned and called out, "This way!"

All the Deverrins caught up with them by the time they reached the topside hatch. It was still open to the light and air of the outside, and Emilie heard the airship's engine. It was possibly the sweetest sound imaginable. It was even better when Miss Marlende poked her head down through the hatch and said, "We've got Daniel aboard . . . What happened?"

"The aether being in Deverrin is dead," Dr. Marlende explained, "Engal and Hyacinth are wounded, and we must get the rest of the Deverrin party onto the airship."

It turned out to be more than fortunate that the Deverrins had decided to come. It would have been extremely difficult to get Lord Engal up and out of the hatch without Brendan and another young man to lift him from behind, especially in the angled position the aether sailer had settled in. Emilie put the translator back into her bag and she and Hyacinth went up the shaft and through the hatch to-gether, it still holding tightly to her arm.

They climbed out onto the top of the aether sailer, clinging hard to the slanted metal. Emilie only had time to take one breath of air before she saw the situation was much, much worse than she thought.

The aether sailer had hit the ridge and now balanced on it, its en-gines keeping it from sliding down into the camp below. Because of the new angle, the airship had been able to avoid the sails and angle much closer. It hung only about twenty feet away, its boarding ladder draped across the aether sailer's hull. The sling and winch was de-ployed, which must be how they had gotten Daniel aboard. Seth, his head bandaged, stood at the railing next to it, watching worriedly. But through the gaps between the sails, Emilie saw the far range of what they had thought were mountains, but were actually piled-up frag-ments of lands brought from other worlds to build this place. They were breaking up.

As Emilie stared, chunks broke off to fly up and away. If the pieces were big enough to see from this distance, they must be huge. With her free hand she pointed wordlessly. Her face set and grim, Miss Mar-lende said, "It's happening all around us." Gripping the edge of a sail to steady herself, she turned to face the airship. "Throw the sling!"

Emilie glanced around in the other directions and saw a giant chunk of blue forest fly through the air. Her throat went dry and she turned back toward the airship. There was nothing she could do about it and looking at it was terrifying. This place was breaking to bits around them.

She was about to ask where Efrain was when he banged out of the airship's door and hurried to help Seth with the sling. They tossed it down and Dr. Marlende and Professor Abindon began to bundle Lord Engal into it.

Members of the Deverrin party were still climbing up from below, confused, staring at the airship. Emilie hoped none of them fell off. Miss Marlende said, "Father, get up to the airship. You need to start working on the spells to get us out of here."

Professor Abindon tightened the last strap on Lord Engal's sling. "Yes, go, Marlende."

Dr. Marlende hesitated, then said, "Take care, and move quickly, both of you."

As Dr. Marlende started to climb the ladder, Emilie said, "Lord Engal, can you carry Hyacinth?" It was huddled beside her and she thought its wound was worse. Between the blood dripping from Lord Engal's jacket and the trail of ichor from Hyacinth, the hull was getting slippery.

Lord Engal held out his arms and Emilie pushed Hyacinth toward him. She had to gently pry its blossoms off her hands. Lord Engal gathered it against his chest, grimacing in pain. Seth and Efrain started the winch and the sling's rope tightened, pulling Lord Engal and Hyacinth up and off the hull.

Dr. Marlende climbed onto the airship's gallery and Miss Marlende ordered, "You next, Mother. Hurry."

The professor hesitated but didn't argue, turning to the ladder. Miss Deverrin moved over to stand with Emilie and Miss Marlende. Miss Marlende asked her, "Is that all your people? I hope so, because if there's someone left in that camp . . ."

"No, that's all of us." Her brow furrowed, Miss Deverrin looked down at the camp, the wreck of the Deverrin airship, as if she had never seen the place before.

"Get them up the ladder, quickly," Miss Marlende told her. Miss Deverrin snapped out of her moment of confusion and called to Brendan. The other Deverrins started to climb, slowly at first, until the hull shuddered under their feet. "Go, hurry!" Miss Marlende yelled.

Emilie clung to the sail, her fingers leaving sweaty prints on the metal. The aether sailer shuddered and she had to swallow back bile. Then Efrain called from above, "Emilie!"

She looked up to see the professor and Efrain at the railing. The professor tossed down a bundle of straps attached to a rope that was secured to the gallery. Miss Marlende grabbed it and shook it out to reveal a double set of safety harnesses. She slung the first over her shoulders, buckled it, and pulled Emilie close to fasten the second one around her. "Here, hold on to the strap on my back."

Emilie gripped the strap in relief, feeling much more secure as Miss Marlende's arm tightened around her waist. The last three Deverrins were on the ladder, only Miss Deverrin and her brother remaining behind. Brendan still seemed muddled, not understanding what was happening. But he moved to grip the ladder and climb when Miss Deverrin urged him on.

When he was almost to the gallery and Miss Deverrin had lifted her foot to step onto the first rung, Emilie felt a swell of relief; they had made it, they had escaped.

Then the hull lurched with a shriek of metal and jerked away from the airship. The ladder yanked out of Miss Deverrin's hands and swung away. Miss Marlende shouted, "Together, Emilie!"

As Miss Deverrin started to slide backward across the hull, Emilie realized what Miss Marlende meant. When Miss Marlende surged forward, Emilie surged with her. They ran right into Miss Deverrin. Miss Marlende wrapped her free arm around Miss Deverrin and Emilie grabbed on to her as well. Miss Deverrin gasped in fear but gripped their arms.

Then they swung free and dangled from the airship's gallery as the aether sailer slid away beneath their feet. Emilie stared down in fascination as the huge craft rolled over and crashed into the remains of the Deverrins' airship. A crack appeared in the far side of the ridge and with horror she watched the whole side of the mountain split open. "It's getting worse," she reported, her voice thick.

Then the rope jerked and they shot upward as the winch reeled them in. The ladder still hung down but Brendan had made it to the gallery, watching them in alarm. As they drew near the railing, lots of hands reached for them and pulled them up. Emilie was dragged onto the metal deck and had to force herself to let go of Miss Deverrin and the harness strap. The professor shouted for everyone to get inside and they all stumbled through the door.

The cabin was crowded with confused people. Miss Marlende tore the harness off and started for the steering cabin. Professor Abindon slammed the outer door, locked it, and called, "Everyone's aboard, get us out of here!"

The airship powered up and Emilie grabbed the nearest person's arm to steady herself as the deck angled underfoot. Then she realized the person she had grabbed was Efrain. He looked scared. He said, "I thought you were going to fall!"

Emilie had thought so too. Her knees still thought so and trembled uncontrollably. She asked, "Where's Hyacinth? And Lord Engal? And Daniel?"

"Up here." Efrain led her toward the front of the cabin, shouldering his way past various Deverrins.

Efrain went through the door into the steering cabin. Dr. Marlende and Miss Marlende sat at the front, working quickly over the control boards. Lord Engal had been placed in one of the chairs toward the back of the room, and Mikel leaned over him, pressing a folded bandage to the wound above his hip. Daniel sat near the door, leaning back against the wall, and Hyacinth sat on the floor like a pile of discarded foliage.

Emilie went to Hyacinth first and knelt beside it. She didn't remember where the translator had ended up. "Is it still bleeding?"

"I don't know." Daniel crawled forward. He looked awful himself. "I'm not sure it's still conscious. It's just been sitting where we put it."

"We need to stop the bleeding." A medical kit lay open on the floor and she pulled out more bandages.

As she looked at Hyacinth more carefully, she saw the blossoms were wilting in two distinct spots on opposite sides. The bullet must have passed right through its body. She tried to press the bandages against the wilted spots, but they were immediately soaked with the clear violet-tinged ichor.

Professor Abindon strode in, dropped her satchel on the deck, looked from Engal to Hyacinth, then said to Emilie, "Try clamps. I'll be with you in a moment," and went on to Lord Engal.

Lord Engal gasped, "No, help Hyacinth. This is an opportunity for a concord between our species—"

"Be quiet," the professor said, and took Mikel's place at the chair. She told him, "You get back to the engine cabin, they may need you." Mikel hurried out.

Clamps, Emilie thought, digging through the medical kit as Efrain held it steady for her. The airship shook as it pushed upward away from the disintegrating hills. Miss Marlende had the wheel now, fighting it to keep the airship on its course. Dr. Marlende leaned over the aether navigator, carefully adjusting it. Emilie asked, "What do clamps look like?"

Daniel crawled over to the medical kit and fished out two metal clips. Emilie took the clamps and handed Efrain her bag. "Look for the translator. Ask it if this is what we should do." She was all too aware that Hyacinth wasn't human and that they could hurt it while trying to help it.

As Emilie fumbled to use the clamp to hold Hyacinth's wound

closed, the sky outside the ports turned dark purple-gray and the airship jerked violently. Miss Marlende cursed. Dr. Marlende said, "Just keep us as steady as you can, my dear." The professor swayed, but stayed on her feet, her hand pressed to Lord Engal's side. She was murmuring something that Emilie hoped was a healing spell.

Efrain got the translator out of the bag. "Hello?" he said into it. "Hello, can you hear me?" He shook his head. "There's no answer, Emilie."

Daniel said, "The mechanism could be broken, or it might need some other power source to work."

Emilie grimaced, realizing he must be right. The translator must have other parts it needed to function, aboard the lifeboat and the aether sailer. With those both gone, it was useless. She steeled her resolve, leaned in, and fixed the clamp around the first wound. Efrain leaned in to watch and winced. Hyacinth didn't react except to weakly move a few blossoms.

Emilie hoped that was a good sign. She moved around to fix the second clamp into place and the deck shuddered violently. Bracing herself, she shifted around and managed to clamp the second wound.

Then Miss Marlende yelled, "Hold on!" Emilie grabbed Hyacinth and Efrain held her arm. The professor dropped into a crouch and gripped the arm of Lord Engal's chair, and Daniel braced himself against the wall. The airship jerked, the deck lifted under Emilie's feet. She, Efrain, and Hyacinth all slid into the back wall of the cabin.

The ports went dark, then suddenly filled with the deep blue light of the aether. The airship went still. Miss Marlende turned, pushing her disordered hair out of her eyes. "Are you all right?"

"I think so," Emilie said, gently disentangling herself from Efrain and Hyacinth. Hyacinth was still alive, though it didn't seem inclined to move much.

Daniel tried to get up, then subsided back to the floor. "We're in the current?"

Dr. Marlende leaned over the aether navigator. "We're back to our first position, where the aether sailer was trapped."

A disheveled and exhausted Miss Deverrin stepped into the doorway from the rear cabin. "We're not all dead, so I assume things are going well." Her voice sounded brittle, as if it took all of her self-control to stay upright.

"The disruption is already shrinking and will soon be gone from the current," Dr. Marlende told her. He sounded a little brittle himself. He asked the professor, "How is Engal?"

She leaned over him again, though he seemed to be unconscious for now. "He'll do. If we can get back home within a reasonable time period."

"That is theoretically possible." Dr. Marlende looked toward Hyacinth, frowning. "That isn't going to help our castaway, though."

Miss Marlende asked, "How is Hyacinth, Emilie?"

"I don't know," Emilie said. It sat in a heap of blossoms, unmoving. She felt a lump of misery take up residence in her throat. Hyacinth had no way to get home, even if it didn't die from its wounds. And they had no way to communicate with it anymore. She picked up the translator from where it had landed against the wall. "We can't even talk to it. This isn't working, it must have needed . . ." She trailed off, because the translator was forming words. It was saying, *Hello, hello. Strange ship, can you hear us?*

Daniel and Efrain leaned over her shoulder to see what she was staring at. Daniel said, "Uh, I think we need to look outside."

The others turned toward the nearest port. Emilie shoved to her feet, clutching the translator.

Some distance away, floating in the aether, was a lifeboat just like the one that they had crashed. *Of course,* Emilie thought. *Hyacinth was supposed to follow them if it couldn't free the aether sailer. When it didn't, they sent someone back.*

Miss Marlende smiled. "Answer them, Emilie."

Emilie leaned over the translator, cleared her throat, and said, "Yes, we can hear you."

* * *

Drawing close enough to the lifeboat to transfer Hyacinth to it was easier than they all expected. The lifeboat was far more maneuverable in the aether than the airship. Emilie watched from the port as it moved in close, guided by Miss Marlende on the translator. Then it turned so that its stern hatchway was just over the airship's gallery and inside their protection spell.

Dr. Marlende ordered everyone else to stay back so the flower people wouldn't become alarmed. It was only Emilie and Miss Marlende who waited on the gallery with Hyacinth.

Emilie had been talking to Hyacinth the whole time, though so far it hadn't been able to reply. Its blossoms had begun to look better, though, and it was able to move by itself when they helped it out onto the gallery.

The ship's hatch opened and two flower people peered out. They were both different colors, one with more yellow blossoms and the other a deep dark green with flowers that looked like grass spikes. Emilie had thought they would all look alike, which she realized immediately had been quite stupid. It wasn't as if humans looked alike, either.

Hyacinth turned to her and the translator started to move in her hands. It said, *I told them to go, but these two are members of my family, and they took their lifeboat to the nearest stable current, and waited.*

Emilie nodded. "That's what families should be like."

Hyacinth curled a blossom arm around her wrist. *And you and I are true companions, even if we do not see each other again.*

Emilie swallowed back the urge to cry, part sadness, part relief that Hyacinth seemed to be getting better. She said, "We are true companions. And thank you for helping us. We would all be dead without you."

It shivered its blossoms at her, in a way she read as amusement. *I suspect you would have thought of something. But we were most clever together.*

Emilie and Miss Marlende picked Hyacinth up as gently as possible and handed it up through the door to the others. Emilie took the translator from where it sat on the gallery and tried to give it to them.

The green one pushed it back to her. The translator said, *Keep this. Then if we find each other again in our explorations we will be able to speak.*

"Thank you," Miss Marlende told them. "I hope one day we do meet again."

The flower people disappeared inside and the hatch swung shut. Emilie and Miss Marlende hurried back into the cabin, and the lifeboat moved smoothly away from the protective spell.

Moments later, both ships entered the aether current again for their long journeys home.

CHAPTER SIXTEEN

It was late evening when they came out of the aether current again, and night by the time they managed to anchor the airship at the Marlendes' airyard in Meneport.

They were greeted by a few sleepy journalists who had apparently been camping in the street outside. Dr. Marlende's students and workmen had been manning the yard waiting for their return, along with some members of the Philosophical Society who Mikel said had probably been watching for them with aether-scopes.

Emilie stood with Efrain, Professor Abindon, and Miss Marlende by the anchoring ropes for the airship, watching all the activity. Miss Marlende had asked a student to send a telegram to Lady Engal to tell her about Lord Engal's injury, and someone else to find a physician to attend him at his townhome, while Cobbier went to arrange transport for everyone. A telegram was also sent off to the Deverrins' country home, to notify Dr. Deverrin's wife of the rescue, and one to a friend of Anton Deverrin, to see if he was still in town. "Hopefully he can take charge of his relatives and sort out accommodation and help for the others until they can be sent home," Miss Marlende said. The Deverrin party was sitting in one of the workrooms, mostly to keep them from wandering off or being taken away by one of the journalists.

Miss Marlende continued, "Our house isn't large enough for this many people, unless we just have them camp out on blankets in the parlor and the dining room." She glanced down at Emilie. "There's room for you, Efrain, and Daniel, of course." She eyed Professor Abindon. "And you as well, Mother."

Professor Abindon just said, "Ah, good. I wasn't looking forward to trying to obtain a hotel room at this hour," and went off to check on Lord Engal.

Miss Marlende added, "And I'd better get a physician for Daniel and Seth, as well. I'll have one meet us at our home. They both seem better, but it won't hurt to take precautions."

As she left, Emilie worriedly surveyed the airyard. Watching her, Efrain said, "You're still afraid of Uncle Yeric, aren't you?"

Emilie eyed him, though they stood in the dark outside the ring of lamps, the airship's balloon blocking out the moonlight, and it was difficult to see his expression. "I don't want to be carried away like a sack of laundry, no."

For a moment it was like they were right back where they had been when Efrain had first stepped into the airyard days ago, as if nothing had happened or changed between them. Emilie's heart sank, but she should have realized this was inevitable. Then Efrain kicked at the ground and said, "I understand why. If I was you, I wouldn't want to leave the Marlendes, either. They really like you."

Emilie felt a twist of hope. Maybe he really did understand. Impulsively, she said, "Why don't you stay, too?"

Efrain thought about it, but said, "I don't think they'd want me around, like they do you. They still think I'm a kid. And I don't hate home the way you do. Besides," he added, "I don't want to leave Emery."

The way Erin left all of us, Emilie thought, *and the way I left you.*

Emilie was digesting this when Miss Marlende returned. Efrain said, "Miss, could I get cab fare to the hotel where my uncle is staying? I think he'll be very worried about me."

Miss Marlende frowned. "Ah. Yes, I'd almost forgotten about that. I think perhaps my father had better take you there himself. I hope your uncle doesn't think we kidnapped you."

"No, I'll tell him I snuck aboard and it was all my fault," Efrain assured her. The fact that he didn't seem the least bit afraid of Uncle Yeric appeared to reassure Miss Marlende, and she took Efrain to go find Dr. Marlende. Emilie followed more slowly.

More carriages and people were arriving, including Dr. Amalus, the advisor to the Ministry and the Ruling Council who had come to the Philosophical Society on the night all this had begun. Then suddenly a man dashed through the gates into the yard. Emilie recognized a hatless and hastily dressed Anton Deverrin. She said, "Miss Marlende, look!" and waved at him.

He saw them and started forward. Miss Marlende pointed toward the work shed where the Deverrins had taken shelter. He bolted toward it and had almost reached the door when Miss Deverrin stepped out, Brendan behind her. They fell into each other's arms.

Emilie's eyes filled with tears, but at least it was for a good reason this time. Dr. Marlende came over to Miss Marlende and stood watching. Miss Marlende put her arm around him and said, "There was nothing to be done. He was long dead before we arrived."

He said, "I know."

Emilie sniffed and wiped her eyes. It was a sober reminder, that there was one person they had failed to rescue.

⊀ ‖ ⊁

Emilie woke the next morning, lying comfortably in a soft bed and under blankets that had been recently aired. It was a very agreeable sensation. She remembered she was on a daybed in one of the Marlendes' guest rooms. Professor Abindon had the bigger bed and the other guest room was being shared by Daniel and Seth, who were staying overnight to make certain their injuries were tended. Mikel and Cobbier had gone to their own homes in town.

Last night, while everyone was still running around sending telegrams and arranging coaches, Emilie had talked a little with Daniel. He had said, "I hope I didn't . . . do or say anything while that thing was . . . I mean I hope that—"

"You didn't," Emilie assured him. "Except, you know, you hit Seth."

Daniel seemed relieved. "Oh, good. Not about Seth, I mean. I already apologized to him."

"Do you remember anything that happened?"

"No, it was all a blank, like I was asleep." He grimaced, obviously thinking about what it would have been like to be aware through the whole terrible experience. "I suppose that's a good thing."

"It would have been very frightening to have been watching and not able to stop." His pained expression worried her, and she said again, "But really, all you did was take over the aether sailer. It was Miss Marlende and I who attacked you."

Daniel smiled a little. "Well, that's nothing unusual."

Now Emilie sat up, peering blearily around. Morning light fell through the gaps in the curtains, and the professor was up getting dressed. She said, "Go back to sleep, if you like. I'm just an early riser."

"Oh," Emilie said, and thumped back down onto the pillow. Then the professor opened the door to the hall and the scent of sausages and hot bread wafted in, and Emilie flung the covers off.

She hurriedly washed in the bathroom next door and dressed, and found her way downstairs to the dining room and the attached parlor, where a number of people, including the Marlendes, the professor, Daniel, Seth, several students, and important members of the Philosophical Society were all eating breakfast, talking loudly, or listening to other people talk loudly. Emilie helped the housekeeper carry in another full platter from the kitchen, then managed to put together a plate of sausage, fried bread, and warm jam, and acquire a mug of tea. She found a chair in a corner and sat down to eat.

The Marlendes' house was not large, but it was airy and comfortable, stuffed with books and framed maps and papers and philosophical equipment. There were no formal rooms; every place looked inviting, as if people often read or studied in every available spot.

"Emilie," Miss Marlende said. "No, don't stop eating. We're going to need everyone to write up an account of their version of what happened to them during the expedition. I'll need one from you, and Efrain if possible, then I'll need your help collecting it all together for our report to the Society."

Emilie nodded, still chewing. Maybe taking a typewriting course at some point soon wasn't a bad idea.

A maid came to the doorway and signaled urgently to Miss Marlende. Miss Marlende followed her away. Emilie finished eating, snagged one of the cream tarts some thoughtful person had brought in a bakery box, and then helped the housekeeper and some of the students clear away abandoned dishes. Daniel got up to help her. "You should be careful of your arm," she told him.

Daniel balanced several cups on a plate. "Compared to what else I did to it, I doubt this will matter."

Miss Marlende came back in and spoke to Dr. Marlende for a moment, then to the professor. They both stood and started out of the room. Miss Marlende beckoned to Emilie to follow. She hurried after them, hoping it wasn't bad news about Lord Engal.

She followed them into a room that must be someone's study. The walls were lined with shelves of books and bound notebooks. There were overstuffed chairs, a big table to lay out the maps that were rolled up in various stands, and a desk piled with papers and books.

Miss Marlende turned to Emilie and said, "Your uncle Yeric and Efrain are here, Emilie."

Emilie froze. "Why? Is he going to try to make me leave with him? I won't. I can go out over the garden wall if—"

"That won't be necessary," Dr. Marlende said firmly. "He didn't seem at all unreasonable last night, but perhaps that was because a journalist managed to hang on to the back of our carriage and follow us there."

Professor Abindon sighed. "They are relentless. That's one good thing about Engal, he keeps them in check without resorting to violence."

Miss Marlende put her hands on Emilie's shoulders and said, "Your uncle isn't your guardian. Even though your older brother isn't available, I don't see how he can legally force you to go with him." She looked thoughtful. "Do you think your older brother, once you do contact him, would have any serious objection to you remaining here with us, in our employment?"

Emilie thought about her conversations with Efrain, the reflection she had done on Erin's behavior. "I would be surprised if he did," she admitted. Erin had undoubtedly had his own reasons for leaving the way he had, though he never mentioned them in the few letters he had written to her. But Emilie had to face the fact that it meant she would never be able to count on him. Accepting that didn't feel nearly as bleak as she had thought it might. Mainly because she felt that now, if she needed him, she would be able to count on Efrain. And he could count on her.

Miss Marlende nodded. "I can summon a solicitor, then. I know Lord Engal has a number of them lying in wait all over the city."

"First, let me just talk to the man," Dr. Marlende said. "We've managed to get along with beings from different aetheric planes, we should be able to settle this."

Dr. Marlende left the study, and Miss Marlende said, "I'd better get back to the others. Just wait here, Emilie. And remember that if you don't want to see him, you won't have to."

Miss Marlende went back to the dining room, but the professor lingered a moment. She said, "I have a great deal of experience leaving people behind in anger. If you would like to talk about it later, I might be able to offer some perspective."

Emilie smiled up at her. "Thank you."

The professor nodded, and went out. Emilie paced for a bit, too nervous to sit down. Then there was a tap on the door and Efrain peeked in. He saw her and slipped inside. "Dr. Marlende said I should wait here."

Emilie nodded, trying not to look anxious. "How was it going?"

Efrain told her, "I think it'll be all right. When the airship lifted off, Uncle Yeric complained to the man who was there from the Philosophical Society, Mr. Elathorn, and I think Mr. Elathorn explained how important the Marlendes are and how Lord Engal is working with them and how important Lord Engal is. And then when Dr. Marlende brought me back to the hotel, a journalist followed us and I guess thought Uncle Yeric was an important person too, because Dr. Marlende went to see him as soon as he got back, and I think that's what they're going to put in the newspaper."

"Uncle Yeric is going to be in the newspaper?" Emilie boggled. She wondered how the village would react. It would be almost a shame not to see it. Almost.

"Yes, it's going to be a big shock," Efrain agreed.

They were still talking about it when Dr. Marlende came in, and said Emilie should talk to her uncle Yeric, that he was of the opinion it would be all right.

* * *

Emilie walked into the downstairs parlor, her heart pounding. This had clearly been the room meant for greeting and entertaining formal guests at some point, but it was now filled with bookcases too, and some of the side tables had papers and writing materials left behind on them, as if some students had been hastily cleared out earlier.

Uncle Yeric stood, clearly still uncomfortable. He said, "Ah, Emilie. Efrain tells me you wish to remain here."

"Yes." Emilie folded her hands and tried not to shift nervously. She could hear everyone upstairs in the dining room talking, which was somewhat reassuring.

Apparently pretending their earlier conversation at the airship yard had never taken place, Uncle Yeric said, "I suspect your aunt will not approve."

"My brother Erin is my guardian—"

"Your brother Erin left his family without a word, with only a letter inadequately explaining his actions." Uncle Yeric controlled himself with difficulty, and said in a more even tone, "I fear what would happen if you ever found yourself in a position where you had to depend on him."

Emilie stared at him, struck all at once by a shocking revelation. Uncle Yeric was just as upset about Erin leaving as Efrain was, as she had been. And he had taken it out on her, just like Efrain and Emery had.

Uncle Yeric and her aunt had always told them all that their mother was an actress and somehow must have passed her feckless ways on to her children. This caused Erin, who had been the oldest, the most favored, the child they had known best and liked best, to leave them without a glance backward. As the only girl, and the next oldest, Emilie had shouldered all the blame, a substitute for her mother and Erin. It wasn't fair, and it wasn't right, but at least she knew now. She said, slowly, "I wouldn't want to depend on him either. But if I have to leave the Marlendes' employ, I can go to my cousin Karthea at Silk Harbor, and help her with her school. She's already said I can, if I want to."

Uncle Yeric cleared his throat. "Ah, well. Your cousin has always been a very respectable young lady, despite her insistence on going to university." He continued, "Dr. Marlende assures me you will be staying under this roof, in the company of his daughter. You must write to your aunt, to let her know what your direction is. And write to her every fortnight, to let her know how you're getting along."

It seemed a small price to pay. Emilie said, "I will. I'll write to her today."

* * *

Uncle Yeric took his leave from Dr. Marlende, and Emilie said goodbye to Efrain in the front parlor. He told her, "Write to me too, and tell me all your adventures."

"I will," Emilie told him. From the stoop of the house she watched Uncle Yeric and Efrain climb into a coach and drive away.

She walked back to the study to sit alone in the relative quiet for a moment, feeling very strange and a little at sea. Relieved to have the whole situation with Uncle Yeric settled, and able to start her new life without worrying about him. Guilty to realize she had abandoned Efrain and Emery just as Erin had, though like her he had probably had reasons he felt were equally compelling. But at least now she was free to visit her younger brothers when she wished. And she was rather looking forward to when Efrain would be able to visit her.

Emilie realized she badly needed to write to Karthea and let her know she was all right, and to her friend Porcia Herinbogel to tell her everything that had happened. Thinking about how she would explain the whole situation to Porcia helped her sort it out more in her own mind. Emilie knew she didn't forgive either Uncle Yeric or her aunt, but understanding their feelings did help somewhat. For one thing, it was going to make it easier to cope if they got angry with her again. Uncle Yeric wasn't going to apologize to her, and the way he and her aunt had treated her would always hurt, even if he didn't seem to believe what he had said anymore. If he ever had.

She was looking around for writing paper when Miss Marlende put her head in the doorway and said, "Oh, there you are, Emilie. Lord Engal is evidently feeling better and has sent a message demanding that everyone come round to his town house and continue the meeting there. Would you like to come along?"

"Yes, miss, I think I would," Emilie said, and followed her out.

ABOUT THE AUTHOR

Lisa Blaschke

MARTHA WELLS has written many novels, including the *New York Times* and *USA Today* bestselling Murderbot Diaries series, which has won multiple Hugo, Nebula, Locus, and Alex Awards. Other titles include *Witch King, City of Bones, The Wizard Hunters, Wheel of the Infinite,* the Books of the Raksura series (beginning with *The Cloud Roads* and ending with *The Harbors of the Sun*), and the Nebula Award–nominated *The Death of the Necromancer,* as well as YA fantasy novels, short stories, and nonfiction.